A Vintage Wedding

I live in the beautiful Cotswold countryside with my family, and I'm a country girl at heart.

I first started writing when my mother gave me a writing kit for Christmas, and once I started I just couldn't stop. *Living Dangerously* was my first novel and since then, I haven't looked back.

Ideas for books are everywhere, and I'm constantly inspired by the people and places around me. From watching TV (yes, it is research) to overhearing conversations, I love how my writing gives me the chance to taste other people's lives and try all the jobs I've never had.

Each of my books explores a different profession or background and my research has helped me bring these to life. I've been a porter in an auction house, tried my hand at pottery, refurbished furniture, delved behind the scenes of a dating website, and I've even been on a Ray Mears survival course.

I love being a writer; to me there isn't a more satisfying and pleasing thing to do. I particularly enjoy writing love stories. I believe falling in love is the best thing in the world, and I want all my characters to experience it, and my readers to share their stories.

Also by Katie Fforde

Huge thanks go to my daughter Briony and (now) daughter-in-law Heidi for getting married and giving me so much wonderful research material. Also to their wonderful husbands – Steve and Frank. I would thank the grandchildren too but they weren't much help apart from being adorable which they don't have to work at.

To the wonderful Lotte and Miles and The Prince Albert which is such an original and great pub it had to go in a book. Do call in if you're ever in Stroud.

To The Old Endowed School which, along with The Prince Albert, has a starring role. The committee works so hard raising funds to restore this fascinating and very ancient building.

To the many people who helped make both weddings amazing, including The White Room who know how to make a bridal party feel special, Siobain Drury who took me to Birmingham Flower Market (at four o'clock in the morning), to Debbie Evans who as always gave me so much inside information about weddings (as well as doing everyone's hair brilliantly). To my daughter's bridesmaids, official and unofficial. Toni, Jo, Carrie, all the hens. You all made your contribution.

To my wonderful editors Selina Walker and Georgina

it's not you! It's not that I'm not grateful but I have the memory . . .

'Thank you, Lindy. Glad to be appreciated,' said Mrs Townley.

Beth remembered she hadn't eaten much that day and helped herself. 'Have a couple!' insisted Mrs Townley.

'It would be rude not to,' said Lindy, encouragingly.

'In which case,' said Beth, and took two.

As she ate, Beth looked around and realised that without the throng of people the village hall would have been pretty dreary. The paintwork was green and maroon and needed redoing. The ceiling was high, with exposed beams and rafters, but it was in desperate need of either a good scrub or total redecoration. 'This could be a lovely building,' she said to no one in particular.

'That's what I thought,' said Rachel. 'But I tend to fall in love with old buildings.'

'Please fall in love with this one,' said Lindy. 'The three groups who use it currently think it's just fine as it is but Mum thinks the roof is about to either collapse or start leaking badly. She says unless people get together and do something about it, it'll fall into total disrepair. She wants to form a "Save the Village Hall" committee.'

'It would be an awful shame to let it just fall down,' said Rachel, staring up into the rafters.

Beth stared up there too and found they didn't look better with closer inspection.

'Here's the wine,' said Lindy after a few moments. 'It may be home-made.'

'I'm sure it's fine,' said Beth. She sensed Lindy was embarrassed about the possibility of home-made wine but to her it felt totally in keeping with what she thought of as life in the country. Beth took a glass being offered by a grey-haired lady wearing a dashing knitted lamé wrap. 'This will be the first glass of wine I've had since I've been here.'

'Are you new here, too?' said Rachel. 'I've only been here ten days. Living here permanently, I mean.'

'Everyone was very excited when you moved in,' said Lindy. 'No one was quite sure who you'd turn out to be. A family? A couple?'

'It's just me,' said Rachel.

Beth couldn't decide if there was a touch of defiance in the way she said this and to cover the slight awkwardness, she said, 'Well, I'm in a rental property.'

'The pretty one with the rundown porch?' asked Lindy.

'That's the one. It's been lent to me by my sister's in-laws-to-be,' said Beth. 'Sorry, that's a bit complicated.'

Rachel frowned. 'Your sister's getting married and her fiancé's parents have lent you a house?'

'Yes! That sounds so much clearer than how I put it. The reason they lent it to me is that I'm organising the wedding.' She paused for dramatic effect. 'Via Skype.'

The other two laughed in surprise. 'That sounds a bit of a challenge,' said Lindy.

'It is – especially on almost no money. But my sister arranged the house for me when I had a major falling-out with my mother and really couldn't go home after uni, so I do owe her. I'm going to try really hard to do a good job,' said Beth.

'Doesn't your mother want to organise your sister's wedding?' asked Lindy.

'Yes!' said Beth. 'She does. But she wants to take over

every single detail so Helena asked me to do it. While she's out of the country.'

'I love the thought of a wedding organised via Skype,' said Rachel.

'You could have the do in the village hall,' said Lindy, 'if we get it restored in time. That would be nice and cheap.'

'That's not a bad idea, actually,' said Beth. 'When is it likely to be restored by? They want the wedding at the end of August.'

Lindy shook her heard. 'Sorry. I didn't mean to get your hopes up. It's not likely to be done this year, not realistically.'

Rachel had been staring at the ceiling again. 'A lick of paint would make a huge difference.'

Beth nodded slowly as the picture formed in her mind. 'It would! With masses of flowers and bunting.'

'Well, I could help with the bunting,' said Lindy. 'I can sew.'

'Is that your job?' asked Beth. 'Sewing?'

Lindy shrugged. 'In a way, but mostly my job is looking after my boys.'

'You've got children?' said Beth. She was surprised. She judged Lindy to be roughly the same age as she was, in her early twenties, and it seemed very young to have children.

Lindy nodded. 'Two of them. Six and three. Little monkeys a lot of the time.'

Beth got the impression she'd added the 'little monkeys' bit for form's sake.

'So, what do you do?' asked Lindy. 'Apart from organising your sister's wedding?'

Beth shrugged. 'Nothing at the moment. I need to find something soon. I've got savings and although Mum doesn't know, Dad hasn't stopped my allowance from when I was at uni, but I'd like to tell him I don't need it any more.'

'Have you just graduated?'

'Last summer. I did what my mother called Facebook and Barmaiding, although there was a bit more to it. I hadn't got the grades I needed for English, which is what she wanted me to do, and picked a course as far away from home as possible. And I'm currently unemployed.' Beth paused, worried that Lindy would think she was a complete flake. 'I did bar work in Brighton up until Christmas but got really fed up.' She made a face. 'My mother said it was my fault for doing such a ridiculous course and did you really need a degree to be a barmaid.' Beth laughed, trying to hide that this had hurt her. 'You don't, really.'

'Do you think university was a waste of time?' asked Lindy.

'Absolutely not. It got me away from home, I learnt loads about life and how to be independent and had a great time.' Beth paused. 'You didn't go?'

Lindy shook her head. 'No. I got pregnant instead. That taught me a lot too!'

'I bet,' said Beth.

'I love this building!' said Rachel, who hadn't really been listening. 'It's got such rustic charm.'

'You'd love it less if you saw the Ladies,' said Lindy.

'Ah. The Ladies,' said Beth, aware of a need now she thought about it. 'Is it over there?'

8

Lindy nodded. 'Through the door marked "TO LETS". Someone thought it was funny to take out the "I".'

Beth laughed and set off for the sign. As she left the others she thought she heard Lindy say, 'Good luck.'

The loo was at least clean but it was freezing cold and the seat had a worrying crack in it. Beth felt that even though the building was used by very few, they might have at least replaced that vital piece of equipment.

As she came out, drying her hands on her jeans, she was stopped by a man of late middle age who was vaguely familiar. 'Hello! You're the young lady living in the cottage above the stream?'

Beth considered. 'That's right.'

'I've seen you round and about. How are you getting on up there?'

'Very well, thank you.' She smiled.

Encouraged, the man went on: 'Well, I'm Bob. I've got the garage on the Cheltenham road. It's nice to see a new young face about the place.'

Beth nodded, wondering how she felt about everyone knowing where she lived and that she was new to the area, but she decided it was part of village life, like excellent sausage rolls and home-made wine.

'A lot of the new people are second-home owners,' Bob went on. 'We need young people who'll settle down here.'

For a second Beth wondered if the village had suffered a Pied Piper of Hamelin-type incident. Then she realised it would be that most of the local young people had moved away because they couldn't afford property in the area. Or there were no jobs. 'It's a gorgeous area. Even in winter it's pretty.'

'It is that.' Bob laughed loudly; then he said, 'And they're just about to draw the lucky programmes. Have you got yours there? It's like a raffle, see?'

Beth, who had worked this out herself, produced her programme from the pocket of her parka as they both moved nearer the stage at one end of the hall. Bob waited expectantly while the announcements went on. He seemed to take Beth's good fortune personally and wanted to see her win something.

Of course she didn't until almost the last number. Looking over her shoulder Bob called out, 'We've a winner here!'

Beth checked her number. She was indeed a winner. Slightly hoping it wasn't the home-made parsnip liqueur that was on the list of prizes, she waited for developments.

'It seems there's some confusion,' said the man behind the microphone. 'We've got two programmes with that number.'

Beth began to say she didn't mind not winning and was happy to resign but her champion wouldn't let her. 'Well, how's that happened?' Bob demanded.

'We'll have to sort that out later,' said the man with the microphone, which he continued to use although people were now clustering round and he didn't need the extra volume. 'Who else has got the lucky programme?'

Lindy appeared with Rachel. 'Here!'

Beth sighed with relief. 'Oh, phew, that's OK. You can have whatever it is, Rachel. I'm sure I won't mind not having it.' Then she worried that she'd sounded rude.

'Do you know what it is?' said Rachel.

'No. Do you?' said Beth.

Rachel nodded. 'It's a really lovely vintage tea set. You probably will mind not having it.' She looked wistful as she said this. 'I have two plates in the same pattern at home. It's Shelley.'

'Then you must have it,' insisted Beth. 'Really.'

'That wouldn't be right,' said Rachel.

'No, really—'

Possibly sensing this could go on some time, Lindy broke in. 'If it were my boys I'd say you had to share it.'

Rachel turned to her. 'What, a timeshare tea set?'

Lindy nodded. 'Take it in turns to own it.'

Beth had now had time to inspect the tea set displayed in a pretty wicker hamper, and discovered that it was indeed extremely pretty. And as she did so she visualised lots and lots of pretty tea sets filled with cake and sandwiches. A vintage wedding: that would suit Helena far better than the glittering champagne affair their mother had wanted for her, and would be much more affordable too. She suddenly suffered a stab of panic when she realised what she'd taken on with this wedding. Really, she hadn't a clue what was involved. She'd have to trawl the internet and find out. One thing she had learnt at uni was how useful eBay and Gumtree and Freecycle were.

'Why don't we go to the pub to discuss it?' suggested Lindy. 'I could ring my gran – she's got the boys – and tell her I'll be a bit later than I said and then we can miss the speeches.'

A short time later the three young women were entering the pub.

11

Beth looked about her. It wasn't quite what she was expecting from a country pub. There was no thick patterned carpet, horse brasses and leather seating areas. It was much more shabby chic, like someone's larger than average sitting room. There was a glamorous black-haired woman behind the bar who seemed to be in charge.

Suddenly Beth remembered how little money she had with her. 'Um, can I suggest, unless we want three drinks, we just pay for ourselves?'

Lindy seemed relieved. 'Good idea. I can't stay for three drinks, anyway.'

They went up to the bar. 'Hi, Sukey,' said Lindy. 'I've brought new people with me.'

Sukey smiled. 'Cool. What are you all having?'

'Red wine,' the three chorused.

'Coming up. And what's that you've got under your arm?'

She pointed to the tea set that Rachel was carrying in the basket.

'It's one of the prizes from the lucky programmes. Beth and Rachel both won it,' Lindy explained. 'There was a mistake in the printing on the programmes.'

'Tricky!' said Sukey and placed two glasses of wine on the counter. Then she reached for another glass.

They carried their drinks to a vacant sofa next to a fire that crackled and spat behind a fireguard. Stretched out in front of the fire was a greyhound, who lifted the last inch of his tail in acknowledgement of the young women.

'Sorry, I wasn't really listening before, but remind me why

you're organising your sister's wedding?' asked Rachel.

'Basically my mother feels it's her absolute right to plan my sister's wedding and have it as she wants it. If she's paying she gets to decide on everything.'

'A Mumzilla,' said Lindy. 'Heard about them. Go on.'

'Well, my sister doesn't want to get married in a cathedral she's never stepped foot inside before and then go to a massive hotel and invite a whole lot of people she's never met.' She paused. 'So I said I'd sort it out for her.'

'I'm assuming there's a good reason why she can't do it herself?' said Rachel. 'I can't imagine letting anyone else organise something so important.'

Beth nodded. 'She and her fiancé have gone travelling. They felt they'd never have the opportunity otherwise. Jeff has got a new job starting in September, so it was now or never. They didn't have gap years to go travelling in.' Beth realised she sounded as if she was apologising for them. 'Anyway, you can imagine how that went down with our mother. Just appalled,' she added, in case her new friends couldn't imagine this. 'And I'm in a new place, currently with no job, so I offered.'

'Goodness,' said Lindy. 'My mum was great about my wedding. She was great about the divorce, too.'

'And is there a reason why your mother thinks it's her right to plan your sister's wedding?' asked Rachel. She seemed a woman who liked to get to the bottom of things.

'I think her mother totally told her what to do and so now it's her chance to have control. She thinks my sister is being totally unreasonable not letting her.'

'What about your dad?' asked Lindy.

'Bless him, he did give my sister money towards the wedding but she spent it on her trip of a lifetime.'

'Didn't he mind?' Rachel gave a little shake of her head. 'Sorry, I seem to be asking questions all the time.'

'It's OK. And he didn't really mind but he was surprised. But Helena said that Mum would still try to control the wedding and she'd rather spend the money on seeing the world.'

'So what's your budget?' asked Lindy. 'If you'd like me to help, I am very good at doing things for almost nothing.'

'Well, that's great!' said Beth, laughing. 'Because that is exactly what my budget is. Almost nothing.'

'I think that sounds a brilliant challenge,' said Rachel. 'I was married – for a short time – and we had a very smart, very upmarket wedding for a very few upmarket friends. I think a budget wedding sounds much more fun.'

'My wedding was fairly small too,' said Lindy. 'But I was pregnant so I didn't really care.' She gave an embarrassed little laugh. 'It only lasted long enough for me to get pregnant again.'

'Don't tell me if you don't want to,' said Beth, 'but how did you get pregnant when you seem so sensible? And then do it again?'

'That is a bit personal,' said Rachel, frowning at Beth.

'No, it's OK. My trouble was, I slept with the wrong brother.'

'Ooh. Big mistake,' said Beth.

Lindy pushed her and grinned. Beth stopped feeling guilty for asking the question. Lindy seemed happy to

14

talk about it. 'I was madly in love – well, of course it wasn't love, it was a crush, but a massive one – with this boy who was much older. Five years older.'

'That's nothing when you're grown up,' said Rachel. 'But it's massive when you're – how old?'

'Sixteen,' said Lindy. 'The brother left to go abroad to study or work or maybe both, I can't remember now. Anyway, his younger brother and I were both upset and got a bit drunk. It turned out he'd had a crush on me but I never noticed because of Angus, his brother. We turned to each other for comfort.'

'That's a word for it I hadn't heard,' said Beth, anxious to keep things light.

'Beth!' said Rachel.

'Sorry,' muttered Beth.

'I got pregnant and – massive disapproval from his parents of course. I had ruined his life—'

'He ruined yours,' said Rachel indignantly.

'Anyway, we rubbed along until I got pregnant again. He got over his crush and we parted.'

'Did you get over yours?' asked Beth.

'Beth! It was a crush. They don't last for ever,' said Lindy, but something about the way she said it made Beth wonder.

She sighed, slightly deflated by Lindy's story. 'So you two are great examples of how marriages can go wrong,' she said. 'Maybe I'd better tell my sister not to bother.'

Rachel and Lindy both protested. 'No! I was only seventeen when we got married,' said Lindy. 'It was bound to fail.'

'And I got married . . .' Rachel paused. 'Well, I did love

him. And I think he loved me. But not quite enough. We drifted apart.' She paused. 'And maybe I wasn't exactly perfect, wife-wise.'

'I'd hate to put anyone off marriage because mine failed,' said Lindy.

'Me too,' said Rachel. She smiled. 'Besides, if you tell your sister not to get married I can't help with the wedding.'

'Do you want to? Are you a wedding planner?'

Rachel shook her head. 'I'm an accountant – freelance – but I'd love to be more creative.'

Lindy nodded. 'I have heard that creative accountants don't have a great reputation.'

Because of her solemn expression it took the others a second to realise she was joking.

'That's why I've had to find other outlets for my creativity,' said Rachel. 'I'd love to have a go at the village hall, for instance.'

'In what way?' said Lindy. 'I'm sure my mother would love to hear your ideas.'

'I haven't had time for ideas yet but I just think it's a lovely building and if it was done up, it could earn its keep. So perfect for a wedding. It's only a short walk from the church. Imagine the bridal party processing across the village green—'

'Dragging their dresses in the mud,' said Lindy.

'—to an old-fashioned feast spread out on trestle tables,' Rachel finished, and then added, 'with bunting.'

Beth looked at her. 'That does sound wonderful. And the sort of thing my mother would absolutely hate. I'll suggest it to Helena.'

'I do think you should do what Helena wants, not what your mother would hate,' said Lindy.

Beth nodded. 'So do I, but I do think Hels would love that. I'll suggest it to her next time we can Skype. What with her being on the move all the time, we can't always,' she added.

'But would she want to get married here?' asked Lindy.

'I think she might. Jeff's parents have connections here. The cottage where I'm living at the moment is their pension. They want to retire somewhere down here.'

'But the village hall is hardly fit for a wedding,' said Lindy. 'You were only in it for a short time while it was full of people. It looks at its best then. It needs a lot of work.'

'Remind me when the wedding is, Beth?' Rachel asked.

Beth shrugged. 'We haven't got a specific date yet. The end of August sometime.'

'Will you still be here then?' asked Lindy. 'Won't your house be rented out?'

'It might be. I'm there now because their insurance isn't valid if it isn't occupied or something. When and if I find a job, I'll be on the lookout for something else. I don't suppose there are many jobs round here.'

'No,' said Lindy. 'You might have to work for yourself in some way, like I do.'

Beth sighed. 'The trouble is, I don't have any skills,' she said.

'Well, look for a job for now and concentrate on your sister's wedding,' said Lindy.

'That'll certainly keep me busy until August,' said Beth.

'Plenty of time to arrange a wedding, if you focus,' said Rachel.

'Not if we've got to do the village hall first,' said Lindy.

'We'll work better with something to aim towards,' said Rachel. 'A big wedding at the end of the summer could be just the incentive.'

Lindy looked at her doubtfully. 'I think you'd better go on Mum's committee,' she said. 'She'll be thrilled. It'll need a lot of enthusiasm.'

'That would be great for me,' said Rachel. 'I'm doing a bit of work in Letterby but it's quite a long commute. I'm hoping to get some work round here. I know there aren't that many businesses but some of them might need me to sort out their finances. Being on a committee might give me good contacts.'

'Of course. Mum will die of joy. An accountant? On the committee? Can I tell her you'll do it?'

Rachel took a breath. 'Only if you two will let me buy you another glass of wine. I'm not sure one is enough for this sort of thing.'

'Well, I think we should have a toast,' said Lindy when Rachel had returned with more wine. 'Meeting you two has been lovely!'

'I think I should toast moving into my own house after months of work,' said Rachel. 'I didn't want to do it on my own.'

'And I think we should all toast new beginnings,' said Beth. 'I know it's not the same for Lindy, who's always been here, but me and Rachel are starting a new life in the country.'

18

'You know what? I think if we thought hard we'd find some sort of project to do together,' said Lindy. 'Not just the village hall,' she added.

'I'll drink to that!' said Rachel.

'So will I! New beginnings—'

'And new friends!' said Lindy, raising her glass.

'Hooray!' said Beth, as she clinked glasses with her two new friends. Life was looking up.

Chapter Two

After they left the pub, Rachel walked with the others as far as she could and then cut off down the lane to her house. She took out her torch and turned it on. She hadn't yet developed the ability to walk about in the near-dark like her country-bred neighbours.

She unlocked her back door and went in, and for the first time the overpowering sense of loneliness she usually felt was missing. Maybe it was because she'd met people. Maybe it was because she'd had a couple of glasses of wine. Or maybe the house was no longer the only thing that mattered to her here.

This house, this charming Cotswold village, had been the focus of her thoughts and dreams for so long, yet when she'd finally managed to throw off the shackles of her city life, it had all felt a bit empty. She had been so sure that if she could only move full-time into the house she had bought partly with some inherited money and now, since her divorce, was hers mortgage-free, she would be happy. And while she did really love making it perfect, paying attention to every tiny detail, somehow it hadn't been enough.

It had taken quite a while to find the perfect property in the perfect location. Chippingford was pretty but not fake; it was more than a destination for second-homers. It was reachable from London and yet it was truly in the country. She had loved planning the alterations, finding the right builders, sourcing the materials, making sure it had all been done to her exacting standards, but moving in had been a little disappointing.

But meeting Lindy and Beth, sharing a slightly odd evening and ending up in the pub had felt positive. Their toast to 'new beginnings' had given her an optimism she hadn't felt for ages.

She went into the kitchen to make a cup of tea. At her insistence, Beth had gone off with the tea set. She lived nearer the pub and it was quite heavy, so they agreed that Beth could have it first. But now Rachel looked at the two plates, propped up against a shelf on her small but perfect antique kitchen dresser and admired them. How would she feel about having more plates, cups and saucers with a pattern? Would it be too much colour? Or would the fact it all matched make it acceptable? And she hadn't been able to check them for chips. If any of it was less than perfect, Beth could have it for ever.

When she'd first taken possession of the house, she'd had it all sprayed white. In the two years since she'd owned it, she had never been able to decide on a colour she liked as much.

Later she'd painted the floorboards white. They were new – far newer than the house, which was Edwardian – and she liked the clean look. Now, as she brought her tea through to the sitting room, she realised she found it cold.

Of course it was cold – there was an unused wood-burner in the fireplace and she didn't have the heating on much. But it was the feeling of the house that was cold, not just the temperature. At first she'd found it cleansing. Now she was ready to add some colour to her life.

She'd felt a bit shy being introduced to Lindy and Beth by Lindy's mother. Mrs Wood had obviously thought Rachel was much the same age as her daughter, but Rachel was thirty-five – a good ten years older than the other two. It didn't seem to matter though, and she really hoped it would go on being like that. She'd often had doubts about the wisdom of abandoning her life in London for this house she barely knew in the country but every time she'd managed to convince herself it was the right thing to have done.

She washed up her mug, dried it and put it away so there would be nothing to mar the perfect lines of her fitted kitchen when she came down in the morning.

As she went up to bed she wondered if actually she was a little OCD about things, as Graham, her ex-husband, had suggested. At the time she had felt she just wanted part of her life she could control. Now she suspected that keeping things tidy was becoming more of an obsession. As she cleaned the bathroom sink thoroughly after she'd brushed her teeth, polishing it with a bit of old towel she kept for the purpose, she wondered some more.

In bed, between freshly ironed, thousand-thread-count percale sheets, she imagined what the homes of her new friends might be like. She shivered slightly at the thought of possible chaos. And yet she'd loved spending time with them and she realised to her surprise that as long as her life was ordered she didn't mind how other people ran their lives.

The following morning her phone went when she was applying a thin layer of polish to her kitchen worktop.

She didn't recognise the number but answered it anyway.

'Good morning! I hope I'm not too early for you. It's Sarah Wood, Lindy's mum. She gave me your card.'

Rachel had given both girls one of the cards she'd had printed in the hope they would bring her business as a bookkeeper and accountant.

'Hello. How can I help?'

'Well,' said Sarah, obviously relieved that Rachel sounded so positive. 'Lindy mentioned you might go on the committee I'm trying to get together? For the village hall? I'd be so grateful to have someone young. And an outsider.' She paused. 'I didn't mean that to sound unkind but when people have lived with something as it is forever, it can be hard for them to visualise anything different.'

Rachel said, 'I like a challenge.' Getting those dusty rafters clean and painted would be very satisfying.

'So will you come to a meeting? I've arranged one for tomorrow night. I'll come and collect you so you needn't feel nervous about going into a room full of strangers.'

'Oh, OK. That should be all right.'

'About seven thirty? Will you have eaten?'

Sarah seemed very anxious to make things as easy as possible for Rachel. 'Seven thirty will be fine.' If she ate at six she would have cleared up by then. And she wouldn't have to actually let Sarah in, so that would be all right.

When she had disconnected, and while she was getting ready to visit the old people's home a little way away, where she did the books, Rachel realised she was quite looking forward to the meeting. It would be good to meet more local people – and as she'd said to Lindy, she might get some work a bit nearer to where she lived.

Sarah had arrived on time the following evening wearing some rather covetable boots, Rachel thought. When Rachel commented, Sarah picked up her leg and admired them. 'Yes, they are nice, aren't they? They were in a sale in a shop in Cheltenham. I always feel I can face the winter better if I've got lovely boots. That and a good coat.' She was wearing one with shearling wool round the hood. 'Are you ready? It's so nice of you to agree to come.'

'Well, you like to do your bit. And you never know, someone might need an accountant.'

'If it's not a stupid question – or even if it is – how did you come to be an accountant? You look like you should run an art gallery or a very gorgeous clothes shop.'

Rachel shrugged. 'I've always liked numbers. I can make them do what I want them to, put them in orderly columns. I think I got it from my father.' Her father had liked things to be tidy too.

But when Rachel and Sarah entered the room upstairs at the pub she realised it was unlikely that the three fairly elderly women and one man present would need help

24

with their spreadsheets or how to minimise their tax liability. They had probably managed their finances brilliantly all their lives with a pencil and a small notebook.

Rachel looked around her as two more people arrived, full of apologies for being late. They were a couple in their early forties and judging by their clothes they were a bit more urban.

Sarah took charge. 'OK, well, we're probably all here. I was hoping for a few more but I know some people don't like going out at night.' She smiled at Rachel. 'Before we start I'll introduce Rachel – she's new to the village but I'm sure she's going to make a great contribution.'

Rachel gulped, not sure if this was a challenge or an affirmation. 'Hello,' she said.

'Right, going round the table...'

Sarah made the introductions. There was an Ivy, an Audrey and a Dot, and the younger couple, who, it transpired, came from London, were Justin and Amanda. The man was called Robert.

Everyone smiled at Rachel, friendly but curious. She smiled back shyly.

'Right,' said Sarah briskly. 'When we've got our committee sorted out we'll probably have daytime meetings.' She paused and sighed. 'I thought having this first meeting at this time would mean a few more – well, you know... We need to drum up some more people, really.'

Rachel understood. Sarah was hoping for some people who worked, ran businesses or had experience of committees and how to raise money and run things. She also realised why Sarah had been so keen to nab her. It was a dilemma. The older people didn't want to go out in the evenings, but working people couldn't attend meetings during the day.

Sarah had a pad, a pen and some bits of paper in front of her. 'We need to elect a chairman.'

'I say, you do it,' said Audrey swiftly and the others all chimed in agreement.

'We should have a vote—'

'Sarah, my love,' said Ivy, 'we don't want to be here all night. We all agree. Just do it.'

Sarah sighed and wrote something down. 'OK. Treasurer?'

No one volunteered. Eventually Sarah said, 'Can I suggest Rachel? She told me she was an accountant.'

Dot, who was sitting next to Rachel, chuckled. 'Ooh, you shouldn't have told her that, my dear. She was bound to pounce.'

'And I did,' said Sarah. 'Now, do we need a mission statement?'

'What's one of them?' said Dot, who appeared to have a pleasing subversive streak.

'They're all the rage,' said Audrey. 'I learnt that when I was a school governor.'

'I don't think we need one,' said Sarah. 'We just want to raise enough money to put the village hall back into a condition where we can rent it out and get some revenue.'

'It doesn't need anything doing to it,' grumbled Dot. 'It's just fine as it is.'

'It'll fall down if we don't do something,' said Justin. 'You can see that just by looking at it.'

'And I don't think it's safe for children,' said his wife, Amanda. 'I wouldn't be happy about mine playing there.

It's dirty and extremely tatty. We thought it might be a good venue for a birthday party but we had people from London coming and we just couldn't use it.'

There were mutterings of disagreement and, 'It was good enough for our little Otto's party,' from the ones who thought the building was fine.

'Do we know how much it will take to make it safe, at least?' asked Rachel. 'And I have to say, if it was redecorated it would get many more bookings. I mean, how many do you get now?'

There was muttering again but no actual replies.

'The Scouts use it,' said Robert.

'And the Cubs sometimes camp in it,' said Ivy. 'They put up their tents and everything.' She paused. 'Only last time most of them rang their mums and wanted to go home.'

'Does the roof leak?' asked Justin.

Sarah cleared her throat. 'We'd need about a hundred thousand pounds to put the building right.'

Through the rumble of dismay Rachel asked Sarah, 'So *does* the roof leak? If it looked better you could still hire it out, earn some money and do the repairs as and when you can afford to.'

Sarah banged on her table. 'Sorry, can we stop talking amongst ourselves? Rachel here has made a very good point. Rachel, would you mind saying all that again, please?'

Rachel had made her point to Sarah to avoid being the young woman from London who thought she knew better than those who'd lived here all their lives. But it seemed she couldn't escape the role.

'I just feel if the hall looked better – if it was totally redecorated and if it wasn't raining, people could hire it. Get some money in and then do the repairs when we can afford them.' The 'we' slipped out. She didn't know if it was likely to offend people, her being possessive about their hall, but it certainly made her anxious. Had she really aligned herself publicly to a collapsing building? Then she remembered how, at the do, she'd spent ages looking up into the rafters, mentally painting them white. She couldn't resist a project, that was her problem.

Rachel lowered her gaze to the table, not daring to check if her fears were justified and that the others were looking at her with distrust and suspicion.

'I totally agree,' said Justin. 'Get it so it looks reasonable and then start renting it out.'

''Ow're we going to get the money to do the decoration?' asked Robert.

'I've got some lovely green paint I could donate,' said Dot.

'Ooh, now you come to mention it, so have I, only it's yellow.'

'No,' said Rachel firmly, in spite of her misgivings about being 'the girl from London'. 'We've got to have the paint all the same colour. White's best,' she added.

There was tutting. 'Shows the dirt, white does,' seemed to be the general opinion.

'I can get you as much white paint as you want,' said a voice from the doorway.

Rachel looked up to see a very scruffy man whose black curly hair needed cutting and whose leather jacket was like a leftover from the previous century. He needed a shave, too. There was no way he would come by that paint honestly, she decided.

Sarah seemed of the same opinion but smiled fondly all the same. 'Glad you made it, Raff, but which lorry did the paint drop off the back of?'

Raff gave a lopsided grin. 'You're so suspicious, Sarah. I promise you it's all kosher.'

'It would save a lot of money,' said Rachel, who, while still suspecting the man of very dodgy dealings, couldn't ignore the financial advantage.

'Raff has a small reclamation yard,' explained Sarah to Rachel.

Raff came into the room. 'Who's this?' he asked Sarah, looking at Rachel. 'A new face? In more ways than one.'

'This is Rachel, and yes, she is new to the area,' said Sarah.

'I'm Raff,' he said, looking down into her eyes in a way that made her feel very uncomfortable.

'Don't you go near young Raff,' said Dot. 'His gran was a friend of mine and even she wouldn't trust him further'n she could throw 'im.'

'Don't you believe all the bad things you'll hear about me,' said Raff, talking directly to Rachel, still looking at her in that disturbing way. 'I don't deserve my bad reputation.' Then he winked, which confirmed Rachel's opinion: he was a man to avoid at all cost.

As he took his seat in between Ivy and Audrey, they twittered coyly. He obviously used his charm on all women, regardless of age.

Rachel wrote 'white paint' on the Emma Bridgewater notebook she'd slipped into her handbag, thinking it wouldn't be hard to avoid him. Raff was so not her type. Her ex-husband was much more metrosexual. He took time and trouble with his appearance: waxing, moisturising and generally making the best of himself. Perhaps she was being unfair, but she wondered if Raff even showered that often.

The meeting went on and people made suggestions for fundraising. Basically, even with the paint being free, there were a lot of other expenses connected to the project.

It was eventually agreed to have a quiz in the pub and put all the money towards decorating costs. An hour had passed and Rachel wanted to go home. She had volunteered to be on the team who did the decorating, but now realised they would never prepare for painting to her high standards and so she'd find it all extremely stressful. If she was doing a job it had to be to her standards.

'OK, everyone. Shall we have another meeting next week? To discuss a good time to decorate the hall,' said Sarah over the noise of people getting their coats on.

'Oh, Sarah, love,' said someone. 'Do we need a meeting? Couldn't we just have a ring round?'

'Better to have something in the diary,' said Sarah. 'Wednesday?'

Eventually a date was fixed for the following Tuesday.

'OK,' said Sarah. 'We'll see as many people as we can then. I'll try and get Lindy to come too. Meeting over. Rachel, I'll email you all the figures I've got so far, from a couple of builders. Then you'll know what we're dealing with.'

'Fine. I'll get it on to the computer and do a spreadsheet.'

'Brilliant! Thank you so much.'

As Rachel was getting her coat on she thought about her white-painted house and shivered. On impulse she said, 'Er, Sarah? Nothing to do with the hall but would you know someone who could sell me some logs? You obviously know everyone.'

Sarah glanced at Raff and frowned slightly. 'Oh yes, I can do that. Leave it with me. I'll think of someone who'll sell you nice dry ones.' She smiled. 'I think all that went quite well, don't you?'

'To be honest,' said Rachel, 'I've never been to a meeting without a PowerPoint presentation before.'

Sarah laughed. 'Ooh, what's one of them? As they'd say round here!'

Rachel laughed too. 'But meetings like this one are much more fun.'

'Sometimes they can be a nightmare,' said Sarah, 'but it was really great having you there. It gives me hope that we will get the hall up and running one day. Maybe not in my lifetime but one day.'

Rachel gave Sarah's arm a squeeze. 'I think you're being a little bit pessimistic but I grant you, it probably won't be done this year.'

'I'll walk you home,' said Raff as people began to head for the stairs.

'No, thank you. I'll be fine on my own, thanks.' Rachel was firm. She had no intention of walking home with Raff.

Sarah, who had been saying goodbye to the others, came up. 'Did I hear you say you'd walk Rachel home, Raff? That would be good. I need to get back. I left a ham boiling and James – my husband – won't hear the pinger and it might boil dry.'

'Really, I'll be fine,' Rachel insisted.

Sarah shook her head. 'I wouldn't be happy about you going on your own. That path is full of potholes.'

Raff held out his arm. Rachel ignored it. She might have to walk home with him but she didn't have to hold on to him. They walked down the stairs in silence. As they passed the main entrance to the pub, Raff said, 'Come for a cheeky half?'

Rachel shuddered. 'No thank you. But please, if you want one, go ahead. I've been looking after myself for some years now. I can walk to my own house without a minder.'

'Another time then,' said Raff, ignoring this. 'Come along. It's dark.'

Because she couldn't physically prevent him walking with her, they set off down the path side by side. As they left the village green the path grew narrow.

'We'd better walk in single file,' said Rachel, having bumped into Raff at least twice. 'Or you could just leave me here? I will be quite safe. You could watch if you were worried, make sure no one jumps out of the bushes?'

'You're very stubborn, aren't you?' he said.

'Yes,' Rachel replied quickly. 'I see it as a virtue.'

He laughed. 'I like a challenge.'

Rachel didn't know what to say. She walked on, wishing she could stop him walking with her. When she got to her gate she halted. 'OK, I'm safely here. You can go now.' She realised she'd sounded churlish but she hadn't wanted him to escort her in the first place.

'OK. I'll be seeing you.'

Rachel didn't turn to watch him go. She could hear him walking down the lane humming. She couldn't bear humming. It was too random.

She went inside the house and looked around her at its white perfection. She had spent weekend after weekend removing years' worth of paint from the cornice so the carving stood out sharply. She realised now she had neglected her husband. She had, as he had claimed, put this house in the country before their marriage. Well, now it was her home. And she would make a go of living here, whatever happened.

Later, before she went to bed, she opened the cupboard next to the bathroom and inspected the piles of sheets, duvet covers, pillowcases and mattress toppers in it. She'd had the cupboard specially built. She needed somewhere to store what she considered a minor obsession. When she was stressed she bought bedlinen. When she lived in London she'd fantasised about one day having a linen cupboard full of lovely sheets, piled in perfect columns. It was the place of safety she went to in her head. Now she had it in real life. She smiled.

Chapter Three

The following day, Rachel was upstairs in the bedroom designated as her office, checking the spreadsheet in front of her for a final time. Her client liked his accounts in hard copy and she was about to put them into the waiting envelope when a movement from the garden caught her eye. She looked out and saw Raff heading down her front path.

Without stopping to think she flew down the stairs to stop him. She didn't want him in her house.

She had the door open before he had time to knock.

'Oh, hello!' he said, surprised, laughing. 'Were you looking out for me?'

There was something about his voice, his accent, which she couldn't place. It didn't go, quite, with the tatty denim, the leather work-boots and the too-long hair. It was unsettling.

'I was just passing the window and saw you arrive,' she said, hoping he wouldn't notice that she was slightly out of breath.

'I've got some logs for you. Sarah told me you needed some.'

'Goodness. I only mentioned it to her last night.'

'And she got in touch with me this morning.'

'I wonder why she didn't ask you last night?'

'She probably didn't think I had dry ones. But her usual supplier obviously didn't have any so she had to resort to me anyway. And here I am. With the logs.'

'Oh, right.' Rachel didn't know what to say. She couldn't ask him to go away until she'd had time to psych herself up for his visit. 'Well, maybe if you could come round the back with them?'

He frowned. 'Now why would I do that?'

'Well,' said Rachel, unable to think of a reasonable answer. 'It's the way it happens. Logs come into the house via the back door.' She really hoped he couldn't tell this was the first load of logs she'd ever taken delivery of.

'And where is your stove?'

'In the sitting room.'

'Which is at the front of the house. Better to have the logs near the stove. Less hefting them about that way.'

Rachel opened her mouth to protest but he was already walking back down her garden path towards his Land Rover, which, she noticed, had a trailer attached to it.

Protecting her home was instinctive with Rachel and rapidly she planned how she could do this. She could ask him to leave the logs outside the front door so she could bring them in herself in a properly organised way but she was certain he'd have some reason why this wouldn't work.

Glancing at him, she saw him lifting a wheelbarrow

35

down from the trailer and knew she only had a few moments to make another plan. Mentally she went through various sheets and old bits of cloth that she might cover up her floor with but then remembered that she'd had a purge and didn't own any sheets that weren't pristine, and the thought of a wheelbarrow going over her thousand-thread-count percale made her feel as if she might faint.

Now she could hear the heavy chunk, chunk, of logs being thrown into a wheelbarrow. How long would it take to fill it?

She'd managed to roll up a few inches of one end of her white wool rug before the first load of wood trundled up the path. It stopped. Rachel continued to try to roll the rug but it was so wide she needed someone at the other end to roll too. She considered asking Raff but somehow the thought of him, in his boots, rolling her rug was worse than anything.

'What are you doing?' he asked.

She looked up at him from her position on the floor, knowing he must think her an idiot. 'Just getting the rug out of the way so it won't get dirty.'

'And how am I supposed to get the wheelbarrow over that lump of carpet? Just put it flat and don't worry about the dirt. There isn't any, anyway.'

Somehow she found herself letting the rug unroll itself and Raff's wheelbarrow went over it. She shuddered. He halted at the stove and began stacking the logs in the inglenook that surrounded it. She had to admit he was doing it quite neatly. She'd redo it herself once he'd gone, of course, but that would be OK.

'This is the perfect place to store logs,' said Raff. 'They'll keep lovely and dry and they'll be handy.' He put the last log in place. 'Have you got anywhere outside where I can put the rest of the load? You've room for another barrowload here but not for the whole lot.'

How could she have forgotten the woodshed? Cursing herself for being such a townie she'd forgotten the selection of sheds that still stood in her back garden. Her builder from London had said they might be useful and she had agreed, planning to disguise them as beach huts, only white, at the first opportunity.

'That's where you should have put the wood in the first place,' she said. 'In the sheds.'

He raised an eyebrow. 'And how much mess would that have made every night as you carried in baskets of logs to make up the fire?'

Although anxious and irritated and a little bit frightened, the words 'baskets of logs' were soothing. It was one of the dreams she'd had in London: that she lived in the country, with baskets of logs by a roaring woodburner. And in the dream she hadn't minded about mess.

'I'll find the key and unlock the door.'

'And put the kettle on, this is thirsty work.'

Stunned, she did as she was told. It wasn't that she was a snob, not at all. Some of her best friends had quite ordinary jobs, but she hardly knew Raff. He wasn't like Kenneth, the builder she'd got on so well with in London – so well, in fact, she had asked him to work on this house, too. He had fully understood her need to put the nozzle of the vacuum up against the hole he was drilling lest any dust land. Raff was a random guy Sarah had misguidedly asked to walk her home and now he was delivering logs.

She took her time in the kitchen, not wanting to see her rug desecrated by his boots tramping over it as if it was just, well, a rug.

'Tea's ready,' she said eventually.

Raff had stacked the logs in a way that almost kept up to her own standards of tidiness. But it threw up another problem. Rachel wasn't so much a townie that she didn't know stacking logs wasn't part of the usual delivery process. He had gone out of his way for her.

'Is that all of them?' she said. She wanted him out of her house.

He frowned slightly. 'No. We've discussed this already. I've over a half a trailer for your woodshed. Now let's have this tea.'

It wasn't so much that he made the place look untidy, Rachel realised, although he did. It was because he was such a large personality. He'd ignored her offer of a chair and was leaning against her kitchen table, dislodging it slightly, drumming his fingers, looking around.

'Your house is very – white,' he said.

'Yes. It's how I like it.' It was hard not to sound defensive when that was exactly how she felt.

'I'm not complaining, just commenting,' he said.

Rachel couldn't meet his gaze. She knew he was looking at her, thinking her weird, and wished he'd leave. She wanted to hoover the rug and see if it had suffered any lasting damage.

'So, how long have you lived here permanently? I thought it was just a weekend place.'

'Not any more. But I haven't been here long. And I don't go out much.' Now she sounded pathetic. She tried to smile.

'Why's that then?'

'I work from home.' Her smile worked better this time.

'Have you any biscuits?'

Rachel wondered if people in the country really were as different from city people as her London friends had warned her. She opened a cupboard and found the packet of digestives she'd bought for the removal men.

'Oh,' he said, looking at the biscuit she handed him on a plate as if he'd never seen one before. 'They're not white.'

'They didn't have white ones at the local shop,' said Rachel calmly. 'They're going to try and get some in for me.'

His smile crinkled up his face, revealing white, slightly crooked teeth. He acknowledged that she was teasing him back and appreciated it.

'They do their best to please.'

'I've found them very helpful,' said Rachel.

'Do you find it lonely, down here?'

Rachel nodded. 'I did a bit, in the beginning, but I'm beginning to get to know people now.'

'Sarah's daughter, Lindy.'

'That's right. I don't know her well yet but she's very nice.'

'She is.'

He drained his mug (porcelain, white, but with a raised pattern) and slammed it on the drainer. Rachel winced. 'Well, I'd better get on with unloading the rest of the logs.'

While Raff went down the garden path with his barrow, Rachel was free to inspect the damage inside once more.

To be fair to Raff, his pile *was* very tidy and the logs, though not white, were pale and Rachel had to admit they softened the look of her sitting room in a pleasing way. The dead leaves and bits of bark on the rug hoovered up very well.

She had a bundle of notes ready when he knocked on the back door to say that he'd finished unloading.

'That's amazing! Thank you so much,' she said, buoyed up by the thought he was going to leave her alone at last. 'How much do I owe you?'

He seemed to take a long time to work it out and yet he must know how much he charged for a load of logs. He didn't need to mentally count the exact number he had provided. 'Let's call it a moving-in present, shall we?'

She could barely suppress a shudder at the thought. 'Oh no. I couldn't do that. It wouldn't be right.' She revealed the notes in her hand. 'Look, I've got cash. How much is it?'

'I said, it's a present.'

'I really wouldn't be happy with that,' said Rachel firmly. 'You must let me pay you or I'll find out from Sarah how much it should be and deliver it.'

He considered this. 'As much as I'd like that, I'd prefer to give you the logs. You can take me out for a drink as a thank you.'

Thinking she'd rather die than take him for a drink, she made one last attempt. 'Really, I want to pay you!'

'And I'd rather you took me for a drink and, as the supplier, I get to choose.'

Then he walked out of her back door.

After Rachel had cleared up the kitchen, resisting the temptation to clean the whole house again, she pulled on her coat and set off to find Lindy's house. She needed to get out, get some exercise. Working from home was great in many ways but it meant she didn't have company on tap when she needed it. Raff had been company but in a very unsettling way. Besides, if she could find out how much a load of logs cost she could find some way of getting the money to him that didn't involve socialising with him.

She found Lindy's little cottage by asking at the shop for directions. It was along a lane where a row of cottages had once housed mill workers. The mill was now converted into several flats.

As she walked down the path towards the house she realised just how tiny it was. And not tidy. Rachel had always believed that the smaller the space you lived in the tidier you had to be. Apparently Lindy didn't agree. The little garden was full of bikes and other toys, many of them plastic. Maybe Lindy kept them in the garden rather than have them cluttering up the house.

She knocked on the door. A worryingly long time later it was answered by Beth wearing what appeared to be a pair of net curtains.

'Thank goodness it's you!' Beth said. 'It could have been anyone. Lindy's on the phone. Come in.'

Rachel stepped over the threshold breathing deeply.

She could cope with other people's mess pretty well but Lindy's house was going to be a challenge. She'd never actually seen such an untidy house before. Every surface seemed to be piled with something: fabric, toys, clothes, newspapers, dirty mugs; it was Rachel's worst nightmare.

'Am I interrupting anything?' She moistened her dry lips, willing her voice to sound normal.

'Not really,' said Beth. 'At least you are, but we don't mind. Could do with the input. What do you think about this dress?'

Beth seemed completely unfazed by the chaos and Rachel found this calming. She tried to sound just as matter-of-fact.

'Truth or tact?' she asked, not wanting to fall out with her new friends.

'If you have to ask it means you agree with us. It's a beggar.' Beth looked down at herself dolefully.

'I'm so sorry,' said Rachel. 'What is it?'

'Well, it might have become Helena's wedding dress.'

'Where did it come from?'

'eBay. Helena bought it thinking if it was cheap it must be a bargain. Bad mistake. She should have left me to do it. I'm the eBay expert.'

'I suppose she thought if it was her wedding dress...' suggested Rachel. 'I mean, I haven't got a sister but if I did and she tried to buy my wedding dress – well, I'd have a fit.'

Beth giggled. 'You wouldn't want to go on *Don't Tell the Bride*, then?'

'What? And have my loutish fiancé make all the

42

decisions about the wedding? Not bloody likely!' For some reason Raff came into her head and with him the sort of wedding he might plan. Her ex-husband would have done a very good job of planning a wedding. Apart from the dress, of course. That would have to be her choice.

'The thing is,' said Beth, 'Helena knows I know all about eBay. She could always reject my choice, but she shouldn't have got carried away.' She turned her back to Rachel. 'You couldn't help me get out of this, could you?'

Rachel saw the dress was made to fit with pins and started on them.

'I do sound bossy, don't I?' Beth went on. 'But when we've only got a tiny amount to spend we can't waste anything.'

Lindy came in with two mugs. 'Hello, Rachel! How nice to see you. I was on the phone in the kitchen then thought I'd get coffees while I was in there. What would you like? Tea or coffee? Tea is a bag in a mug and coffee is value instant.'

Rachel's ex had been a coffee purist and it had rubbed off on her, a bit. 'Tea, please. Just a dash of milk, no sugar.' She smiled. She felt she was getting the hang of chaos.

'Rachel thought the dress was only fit for dusters, too,' said Beth.

'I didn't say that!'

'But it is, though, isn't it?'

Lindy surveyed the pile of grubby lace lying over the arm of a chair. 'At the moment, yes. But I could turn it into a nice dress for someone...'

'And I, with my eBaying skills, could sell it. You'd get

the money, Lind. You'd be doing the work.' Beth seemed pleased with this suggestion.

'We could work something out,' said Lindy. She picked up the dress. 'It would look better if it was ironed.'

'Can I do that?' asked Rachel. 'I love ironing.'

'You like ironing?' said Lindy incredulously as she hefted a big pile of something that turned out to be curtains from a surface that currently cut across the sitting-room floor leaving very little space for walking about. It was an ironing board. 'Really? I wonder if I might like it if I ever had time to do it. But I don't. Gran's curtains need doing desperately. I altered them for her and still haven't pressed the hems. I never got further than setting up the ironing board.'

'I'll do them,' said Rachel, hoping she wasn't showing insane eagerness to get creases out of things as she clambered over the clutter to get to the ironing board as if it were a life raft.

Lindy handed over the dress. 'If you iron it, Beth can put it on again and I'll see what I can do.'

'You know what I've been thinking?' said Beth.

'No,' said Lindy. 'We're not psychic.' She glanced at Rachel who was organising her ironing pile. 'At least I'm not.'

'Remember our toast? To new beginnings? I think this could be a new beginning.'

'What could?' asked Rachel.

'I think we should set up a little company, doing what we're good at.'

'I am good at ironing,' said Rachel, 'but I don't want to do it as a business.'

44

'Not ironing! At least, not only ironing, but combining our skills: my eBay talent, Lindy's sewing, Rachel, you doing what you do when you're not ironing—'

'Accounts,' said Rachel.'

'Perfect!' said Beth. 'You always need someone who does accounts.'

'And I do lots of other things as well,' said Rachel, liking the sound of what Beth was saying.

'We could arrange weddings for people, on the cheap,' Beth finished.

'Catchy name!' said Lindy. '"Weddings on the Cheap"! That'll get people flocking to us.'

'You never know,' said Rachel. 'It might. But a better name would be "Vintage Weddings".'

'Vintage doesn't mean cheap, does it?' asked Lindy.

'No, but it always means second-hand, or "pre-loved",' said Rachel. 'It would fit in with revamping old wedding dresses.'

'Oh, I like that!' said Beth. 'And if we did a few for other people, we'd know more what to do for Helena's.'

'We'd have our day jobs as well, of course,' said Rachel, pausing in her ironing, 'until it takes off. But it would be brilliant fun. Or it might be. Have you got a sleeve board?' she asked Lindy.

'Somewhere. There!' said Lindy triumphantly. 'It's being a skateboard ramp for superheroes.'

Rachel accepted the offered board. 'Don't you find it difficult working in such...' She paused, aware she might cause offence.

'In such a mess?' asked Lindy. 'Well, in a perfect world I'd have a huge space to do dressmaking and things but as it is, I just have to focus on what I'm doing and ignore everything else.' She smiled wryly. 'My mum says it's a special gift. What she means is, I should tidy up more. But there seems no point.'

Rachel swallowed and concentrated on the frill on the sleeve. Unknowingly, Lindy had just told her the whole focus of her own life was pointless. Rachel was trying very hard to work out if she was right.

But at least her ironing skills were useful. A little while and a cup of tea later, she handed back the dress, laying it over Lindy's arms. 'It's still dreadful but at least it doesn't need ironing any more. Mind if I get on with these curtains?'

'Knock yourself out!' said Lindy. 'Gran will be thrilled. She does so much for me and I can't even get her curtains finished for her.' She paused. 'Put the dress back on, Beth. Let's see what I can do with it.'

Lindy had cut a sweetheart neckline and was pinning in a cap sleeve in place of the wrist-length ones when she remembered something. 'Sorry, Rachel. You didn't actually come round here to do my ironing.'

'That's OK. I love ironing.'

'But why did you come?'

Rachel shrugged. 'I just needed company. I had a load of logs delivered and—'

'Oh no,' said Lindy, looking at her, worried. 'Don't tell me Mum – er – who delivered the logs?'

'Raff.'

'No! Mum really should know better.'

'To be fair, I think she did try to get some from someone else first.'

'So what's wrong with Raff?' asked Beth.

'He's a nice guy and all that,' said Lindy, 'and his logs are really cheap, but...'

'What?' asked Rachel.

'Well, you're new to the area. He's bound to be interested and – how much did he charge you for the logs?'

Sensing Lindy would be sympathetic to her outrage, Rachel put down the iron. 'He didn't charge me. He said I was to take him out for a drink instead.'

'That's all you need!' said Lindy. 'Raff McKenzie hitting on you when you've only been here five minutes.'

'He was a bit – full on,' admitted Rachel.

'Don't get me wrong. He's nice. But he's a bit – well, you know – love 'em and leave 'em.'

'Has he ever tried it on with you?' asked Beth.

Lindy shook her head. 'No. But there was a girl who broke her heart over him and left the area.' Lindy went on: 'We don't want Rachel leaving if she's going to be so useful!'

Rachel laughed. 'I promise I won't let him break my heart. It took me years to get to live here. I'm not going to be driven away by a man. Even if he does look a bit like the dark-haired one in the Ladybirds.'

Lindy's eyes widened. 'Yes! He does, now you come to mention it.'

'He sounds lovely,' said Beth wistfully. 'Maybe he just needs the love of a good woman.'

'Maybe,' said Lindy, sounding sceptical. 'Or maybe he just plays around.'

'Anyway,' said Rachel. 'If you could just tell me how much a load of logs is, and his address, I can post him a cheque. Cash even,' she added.

'I'll have to ask Mum,' said Lindy. 'And tell her off at the same time.'

'I can't imagine telling my mother off,' said Beth.

'I couldn't imagine that Lindy would make that dress anything other than vile,' said Rachel, 'but it's looking quite nice now.'

Rachel had become accustomed to value tea bags and had got through quite a considerable heap of ironing before Lindy suddenly squealed and realised she should have picked up her boys ten minutes ago.

'Don't go!' she called as she shot out of the door. 'We'll have beans on toast when we come back.'

'I'll go and get a couple more tins of beans and some bread,' said Beth as the door closed behind Lindy. 'I don't think Lindy can really afford to feed us all.'

'Here, take some money,' said Rachel. 'I can stand us beans on toast. I have a few paying clients, at least.'

A little while later, two boys rushed into the house shouting but abruptly stopped when they saw strangers there.

'Hi, guys!' said Beth, gathering up the scraps of lace that Lindy had ruthlessly pruned from the dress.

'Hello!' said Rachel, striving for the same casual tone that Beth had used. She wasn't used to children and never knew how to be with them. There was always the fear that they'd be sticky and make her sticky too. Fortunately they rushed into the kitchen making aeroplane noises.

'It's really kind of you to iron the boys' things,' said Lindy, seeing the pile. 'It's wonderful enough that you did Gran's curtains.'

'Don't you normally iron the boys' things?'

'Frankly, I get a sense of achievement when I get a load of clothes in the washing machine. Getting them dry is enough of a challenge.'

Rachel realised that without a tumble dryer, this would be extremely difficult.

Somehow, Rachel got through the beans on toast with the boys. Lindy's kitchen table was just about big enough for them all to sit at and while Rachel ended up sitting next to Billy, the youngest and potentially stickiest, she was able to keep out of his reach. He was rather sweet, she concluded, and very cheerful.

She made her excuses as soon as she could. She'd enjoyed herself but her tolerance for mess and confusion was low. She waved cheerily at the boys and set off towards order and calm, leaving Beth to read bedtime stories. She wanted to work out a bit of a business plan for Vintage Weddings. She had very little to go on, but it would be good to make a few notes.

Chapter Four

A few days later, Lindy was feeling cheerful as she walked away from her grandmother's house, leaving her two boys in it, watching *Peppa Pig*, having been fed and bathed. She and Gran had done it together, as they often did, and now Lindy was off out.

Not, she admitted, smiling to herself, that a meeting about saving the village hall was exactly a hot date, but she'd long since stopped hoping for them. This was sad for a woman of only twenty-three but so far her life had not turned out as she'd planned.

Turning her mind to happier things, she thought about the wedding dress and was pleased. With the aid of a few crystals and a lot of skilful hand sewing, she'd turned it into something very glamorous. She had loved working with the fine fabrics, even if they weren't the pure silk and lace she'd have preferred. It was still a dress any bride – well, any bride without a fortune to spend on her dress – would be happy to get married in. Sadly, it wasn't ever going to look good on a bride without a tiny waist, so it wasn't suitable for Helena, but it was still lovely.

Although she often thought about how lucky she was – two beautiful boys and very supportive parents and grandmother – Lindy spent a lot of time yearning for something different. Not very different, she always insisted to herself, but a bit. A more creative outlet; work that wasn't just making curtains and hemming jeans. Vintage Weddings could give her this and the thought was heart-warming.

She'd never want to do without all the advantages of bringing up her children in the same place as she'd been brought up herself, but she often felt she was the youngest middle-aged housewife on the planet. She sometimes wondered if she could have worked harder at her marriage, overlooked Edward's lapses, gone for counselling. In her heart of hearts, though, she knew that wouldn't have worked. Her marriage to Edward had been doomed from the start.

But having Rachel and Beth move into the village had given her a much-needed boost. If only their plan to set up a little business to arrange budget weddings came off – it would give her a way of making money for doing what she loved. While she was perfectly happy to make curtains for people she longed to do something a bit more exciting.

She saw Rachel hovering by the end of her lane and hurried to catch up with her. Lindy had offered to call for her but Rachel had insisted she'd be fine, she'd been to a meeting before; however, Lindy sensed that really, she'd like to have someone else to walk into the pub with. Rachel would soon realise, if she hadn't already, that the Prince Albert was not like other pubs, it was far more female-friendly.

'Hi, Rachel!' she called as soon as she was within earshot. 'I can't tell you how thrilled Mum was about getting you on to this committee. And Beth's coming too.'

Rachel laughed. 'I sort of offered, going to the first meeting.' She paused. 'So, have you finished the dress?'

'Yes! It's amazing. Even though I shouldn't say that really. I've got some pictures on my phone. I can't wait to show Beth.'

'Show me what?' said Beth who swung into step beside them on the threshold of the pub.

'The dress. It looks really good.'

'Ooh, can't wait to see it.'

They filed up the stairs to the meeting room. Lindy spotted Raff, chatting to Audrey and Ivy who were treating him as though he was their long-lost nephew.

'Let's sit together,' said Lindy, rearranging chairs to make this possible. She was slightly annoyed with herself when she realised this now meant Rachel was sitting next to Raff. 'Hey, Mum!' she called as Sarah entered the room. 'Had you better have Rachel next to you? If she's treasurer?'

'It's OK, love,' said Sarah calmly, taking off her coat and rearranging her scarf. 'I'll sit on her other side. Ooh, Sukey's provided water.' Sarah poured herself a glass. 'Right!' she said, looking round the table, checking out who was missing.

Lindy resolved to give her mother a firm talking-to about Raff and his ways. She really didn't want Rachel getting messed up by him. Lindy sometimes felt that having children so young had made her maternal instinct a bit excessive but she sensed that in spite of outward appearances Rachel was a little fragile. Raff could be very bad for her just now.

At last everyone was seated and was catching up with those they were seated next to. They obviously wouldn't stop talking until they were made to. Sarah had told Lindy that she'd managed to strong-arm a few more people into coming to this meeting.

'OK!' Sarah tapped her water glass with her pencil and eventually everyone settled down.

'First thing on the agenda: getting the hall painted. We've got the paint – thanks, Raff – all we need is the manpower. I've got a list of people who offered last time. Lindy? Beth? You weren't here at the last meeting; are you up for painting the hall?'

'Of course, if Gran will have the boys for me.'

'A weekend would be best, I think,' said Sarah, looking at Justin and Amanda, who had been at the previous meeting but hadn't signed up for decorating. 'Maybe this Saturday? Do you think you might make it?'

Justin was quick to reply. 'Unlikely. We've got our own house to upgrade. I don't really want to waste a weekend slapping on emulsion.'

Lindy happened to be looking at Rachel when he said this and saw her wince. Given how scrupulously she'd done her ironing, Lindy didn't think 'slapping on emulsion' was quite her way of doing things.

'I'll do it,' said Raff. 'I'll provide ladders and a scaf-folding tower. We'll need one for the ceiling.'

'So are all the materials donated?' asked Rachel, pencil poised. 'If not, how are we going to pay for the ones that aren't free?'

'Until we've done some fundraising, there is no money,' said Sarah. 'I was hoping we could come up with some concrete plans to do this tonight.'

'Bit of a chicken-and-egg situation,' muttered Audrey. 'Maybe we'd be better to just leave things as they are.'

'Maybe if we all chip in – say fifty quid?' said Justin. 'That'll give us roughly five hundred pounds' worth of working capital.'

He might as well have suggested everyone present donated an organ in order to make a new, better person.

Sarah broke through the protest. 'That's actually a good idea, er, Justin, but most people here couldn't manage that sort of donation.'

'We'd pay it back, when the money started coming in,' said Rachel.

'Still far too much,' said Sarah. 'What about twenty? Two hundred will buy us quite a lot. And we could ask people not here tonight to put up some money.'

'I'm on a pension. I already suffer from fuel poverty,' said Ivy. 'I can do a couple of quid and that's my lot.'

Lindy saw Raff give her a sympathetic glance and realised she wouldn't be surprised if this elderly pen-sioner didn't find a load of logs by her back door in the near future. He'd be a really nice man if he didn't play the field so much.

There was more chat and then Rachel tapped the side

of her glass. 'As it's unlikely we're going to reach a figure we can all afford that will still give us a useful amount of money, I suggest we all contribute according to our means. And it is only a loan and will be paid back as soon as we get our first booking.' She looked around. 'Justin? I'll put you down for fifty pounds.'

'Hang on, isn't it a bit complicated, us all donating different amounts?' said someone.

'It's a loan, not a donation, and it's not at all complicated if we keep proper records,' replied Rachel smartly. 'Probably best if people write down their names and the amount they want to give and I'll record it. It'll be private that way.' She looked around her at the disparate group. 'I don't know any of you; I won't judge you if you put in two quid and drive a Rolls-Royce.'

People chuckled.

'We'll do that after the meeting,' said Rachel and looked up at Sarah expectantly.

'Right,' said Sarah, looking, thought her daughter who knew her well, a little pink. 'Just one more thing – I've taken a booking.'

'For the hall?' asked Rachel, aghast.

Sarah nodded. 'It's for a wedding. It's the daughter of one of the farmers I look after.' She paused. 'I'm a farm secretary, for those who don't know.' Rachel and Beth nodded. They hadn't known this.

'Wasn't that a bit rash?' said Justin. 'Think of the state of the place!'

'I think it's good we have a target,' said Rachel. 'It'll make us get on and do it. When is the wedding? Some time in the spring?'

Sarah still looked embarrassed. 'It rather depends on when you think spring begins. Valentine's Day – this year.'

'That's the fourteenth of February,' said Justin.

'That's early!' said someone.

'Same time every year,' said another. 'It's not like Easter.'

'That's only a month away,' said Rachel.

'It's a big ask,' said Justin.

'I know,' said Sarah apologetically, 'but April's mother died when she was quite little. She asked me for help with her wedding. I couldn't not.'

'I think that was rash, Sarah,' said Audrey, shaking her head.

'Oh come on,' said Raff. 'We can do it if we try. If Sarah's got us a gig, we have to go for it.'

No wonder her mother kept saying he was kind, thought Lindy, he was.

'Although of course I couldn't ask a lot of money for the hall,' Sarah went on, sounding a bit apologetic. 'Even painted it'll be fairly ... primitive.'

'Rustic sounds better,' said Rachel, 'and it's going to be lovely. Although we will be really up against it,' she muttered sotto voce.

'So thirty quid is an acceptable fee?' Sarah continued. 'They haven't much money.'

'Get them to pay in advance; the money can go towards materials,' suggested someone.

'Good point,' agreed Rachel. 'Will they be able to do that, do you think?'

Sarah shrugged. 'I'll ask them.'

'Oh, for goodness' sake,' snapped Amanda. 'If they can't afford thirty quid up front, they can't afford to get married! Have they any idea how much a wedding costs? The average is nearly twenty grand.'

'That's an average,' said Rachel. 'It means lots of weddings are far cheaper.'

'Good thing!' muttered Beth.

'I told the bride you'd ring her,' said Sarah, addressing Beth. 'That you three girls could help?'

Lindy wondered if her mother realised they wanted to organise vintage weddings for money, not to help out other broke women.

There was more discussion about checking with the Parish Council that they could rent out the hall, Sarah being apologetic for being so impulsive and telling April she could have the hall, and then someone agreed to put it to them at the next meeting. The general feeling was that the Parish Council found the hall a huge embarrassment and would be grateful if someone did something about it.

At last Sarah declared the meeting closed.

'I'll collect the donation pledges,' Sarah said. 'It'll be easier for me and it might take a little time. If you three are going for a drink I'll join you.'

'So – downstairs for a quick one?' said Beth to Lindy and Rachel.

'Yup. That would be good. I can show you the pictures of the dress,' said Lindy. 'And we can discuss this fine mess my mother has got us into.'

The other two laughed affectionately. 'Not really a mess,' said Beth. 'A chance to practise.'

'I have to say,' said Rachel, 'I'm really doubtful that we'll be able to get the hall done in time.'

'We've got a month,' said Beth. 'Surely that should be plenty of time.'

'Not if we're going to do it properly,' said Rachel.

'I don't think we've got time for that,' said Lindy, hoping Rachel would never find out that she had been known to decorate without moving the furniture. 'But we'll have to do our best.'

The three bagged a table near the fire and were soon discussing what they could do for the Boracic Bride from the farm.

'I'm not letting that dress go for half nothing,' said Lindy firmly. 'Even to please my mum.'

'Totally agree!' said Beth. 'That's going on eBay as soon as we can get it properly photographed.'

'We'll find BB another dress,' said Lindy.

'Brigitte Bardot?' asked Rachel, confused.

'Boracic Bride,' said Lindy. 'I was just playing around with names. You know, rhyming slang – boracic lint, skint.'

'No,' said Beth. 'It's too negative and reminds me of sprouts. Vintage Weddings is a much better name.'

'Oh, OK,' conceded Lindy.

'She's right,' said Rachel. She frowned. 'I do have to say I am really worried about getting the hall painted in time. By the time we've washed the walls, and all that woodwork in the rafters, sanded it—'

'We'll have to do our best,' said Beth firmly. 'And remember that we can cover up the rafters with things and go back and do the job properly afterwards.'

'But people never do. They always say, "We'll put up

with this for now," but they never go back and do it right.'

Beth put a calming hand on Rachel's. 'But they don't have you to make sure it gets done properly eventually.'

Beth was very good with people, Lindy noted, seeing Rachel smile and look slightly less stricken.

Rachel got to her feet. 'Can I get us some wine? I need help if I'm going to get over the thought of getting that hall looking OK in time.'

Just then Raff appeared.

'Evening, ladies. Rachel?'

Lindy saw Rachel blush and hoped fervently it was just embarrassment and not because she fancied Raff.

'How's that wood burning?' Raff was focusing entirely on Rachel.

'Er – fine! Good!'

'Pushing out lots of heat, then?' went on Raff.

'Oh yes,' Rachel said, 'lots of heat.'

'Good.' Raff continued to look at Rachel.

'Yes?' said Rachel, getting pinker with every moment.

'You never bought me that drink.'

Rachel smiled as if with relief. 'And isn't this the perfect opportunity? I'm just going to the bar. What can I get you?'

He shook his head. 'Too easy. Besides, I can tell you girls are working.'

'We wouldn't mind you joining us, just for a short time,' said Rachel, sending a wild look in the direction of the other two.

Raff shook his head. 'Nope. I want you to ring me up and ask me out for a drink at a time that's convenient for both of us.'

Rachel shook her head. 'I'm sorry, I can't do that.'

'Why? Have you lost my number?'

'No,' said Rachel. 'I didn't lose it. I tore it up into little pieces.'

Lindy wasn't sure what she was expecting him to do when he heard this but Raff laughed and she sensed respect in his expression.

Beth also seemed to be smiling behind her hand.

'Well,' he said, producing a card. 'Let me give it to you again. And if you don't ring me and ask me for a drink you'll owe me for a load of wood.' And he moved off.

Rachel sat down and stuffed the card into her pocket. 'Did you ask your mum how much a load of wood costs? Then I can just pay him. I'd so much rather.'

Lindy shook her head. 'I'm sorry, I forgot.'

Rachel sighed. 'I'll get the drinks,' she said. 'Will wine still cut it? Or do we need vodka?'

Lindy laughed. 'You're the one who needed alcohol to calm your nerves.'

When Rachel came back with a bottle of wine and some glasses, Lindy said, 'You haven't actually lit your wood-burner yet, have you?'

Rachel bit her lip. ''Oh, God, is it that obvious?'

Lindy chuckled. ''Course not! I just guessed.'

'I don't know how to light a fire,' said Rachel. 'I'm so embarrassed. I move down from London to live the country life and I don't even know the basics.'

'You need something to light it with,' said Beth. 'I only learnt how to light one when I was really cold. Moving into the cottage just after Christmas, it was freezing! I've just about got the hang of it now. Candle ends are good.'

'So, what's your cottage like, Beth?' asked Rachel, possibly wanting to direct the conversation away from her failures as a countrywoman.

'It's a bit soulless, to be honest,' said Beth. 'Very like a lot of holiday accommodation. But it's free and I'm very grateful to have it to live in.'

'What you really need is dry kindling,' said Lindy, still thinking about Rachel's need to learn about firelighting. 'One day I'll take you to my favourite kindling place with the boys. But I'll try and drop some over to you before.'

'We really ought to use every spare minute to do the hall,' said Rachel. 'I can't worry about fires now. So don't worry if you don't have time.'

'I'll ring April,' said Beth, 'and tell you when she can meet us.'

'You mean our Boracic Bride?' Lindy couldn't resist.

'We must stop calling her that!' said Beth.

'Otherwise I'm bound to do it to her face.'

'I wouldn't want to take the boys to that meeting. Can we wait until the weekend?' said Lindy. 'And would we go to her or should she come to us?'

'I think we should go to her,' said Rachel. 'Otherwise she might want to see the hall and then she'd take away her thirty pounds and have her wedding somewhere else.'

'But is thirty quid worth worrying about?' said Beth. 'It's such a tiny amount. I can't believe we couldn't get more for it, even as it is.' She took an iPad out of her bag. 'Excuse me. Do you mind if I do a bit of research?'

Lindy suddenly felt downhearted. 'I've just had a thought. If we kill ourselves to get the hall into some sort of decent state we'll only get thirty pounds for it. Wouldn't it be better to turn down the wedding and give ourselves a proper length of time to do it?'

'It would be letting your mum down, though,' said Beth, still looking at her iPad. 'It would be good to have a target. And I know it doesn't sit well with Rachel, but it really doesn't have to be perfect.'

She looked up from the screen. 'It seems you can rent village halls very cheaply but we really must make sure ours is wonderful. Then that's one less thing we have to worry about when Helena's wedding comes around.'

'And I bet ours has better architectural features. Painted, it could look gorgeous. Imagine it filled with flowers,' said Rachel.

'Garlands!' said Lindy. 'Bunting, of course, but it's a bit – well – overdone these days, don't you think?'

'Garlands would be lovely for a wedding,' said Beth. 'I wonder if we could buy them cheaply?'

Lindy shook her head. 'No. If we have garlands we make them. For nothing.'

'We're not all good with our hands,' said Beth. 'I'm good at computers and eBaying but otherwise I'm fairly useless. Although I did like art at school.'

'Oh,' said a voice from behind them. 'That's a shame. I was wondering if any of you wanted a job?'

'Me, please,' said Beth, putting up her hand the moment she saw it was Sukey, licensee of the Prince Albert, who had asked the question. 'I can do bar work.'

'Brilliant!' said Sukey. 'Milly is leaving and I know we're going to be really busy. We've got several music nights coming up. When can you start?'

'Whenever you want me!' said Beth.

'I was going to say yes, too,' said Rachel. 'But I do have a day job.'

'I could keep you in reserve, if we get very busy. Have you got experience?'

'A little bit. And I'm a very quick learner,' said Rachel.

'She's an accountant,' said Beth. 'She can probably do the change thing.'

'Well, I'll keep you in mind if it looks like I need you. Being a single-handed licensee means things can get busy. So as long as you can wash glasses, you'll be fine,' said Sukey easily, heading back to the bar. 'Come and see me at lunchtime tomorrow and we'll work out the details.'

'We can collect kindling after you've done that,' said Lindy. She sighed. 'I wish I could get a job in a pub. I love what I do, sewing, making things, painting cards, but it's quite lonely sometimes.'

'Couldn't you get childcare if you wanted to work outside the home?' asked Rachel.

'I couldn't make enough money to make it worth the cost of the childcare and I rely enough on Mum and Gran as it is, even with school and the nursery, and Billy only goes there part-time. Mum works pretty much full-time and it would be too much for Gran to have them all the time. That's why I just do things I can do at home.'

Beth, who'd obviously never had to consider the cost of childcare, took a moment. 'You make cards?' she said. 'Brilliant. You could do bespoke invitations. Hand-painted. They'd be really expensive.'

'And really time-consuming!' objected Lindy. 'I think

I'd have to design them and do a few and then we'd set up a production line.'

'I can write really tidily,' said Rachel, 'even have a go at calligraphy.'

'Between us we have all the skills,' said Beth, 'although mine is mainly sourcing stuff at bargain prices. But what's our schedule? Collect kindling after we've had a chat with Sukey, then go and see our Vintage Bride?'

Lindy laughed. 'That's worse than Boracic. It makes her sound old. I'll get her contact details off Mum – Oh, here she is.'

Sarah collapsed on the sofa and opened her handbag. 'Get me the biggest glass of wine you can carry,' she said to Lindy, handing her a twenty-pound note. 'And whatever you girls want. And if ever I volunteer to be on a committee again, shoot me.'

Chapter Five

Beth's phone buzzed horribly early. It was a couple of days after the village hall meeting and she and Rachel had arranged to go and visit their first bride, in her home. Lindy was at home, looking after Billy.

Beth spat out the toothpaste and ran back into the bedroom and just caught the phone in time. She had a hunch it would be Rachel and so wasn't surprised when her number was displayed.

'Beth? It's me, Rachel. So sorry to ring you so early but a job has come up at the last minute. I'll have to do it. It means I can't come with you to the farm.'

This was disappointing. 'Well, never mind. I'm sure we can reschedule.'

'No need. I've arranged it. Sarah will take you, then pick you up later.'

'That's very kind of her!'

'It is, but she didn't mind because she got us the gig. And she said it was on her way to some other farms she works for.'

'That's fine then.

'It does mean you might be there rather a long time. Is that OK? Sarah thought April would be fine with that.'

Beth blinked. Rachel was being super-efficient. 'I'm sure it's fine,' she said. 'It'll be nice to have a day out.'

'I am sorry to let you down but I don't want to turn down paying work – it might lead to more. But I feel bad about this morning.'

'It'll be fine,' said Beth. 'I might have to make some decisions on my own though, about things we haven't discussed.'

'We trust you. Now, Sarah will be with you at about eleven. That OK?'

'Oh, yes. I promised Sukey I'd do her a website so I'll do a bit of work on that. Then I'll start designing ours.'

'Oh.' Rachel sounded surprised. 'Have we got anything to put on it?'

'We certainly will very soon. I want to take lots of pictures of the church and the surrounding area.'

'Oh, I know. Like when you're looking at a house on the internet and there are fifteen pictures of the garden and three of the inside.'

'Certainly not,' said Beth. 'Or at least, only a bit. But we've got to get an online presence as soon as possible.'

'I know you're right. And once we've done this wedding we can get April to give us a testimonial.'

'I just hope we get on!' Beth suddenly felt nervous. 'I've never done anything quite like this before.'

'Nor have any of us,' said Rachel. 'And you'll be fine.'

Sarah was prompt and Beth, who had been watching for her, ran out to the car. It was a beautiful winter's day. Bright, cold, with a blue, sun-tinged sky that made spring seem imminent.

'It's lovely having this little tour,' said Beth, looking out of the window at the countryside. The gentle hills were covered with a mixture of farmland and woods and today the leafless trees stood out against the duck-egg sky.

'I love days like this,' said Sarah. 'I think I almost prefer the trees in winter. I like seeing every little branch and twig outlined. Of course it is gorgeous in summer, too, but days like this are special.'

'You're right!' said Beth, thinking of photographs and the website. 'Not having a car means I've been stuck with places I can walk to. I didn't realise how much really great scenery there is just a little further away.'

'But you can drive?'

'Oh yes. I saved up lots of money when I was working, as a student, but when it came to it, I felt a car was more than I could afford really.' She paused. 'Although maybe I should have got one. At least then I would have more choice of jobs.'

'This isn't the best area for jobs if you've got to walk there,' said Sarah. 'Although there is the pub.'

'I know. I'm starting there tonight. When Sukey heard how much experience I had she said I could start straight away. She is so lovely.' Beth paused, waiting in case Sarah had something bad to say about her new employer.

'She is. She has really turned that pub around. She only moved here a few years ago.'

Reassured, Beth went on: 'Aren't there any other busi-nesses that might need someone like me? I've got skills that could be useful for a small business. You know, I could set up websites, help with marketing, write blogs for small firms who don't have an online presence but need one.'

Sarah shook her head. 'Not within walking distance. I'm a farm secretary but I only work part-time and I couldn't even do that if I didn't have a car.'

'Oh well. In the meantime I could help any locals get online so they can send emails, or Skype, if they've got computers and don't know how to use them. That would be for nothing, of course.'

Sarah shot her an approving look. 'That's kind. I'm sure there are a few people in that situation.'

'But I'm obviously going to need a car if I'm going to get a proper job.'

Sarah nodded as she changed gear. 'Lindy has the same problem. She'd love to do something that gets her out of the house a bit, but with no transport and the cost of childcare, she has to do stuff from home.' She paused. 'It would be wonderful if you girls could make a go of your business. Just hearing about it in the pub the other night got me all enthusiastic.'

'But it will take ages before we're actually able to make money from it,' said Beth. She thought for a few moments. 'We can use Rachel's car, I suppose, but we ought to have a works van or something.'

'You're right. You need wheels. I'll have a think. Lindy's never managed to afford one on her own – even with us helping her – but if there was something she could occasionally have the use of to help her get to bigger towns to get materials, deliver things, it would be really useful. There are busses of course, but not at very convenient times.'

They fell into a friendly silence. Beth reflected how nice it must be to be able to just chat to your mum without there always being undercurrents. Beth's mother wanted to micromanage every corner of her daughters' lives. It was silly; if she weren't so bossy she'd see more of them, Beth and Helena both acknowledged.

They had climbed up out of the valley and on to the hill and now the views were more far-reaching, across the Severn Plain to the hills beyond.

Sarah pulled up at a gateway with 'Spring Farm' written on it. 'What amazing views!' said Beth.

'You should see them from the farm!' said Sarah. 'As it's not very far, do you mind going the rest of the way on your own? If I come I'll have to talk to Eamon, April's father, and it'll make me horribly late.'

'No, that's fine,' said Beth.

'I'll pick you up at three? April will give you something to eat, I'm sure. Sorry this is such a rush!'

Having assured Sarah this was absolutely fine, Beth set off. She wasn't exactly filled with trepidation but she did wonder what she'd find at the end of the farm drive on the top of the hill.

The farmhouse was just round the corner and there was a young man on the doorstep. He was wearing overalls tucked into wellington boots and dark blond hair that curled slightly.

'Hi!' he said, smiling. 'You're Beth? Here about the wedding? April asked me to look out for you. She's just upstairs.'

'That's me.' The young man was looking at her in a way that said 'interested'. As a barmaid she'd had her fair share of chatting up and casual dating but in spite of his working clothes, this guy had something about him. She smiled shyly.

'Well, come in! I'll give April a shout.' He grinned. 'I'm Charlie, her brother. I'll put the kettle on, then I'm off. I'll leave you to do the girly things.'

Beth stepped into a little porch that led into a large kitchen that was obviously the centre of the house, where everything went on. She could tell no one had done anything about decorating it for several decades and it had an easy chaos about it. An open fire with a cream-coloured, crazed stove-enamel surround flickered, and at the back of the room Beth could see some sort of solid-fuel range. The place was definitely tatty and untidy but it was warm and comfortable and she relaxed a little.

A young woman wearing a dressing gown, with long, curly brown hair round her shoulders, came into the room. 'Are you Beth? I'm April. Sorry not to be dressed. I've been trying on my mother's wedding dress. I'll get my clothes on.'

'Don't do that!' said Beth, seeing a solution to a major expense right there. 'Let's see your mother's dress.'

April shook her head. 'Can't get near it. My mother was tiny. I know I said I'd diet before the wedding but even if I starve myself I won't lose two stone in a month.'

Beth was firm. 'Lindy – that's Sarah's daughter: do you know her? – she's brilliant at making wedding dresses fit, and flatter. And the dress is a major expense in a wedding. If we could use your mother's dress, even factoring in the alterations, that would save a lot of money.'

April looked pained. 'That's what I thought but—'

'Let's have a look, shall we?' said Beth.

Beth followed April up a creaky staircase with faded floral walls, wondering if the house was wonderfully 'vintage' or dreadfully out of date, and deciding the former. There were patches where water had obviously come in at some point and the paintwork was chipped but it had a lovely ambience.

It got better. April's bedroom made Beth think of girls' bedrooms described in the pony books she used to read so avidly as a child. The single bed was covered by a patchwork counterpane and there was a dark oak dressing table. Rosettes formed a frieze round the top of the rosy wallpaper and photographs of April on various horses covered the walls. Beth loved it. Her own girlhood bedroom had been designed by her mother. Pictures were only allowed on one section of wall and her mother had had a large say in which bands were featured.

'What a lovely room!'

'Do you think so?' said April, surprised. 'It's dreadfully old-fashioned but I like it.'

'It's gorgeous!' Beth looked around her and spotted horsey plaster ornaments, odd vases and souvenirs from gymkhanas and holiday destinations. 'But then I really like vintage things. Now let's see this dress.'

'It's actually in here,' said April, leading Beth to another room. 'I just needed to get my hair clip. The dress looks a bit better with my hair up.'

The dress was hanging over the back of a chair. April

had obviously put it there when she heard Beth arrive. Beth picked it up. She couldn't tell what period it was, although she assumed it must be eighties. It was like a coat, with covered buttons all down the front, a high neck, narrow waist and leg-of-mutton sleeves ending with a frill at the wrist. There was a frill at the neck and a sash that could have been done up at the front or the back, Beth couldn't tell.

'This is amazing!' Beth would have said something nice, out of politeness, but she really meant it. 'Have you seen that programme when the bride has to decide whether to have a new dress or wear her mother's? The ones I've seen have always had awful dresses but this is really special.'

'I know it is,' said April glumly. 'I remember my mum telling me how expensive it was – but I can't fit into it.'

The buttons were already undone. 'Let's see. I'm sure Lindy could alter this and it's so lovely. It won't look like it was your mother's, just fabulously vintage.'

'I like the idea of having a vintage wedding,' said April. 'It sounds elegant. A wedding on the cheap doesn't sound nearly so good.'

'Mm,' said Beth, helping April get the dress over her shoulders. 'We're thinking of calling ourselves Vintage Weddings – our little business that sorts out weddings for people.'

'What do you provide, exactly?' asked April, in the dress now, but with none of the buttons done up.

'We haven't worked out the details yet – you'll be our first client – but I promise we'll be amazing value for money and get you a wedding for less than you could do it without us.' Beth realised this was a massive assumption but why would anyone use them if it wasn't true?

She looked at April and took hold of the sides of the dress. They didn't meet over her stomach.

'I'm so fat!' said April.

'No you're not, at all. You're healthy and people were thinner in the eighties.' She considered. 'This is such a lovely dress we must get you into it. I'm sure Lindy could do wonders with it. It needs a panel or something added to the middle. It fits OK on the arms and shoulders.'

'I would love to wear it. Dad would be so pleased. And not just because it'll be cheap.' April paused. 'How much would a new dress be?'

Beth, who had done quite a lot of research before she came, said, 'Average is a thousand, but of course lots and lots of dresses are much cheaper. What's your budget?'

'I don't exactly have a budget but Tristram and I are going to share the cost with Dad and Tristram's parents. None of us has much money though, so it has to be really cheap.'

'Well, Lindy could alter this for you for far less than the cheapest dress and it'll be fabulous. And I'm not sure the cheapest dress would be all that nice. This is such gorgeous material.'

'There's some more of it in the attic. Offcuts,' said April.

'Perfect! Well, that's one big tick. Shall we go and sort out what else we might be able to help you with?' Beth felt really excited. Although she enjoyed creating websites – something she learnt during her much despised university career – it was much more fun to deal with real human beings.

After fiddling with the dress, the spare material and other bits and pieces, April led them downstairs. Here they sat at the kitchen table sipping tea. April had a folder decorated with ponies that Beth really hoped was an old one. She didn't want their first client to still be pony-obsessed in her mid-twenties.

'I really want to arrive by pony and trap,' said April, giving Beth a frisson of anxiety about ponies. 'But Dad can do that. There's a lovely one in the barn. Needs a bit of cleaning up but Charlie can drive me.'

'Great,' said Beth, crossing 'transport' off her list. Then she had a thought. 'Do you think he'd be happy for us to hire it for other weddings?'

April shrugged. 'Probably. If we've got to clean it for mine we might as well use it. We've got the perfect pony, and Charlie's very good at driving.'

'What about if it rains? It will be February, after all.'

April made a face. 'It'll have to be Dad's Range Rover.'

'Well, that sounds smart and we can put ribbon on it.'

'It's not smart,' said April, giggling, 'but we could put ribbon on it.'

'That's another expense we don't need then. Now what sort of food do you want?' Catering was one of the things they hadn't properly worked out. They'd agreed they needed to offer it as it was such a big part of the wedding, but neither Lindy nor Rachel had declared a passion for making canapés, and they hadn't yet found another solution.

'We fancy a proper meal but maybe people could serve themselves? A sit-down do would be very expensive, wouldn't it? Of course we would sit down to eat it. We wouldn't expect them to stand around, chomping away.'

'What sort of food? Roast beef and Yorkshire pudding? Or something a bit easier to serve?'

Beth then realised she had no idea what the kitchen arrangements were like at the hall and that they'd have to hire in hotplates and things. She made a note. 'If you went for the easier option, with people serving them-selves, it would certainly save on waiting costs and there are lots of women locally who produce great food. I went to an event at the hall – which will look amazing by the way – and the nibbles were excellent. We just need to find out who did them.'

'Dad has lots of goodwill locally – because he's a widower, I suppose – so I'm sure we could find people to make food. We'd pay for the ingredients, of course, although we can provide a ham. And my auntie wants to make the cake.'

'This wedding will turn out very reasonable!' said Beth, pleased. 'I wonder if your auntie might like to make cakes for other clients?'

'I'll have to ask her. I'm not sure. But there are always people willing to make a cake. At Mum's funeral – I was ten – I remember tables full of cakes.'

'Does your auntie do icing?'

April shrugged. 'Not sure.'

Beth made a note. Cake-decorating, like catering, was fairly important.

Just then Charlie appeared. He'd obviously come in through the back door. 'Any soup on?'

'No, sorry,' said April, getting up. 'You did the lambs for me; I'll make lunch. You talk to Beth.'

Charlie joined Beth at the table. 'So, tell me all about yourself. You're new to the area, aren't you? I certainly haven't seen you around.'

'I am new,' Beth agreed.

'So, what brought you here? Not the amazing nightlife.'

'Just luck really. I've been lent a house – a holiday let – to live in for the winter. But I love it here. It's really pretty and I'm meeting great new people.'

'I'm meeting great new people too!' said Charlie, twinkling. 'Or maybe just one person.'

'Charlie!' said April, laughing. 'Leave her alone. She doesn't want to be hit on.'

'No, I'm working,' said Beth but she smiled, to indicate that she actually didn't mind at all.

'So, what are you working at, exactly? To me, if it doesn't involve tractors or livestock, it's just having fun.'

Beth laughed lightly. 'I know farming is important but so are other things. We – two friends and I – are just in the process of setting up a business and April is our first client.'

'Beth and her colleagues are helping me with the wedding,' said April. 'Sarah's daughter Lindy is one of them.'

'So what's the business exactly?' asked Charlie.

Beth realised they needed a simple sentence that embodied the services they offered.

'We offer a service to couples who want a nice wedding but have very small budgets. Currently we're only doing it in this area, offering the village hall – suitably prettied-up – for receptions but we could arrange other venues, marquees for example, if that's what the couples would prefer.' Considering she hadn't had long to think about it, she was pleased with how this sounded.

'Cool,' said Charlie. 'And what are you doing for my sister?'

'Loads!' said April. 'Lindy is going to alter Mum's wedding dress for me. And we're having the do in the village hall.'

'I don't know why you're not having it in the barn,' said Charlie. 'It just needs a bit of clearing out.'

'Charlie! The barn would take for ever to clear out and besides, it's next month. It'll be bloody freezing in the barn in February. At least there is some sort of heating in the hall.'

'Although if you did ever clear out the barn,' said Beth, 'one day, you could hire it out as a venue. Bit of diversification?' Beth's pen hovered over her pad. She could imagine lots of brides wanting to get married in a beautifully decorated barn. She quite fancied it herself.

Charlie nodded. 'Not a bad idea. It would take a bit of fixing up though. Pity April's getting married in such a hurry.'

'You know it's because Tristram's got a job in the States and we have to be married so I can have a visa. I thought I'd told you.'

'Sorry. I don't think I took that in about the visa,' said Charlie.

'I don't want Beth to think I'm pregnant or something.'

77

'Really, these days so many people get married after they've had their children,' said Beth.

'I know,' said April. 'But Dad really wouldn't have liked that!'

At that moment April's dad appeared, wiping his feet hard. 'It's getting cold out there!' he said. 'Oh, company!'

'This is Beth, Lindy's friend. She's helping with the wedding,' said April.

Beth smiled and got up. 'Hello, nice to meet you, Mr Williams.'

'Eamon,' said the farmer. 'Very nice to meet you too. I was so grateful when Sarah said she knew someone who could help April.' He smiled a little ruefully. 'Wedding on a budget!'

'Our speciality,' said Beth. 'And we've already found lots of ways to really save money.'

'The dress, Dad. Lindy can make it fit me!'

'It'll look wonderful. Such a lovely dress.'

Eamon became a little misty-eyed. 'It *was* a lovely dress. Your mother gave up a lot to marry a farmer in the back of beyond.'

'But she loved it here,' said April. 'You know she did.'

'I know, lass. But she could have done better.'

'Come on, you two!' said Charlie. 'Let's not get too sentimental. Time for that on the wedding day. Now, are those sandwiches ready?'

Beth could have hugged him. For several reasons. Firstly she was grateful for him changing the mood before everyone started crying and secondly, well, he was very fit.

*

After lunch, Beth helped April clear up while the men discussed the farm. Eamon made his apologies. 'Must be getting on, but thank you for coming, Beth. With no mother to help her—'

'It's my absolute pleasure,' said Beth quickly before Eamon could get mournful again. 'This is going to be great fun.'

Charlie lingered a little. 'How are you getting back?' he asked Beth.

'Sarah's coming for me later. At about three.' She realised how late that was. However she dragged it out, she couldn't usefully do much more than another hour with April.

'I could drop you back in an hour if that would suit you,' said Charlie. 'Unless you've more to do, of course.'

Beth looked at April. She probably had things of her own to be getting on with. 'Well, the next thing is to arrange a time with Lindy to see about altering the dress, so if you wouldn't mind giving me a lift . . .'

'I'd be delighted,' said Charlie with a grin.

'Hope you don't mind this old van,' said Charlie a little later.

'Er, no, it's fine,' said Beth, trying to breathe through her mouth to avoid the smell.

'It's a bit tatty, but it goes fine.' To prove this, he changed down a gear and roared round a corner. 'Got plenty of grunt,' he said.

'And that's good?'

'Of course. Do you drive?'

'Yes, but I haven't got anything to drive at the moment.'

In spite of this she currently had her right foot pressed to the floor, braking hard.

Charlie noticed this. 'Sorry, am I going a bit fast for you?'

'Yes,' said Beth, holding on to the door. 'Just a bit.'

'It's because I know these lanes really well,' he said, slowing down to a speed more acceptable to Beth. 'I really wouldn't want to frighten you,' he added.

Beth smiled at him. At first she'd thought he was driving fast to show off, but Charlie was obviously considerate.

'I'm so pleased April's got you to talk about the girly things with,' he went on. 'It's been hard for her since Mum died – harder on her, really, than me and Dad. Dad still misses her dreadfully, although it's over ten years ago now.'

'Obviously, we're happy to be able to help.'

'So what did you do before you set up this wedding thing?'

Beth laughed lightly. 'Well, I was a barmaid mostly, and will be again tonight.'

'I'll come and visit you!'

'Good! But my degree involved online marketing, websites, stuff like that.'

'So why aren't you doing that?'

Beth felt a bit challenged and obliged to justify herself. 'I haven't been here long enough to get any clients, although I hope working at the pub will help. But I also really like the idea of working with other people. Freelance work is convenient – especially as I don't have transport – but it's a bit lonely.'

'How about if I sorted the transport problem?' Charlie shot her a grin that made Beth's stomach give a little jolt. 'Maybe better for the wedding thing than your job, but if you wanted it, you could have this van.'

Just for a second she wondered if this van was too smelly for Vintage Weddings and then realised that was ridiculous. They'd get rid of the smell, do it up, maybe put 'Vintage Weddings' in lovely signwriting on the side. 'How much?'

'I can't go lower than three hundred. But I will make sure it's mechanically completely sound.' He grinned again, having the same effect on Beth's stomach as before. 'I'll even have it valeted!'

Half an hour later, Beth waved Charlie goodbye with a happy smile. He had promised to come and see her at the pub, and she had really enjoyed chatting to him on the journey home. And he'd made a suggestion she couldn't wait to pass on to the others.

Chapter Six

꒰꒱

By the time Lindy arrived at the pub, having had a call from Beth and leaving her father in charge of the boys' bedtime stories, Beth knew her way around behind the bar. She was to work when the other barmaid, Ilana, couldn't. Or when they were both needed. It was a quiet night, and Beth was glad to have the opportunity to get her bearings. She'd also written a quick blog post about an upcoming event at the pub. Sukey had been delighted. 'That would have taken me ages!' she said.

'Tell your customers, please! I'm also hoping to help get some locals online. Although obviously I wouldn't charge for that.'

'Hey!' said Beth as Lindy appeared, delayering now she was in the warmth and perching on a bar stool. 'What can I get you? On me. Drinking my wages in advance.'

'As long as you don't drink too much,' said Sukey, 'I don't mind you buying drinks for the customers. But this is on the house. Beth did me a lovely blog post that's definitely worth a couple of glasses of wine, or whatever you want.'

'Red wine, please, if you're sure,' said Lindy.

While Beth retrieved the bottle from the shelf behind her, Sukey leant on the counter. 'So, Lindy. How's your mum?'

'She's fine. She'll be in later,' said Lindy, 'she wants to arrange the quiz.'

'Excellent,' said Sukey. 'A pub quiz always gets them in.'

'This will be in aid of the village hall renovation,' said Lindy. 'There'll be a raffle, of course. No fundraising event would be complete without one.'

'I can donate my services as a prize,' said Beth, having filled two glasses. 'Lots of old people get given old laptops by their families and then have no clue how to use them.'

'Good idea,' said Sukey.

Lindy picked up her glass. 'Cheers for this. I could offer a bit of mending. Mum asked me to think of something. She wants good prizes. That tea set, donated by Raff's mother, was great.'

'Oh, you mean the timeshare tea set?' said Beth. 'That led to great things, I think.'

'Definitely!' agreed Lindy. 'So what's this news you wanted to tell us?'

'Let's wait for Rachel,' said Beth. 'She should be here in a minute. So your dad's OK with babysitting?'

'Oh yes. He has some DVDs at my house that Mum doesn't like. War films, mostly.'

The door opened with a blast of cold air and Rachel hurried in. 'Sorry I'm a bit late. I had things to do at home.'

Beth thought she looked a little bit guilty as she said

this but didn't comment. 'What can I get you? White wine? Red?'

Rachel considered. 'I think red. As it's cold out.'

'You could have a ginger wine?' suggested Beth. 'That's nice if you need warming up.'

Rachel shook her head. 'No, no, red wine is fine. I'm desperate to know what this news is, Beth!'

'Well!' said Beth, relieved to be able to impart her news at last, and anxious to do it before Charlie arrived. 'We've been offered a van.'

'A van?' Rachel's nose wrinkled.

Seeing the wrinkle, Beth bit her lip. 'Yes. And I have to say, it is a bit pongy. But it goes well! And Charlie – April's brother – said he'd have it valeted.'

'That sounds brilliant!' said Lindy.

'I do have a car,' said Rachel, obviously not so keen on an ex-agricultural vehicle.

'Yes, but you need it for work. And the business should have its own transport,' said Beth.

'How much does he want for it?' asked Lindy.

'Three hundred pounds,' said Beth.

There was a brief silence. 'I have got it in savings,' began Rachel.

'No, we're not going into your savings unless we absolutely have to,' said Beth. 'I've got savings too, but I'm currently living on them. That, and a bit of money from my dad.'

'We've got the eBay dress to sell,' said Lindy. 'That might get us three hundred?'

'Yes,' said Beth. 'It might easily get that. A bit more, even.'

84

'But Lindy did all the work to make it worth that,' said Rachel. 'She should have the money. Apart from the bit Helena put in, buying the dress in the first place.'

'Helena can contribute that,' said Beth firmly. 'She owes us.'

'And I really don't mind about the money going towards a van,' said Lindy. 'If I could use it too, it would be brilliant.'

'Well, of course you could use it,' said Beth. 'And I could too. It would make getting any sort of paid work so much easier. But are you sure?'

'Absolutely!' said Lindy.

'From a business point of view that would work,' said Rachel. 'Eventually we should be able to pay ourselves salaries. But not just yet, obviously.'

'That's very good,' said Beth. 'I'll tell Charlie. He's coming in a bit later.'

Rachel narrowed her eyes. 'Are you going a bit pink, Beth?'

'No! I probably put too much blusher on.'

'So why are you wearing make-up?' asked Lindy. 'You don't usually.'

'Because I'm being a barmaid. Duh!' Beth blushed even more. She'd had several jobs as a barmaid and she'd never worn make-up for any of them. But Lindy and Rachel weren't to know that. 'Do you want to know how I got on with April?'

'Oh yes,' said Lindy. 'You said her mother's dress is amazing?'

'Well, it doesn't fit but there's extra material and I'm

sure you can do something with it,' said Beth. 'With your magic fingers and all.'

'If we could adapt brides' mothers' wedding dresses as part of the vintage package, that would be really good,' said Rachel.

Lindy and Beth regarded her. 'Because, mostly, you have a life,' Beth commented, 'you won't have seen the programme where they do that: bring out the dress and try to convince these lovely girls to wear these bits of outdated tat you wouldn't put your dog in.'

Rachel nodded. 'OK. But April's mother's dress is different?'

'Yup,' said Beth. 'It's gorgeous, potentially. But although I think it would be great if Lindy could work her magic on the mothers' dresses, not all of them would end up lovely.'

'I can't wait to see April's mother's,' said Lindy. 'And if brides and their mothers were willing to donate the dress so I could pimp it up a bit and sell it, we could take it off the cost.'

'Mm, we'd have to be careful,' said Beth. 'We don't want a whole lot of dresses we can't do anything with.'

'OK, designer dresses only,' said Rachel. She frowned. 'Not sure I'd want to have my mum's wedding dress put on eBay.'

'We'd have to check, of course. What else do we need to sort out for April's wedding?'

'Well, her auntie is making a cake but April's not sure she'd be up to fancy icing. One of us should learn. Me, maybe. Currently I'm only good when I've got a

86

computer to help me.'

'Good plan,' said Lindy. 'There would be lots of people who've got an aunt or a mum who can make a nice cake but they've got to look good.'

Beth suddenly doubted being able to learn to ice cakes. 'Lindy, this wouldn't be more your thing than mine?'

'No,' said Lindy firmly. 'I'm pretty good at Buzz Lightyear and Thomas the Tank Engine cakes but I haven't done anything more ... delicate. I mostly mould it in my hands and stick on sweeties. I'll tell what would be helpful though: the Lakeland catalogue.'

'Oh, Lakeland!' said Rachel dreamily. 'One of my favourites.'

'They have amazing gadgets. My mother and gran drool over them.' Lindy sipped her wine knowingly.

Aware that she'd somehow missed out on something that obviously made others very happy, Beth accepted her mission. 'OK, I'll see what I can learn through YouTube and practice,' she said. 'Oh, here's a customer.' She turned to him. 'What can I get you?'

After she had pulled a pint of ale from the local brewery, Rachel said, 'I might be up for making sugar flowers. I love fiddly things.'

'Wonderful. We'll be fine. Oh, here's Charlie.' Beth put on an especially welcoming smile.

Rachel and Lindy looked at each other. 'Shall we get out of Beth's way?' Rachel said. 'We don't want her to feel awkward.'

When they had taken their glasses to a table, Lindy said, 'I think I remember Charlie from school but he was a few years above me. Beth seems to really like him. Mum

87

will know him from the farm. We'll get her to update us.'

'Do you like living where your family all live?' Rachel asked. 'It's something I can't imagine doing, really. But you've got your parents, your gran – with your boys, there's four generations of you.'

'It's all I know,' said Lindy. 'I do wish I'd had a chance to get away, but this is a brilliant place to bring up children. What about you? Where's your family? Have you got any siblings?'

'No, I'm an only child. My parents moved up north when Dad retired early, and my grandparents always lived in Ireland. I never knew my grandparents that well. Loved them, but we were always visitors.'

'In lots of ways I stayed here because I got trapped. I meant to go to art college, be a student, all those things, but I got pregnant, so I had to stay. Now my top tip to people about to have babies is live near your mum. And if you've got your gran too, well, that's even better.'

'And it is a really beautiful part of the country. Anyone would be lucky to live here. That's why I picked this area.'

Lindy thought about this. 'I am lucky, I know, but I do still wonder what the rest of the world is like.'

Rachel laughed softly. 'I've travelled quite a bit and I'll tell you what it's like: not as nice as here, mostly.'

Lindy joined in the laughter. 'I'm sure but I'd kind of like to find that out for myself.'

'You're still very young. There's plenty of time for travel when your boys are bigger. Or grown up even. That's the joy of having your children young. I've left it a bit late.' She didn't want Lindy to know that the thought of children and all the mess and disruption they would bring terrified her.

'Come on! You're not exactly ancient,' said Lindy. 'You've got plenty of time to have children – but only if you want them.'

'Don't you think everyone should have children then?'

Lindy shook her head. 'I adore mine but parenthood's not for everyone.'

'But you like it?'

'Part of me wonders if I'd have preferred a stunning career in fashion, but I don't really believe that anything I could have created would be as wonderful as my boys. Who's to say?'

'Oh,' said Rachel, as a thought struck her. 'I forgot to say thank you for the kindling. I found it when I got in from work. It was so kind of you. Especially when you're so busy.'

Lindy shook her head. 'I didn't leave any kindling, Rachel, I never got round to it.'

Rachel sighed. There could be only one other person who might have done so. 'You think Raff left it?'

Lindy nodded. 'I do. It's just the sort of thing he would do. And he likes you.'

Rachel flopped back into the chair. 'I don't like him.'

'Good. He's such a player. Just don't go there. Oh, here's Mum!' She waved. 'Over here!'

'Hi, girls! What can I get you? Wine? Shall I get a bottle?'

'Sit down for a bit, Mum,' said Lindy.

Sarah slumped into a chair. 'I've had a really busy day but I bumped into April's dad, Eamon, this afternoon at one of the farms I was at and he is so pleased with what you've done already.'

'Beth was the one, you must tell her,' said Rachel.

'I'll do that now. What are we drinking? Red wine? I'll get it.' And she headed for the bar.

'Your mother is lovely,' said Rachel. 'She was so nice when I rang her before dawn to explain about not being able to go with Beth.'

'She is fun. She gets involved in too many things though. Dad worries that she does too much.'

Rachel, who happened to be looking towards the door as it began to open, suddenly said, 'It's Raff!' Her heart flipped in panic. She wanted to hide. 'Can we join the others at the bar?'

'Oh, OK,' said Lindy, picking up her glass.

They were at the bar, deep in conversation, before Raff had fully entered the pub. Rachel had her head close to the others, hoping Raff wouldn't notice her.

'. . . so we've got to get as many teams as we can,' Sarah was saying. 'We'll have a raffle, with lots of good prizes.'

'I could offer to do someone's books for them,' said Rachel, her head turned as far away from Raff as it would go, given she wasn't an owl. 'That would be worth quite a lot for someone. And we're painting the hall this weekend?' she went on.

'As many of us who can,' said Lindy. 'It would probably be better for me to send Dad to do my stint, than have him look after the boys.'

'Do it in shifts,' suggested Sarah. 'When Dad gets tired, he can take over from you with the boys.'

Raff joined them at the bar. 'Good evening, everyone.'

Rachel nodded in his direction and then hid behind her glass.

'Evening, Rachel.'

It was hard to ignore the piercing blue eyes fringed with curly lashes that regarded her from a rugged, unshaven face.

'Hello, Raff.' She paused. 'Did you leave some kindling by my back door?'

He raised an eyebrow in reply. 'I knew you'd never light the wood-burner without any and I have plenty that's really dry.'

'That was very kind of you,' she said. And as it seemed the moment for taking the bull by the horns, she went on, 'Would you like to come for a drink sometime?'

'Very much. But not here.'

Rachel was alarmed. 'Not here? Where else is there to go?' She felt safe in the pub – she didn't want to be with someone who was so unsafe without feeling happy in her surroundings.

'Strange as it might seem to you, coming from London, there's a whole world of nice country pubs that aren't full of people you can chat to instead of me.'

She was aware that Sarah and Lindy had moved a little away from her and she felt exposed. 'We could sit in the corner, if you insist. But I never drink and drive so I wouldn't want to go anywhere I couldn't walk to.' She felt she'd saved a point – not the same as winning one – but for now she was safe.

Sukey passed a glass to Raff without him having to ask. It was beer. He took a sip. 'There is a lovely little pub just over the hill. We can walk.'

Rachel shook her head. 'I'm not tramping over the fields in the pitch dark.' Silently she added, 'With a man I don't know and certainly don't trust'.

'We'll go at lunchtime. Do you work?'

'Yes!'

'But freelance,' said Sarah, who couldn't help herself. 'You're like me, surely, and work in bits and pieces?'

'Mum!' said Lindy, aghast, and grabbed her mother by the arm.

'Just trying to be helpful!' said Sarah.

Rachel could hear Lindy muttering darkly.

'OK!' said Rachel. 'What about tomorrow?' Taking Raff out for a drink was becoming more and more of a big deal and it hadn't been a small deal when he'd first suggested it.

Raff smiled a little crookedly. 'I'm terribly sorry, I'm having lunch with my mother tomorrow.'

Rachel beamed. She was so relieved. Although they'd have to reschedule, she'd done her duty for now. 'Oh, what a shame! And I'm terribly tied up next week. But maybe the week after?' She'd be able to come up with some reason not to go then.

'Well, no great hurry,' said Raff. 'I can wait. Now I'm just going over there to chat to a friend.'

Although she should have felt reassured by this casual acceptance of her busyness, she actually felt a whole lot worse.

'God, I'm so sorry about Mum saying that to Raff,' said Lindy when Raff had gone across the room. 'She doesn't get what he's like. She just says how kind he is. Yes, Mum, I am talking about you!'

'He is a nice man,' said Sarah firmly. 'But if you girls want to slag him off, I'll go and talk to the darts lot. Persuade them they want to bring a team to the quiz.'

Not wanting to slag him off, or even think about him, Rachel turned to Beth. 'So, Beth, tell us about Charlie!'

Beth's smile was definitely a bit silly. 'Well, as you know, he's April's brother. And I've told you about the van.'

'Oh, you. You know what I mean,' said Rachel with a smile.

'We'll have to get on with selling the wedding dress, to get the money for it,' said Lindy, ever practical where money was concerned.

'We'll need to get a good picture of it to put on eBay, and it might be better if someone – me probably, as it fits – models it. It's one of those that looks better on a body than on the hanger.'

Rachel nodded. 'I've got a nice camera and I don't take bad photos.'

'We'll get together at mine when it's ready,' said Lindy.

'Or mine,' said Beth.

'I'd rather it was at mine, if you don't mind, Beth. I don't like asking my family to babysit if I can avoid it.'

'Oh no, that's OK! Mine's really small anyway.'

Lindy went on, as if worried in case Beth was offended: 'I've always been a bit frightened of putting things on eBay. I need to learn how to do it.'

'I'll show you. It's not that hard,' said Beth.

'We've all got a lot to learn, one way or another,' said Rachel. Although she wasn't looking at him, she was thinking about Raff. What she needed to learn was how to deal with people like him.

The girls chatted some more and then Lindy and Rachel left Beth to her serving duties and headed home. The pub became busier as the evening wore on and Beth certainly earned her keep. Her mother might not think being a barmaid was up to much but Beth really enjoyed it and was gratified that Sukey seemed very pleased with her. And it had been great to see Charlie again, albeit briefly as he'd had to dash off to sort out something on the farm. All in all, it had been a lovely evening.

Chapter Seven

It was Saturday and Beth and Rachel were standing outside the hall, having both arrived at the same time. It was Chippingford Village Hall transformation day – or a giving it a fresh lick of paint day anyway.

'At least it won't show if you get paint on it,' said Beth, looking at Rachel's pristine boiler suit with surprise. A pair of old jeans and jumper had been enough for her but perhaps Rachel didn't own such things. Beth thought perhaps she didn't; Rachel was always so well groomed.

Rachel shrugged. 'That's what I thought.'

'Is it new?' asked Beth, obviously not ready to ignore what Rachel considered the proper gear for painting in.

'No. Just clean. Now, what's the plan?' Rachel wanted to get on with it. She hadn't been in the hall since the night the three of them met and she wanted to see just what sort of condition it was in.

'It's unlocked and people have arrived already. Lindy will come if she can but obviously on a Saturday she's got her boys, and I'm not sure if her dad can help out or not.'

'Well, let's get in there!'

Rachel checked that Raff wasn't one of the early arrivals and then chatted for a bit with the people who were there. There was Bob, whom she remembered from the first event in the hall, and a couple of people she'd spotted in the pub. Then she did what she was desperate to do: investigate the decorative order of the hall. The fact it was so gloomy even though all the lights were on and it was a bright day did not bode well.

Rachel found Sarah in a cubbyhole with a sink and a broken electric cooker that described itself as a kitchen. 'So who's in charge of the painting?'

Sarah, who had a smudge of dirt on her face already, regarded Rachel. 'As chairman I appoint you to be in charge of anything you'd like to take charge of. I'm worrying about this kitchen, which you wouldn't cook dog food in, given a choice.'

'Did you tell April there was a kitchen in the hall?'

Sarah shook her head. 'I can't remember what I told her. I just wish I hadn't had this mad idea. This place is a dump and we can't change that in just under a month.'

Rachel, who had been feeling pretty pessimistic about it all herself, instantly felt proactive and protective. 'Don't worry. We can sort this. When Raff gets here I'll see if he can get one of those paint sprayers. We can have the whole place white and clean-looking in a couple of days.' Although as soon as the words were out of her mouth she realised how incredibly hard they'd have to work.

Sarah looked sheepish. 'Lindy said you weren't to have anything to do with Raff and I mustn't encourage him to go near you.'

Rachel smiled. 'I can handle Raff. Lindy needn't worry.'

As she left Sarah looking at her list of contacts on her phone, trying to find a plumber, Rachel couldn't help laughing at herself. When she'd decorated her home she'd spent weeks and weeks on preparation, only allowing herself to apply the final coat when the surfaces had been sanded back to silky perfection. Now she was blithely suggesting something that would probably mean painting over the cobwebs, let alone the dirt of ages.

Fortunately her weird euphoria over the size of the challenge didn't instantly evaporate when she turned round and saw Raff and Bob coming through the door with a scaffold tower.

She went up to him with an I-need-a-favour smile. 'Hi, Raff. I was just talking to Sarah in the kitchen – if you can call it that – and we decided we need one of those sprayers so we could just spray the entire hall white, really quickly.'

'Good morning, Rachel. Very nice to see you too. Lovely day, isn't it?'

'Oh – hello – yes – lovely day,' Rachel said impatiently. 'So what do you think about the spray thing?'

'Put on a mist coat, you mean?'

'Oh,' said Beth. 'Like that programme when the man redesigns people's houses for them? And makes everything white so they can get a sense of the space?' Beth cleared her throat. 'Sorry. I probably do watch too much television.'

'Not from now on,' said Rachel. 'We have a hall to decorate.'

'That's not a bad idea, actually, the mist coat,' said Raff.

Rachel had a flicker of satisfaction at praise from Raff. 'So, can you get the equipment?'

He seemed to take this question as a challenge. 'Yes. I've got a friend who's got the kit. I suppose you want it now?'

'If possible. Although I suppose later today would be OK.'

'You're very demanding. But I like that in a woman.'

Rachel scowled and made Raff laugh again. 'OK, I'll make some calls. Maybe you could have it tomorrow. Is that soon enough for you, Ms Impatient?'

'Absolutely soon enough, Mr Fix-it!'

As they watched Raff stroll into the corner of the room to make his calls, Beth, who'd watched the conversation as if it were a tennis match, said, 'But what shall we get on with until we can do that?'

'Wash,' said Rachel. 'Get as much loose dirt off as we can. It's filthy so it'll be hard work. Did we all bring rubber gloves and things? I've got some spares if you want them.' Rachel didn't explain that she'd gone through a phase of buying rubber gloves along with her phase of buying bedlinen, and produced four pairs from the bag slung over her shoulder.

'You have got a lot of gloves in there,' said Raff, rejoining them at just the wrong time for Rachel.

She decided to go on the offensive. 'Are you any good at plumbing? Or electrics? If so, Sarah needs you in the kitchen. That's the cupboard down the end.'

Raff inclined his head in acknowledgement of this

request and went off to find Sarah.

'My God, Rach! Respect. You've got him well trained, haven't you?' said Lindy, who had quietly joined the group.

'Thank you,' said Rachel. 'I just feel really determined to get this hall done. But I have realised that we're going to have to do all this washing in cold water!'

There was some discussion as to whether the rafters needed washing when no one would really see them but Rachel was firm. 'No, we must. We're going to decorate properly at some time – it would be mad to paint over dirt.'

'Well, who's going to get up there and do it?' objected Justin, who'd managed to donate an hour of his precious time to the project.

'We have a scaffolding tower in case you hadn't noticed,' said Raff, who had done as much as he could for Sarah and rejoined the others.

'Sorry, mate, I had noticed, but I don't do heights.'

Several other people said they didn't do heights either. Rachel suspected it was really that they didn't do washing in cold water. 'I'll do it,' she said. 'I'm OK with heights. And my rubber gloves are lined.'

Rachel had changed the water in her bucket several times, climbing up and down the scaffold tower intent on her task before she realised that everyone else had gone. Except Raff.

'Oh,' she said, startled, about to refill her bucket and go back up there. 'Did you want this back?' She gestured to the tower.

'Not right this minute, no. But we have to go.'

'No, it's all right. I've got the key. I can lock up when I've finished. But you don't need to stay.'

'It's five o'clock. We've been here since nine without a proper break. I'm hungry and you must be too.'

'I'm fine! Do go.'

He shook his head. 'Not without you. I'm taking you to meet my mother.'

Rachel blinked at this, but found her sense of humour. 'That's a bit early in the relationship, isn't it?'

He grinned. 'Nice that you think we have a relationship.'

Rachel stopped being amused. 'We haven't. And didn't you have lunch with her yesterday?'

'I couldn't make it so I promised to come today instead. And I'm going to take you with me. Now, do you want to go home and change? Or go as you are?'

In spite of being tired – something she had only just noticed – Rachel was feeling strong. She'd really enjoyed scrubbing away at rafters that probably hadn't seen a cloth since they were last decorated in the fifties.

'OK, so if I agree to go with you to meet your mother, does that count as our date? For the wood?'

'Rachel!' He shook his head reproachfully. 'What do you think?'

Rachel didn't know what she thought and she didn't know what Raff thought either.

'So? Change or as you are?' he said.

'Shower and change,' she said. 'I'll meet you somewhere in an hour.'

He shook his head. 'I'd rather wait at yours.'

'Don't you want to get changed yourself?'

'No. I can shower and change at my mother's.'

'Well, you can't stay at mine,' said Rachel firmly. 'Wait in the pub.'

'Closed for a private party.'

'Knock on the door. Sukey will let you in.'

'Sukey is out. Besides, why won't you let me in? Do I make the place look untidy?'

Rachel gritted her teeth. There were two reasons why she didn't want Raff to be in her house while she showered and changed. One was because she didn't know him well although her logical mind told her she shouldn't worry: he was well known in the village, Sarah thought he was a good man and while Lindy said he was a womaniser, no one had implied he wasn't safe. The other reason was exactly as he'd expressed it: he made the place look untidy.

'Listen,' he said, 'I do have a deep desire to...' He searched for the word. 'Rumple you—'

She gasped with shock.

'But I promise I won't.'

'That would be assault!' Rachel realised that sounded as if she was afraid of him and now she thought about it, she knew she wasn't.

'It wouldn't be assault if you wanted it too.'

Rachel felt as if she'd hardened her muscles to take a blow from one direction only to find herself knocked from somewhere else altogether. 'That will never happen!'

He shrugged. 'I'm prepared to wait. Now come along. Time for you to get clean and prettied up and me to sit in your white house and wait.'

She glared at him. 'It's not white, it's "wevet".'

She left him, still in his coat, in her sitting room reading a copy of *Country Living* that she produced from a drawer. She showered and washed her hair at a speed unknown to her previously. She didn't iron her hair. This was a big deal for Rachel, who preferred her reddish locks to be sleek and controlled, not rioting round her head like damp candyfloss. Having dried herself (but not between her toes and with no application of body lotion – almost unheard of) she pulled on some black velvet jeans, boots and several layers of jumper and cardigan. She didn't usually wear a lot of make-up but now it was only a smear of foundation round her nose and some mascara. Then she flew back down the stairs.

'That was quick!' Raff said, putting down his magazine and inspecting her. 'There's no great hurry. Still, you look great. I like your hair like that.'

'Thank you,' said Rachel, feeling wrong-footed. Why had she felt obliged to rush so? Why hadn't she taken her time and got ready properly? Now it looked as if she was desperate to see him. In fact, it was because she was desperate to get him out of her space. Even if she had to get out of it too.

'You obviously don't feel the cold,' he went on.

'Er – why do you say that?' She *was* feeling the cold at the moment – damp hair in winter was chilly. She searched her mind for where she'd put away her hat. Unusually for her, she didn't instantly know.

'Because you haven't lit your wood-burner although you've got dry wood and dry kindling.'

'How do you know?' she demanded.

'There is no soot or anything inside the stove.'

She felt embarrassed. 'It doesn't seem worth it for just me.'

'Why don't you go and dry your hair properly and I'll light it? Then you'll come back to a warm house.'

Rachel shook her head. It was her wood-burner, chosen and paid for by her: she should be the one to light it first. 'No, I'll do it.'

'Come on then.'

'No. Not with you looking at me.'

'Why not with me looking at you?'

She exhaled sharply. 'Because I've never lit a fire before!' She felt as though she was declaring she never gave money to charity or smiled or had had a good friend: a terrible confession.

Raff didn't seem shocked or surprised or even particularly bothered. 'Would you like me to help you?'

Rachel suddenly felt less pressured. He didn't seem to think it was awful and, more importantly, didn't want to know why, even though it was winter. But she did inwardly take a deep breath and put her shoulders back in preparation for doing something difficult. Not difficult because firelighting was beyond her – it probably wasn't; Boy Scouts did it all the time and they weren't all Ray Mears. No, it was hard because lighting the wood-burner would spoil its pristineness. She'd made excuses to herself and others – having to get wood, finding out about kindling – but really she was afraid that lighting a fire in it would spoil it. But if anyone was going to do it, it would be her.

'I think I know the basics,' she said. 'But you can

mention it, politely, if I look like going completely off track.'

He laughed and Rachel realised she liked having made him laugh. He wasn't laughing at her, he was laughing because she'd been mildly funny. It was a satisfying feeling.

She knelt on the rug in front of the stove and opened the doors. She tried to remember what Beth and Lindy had said about firelighting. There was something about candle ends, which she had, but could you just put them straight on to the bars? The kindling was in the shed. She got up to fetch it. 'I'm getting the kindling,' she said, hoping she didn't sound defiant or, worse, apologetic.

'Newspaper first,' said Raff when she was at the door.

'What? I don't have any. I read them online.' She felt bewildered. She didn't have paper she could just burn. She didn't have things in her house she didn't need. Magazines were different. But she didn't think they would burn well and besides, they were for filing, for research and making mood-boards, not for burning.

Raff shrugged, not sensing the panic his casual instruction had caused. 'What? Even the local rag? I've got one in the van. Wait.'

While he was away she rushed upstairs and started to straighten her hair, but then realised she wouldn't be able to do it to her usual standards. She ran her fingers through it a few times in lieu of brushing. She'd never get a brush or comb through it now.

'You've done something to your hair,' he said as he strolled back into her house and on to her rug with a newspaper under his arm. He considered her. 'As we do have a bit of a schedule, shall I light the fire? I'll teach you how another time.'

She shrugged. She could make sure there either wasn't another time or, preferably, learn how to do it beforehand. If she had to have newspaper she could keep it in the shed.

'Fine. Whatever. Or we could just leave it?'

He shook his head. 'It's time this wood-burner lost its virginity.'

Chapter Eight

Shivering with her still slightly damp hair, in spite of layers of cashmere and wool, and tired after her hard day's cleaning the hall, Rachel watched Raff lay the fire.

He was careful, selecting twigs from the pile, assessing their thickness and creating a construction of sticks and then laying bigger ones on top. She was fascinated.

'Have you got a match?' he asked.

Rachel had a box of especially long, French matches and a gas lighter. She handed him the gas lighter. The matches weren't for using; they were for aesthetic purposes.

She watched as the fire began to crackle with life and felt as if it was the first fire ever. Although it had created an awful mess – Raff had been careful in his selecting but not about the bits that dropped off all over her rug. But somehow she didn't mind.

Raff put on some more logs, fiddled with the knob under the stove that Rachel realised she'd have to learn about and then shut the doors. The fire blazed cheerily.

'With luck, when you get home, you'll be able to open

up the draught and it'll come back to life.' He paused. 'I'll come in and do it for you.'

She felt instantly wary. 'It might be better if I do it myself. I've watched you do it, I should be able to remember.'

He gave his crooked smile. 'We'll see. Now come along and meet my mum.'

Rachel sat in the front seat of Raff's pickup truck wondering what on earth she was doing there. Why was she in a pickup truck? It was not a vehicle she had ever imagined she would travel in. And why was she going to visit the mother of a mere acquaintance? Supposing his mother took it to mean there was something going on between Rachel and her son? It would be so embarrassing. And shaming! Her and Raff? Honestly, unsuitable pairings weren't in it. She cringed at the thought she was fundamentally snobbish and yet she couldn't shake off the notion that Raff was 'rough trade'. Why had she let herself be talked into getting into his truck? She must have been sleepwalking or something.

'Erm – I don't think this is a good idea,' she said, trying to ignore the empty can that was rolling around in the footwell, to rise above her fastidiousness. 'Your mother doesn't know me. She won't want me visiting her.'

'She won't know you if she doesn't meet you and she likes people. She's got a cottage pie in the oven. I don't know about you but I'm bloody hungry.'

'Fair enough. But you don't have to drag me along. She will have done cottage pie for two, not three.'

He laughed. 'Sorry, but my mother has no notion of

cooking for two. She reckons it's not worth the bother if you're not feeding at least half a dozen people.'

'It's not a dinner party, is it? I'm not dressed—'

Raff found this idea so hilarious he could hardly drive. 'I'm not saying we'll be the only ones there. I don't know. We might be, we might not. But it won't be a dinner party.'

Rachel hunched down in her seat, embarrassed. His mother was probably a simple country soul cooking wholesome country food for her boy, of whom she was probably terribly protective (not knowing any better) and here was she, an overly particular London woman, about to invade her humble (but scrupulously clean) home.

'I expect you love your mum, don't you?' Rachel was trying another angle.

'Of course. She's the best.'

'Then why are you inflicting me on her?'

He didn't answer for a worryingly long time. 'Because I think you'll like each other.'

Twenty minutes later, Raff turned the truck into a drive, rutted and muddy but long and obviously leading to a substantial property. When he turned round a bend, Rachel could see just how substantial.

'Does your mother live in all of it?' she asked. 'Or just an apartment?' She instantly had a vision of his mother being a family retainer, allowed a couple of rooms as a reward for years of faithful service.

'All of it that's watertight. Fortunately with a house this size it's easy to just abandon one room and move into another.'

Rachel couldn't conceal her horror. 'I couldn't live in a house that I couldn't live in all of,' she said and then realised she probably sounded mad. And why did his mother live in such a huge house? Maybe she'd married into 'the Mob' and inherited a house acquired by ill-gotten gains?

'I still think you and my mother will get on. Come and find out.'

Raff led them round the side of the house to the back door. He opened it and went in. 'Mum!' he called. 'We're here!'

An old black spaniel appeared and ambled over to them. He seemed moderately pleased to see Raff. Rachel he ignored.

'In the kitchen, darling!' called a voice – a very aristocratic voice, Rachel had time to note before she was following Raff down the passage and into the room.

It was a kitchen but for a moment Rachel thought it could have been a film set. It was dimly lit and cave-like and very, very full of stuff. Furniture, ornaments, china, glass, and she couldn't see what colour the walls were because when a bit of wall wasn't covered by a cupboard or shelves, there were pictures. Before she could suffer an attack of sensory overload, Raff's mother appeared from behind a loaded countertop.

'Hello!' she said warmly.

She had a lot of white hair curled into a bun on the top of her head. She was dressed in varying shades of purple and blue but it was hard to define what the actual garments were. Layers of skirt, cardigan and shawl blended into a pleasing melange of colour. She was holding a wooden spoon but just for an instant Rachel imagined it was a wand. Seeing her son she flung her wooden spoon over the counter where it landed in the sink. She took her son in her arms and squeezed him tight. He returned her hug and then drew Rachel forward.

'This is Rachel,' said Raff. 'She's not sure she's welcome.'

'Darling!' Rachel was embraced too. 'Why wouldn't you be welcome? There's always plenty. One thing I can't abide is an under-caterer.' Forget-me-not-blue eyes peered into hers. Rachel examined her conscience and was grateful to discover she had never been guilty of under-catering: she was far too anxious to allow it. But there was something about those eyes that belied the Mrs Pepperpot cosiness of Raff's mother.

'Raff!' went on his mother. 'Drinks! And my name is Belinda.'

'How do you do?' said Rachel, wishing she didn't sound so formal.

'Wonderful, darling. Now please sit down and let's have a drink and a chat while we wait for the pie to brown.' She caught Rachel looking at a steaming pot. 'That's soup for tomorrow. I'm visiting an old man. I'll take it with me.'

Rachel pulled out a chair and sat at the table. Looking around her she realised she'd never been in a place so cluttered and untidy in her life, apart from Lindy's, and that was tiny so she had an excuse. In fact, if all her possessions were gathered together and put on the table they would just disappear, camouflaged by the vast amount of stuff already there.

'Raff! Take her coat, give her a glass of wine and tell me what you've been up to.'

Rachel felt it would be rude to stare but the room and the crowded table made it almost impossible not to look around her.

Belinda, possibly catching her bewilderment, said, 'I'm doing some life laundry, darling, so I've emptied a few cupboards.'

Raff found a space for a glass of wine near Rachel. She noted the glass and realised it was probably an antique. 'Really, Mum?'

Rachel noticed his accent had become less estuary and more like his mother's cut-glass tones. She wasn't sure she approved of this ability to change. Maybe it meant he was even more shifty than she already thought him? The fact that he was less 'a bit of rough' than she'd thought he was didn't make him any less unsettling.

'Sweetheart, I know you think I'm wedded to my possessions but I'm really not! I've just never been able to face doing anything about them before.'

'So why now?'

'I've been thinking it might be time to "downsize".'

'Good God, Mother! Why now? And I didn't think you even understood the concept.'

Rachel had noticed she said the word as if for the first time.

'Of course I understand it!' Belinda said indignantly. 'I've just always had more interesting things to do before. As for the downsizing, well... I do rattle around here a bit. Or I would if the walls weren't well padded with furniture and pictures.' She winked at Rachel, as if sensing she felt as if she was in a very unfamiliar world. 'Raff's father died when he was very young and it's possible I've become a bit eccentric, being a single parent for so long.'

'You'd have been eccentric whatever had happened,' said Raff, who seemed to have taken being fatherless in a very relaxed way.

'Well, maybe,' said Belinda before retreating behind the counter and opening a door of the Aga and peering in. 'Hmm. Needs a few minutes yet.'

She came and joined Rachel and Raff at the table. 'So tell me, Rachel, have you lived in the area long?'

'Well, I've actually had my house for a while but I haven't lived in it full-time until recently.'

'And do you like it down here? Did you come from London?'

'Yes, to both,' said Rachel. 'It's still a bit new and strange but I've wanted to live here permanently for ages.'

'What sort of house?'

Rachel paused, trying not to feel interrogated. She was sure Belinda meant well.

'Rachel's house is very...' Raff paused and Rachel tensed, waiting for him to expose her as OCD and neurotic. 'Very wevet,' he said.

Rachel sighed. 'He means white.'

'So why did he say wevet?' Belinda seemed confused.

'It's white,' said Rachel. 'Wevet is a shade of white, on the Farrow and Ball paint chart. It comes from an old Dorset word for cobweb.' She would undergo torture before she'd admit how long it had taken her to choose that particular shade. Nor would she tell anyone that paint charts were her comfort reading and she knew many of the names by heart.

'I never knew white came in shades,' said Belinda.

'Nor did I, until I met Rachel,' said Raff.

Just for a moment Rachel felt there was something special in the way he said the words and then she pulled herself together.

'Why don't you top up Rachel's glass and take her for a quick tour while we wait for the pie to brown?' said Belinda.

'Would you like that?' said Raff.

'Yes please,' said Rachel. 'I'd love it.' She got up from the table feeling slightly odd. It couldn't have been the wine because she hadn't drunk much of it. She wondered if it was because she was absolutely surrounded by clutter and quite possibly dirt and yet she was entirely calm. Maybe it was because she had begun to know Lindy, who also lived in chaos, or maybe it was because this place was more like a museum or National Trust property than an actual home.

'Follow me, then.'

He led her out of the kitchen through a couple of passages. 'This is the hall.' He switched on the overhead light, which cast an eerie glow over the large, dark furniture that filled the space. 'It's all a bit Gothic.'

'There are some lovely pieces, I think,' said Rachel. 'But I expect the house needs rewiring.'

'I know damn well it does! Mum wouldn't ever let me sort it out because it would mean moving too much stuff.'

'But if she's going to move, I don't expect she'd want to bother.'

'I'm not sure about this moving thing. I keep telling her she'd do better to sell off part of it and stay here. She's lived here all her life – it was her parents' house, and before that, her grandparents'.' He opened a door and ushered Rachel through it. Again the light from a dim bulb did little to illuminate the room, which was big. And yet the clutter was evident.

Every surface except the seats of the chairs was covered. There were lots of tables of various sizes scattered round and every one of them was covered. Piles of magazines, which turned out to be copies of *Country Life* going back decades. Another table was covered in books: art books; big, illustrated books about country houses; gardening books; wild-flower books; bird books.

'Goodness me,' said Rachel, moving from table to table. 'There's quite a large shop's worth of books here.'

'My grandparents collected them; so did my parents. I think my mother has stopped now.'

The surfaces not covered in books were covered in china. Figurines, dishes, jugs, bowls, whole dinner services and tea sets, piled up and, Rachel discovered, dusty.

Round the edges of the room were glass-fronted cabinets, equally full of china. Rachel longed to get a torch or a table lamp so she could inspect it all properly.

'I think if your mother really wants to downsize she should just turn her house into an antique shop until all the stuff is sold. This lot must be worth a fortune!'

'I don't think my mother would be able to cope with

people wandering about her house arguing about the price of things.'

'No! That would be awful. You'd have to do it for her. Even sell it in your yard.'

He grinned. 'Maybe I should suggest it. I'm sure she'd love the thought of her antique china being sold alongside cast-iron guttering and chimney pots.'

'Or put it on eBay and sell it item by item. Beth would do it for her. For a commission, I expect. Or you could have a separate department selling smaller items. Beth would design a section of your website, making it all look gorgeous. You have got a website?'

Raff frowned. 'I have, but it probably needs an upgrade. I'll talk to Beth about it, if she's good.'

'She's brilliant. She's doing one for Vintage Weddings as soon as possible. No business can survive without an online presence.'

Belinda came into the room. 'So are you setting up a business, Rachel?'

'Yes, with two friends. Lindy you may know? She's Sarah Wood's daughter? And Beth, who's new to the village like me.'

'Well, let's go and eat and you can carry on telling me about it. I like to hear about "women doing it for themselves".' Belinda sent her son a challenging look. He laughed.

The kitchen table had been as heavily laden as the rest of the surfaces in the house, but once cleared had just about enough room for three people to eat. Rachel sat at her place and sipped more wine. She felt strangely happy, as if she'd gone to a theme park and enjoyed a roller-coaster ride when she hadn't expected to. There was so much clutter she could no longer feel bothered by it. It was like some sort of therapy.

'Do start,' said Belinda, pouring more wine into her glass.

Rachel glanced at Raff, who was already forking up cottage pie. Had he brought her here to cure her of something? If so, it was outrageous. She moistened her lips to speak. 'This is the most delicious cottage pie I have ever eaten,' she said. She wasn't sure that had been what she'd intended to say but it came out, because it was true.

'Thank you, darling,' said Belinda. 'We had a truly massive joint the other day so this is actually made from leftover beef. That and equal quantities of butter to potato makes a very nice pie, though I say it myself.'

The plates were red hot and cracked and discoloured. They had once been very good quality but Rachel decided that if Belinda made a habit of heating them to such searing temperatures they were bound to deteriorate. Somehow it didn't seem to matter.

'So, tell me more about this business you girls are setting up.'

Rachel explained as succinctly as she could. She had never met anyone like Belinda before and found her daunting. She seemed unpredictable and strange. Her values were unlike those of anyone Rachel had known. She was obviously kind and welcoming, but the clutter? What sort of a person let things pile up like that? It was weird.

Belinda produced bars of chocolate for pudding,

tossing a selection on to the table. 'Help yourselves. They were on offer. Coffee? Tea? Or brandy, Rachel?'

'Er, tea, please.'

They sat at the table eating chocolate and drinking tea, Belinda and Raff catching up with each other's projects.

'So, Rachel, what do you do? Apart from the wedding thing?' The forget-me-not-blue eyes were intense. Rachel realised mother and son shared both the colour and the expression.

'Well, currently I'm an accountant, bookkeeper, that sort of thing.'

'So you'll be useful to this plan to clean up the village hall?'

'Yes. The thing is, there's going to be a wedding there. Which means we have to hurry up and get it presentable.'

'We're mist-coating it tomorrow,' said Raff.

'White, I assume? Very minimalist then,' said Belinda.

Rachel assumed she disapproved. 'To begin with, yes. We might introduce some colour later.' Not if she had anything to do with it, of course, but she was aware she wasn't actually the appointed interior designer.

'Well, that sounds nice. I'm leaning towards minimalism myself,' she said. 'Hence the downsizing thing. I'm going to get rid of everything I don't need.'

'Maybe you mean decluttering?' said Rachel bravely.

Belinda shook her head. 'No. That would be implying my things are clutter.' The blue eyes were piercing and Rachel was sure she had offended her. 'I don't think they are because many of them are beautiful. In fact, I have some things you might find useful in your new business. Follow me.'

Still unsure if she had caused terrible offence by her use of the word 'clutter', Rachel followed Belinda down a dark passage. Belinda opened a door and switched on a light. It was a dining room. The table was loaded with china, piles and piles of it. It was all gorgeous – the sort of thing that gave the word vintage a good name.

'It's all yours if you want it but you'll have to take it away,' said Belinda. 'I starting sorting some of it but gave up.'

Rachel went into the room and nearer the china, amazed that there was even more than she'd seen already. It was lovely. Old, elegant, not in perfect condition but still beautiful. 'You could sell this on eBay,' said Rachel.

'So could you. I can't be bothered with selling things. I've got enough to live on and can't see the point of having more money than you need.'

This was a surprising concept. 'But Raff would do it for you.'

'Look, darling, if you don't want the crockery, all you have to do is say so. I'm sure Raff could get someone to take it all away.'

'I – er – we do want it,' said Rachel. 'I just need to think of where we could store it.'

'Haven't you got a house?'

'Yes, but—'

'There you are, problem solved. I'll get Raff to bring it round to you.'

Rachel took a few calming breaths. She couldn't have rejected the china: it was a hugely generous present. But the thought of her spare room being full of random plates and saucers, soup bowls and tureens made her panic. She forced herself to be rational. She could put some of it in the other shed and it wouldn't be for long. Beth could probably sell a lot of it, and earn them some money. It would be fine.

'That's so incredibly kind of you,' she said and then, out of nowhere, came, 'When we've got the hall sorted I'd be glad to come and help you with your reorganisation.'

Belinda beamed. 'Thank you, darling. That would be wonderful!'

Chapter Nine

❧

Lindy had felt a bit guilty to be leaving the working party – Rachel scrubbing away at the rafters, the others round the skirting and walls – to go back to her boys. Her father had done an hour or so and now they were with her grandmother and Lindy knew they would have been making cakes. Thus, there would be hot tea and cake waiting for her. She was looking forward to getting her boys home afterwards, bathing them and then curling up on the sofa with them to watch a film. She was just wondering which of their DVDs she could bear watching again when she almost bumped into a man coming along the path to the hall.

'Oh! So sorry! I was miles away!' said Lindy and then looked up. The man was both strange and familiar, and it took her a few seconds to see that the person she thought she recognised in him was in fact her own little boys. Then she realised who it was.

He stared down at her. He too was frowning. 'Lindy?'

Lindy laughed. 'Hello, Angus.'

He gazed down at her for a very long time. 'It seems

a bit of a cliché to say: my, how you've grown, but you are ... very different.'

'I'm bound to be. It's been years. So much has changed.' And so much hadn't changed, she thought. 'You didn't come to the wedding.'

'No. I should have done. But I was a long way away and ... my parents didn't think it was a good idea.'

'Don't worry about it. It wasn't worth the trip. The marriage didn't last long.'

He shook his head, obviously not sure if he should laugh or commiserate. 'I know.'

Lindy cleared her throat, suddenly embarrassed by his scrutiny. 'Don't let me stop you. You were obviously going somewhere. The hall, presumably.'

'I was going to the working party. I heard about it in the shop. Is it over? You're leaving?'

'My grandmother has got my boys. I skipped out early. But it's still going on.'

'I've come back to the area after a long time away. I wanted to get involved. I went to my first Cub Scout meeting in that hall.'

Lindy laughed. 'Goodness me. Well, if you want to help, my mother is in there. She'd be delighted to have you on board, I'm sure.'

'Well, she might be. I'm an architect.'

Lindy nodded. She didn't tell him she knew that. 'That will be useful – later, anyway. At the moment we're just redecorating so we can hire it out, raise a bit of money for repairs. The roof is in a bad way. Although you'll find out all about it if you find Mum.'

He nodded. 'I'd better get in there then. But, Lindy, I

hope to see you around? I haven't seen my nephews for years, not since they had a day out with Edward.'

She nodded. She remembered the time her ex took the boys out for the day and brought them back in the middle of the night. She thought she'd die of worry. Fortunately for her, he never showed any interest in taking them out again and shortly afterwards left the country.

'Billy was just a baby,' she said.

'I'd like to catch up with them. Be an uncle.'

'They'd like that.'

'And would you like that?'

She smiled. 'Well, you wouldn't be my uncle.' And although she longed to stay and talk she was already late. 'I'd better go and pick them up. Go in and talk to Mum.'

Lindy walked to her grandmother's house with a smile on her face. She remembered Beth asking her if she'd got over her crush and she hadn't properly answered the question. Because, seeing Angus again just now, she wasn't convinced she had. It was obviously true that absence – several years' absence in her case – made the heart grow fonder. She laughed. What was she like!

As she went through the bathtime routine, the twenty-nine readings of the *Gruffalo* and other sleep-inducing rituals, she thought, which she hadn't done for ages, what it would have been like doing all this with a partner. The thought made her sigh a little. Even when he had been around, Edward hadn't been the most dedicated of fathers. She and Edward had had Billy in the faint hope it would help mend their relationship. Lindy would never regret having him, but he hadn't worked as glue. And she had always been secretly grateful Edward had made the break in the end, by having an affair. It meant she kept the kids and the moral high ground. But even with her very supportive family it had been tough bringing up the boys on her own.

Beth hurried to get ready. She was due at the pub in ten minutes, having stayed in the hall far too long. She hadn't wanted to abandon Rachel and the others and now was in a rush.

She arrived at the pub, pink and a bit damp, just on time.

Sukey was behind the bar, relaxed and welcoming. 'You did well to get here on time, Beth,' she said, replacing a glass on the shelf. 'I know you were scrubbing the hall earlier.'

'Well, I didn't think I'd worked here long enough to allow myself to be late,' said Beth.

'As you can see, we're not rushed off our feet yet. It will get busy later. You come and settle yourself in. I've got things to do. Ring the bell if you need help. Ilana will be in later.'

Beth went behind the bar and looked around her. It was such a welcoming place she felt very lucky to be working here. It was money, company and free heating, all at the same time. The fire was roaring, currently being enjoyed by at least four dogs. Beth still wasn't up on which dog was whose. She was fairly sure there were a couple of pub dogs, but the others must belong to regulars; however, as there always seemed to be a different combination, she couldn't be sure.

One of the regulars came up and ordered a pint of Albert Memorial.

'I hadn't heard of that before I worked here,' said Beth as she pulled the handle.

'It's special to here. It was created for the pub's centenary. It's really good.' He grinned. 'I was on the tasting panel. I'm Pete, by the way. I'm in here a lot.'

People began to drift in and Beth found herself getting busier and busier. Where was Ilana? She was just about keeping up although she was aware of a lot of glasses that needed washing when Sukey came down to join her. 'You've done well! Ilana phoned in sick and I should have been down earlier really. But I was fairly sure you could cope and I've nearly finished my paperwork. I got a bit behind when we had a guest for a few nights.'

'You don't do much B and B, do you? Do I need to cook breakfast?'

Sukey shook her head. 'No, not much. Only if people really want it. Being single-handed means I don't have much time. But the rooms are there if people are happy to muck in.'

Beth nodded. 'If you don't mind I'll get some of those dirty glasses and then wash them.'

'Knock yourself out!' said Sukey. 'I usually have to remind people to do that.'

Beth made a point of wiping all the tables after she'd collected the glasses. She loved the way every table was different and nothing seemed to have come from 'pub central', which made it all so much more homely. She also loved the stripped floors – so practical – the worn rugs, and the ancient leather sofa that made you just want to curl up in it.

Something made her look up the next time the door opened and she wished she'd taken more time to get ready. It was Charlie.

She let her initial delighted flush die down a bit before she approached the bar, cloth balled up in her hand so he couldn't see it. 'Hi!' she said casually, before slipping behind the bar. Why hadn't she done more to her hair than just wash it? The short style benefited from a bit of styling foam.

'Hi!' he said. 'I'm glad you're here. I wanted to see you.'

Beth allowed a frisson of joy waft over her. 'Oh?'

'Yeah. It's about the van. I've done it up a bit and wondered if you'd like to come up and see it tomorrow?'

Beth examined her conscience. As far as she had gathered, the mist coat would be going on to the hall tomorrow and they wouldn't need her to help do that. 'Should be OK,' she said, hoping he'd think she'd been mentally running over her busy social calendar. 'What can I get you to drink?'

Charlie examined her with eyes that told Beth he was very interested in her. She didn't dare meet his gaze for long so she picked up a glass. 'Albert Memorial?'

'Cool. But it had better be a half. I'm driving.'

Beth filled his glass dreamily. Charlie was really cute. It wouldn't be enough to make him eligible in her mother's pernickety eyes, but it worked for her. Her mother would take exception to the ring in his ear and the bracelet around his wrist. In her book, men only wore signet rings and, possibly, wedding rings. But by anyone's standards (except her mother's) Charlie was gorgeous. It had been a while since she'd really fancied anyone.

'So, I'll come and pick you up and if you're happy with the van you can drive it back.'

'What about insurance?'

'Oh don't worry about that.' He raised an eyebrow. 'You do really drive, don't you? Not just one of your mates?'

'Yes! You asked me before.' She paused, suddenly full of doubt and not only about driving the van without insurance, even for such a short distance. 'The van is roadworthy, isn't it?'

'Yes! You know it is.' He smiled to show he wasn't offended. 'It's not great-looking but it's in good mechanical order.' His smile became a wicked grin. 'I've cleaned it inside and out but I'll throw in a Magic Tree to get rid of the smell if you still think it's there.'

'Hmm.' Beth was doubtful about Rachel approving a synthetic perfume like that. She'd probably prefer something more upmarket. But Charlie was being really helpful.

She realised he must think she was doubting the van's abilities. She had been in it before but she hadn't really taken that much notice, not as anything other than a ride home. She'd pay more attention this time.

'Tell you what, you come up and see it tomorrow and if you still think you'd like it I'll sort out anything you're unhappy with.'

He gave her a smile that made her wish he wasn't

talking about vans, even though he was being kind as well as helpful.

'So are you busy, on the farm?' said Beth, polishing glasses so it looked like she was doing more than chatting.

'Always busy on the farm. We've got work on with the sheep at the moment.'

Beth's mind instantly turned to fluffy lambs curled up against their mothers against a backdrop of straw bales. It seemed idyllic. 'How lovely.'

Charlie laughed. 'You'll see how lovely you think it is tomorrow. Spend some time up at the farm. I'll pick you up at nine. Is that too early?'

'No, that's fine.'

'I'll be there at nine, then.'

It was all Beth could do to stop herself sighing as Charlie moved away.

Chapter Ten

The following morning Lindy's mother rang fairly early. 'Sunday lunch?' she said blithely, as if there wasn't a village hall in desperate need of refurbishment.

'Love to, but Mum, haven't we got to go and sort out the hall? We haven't got long.'

'Raff is doing that spray-painting so there's not much we can do until he's finished and it's dry. We can have lunch. Dad bought a huge leg of lamb yesterday. He'd be disappointed if he couldn't cook it.'

'Well, if you're sure. What time would he like his sous-chef to arrive?'

'Well, Angus is coming at one, so half eleven would give you both plenty of time.'

'Angus?' This was a bit of a shock although a second later Lindy realised she should have predicted her mother would invite him for lunch. Angus and Edward's parents no longer lived in the area and if Sarah even half expected that someone would be without lunch on a Sunday she would invite them. Lindy wasn't sure how she felt about it. She'd met him last night, of course, but she'd have her boys with her at lunch. She'd be in full Mummy mode and she wasn't sure that's how she wanted him to see her. Although he had said he wanted to be more of an uncle to them... She sighed. Seeing him again had stirred up all sorts of emotions and she wasn't sure she liked it. She might occasionally feel her life was rather like a still mill pond and long for something to cause the odd ripple but was Angus a ripple she wanted or needed right now?

'Yes. He was so helpful about the hall yesterday, getting stuck in with getting it ready for painting, it seemed the least I could do. He's staying at the pub because he's just bought a house that's not habitable but Sukey's not doing Sunday lunch at the moment...'

'So you asked him.' Lindy had never told her mother how she felt about Angus but suspected even if she had, her mother's matchmaking habits would not have been affected. Any young man – even if he was related to the unreliable Edward – was fair game. 'Well, that's OK. So will you and Gran take the boys to the swings as usual?'

'And let you and Dad peel and scrape? Absolutely. And I bought a new jigsaw puzzle we can all do afterwards.'

After they had discussed arrangements some more, Lindy went to find clean clothes for the boys. Sunday lunches had become a much-loved routine. Her father cooked, she assisted and made pudding while her sons spent a happy hour running round like mad things with their more mature female relatives. With luck, some Sunday afternoon P and Q, as her grandmother referred to it, could be had with the aid of a DVD, during which most people had a little nap. But if Angus was there, it would be different – slobbing out would not be appropriate. On the other hand, it would be lovely to catch up with him. She had no idea what Angus had been up to recently, for even on the rare occasions she communicated with her ex, Edward was not one for family gossip – to be fair, in part because he knew she was sensitive about their lack of interest in the boys. But Angus seemed to want to get more involved. She would just have to brace herself for him mentioning a long-term girlfriend or something. If he had children, he probably would have mentioned it when he was talking about the boys.

'Grandpa!' yelled the boys as he opened the door. They flung themselves at him and somehow he managed to get both of them up into his arms although Ned was tall for a six-year-old.

'One day those children will realise that I'm quite nice to them too,' said Sarah mildly.

'They adore you, Mum,' said Lindy, who was always slightly embarrassed by her boys' overt preference.

'I know they do. They probably just want a father figure or something,' said Sarah. Billy, the three-year-old, went up to her and hugged her legs. Sarah picked him up. 'So? Who's coming to the swings! Yay! We're meeting Gran there.'

'Can we make biscuits, Sarah?' asked Billy, who always wanted to bake.

'Maybe later but now we're going to the swings with Gran. If we don't join her she'll feel silly playing there on her own.' Sarah had decided it was far too confusing to have two 'Grans' in the family and had insisted on being called Sarah. It was absolutely nothing to do with her feeling too young to be called Granny, she insisted.

James, Lindy's father, said, 'We'd better crack on. If you want to make a fancy pudding because we've got company you'll need to start.' James was a keen cook and loved cooking large meals for family and friends but he ran a tight kitchen and he liked things to be served at the time he had declared they would be.

'I'm not doing anything very fancy but if there are still apples, I'll make a pie,' said Lindy.

Later, as Lindy set the table, she was aware she was nervous. Suppose the boys didn't behave well? Angus might go off and never want to see them again. Their father hardly saw them and Angus was only their uncle. Although she didn't think her boys actually preferred her father to her mother, maybe her mother was right and they did want a father figure? It was something she had never really been able to get her head round, introducing another man into their lives. She knew she would hate it if someone else disciplined them. She didn't even like her beloved parents telling them off at all crossly. But having an uncle would be good for them. Her uncles had always been great fun when she was little. But would it be good for her though? Especially when said uncle had been someone she'd once adored? As she took her crumble-topped apple pie out of the oven, she hoped that Angus liked his crumble topping ever so slightly singed.

Angus, Lindy discovered, was not one for small talk. He'd always seemed very aloof but that was normal for a twenty-one-year-old in the presence of the sixteen-year-old friend of his brother. She couldn't help reflecting that while Raff had a lot wrong with him, he didn't create awkward silences. Angus, who seemed rather too smartly dressed for a Sunday lunch that involved small children, seemed quite content to answer questions with more polite versions of 'yes' and 'no'.

Lindy wanted to ask if he was likely to be around long but hadn't been able to think of a way of putting it that didn't sound rude. To be fair to Angus, he had asked James about the garden but as James didn't do gardening and had no interest in it either, this didn't create a lot of chat.

After a particularly long pause, Lindy bravely said, 'So have you been to see your family up in Northampton? Are they well?'

'Yes,' said Angus. 'They're both on good form. Dad still plays golf three or four days a week. My mother runs a lot of local charities – environmental ones mostly. She's very keen on recycling.'

'Oh, so are we!' said James.

Lindy, who'd been on the receiving end of some of Angus's mother's recycled gifts, was less enthusiastic although she didn't comment. Angus's parents, her boys' paternal grandparents, were of the school that 'children had far too many toys these days'. Lindy, who was bringing up hers with the minimum financial support the law would allow from their father, felt in her boys' case this wasn't actually true. Fortunately for her and her children, they rarely visited.

The two families had never really got on. Much to

Eleanor, Lindy's grandmother's indignation, Edward's family didn't feel Lindy was good enough for their son. Eleanor said the only difference between the two families socially was money. Edward's family had lots, Lindy's very little. But breeding? Eleanor, who wasn't usually remotely snobbish, said the Fredericks were 'nouveau riche' and not nearly as posh as they liked to think themselves.

It was generally felt that the Fredericks moved away from the area to escape the shame of having a son who, having got her pregnant, was forced to marry a girl who'd been to a comprehensive school. Since then, they'd disapproved of her from a distance.

But she'd never really known Angus. He'd been kind, polite and studious. She wondered now why she'd thought he was so amazing when she hardly knew him. But she *had* thought he was amazing and he was still polite; he'd brought a very nice bottle of wine and flowers for Sarah. He just wasn't much of a one for chat.

Lindy, her father and Angus had been standing in the sitting room clutching glasses, seemingly for hours, when at last they heard the boys' arrival, signalled by the sound of the front door opening and a loud 'Raaaaaaaaa!' Then a small herd of elephants rushed along the corridor and entered the room. They both fell abruptly silent. A moment later, Billy burst into tears and ran behind his mother. Ned stood in the middle of the room as if wondering how he'd got there and how to escape. There was a stranger present.

'Oh God, I'm so sorry,' said Sarah, following them into the room, 'they're not usually as noisy as this.'

Lindy, embarrassed by her sons and annoyed by her mother apologising for them, said, 'Billy will be fine in a minute. He just wasn't expecting to see you, that's all. Billy, Ned, this is your Uncle Angus – Daddy's older brother.' Billy was still clinging to her and Ned was looking nervously from his mother to Angus.

'Hello, Angus! Glad you could come! Lindy, Billy got upset when Gran didn't come back with us,' Sarah went on. 'She's having lunch with a friend.'

'I don't know if it'll make things worse, but I have got presents for them.' Angus put his hands in his pockets. 'Of course I have no idea what might be suitable so feel free to take them away if they're all wrong.'

Lindy, who knew how that would go down, hoped he hadn't got them fireworks.

Angus handed them each a parcel. Ned got his open first. Lindy's heart plummeted. It looked horribly like a penknife. But as Ned inspected it she saw it had a lot of gadgets on it but none of them seemed to be sharp.

'It's like a Swiss army knife,' said Angus.

'Cool!' said Ned, smiling now.

Billy got his wrapping off and revealed a torch. 'Cool!' he said, sounding very like his older brother. 'I love torches!'

'Goodness me, Ned,' said James. 'That looks a jolly useful bit of kit. Can I have a look?'

'And that's a lovely torch,' said Sarah, ever the diplomat.

'If you twist the end it changes colour,' said Angus.

Just for a few moments everything went well but then, inevitably, they began to squabble, wanting to play with the other's gadget.

Sarah swept in. 'Boys! Come with me into the kitchen. I've got special drinks.'

'I'll see to them,' said James. 'I want to check on the spuds. Come on, chaps.'

After minimum discussion about what the special drinks consisted of, the boys were herded out of the room by their grandparents.

'I'm sorry!' said Angus. 'I obviously gave them the wrong things and caused a riot.'

'Not at all. Honestly, they get given really boring things, like gloves and scarves, and still fight over them.' She tailed off, remembering who gave them the gloves and scarves. 'They get over it very quickly. Most of the time.' She didn't want Angus to be put off being a more interactive uncle. It meant a lot to her that he was trying.

'Your parents seem to enjoy being grandparents.'

'Yes, thank goodness. I'd be stuck without them. And my grandmother.'

'My parents are too wrapped up in their own lives to care much, I think.'

Lindy totally agreed, but she said, 'Well, to be fair, becoming a grandparent is something that happens to you and you don't have any choice about when it happens.' She was aware how her motherhood had affected her family. They'd been wonderful but it must have been a shock, becoming grandparents so young. It had been quite a shock for her, too, but at least it had been as a result of her actions, not another's.

Angus opened his mouth to speak and then changed his mind. At that moment the boys thundered back into the room, Billy trying to grab Ned's gadget and his older brother pushing him away. They rushed round the room, squabbling loudly as Sarah hurried in after them. Sarah eventually managed to calm them down and collapsed on to the sofa where Billy climbed behind her so he was completely hidden, just as Ned picked up a gas firelighter and started playing with it.

Lindy tried to distract him with one of his favourite toys but he held on to it, teeth clenched. 'It's mine,' he said stubbornly. 'You can't have it!'

'It's not yours, it's Grandpa's,' said Lindy, calm in appearance only. 'Now give it back to me.'

'Nooo!' said Ned.

'Ned!' Lindy used her 'warning' voice. 'Darling. Please remember you are a schoolboy, not a baby.'

'I'm not being a baby,' Ned declared. 'I just want this.'

Had he not clicked it on at that moment, Lindy would have lived with the situation, but as the house going up in flames seemed a real possibility, she felt she had to act.

'Please don't do that. And give it to me. Now.'

God, what must Angus think of them all? Billy would hardly show his face and when he did he bickered with his brother, and Ned was being beastly. And here she was seemingly unable to control her own children. Angus might not exactly be Mr Tumble but he might have taken them fishing, something she was not prepared to do herself. She only hoped he wasn't completely put off.

'I want it,' repeated Ned. He flicked it on again.

'Tell you what,' said Angus. 'If you let your mother have that, I'll show you my knife. It has twelve functions. Some of them are lethal if used in the right way.'

Lindy wasn't sure that Ned knew what 'lethal' meant

but he obviously picked up that the knife was dangerous and therefore desirable. He dropped the lighter.
Lindy had been about to revise her opinion of Angus's
suitability as an uncle but now she was just grateful that
he'd managed to achieve what she hadn't. He smiled at
her now as she picked the lighter up and went with it
into the kitchen. 'Is lunch nearly ready, Dad? The boys –
well, Ned really – are being a nightmare.'

Somehow the meal passed. The boys were calmer,
probably tired out, and Ned had even insisted on sitting
next to Angus. Lindy half listened as her mother and
Angus – in between chatting to his nephew – discussed
the state of the hall. Angus seemed much more talkative
now – but then her mother had that effect on people. She
tuned out the chat, lost in thought. When she'd first seen
Angus outside the hall, her heart had fluttered. She was a
young and healthy woman; it was natural to fancy attractive men, especially if they were probably her first love.
It was one thing to fancy someone, but could she actually
have a proper relationship with a man? A proper relationship would involve her boys. Apart from her family, she
and the boys had been a close little unit for so long now,
would it feel safe to let someone new in? And what if the
boys weren't happy about it and showed it? She couldn't
be torn between a man and her sons. Her sons would
have to win, which meant, realistically, that she couldn't
have a man. And boys were notoriously protective of
their mothers. She did sums in her head. She worked out
she would have to be her mother's age, late forties, before
she could safely assume her boys had left home. It was

rather late to be embarking on a romantic journey. She would probably have shrivelled up entirely by then. She laughed at herself and tuned into Billy who was refusing the green beans his grandfather was trying to persuade him to eat because they squeaked. It was a lost cause.

'More pudding, anyone?' asked Sarah, looking hopefully round the table.

'At the risk of seeming incredibly greedy, I'd love some,' said Angus. 'I was living on hotel food before I found my house and now I'm at the pub. Sukey does great food but a proper home-made pudding is a treat.'

Sarah, who was a feeder, scraped the last of the pudding into Angus's bowl and passed the cream and the ice cream. 'So how long will it be before you can move into your own house?'

'There should be a usable kitchen fairly soon. But the house itself is a very long project.'

'Like the hall,' said James.

'We're doing really well with it though,' said Lindy, feeling protective of it for some reason. 'Raff and Rachel are putting a mist coat on it today.'

Billy splatted the back of his spoon into his pudding. Lindy took the spoon away from him. 'I should think you two could get down now.'

'Please may I get down please!' the boys chorused and ran off.

'You're such a brilliant cook, Sarah,' said Angus.

'Well, I am, of course, absolutely brilliant,' said Sarah, 'but James cooked the main course and Lindy made the pudding.'

Angus looked at Lindy. 'Goodness! Well, it was delicious!'

'Thank you! I'll go and make some coffee,' said Lindy.

'I'll do it!' said Sarah.

Lindy shook her head. She knew perfectly well Sarah was trying to keep her and Angus together. While Lindy was quite keen to spend time with him, she wanted it to be because she wanted it, not because her mother was such a matchmaker. 'Why don't you get out the puzzle?'

'I like puzzles,' said Angus.

'I like them too,' said Ned, who looked up from his game. 'But I like knives better.' Then he flushed. 'I liked your present,' he said, addressing Angus, but clearly unsure what to call him.

Lindy left the room. She didn't want to ask Angus if he'd like to be 'uncle' because it seemed to carry more weight than just being a name. When she came back with the coffee and some chocolate Rice Krispie cakes the boys had made recently, she assumed the matter had all been sorted out. She'd ask the boys.

Referred to as uncle or not, Angus proved a good jigsaw puzzler. He handed Billy pieces facing the right way up so he could easily see where to put them. The pieces were fairly large and on his own Ned would have finished it quite quickly. But Ned was a good older brother when he wasn't snatching his brother's toys from him, and made sure Billy was included. It was all going so well that Lindy felt she could go and clear up the kitchen and load the dishwasher. While Angus had said he wanted to see the boys, he hadn't said anything about wanting to see her.

*

139

At last it was time to go home. The jigsaw pieces were put away, coffee drunk and the boys' various items of outdoor clothing found.

'Angus will give you a hand getting the boys home, I'm sure,' said Sarah.

'I think I can manage, Mum! I have been taking them home on my own for a few years now.'

Not content with trying to get Rachel hooked up with someone who was just wrong for her in every way, she was throwing her and Angus together in a really embarrassing manner. After a shaky start the day had gone well but Lindy's feelings for Angus were still somewhat confused. She'd been a different person when she'd first fallen for him. It was one thing the boys getting to know him properly, but for her it was much more complicated. The last thing she needed was her mother interfering. She knew what Sarah could be like: everything was done with the best intentions but once she had an idea in her head there was no diverting her.

'Actually,' said Angus, getting up, 'I will walk with you a little way if you don't mind. I want to go into the hall and see what's been happening. I really enjoyed helping out yesterday. And I've got a key. Sarah kindly gave me one.'

Sarah nodded. 'With all the renovations, I didn't want to be the only one with a key so I had lots cut and shared them round.'

'Rather takes away the point of locking it, doesn't it?' said James. 'If so many people can get in.'

'Local people aren't going to do anything bad,' said Sarah. 'I was a bit selective about who got one.'

Lindy laughed. 'And actually, it's highly likely that Raff is still there. He was going to do the mist coat.'

'What is a mist coat?' asked James. 'People keep talking about it!'

'You put a very fine mist of paint over everything. It's usually white,' said Sarah, with the confidence of one who'd had it all explained to her quite recently.

'There's probably not a lot happening but we could certainly go and see,' said Lindy. 'Boys? We're going!'

'Is he coming?' asked Billy, looking up at Angus.

Not sure if she was making a serious mistake, Lindy said, 'For a little of the way.'

'Oh, good,' said Billy, satisfied with this reply. Ned was chatting away happily to Angus. Lindy wasn't sure if she was pleased about the boys' acceptance of him or not.

At last they were out of the house walking towards the hall. There were lights on. 'I think Raff must still be doing the mist coat. I wonder if it's safe to go in?' She had visions of her and the boys coming out looking as if they'd been in a flour fight.

'I'm prepared to risk it,' said Angus. 'I'd like to see if there's access to the roof space and have a look at what's going on up there. I didn't get a chance yesterday.'

Lindy wasn't going to let Angus know more than she did about the hall. It was Vintage Weddings' project. 'I'll come in with you, then. I'm desperate to see what it looks like.'

Angus opened the door and they went in. The hall looked very, very different. 'It's like – fairyland!' said Lindy to Rachel, who was wearing her snow-white boiler suit. She had obviously decided she didn't quite trust Raff to mist-coat without her supervision.

'It's lovely, isn't it? Such an improvement. I just wish they'd let us keep it white, but I don't expect they will.'

'I don't know,' said Angus, having a good look round. 'You could maybe convince them to go the Strawberry Gothic route. It could look brilliant in here.'

'What's that?' asked Lindy.

'It's Gothic buildings painted light colours, more or less,' said Rachel. 'I'll show you on my phone.'

While Rachel was tapping on urls to bring up a picture and Lindy was keeping an eagle eye on her boys, Raff came up.

'Do I remember you from school or something?' he said to Angus. Raff had gone off to collect the mist-coating machine when Angus had been helping out the day before.

'My parents lived here until about seven years ago,' said Angus. 'But I went to boarding-school and wasn't around in the holidays all that much. You do look familiar though.'

Raff nodded, beginning to grin. 'Skateboarding! You used to skateboard with us. We called you "Posh Boy".'

A rueful smile spread over Angus's face. 'That's right. But then I did my knee in and had to give it up.'

'Well, nice to see you back,' said Raff. 'We must have a pint sometime.'

Lindy, having seen a picture of a white-painted church in Herefordshire that looked glorious, decided her boys had used up their supply of good behaviour and needed to go home.

'Well, I'll vote for Strawberry Gothic,' she said. 'Guys! Time to go now.'

'It's time we went too, Rachel,' Raff said.

'I'll stay for a bit longer,' said Angus. 'I can lock up.'

'Will you be all right?' asked Lindy. Then she shook her head, annoyed with herself. 'Sorry. It's being a mum. It makes me a bit... mum-like.'

'Not a bad thing, Lindy,' said Raff.

'As long as I don't cut up people's food for them, I suppose it's OK. Come on, boys! We're off!'

Chapter Eleven

Meanwhile Beth, too, was having a different sort of Sunday to the one she was used to. She had been shattered when she got home just after midnight having washed and put away, she was sure, more glasses than the pub actually owned. She was very keen to make a good impression and perhaps get more shifts at the Prince Albert. She needed the money and she loved the work. She now knew that Charlie was pretty much a regular although he never had more than half a pint.

She had set her alarm for eight and fallen into bed. If it hadn't been Charlie who was picking her up at nine she might well have set it for half past eight, but although it wasn't a date, she really wanted to look as good as you can do in jeans and jumpers.

She pulled her trapper hat with ear flaps on over her damp hair and waited, trying not to be spotted by him looking like the Lady of Shalott, staring desperately out of the window.

She couldn't see his Land Rover and assumed he'd parked it round the corner. She retreated into the kitchen, taking time to rinse her mug and put it on the drainer before she answered his knock.

'Hello!' she said gaily and then hoped her girlish enthusiasm wouldn't put him off her.

'Hello!' He flapped the tassel on her hat. 'Glad to see you're dressed for the weather. Have you got wellies?'

'Oh yes.' She indicated the bag in her hand. 'I thought I might need them.' She grinned. 'I'm not a complete townie, you know!'

'You look great, by the way,' he said, giving her a peck on the cheek. 'Good and workmanlike.'

'Do I need to be workmanlike? I thought we were just looking at the van?'

He laughed. 'You never know what you'll be asked to do when you visit a farm . . .'

He took her arm in a friendly way and led her round the corner. There was no Land Rover, just the van.

'So there she is,' said Charlie proudly, standing in front of the bright red vehicle that reminded Beth strongly of Postman Pat. 'I've done it up a bit. Should do you nicely.'

'Wow!' said Beth, not knowing quite what else she should say.

'Like it?'

'It's very red.' He might have washed it but the paint was still very faded in places. What would Rachel think of it? Would she want it resprayed in white?

'It doesn't get any better-looking by you staring at it. Get in!'

Beth walked towards the passenger door.

'No.' Charlie opened the driver's door. 'This time, you're driving.'

145

Beth kept her dismay concealed. It wasn't only the insurance. Still, she could sort that out when she got back. Her first problem was that she hadn't driven for a while and would have preferred to get some practice on something a bit more familiar. And had he managed to deal with the smell? She walked round to where Charlie was waiting for her and got in.

She had a few seconds to familiarise herself with the van before he joined her. The smell was slightly better – which did help.

'Let's get going then!' he said.

'Don't you want to see my driving licence or anything?' she asked, wanting a little longer to get used to the driving position.

'This isn't a driving test, it's a test drive.'

'OK,' she said. 'I should be asking you all sorts of probing questions.'

'Ask away,' he said glibly.

'I will when I've thought of some,' she added, thinking that one of the downsides of leaving home was that you couldn't get your dad to help you buy a car. Maybe Lindy's dad would give it a once-over to make sure they weren't making a mistake.

She took her time adjusting the seat and the mirror.

'The visibility isn't as good as I'm used to,' she said.

'You'll soon get used to using your wing mirrors.' He waited for a few seconds. 'Crack on. Turn right when you get to the end of the lane.'

Beth began to enjoy herself. The van was easy to drive and she'd always liked driving – and the smell hardly bothered her at all now. It was a lovely day and perfect for exploring the countryside. 'This is fun!' she said. 'The farm's in this direction, isn't it?' She was fairly sure that Sarah had gone off at the left fork when she'd first taken Beth to the farm.

'We're not going to our farm. Carry on in this direction for a bit. I'll direct you.'

'OK!'

'So, how do you like country life?' he asked a little later.

'It's great! It's certainly better now I've got a job and some friends. I'll need some proper work of course – I think I told you, didn't I, that I design websites and do online marketing? But if the van turns out all right – and it's going OK so far – I should be able to borrow it and look for clients further away than walking distance.' She laughed gaily.

'So your parents wouldn't help towards a car of your own?'

'No. To be fair, they did give me some money but I'm afraid I used it to run away from them. Or rather, not go back after university, as they wanted to me to.'

'Run away? That sounds a bit drastic!'

She laughed. 'My mother is a bit on the controlling side. It's why I'm organising my sister's wedding. But I don't expect you want to hear about that!'

'No. Even my sister's wedding is getting a bit much for me.'

'Well, tell me what's going on at the farm!' Beth's barmaid training meant she always asked people about their work.

'We're just coming up to lambing so it's the calm before

the storm,' said Charlie. 'Which is why we're taking the day off.'

'On a magical mystery tour? You still haven't told me where we're going?'

'We're going to visit a ram. And some of his progeny. I'm interested in a rare breed of sheep and I'm thinking about breeding them.'

'And you thought I was your ideal chauffeur to get you there?'

He grinned. 'That's right. I thought you might be my ideal all sorts of things.'

Beth kept her eyes on the road, which was becoming more a lane. She was trying very hard not to grin back at him.

At last they found the farm in a fold in the hillside. The small stone house was surrounded by outbuildings, some modern, some old and ramshackle. The last bit of track was potholed and stony and Beth took it slowly. She now felt the van was theirs – hers and Lindy's (she still doubted Rachel would want anything to do with it) – and was determined to be careful with it.

A man wrapped up in tweed, a sheep dog at his heels, emerged from the house.

Beth and Charlie got out. Beth stayed close to Charlie, not happy with the expression on the face of the sheep-dog. Charlie put his arm round her and she felt better. To be fair to him, the dog didn't say anything unfriendly.

'Come to see this ram, then?' said the man, not wasting time on preliminaries.

'That's right,' agreed Charlie. 'And some of his

148

progeny, if I may. I want to make sure Balwens are the right breed for me.'

'This way then,' said the farmer.

The sheepdog left his side and followed the little group. Beth felt she was appearing in an edition of *One Man and His Dog* and might be herded into a pen at any moment.

Beth let the men walk ahead. She was sure Charlie would be happy to have her near him but sensed the farmer wasn't used to young women and felt a little shy in her presence.

'So, what are the best things about Balwens, then?' asked Charlie.

'You'll have done your research. Good feet, easy lambing, excellent meat. Not too big, easy to sell to housewives.'

'Right.'

The talk got more technical and Beth stopped listening. She was wondering if she'd like living on a farm. Would she take to it? Become one of those women who reared orphaned lambs in the Aga and had a flock of chickens round her back door, all with names like Esmeralda, Philomena and Cleopatra? This was a pleasant enough daydream but she did slightly wonder if she'd be lonely, up at Charlie's family farm day after day. Skype was brilliant but it wasn't the same as a flesh-and-blood human.

At last the sheep-viewing was over (they were extremely pretty sheep, she had to agree, when asked), and a certain amount of vintage-tractor-viewing (for which Beth managed to fake enthusiasm), it was time to leave the farmer to his Sunday roast.

'You drive,' she said to Charlie, handing him the keys to the van. 'I want to admire the scenery.'

'OK,' he said. 'Now, what about lunch? Are you fed up with pubs, seeing as you work in one? I know one that does a very good Sunday lunch?'

She was thrilled that he cared enough to ask. 'What's the alternative?'

He gave a rueful grin – one that sent Beth's heart racing. 'I don't know!'

'A pub is fine,' said Beth. 'Fortunately, considering I'm back on duty tonight, I really like them.'

The pub was much more 'gastro' than the Prince Albert would ever be, and although it was nice enough, Beth knew which one she preferred. Though she accepted it might just be loyalty.

'So, what are you drinking, lovely?' he said.

Beth warmed to the endearment. 'Red wine, please, if we're having Sunday lunch.'

'Red it is. Just a glass? Or a bottle?'

'A glass,' she said, keeping her sigh of happiness for when he'd gone to the bar and wouldn't hear her.

Halfway through her wine she offered to stop drinking so he could have more than the half of lager he was drinking. He wouldn't hear of it. 'This is your day off,' he said.

After lunch they drove some more and then he took her for a walk, to where a view of the entire Severn Vale and the Malvern Hills beyond could be seen. They went to the viewpoint, Charlie's arm tightly around her. They stood for a few moments admiring the view. 'Look, there's Wales,' Charlie said. 'My mother came from Wales. I like coming here, to see the Land of My Mothers.'

'You must have been very young when she died.' Beth, who'd had a second glass of wine with her lunch, was feeling sentimental.

'I was twelve.'

'I'm so sorry!' she said.

'Don't worry. It wasn't your fault.' Then he took her into his arms and kissed her.

At first it was clumsy and then rapidly it became intense. Beth was short of breath, passionate and enthusiastic. But for some reason when Charlie's hand pushed its way up her back, under her T-shirt, fingering the fastening of her bra, she pulled back.

'You're right. It's far too cold for this here. Let me take you home.'

On the way home, Beth's desire fought with her brain. Her body said: Yes, yes please! But her head thought it was just a bit soon.

She was still undecided when they reached her front door. She and Charlie chased up the path to the door and she let them in.

'Would you like tea or something?' she asked.

He laughed. 'What do you think? Come here!'

Her body told her head to be quiet and she led Charlie into the bedroom. They sat on the bed for a bit, kissing, while he undressed her top half. Then he pushed her gently back and concentrated on kissing her senseless.

Then his phone rang in his jeans pocket.

'Dad! What's the problem!'

Beth couldn't hear what his father had to say, but she

gathered pretty quickly that it was an emergency and Charlie had to leave.

'I'm sorry, kid. There's a ewe in trouble and Dad wants me there. He could cope really but I said I'd be back an hour ago. I'll have to leave.' He kissed her thoroughly, and then pulled on his sweater. 'I'll be in touch.'

Beth pulled her own T-shirt and sweater on slowly. She was confused. Was she desperately disappointed or relieved?

Under the shower a little later she decided she was disappointed.

Chapter Twelve

It was a week before April's wedding. The girls had all been working hard on different aspects of it and hadn't had a chance to have a proper catch-up with each other. Or, as Rachel would have it, a meeting. Now they were assembled in Lindy's crowded sitting room, so she didn't have to get a babysitter. It was seven o'clock and Lindy had half her mind on her boys upstairs. Billy was asleep but if she wasn't careful, Ned, who quite audibly wasn't, would wake him up.

'Sorry, you two!' she said now. 'Why don't you start without me?' She ran back up the stairs hoping Ned's loud singing hadn't already woken his brother.

She was back down five minutes later, wondering, as she often did, if bribery was really as bad as all that if it worked.

'OK. It should be fine now. Ned's in my bed with a book. I'll move him later. So, where are you?'

'Well,' said Rachel, who had her ubiquitous Emma Bridgewater hardbacked notebook on her knee, 'we were just ticking things off the To Do list, where we can.'

'Please let some things be crossed off,' said Lindy. 'I've got a very long list of things that aren't.' She wasn't looking forward to admitting the major one.

'OK, well, the hall is sort of decorated,' said Rachel. 'Not properly but—'

'It looks a-mazing!' said Beth. 'You just wouldn't recognise it from the night we met there. Everything white. The walls. The beams. The woodwork. It's like a snow scene.'

'I know!' said Lindy. 'It's lovely.

'It is but we'll probably need to change some of that,' said Rachel. 'The paintwork needs to be a different colour. Maybe a pale grey—' She stopped, aware the others were looking at her.

'Is pale grey really a colour?' said Lindy.

'Whether it is or isn't, we haven't got time to do more painting now. We'll have to jolly it all up with wreaths and things,' said Beth.

'But—' said Rachel.

'No, really, we haven't time,' said Beth firmly.

'So that's the hall,' said Lindy, knowing they were depending on her for 'wreaths and things'. 'What about the catering?'

'That's all in hand,' said Beth. 'Lots of local people are donating their time and even ingredients. With April not having a mother, people just want to help.'

'So what are we having to eat?' Rachel seemed to need to write this down.

'One woman is doing some massive pork pies as well as about five Victoria jam sponges – I've done quite a lot of bartering, teaching older people how to email in exchange for a plate of sausage rolls. Not only sausage rolls,' she finished, seeing the expression on Rachel's face.

'Cool,' said Rachel, ticking something. 'Oh, and is the wedding cake sorted?'

'It's made. But it does need to be iced,' said Beth. 'I've been practising like mad. I've got quite good, although I say it myself.'

'Well done, Beth!' said Lindy. 'Now, Rachel brought some wine. Anyone?'

'Oh yes please,' said Beth. 'Would you like me to get it, Lind? You look as if you need to sit down for a bit and you've been working so hard.'

'We all have,' said Lindy, 'but if you don't mind... And when you come back, I've got something to confess.'

'Cheers!' said Beth brightly when she had returned with glasses and filled them.

'So what's your confession, Lindy?' asked Rachel, looking worried.

Lindy sighed. 'I haven't finished the dress.'

'But the wedding's in a week!' said Beth.

Lindy nodded hard. 'I know! The trouble is, April and her fiancé got a deal and went off for a few days in the sun. Tristram's got to start work the moment they reach America, so it's a sort of honeymoon.'

'Just before her wedding?' said Rachel. 'Unusual.'

'She did sort of ask me if it was OK, but I could hardly say no. Anyway, I haven't been able to get hold of her for fittings and when she did come for one we realised I'd have to move all the buttons, which meant new buttonholes. There's really quite a lot of work involved. It's not that I can't do it,' she went on, suppressing a mild feeling of panic, 'but I don't have that much time. And Ned's been off school.'

'Of course you're really busy,' said Beth. 'You're a mum and that's your most important job.'

'Why don't you let me do the decorations for the hall?' suggested Rachel. 'I could take that off your hands, at least.' She frowned. 'Not sure quite when I'd fit it in but I'm sure—'

'No!' Lindy felt protective. 'It's OK. I love making wreaths and things and it would be relaxation after finishing the dress. I won't be able to do it until the day before anyway, and if I haven't finished the dress by then we're in real trouble.'

'It'll be fine, I'm sure!' said Beth breezily. 'I'm looking forward to doing the cake actually. I can do that a couple of days before, as long as I've put the base coat on, so to speak.'

'Oh God! Beth!' Lindy bit her lip. 'I'd forgotten. I told April it would be possible to copy the design of the lace to put on the cake.'

Beth's breeziness dissipated. 'I've only practised roses – her mother's favourite flower. I was just grateful it wasn't orchids or hyacinths or something really complicated.' Her Charlie-induced happiness dimmed slightly.

'I suppose I could tell her it's out of the question but she will be disappointed,' said Lindy. 'She particularly wanted it because it was what her mother had. It's her mother's dress. She wanted the same.'

Beth sighed. 'I'll do it then.'

'Surely transferring lace patterns on to cake isn't something you can just do straight off, is it?' Rachel sounded sceptical and worried.

'There is absolutely nothing you cannot learn from YouTube,' Beth said. 'I have quite tidy handwriting and I'll practise of course. Lindy, I might need your help tracing the lace pattern, but I'm sure it'll be OK.' She paused. No one spoke. 'I watched a lot of *Cake Boss* when I was at uni. Me and my flatmates had a bit of a cake thing going on. And as I said, I have been practising.'

'Well, if the lace thing doesn't work, April will just have to make do with the roses,' said Rachel, writing something down. 'So when is she coming for a fitting?'

'I'll set one up with her soon. It should be fine,' said Lindy.

'Right,' said Rachel. 'Actually, I've got something to tell you. Something that should make us a bit of money.'

'Fantastic!' said Lindy. 'We need some good news.'

Lindy and Beth looked at Rachel expectantly.

'So?' asked Beth when Rachel hadn't answered after several tense seconds had ticked by.

'I should say,' said Lindy, 'if it's anything to do with lap-dancing, I'm not up for it. Just so you know.'

But seeing Rachel's expression she realised she wasn't in the mood for flippancy.

'It's to do with Raff,' said Rachel.

Lindy groaned. 'Oh God! I am so sorry, Rachel. It's all my mother's fault, she means well, but—'

'No, it's OK,' said Rachel. 'It's not your mother's fault, it's Raff's.'

'Raff's mother?' said Lindy.

'I can't quite imagine him having a mother,' said Beth.

'Most people have, at least at one time in their lives,' said Lindy.

'It's not even Raff's fault. I didn't have to go to dinner with his mother.'

'You went to dinner with his mother?' said Lindy.

'What's she like?' said Beth. 'And why did you go to meet her? Back up a bit, Rachel. I didn't know you were even seeing Raff.'

'No!' Rachel almost shouted. 'We're not! Seeing each other, I mean. After we did the decorating that Saturday he invited me to his mother's for a meal.'

Lindy was surprised. 'I didn't think you even liked him.'

'I only like him as a friend!' said Rachel, sounding defensive. 'We've been out for a drink a couple of times and for a walk but I've always kept him – well, you know – at arms length. But we were both so tired and hungry. And Raff has been – helpful. And he let me do the mist coat on that Sunday. I got to use the machine.'

'Actually I get that,' said Beth. 'It must have been fun.'

'It was heaven,' said Rachel. 'I love turning things white. I was the Snow Queen in a past life,' she said.

'We saw the mist coat; don't try and change the subject. Go back to his mother?' said Lindy.

'Her house is amazing!' said Rachel. 'Like something the National Trust has just been left, where nothing's been thrown away for generations. Although in this case, it's probably just for decades.'

'Long enough, anyway,' said Lindy. 'I have met Raff's mother a few times and she has a certain style. I wouldn't have put her down as a hoarder, in an unbalanced way.'

Rachel considered. 'Perhaps I was unfair. The house isn't full of rubbish but it's very full. Of everything.

I think I offended her when I said clutter.'

'Now my mother is prudish,' said Beth. 'I mean really prudish, but even she wouldn't object to that particular "c" word.'

'Agh!' said Rachel. 'You know what I mean! Anyway, her dining room had a massive table in it, absolutely covered with china. She said we could have it.'

'What sort of china?' asked Beth. 'Shepherdesses and dogs?'

'No. Eating-off china. All sorts. Whole dinner services – tea sets – we'll never need to buy anything for weddings and we could probably sell quite a lot of it. Some of it's really good stuff: Minton, Wedgwood, Crown Derby – all the big names.'

'Why doesn't Raff sell it for her?' said Lindy. 'I always thought he was quite good to his mother.'

'I said that, but she's not into selling things, even if Raff did it,' said Rachel. She paused. 'I did offer to help her sort out her house, of course.'

The other two nodded. 'It's an amazing offer,' said Beth. 'And imagine being able to serve food on vintage china. The proper stuff, not just car-boot finds that are called "vintage" because they're not new.'

'The village hall does have china,' said Lindy. 'Functional, but not special.'

'Even my mother will be impressed if she's eating her smoked-salmon sandwiches off vintage Derby plates.'

Everyone laughed but then Rachel said, 'Although if there is any vintage Derby, we'd probably be better off selling it.'

'When will you go over and have another look?' said

Lindy. 'If it's a weekday and it's not a nursery day for Billy and I can get Gran to look after him, can I come?'

'I think we should all go if we can,' said Rachel. 'There's so much of it. We can't go until after the wedding, I've already told Belinda that.'

'It sounds so much fun,' said Lindy. 'Something to look forward to after the stress of the wedding.'

'OK,' said Rachel, who was looking at her notebook again. 'What's the news on the van?'

'It just needs another valet, and it's ready,' said Beth and went pink. 'He's taken a while to get round to it.'

'I took the cash out to pay for it the other day,' said Rachel, reaching into her bag and producing an envelope. 'Here you are. Don't lose it between here and home.'

Beth put the envelope in her own messenger bag and zipped it up. 'I'll be careful.'

'And is there anything else you'd like to tell us, Beth?' asked Lindy gently. 'To explain why you're blushing? I'm assuming you're not planning to run away with our money and spend it all on sweets.'

Beth giggled nervously. 'No! But Charlie and I did spend an amazing day together. And he has taken me out for a drink since. He's been lambing night and day, so it's been difficult. And it's early days, of course, but I do like him.'

'Young love,' said Lindy. 'So sweet.'

'I have to admit, I was getting a little jealous of my sister,' said Beth, who was obviously happy to talk about Charlie. 'She's so loved up. I just thought it wouldn't happen for me. But as I said, it's early days, plenty of time for it all to go wrong.' She sighed.

'Why should it go wrong?' said Lindy. 'You're lovely. Any man would be proud to have you on his arm.' She paused. 'Oh, did I sound like my gran just then?'

The other two nodded. 'But that's OK,' said Beth. 'I met her in the shop the other day and she was lovely.'

'And you're a bit young to be so pessimistic about love,' said Rachel. 'That usually happens at about my age.'

'Well, you're young too,' said Beth. 'And you've got Raff.'

'I have absolutely not got Raff!' said Rachel. 'We are so unsuited it isn't even funny suggesting there's anything going on between us!'

'What is it my gran says? "I think the lady does protest too much." I think it's Shakespeare,' said Lindy.

Rachel shook her head. 'No, really. He's far too – unkempt for me. I like my men well groomed—'

'And well heeled?' suggested Lindy.

'Not necessarily! But I do like them to have a proper profession.'

'But Raff has a business,' said Lindy. 'Isn't that OK?'

'Lindy! You were the one who said I shouldn't have anything to do with him,' protested Rachel.

'Not because he has a reclamation yard; because he's unreliable with women,' replied Lindy, suddenly anxious that maybe Rachel was a bit of a snob.

'Well, whatever the reason is, I'd better get off,' said Beth. 'I've got to gear up my cake-decorating skills to whole new heights. How soon could you trace the lace pattern for me, Lindy?'

'I'll do it now if you can hang on,' said Lindy. 'And, Rachel, sorry if I sounded a bit judgemental.'

'No, no,' said Rachel. 'I realise how it must have sounded. But I promise you that my problems with Raff are nothing to do with him being a posh form of scrap-metal merchant.'

The other two laughed and finished their wine. Then they said their goodbyes.

Beth went home clutching a bit of baking parchment with a leaf pattern on it pressed between the pages of a novel she'd borrowed for when she couldn't cope with icing any more. She hoped Lindy didn't feel abandoned when she and Rachel both rushed off, but she was hoping Charlie might ring and if he did, she wanted to take the call in private.

But she was not going to hang about waiting for a call. She would get on to YouTube and see if she really could learn to decorate cakes – and not just with roses – from it.

At eleven o'clock, when she was beginning to get boss-eyed from staring at her laptop watching piping bags dance over icing, creating flowers, swirls and filigree with unbelievable skill, she finally decided to go to bed. There had been no phone call from Charlie. She was terribly tempted to text him but couldn't think what to say. A 'good night!' didn't seem appropriate this early in their relation-ship. Maybe she could say 'Any news on the van?' Then she thought about it. Charlie was a farmer. Lambing was probably still going strong and he wouldn't want a text this late. No, she wouldn't text. But how she wished that he would. She was fretting a bit about how things had been left after their day out together. She'd seen him in the pub since, and he'd seemed fine – as friendly as ever

– but she still worried that he'd think her a tease, even though it had been his phone that had stopped them. And while she had been disappointed, she had now begun to feel that they had been going a bit too fast too soon.

Beth was in a very deep sleep when she gradually became aware of someone banging on the front door. It sounded so urgent she just fell out of bed and made her way downstairs, blinking, trying to wake up. There must be an awful emergency – perhaps someone was ill, or there'd been a car crash or something – and she ought to be alert and able to help. She debated pulling on her jeans for decency but decided if there was an emergency, no one would notice her thighs.

The man on her doorstep, grinning and dangling car keys, was Charlie. Beth had been so sure it would be a policeman or an anxious stranger she took a second to register it was him.

'What are you doing here?' she asked huskily, checking her brain to see if there'd been arrangement to drop in on her insanely early after delivering something locally.

He grinned. 'I've brought your van after its second valet. Not even toffee-nosed Rachel will complain about the smell now. Are you going to ask me in?'

She flinched inwardly at this slur on Rachel, but she didn't comment. 'Of course. Come in.' She waited until he was in the hallway and then said, 'I'll just get some clothes on.'

'I think you look fine as you are,' said Charlie. He gave her a long, lazy look that told her he was all ready to carry on from where they left off last time he was here.

Beth didn't know how she felt about this and didn't comment. 'I won't be long,' she said and retreated to the bedroom.

Maybe it was the fact she was wearing an outsized Hello Kitty T-shirt she'd worn in bed since she was twelve, but she didn't feel she wanted to get straight back into bed with him. She needed a bit more wooing, she decided.

She didn't spend much time getting dressed. She more or less pulled on what she'd taken off the night before, brushed her teeth, gave her hair its usual ruffle and joined Charlie in the sitting room. 'Good morning!' she said, feeling cheerful now she was wearing knickers and had cleaned her teeth.

'Good morning, beautiful. I'm a little bit disappointed that you felt you had to get dressed just for me, but maybe I'll forgive you if you make me breakfast.' He pulled her too him and kissed her in a way that made her wonder if she was actually breakfast.

'You should have had it already, being a farmer and up at dawn,' she said teasingly when he let her go.

'I've had coffee and a bit of bread and butter already, but now I need food.'

Beth went into her tiny kitchen. As it happened, she did have a packet of bacon and one of her newly online older friends had given her a box of fresh eggs as a thank-you present. She dug out her frying pan.

There wasn't a lot of difference between a hung-over student and a hungry farmer, she decided as she loaded up his plate. She'd made toast for herself but Charlie had several rashers of bacon, a mountain of scrambled eggs, fried mushrooms and tomatoes and fried bread. She'd been a breakfast chef for a while one vacation and knew how people appreciated an overloaded plate. She put it down in front of him with a proud flourish.

'Awesome!' he said. 'You rock!' He pulled her to him in a hug and patted her bottom.

She went and fetched her tea, examining why that innocent little pat made her feel a bit – tawdry.

'Well, that was delicious,' said Charlie, wiping his plate with his toast. 'If there's nothing more you can offer me, maybe you should drive me home?' He drained his tea mug, keeping his eyes on hers, making sure she didn't misunderstand him.

She smiled. She didn't want to turn him down but she didn't want to take him to her bedroom, either.

'Toast? Peanut butter?'

He shook his head but with a wicked grin. 'Not quite what I had in mind. But no hard feelings. I need to get back to the farm. Time to relieve Dad on lambing duty.'

Beth returned his smile. She liked him for not forcing the issue. She wasn't a prude but she had an internal clock that told her when it was right to take a relationship to bed. Although it was nearly right, she felt that she and Charlie hadn't quite reached that point yet. He probably realised he wouldn't have to wait too much longer and could be patient.

She'd pulled on her jacket before going with him to the van. She pulled open the door and sniffed. There was still a smell – it was hard to pretend otherwise – but it was far less than it had been. Rachel (whom she refused to think of as toffee-nosed) could use her own car. Lindy wouldn't mind the van smelling a bit agricultural.

'Fantastic! I now pronounce it smell-free!' she said. 'I'll just go and get the money.'

She nipped back into the house and took the pile of notes from where she'd hidden them under her suitcase on the top of her wardrobe.

'Here you are. Used, non-sequential notes,' she said as she handed them over. 'Count them.'

Charlie barely glanced at the bundle. 'I trust you, Beth. And if the money is short, well...' He grinned. 'I know where you live.'

Beth decided at that moment that she'd been far too prudish and should have just got straight into bed with him without getting dressed first, or giving him breakfast. It was too late to go back on the decision but, oh, how she wanted to! She gave him a very long kiss goodbye after she had dropped him off.

That evening, Beth tucked her hair behind her ears reflecting, for the zillionth time, on how high maintenance really short hair was. It was easy to wash and quick to dry but without a lot of products it didn't look right. It needed cutting horribly often, too. Maybe Lindy would do it for her. She was so multitalented she was bound to be able to cut hair.

Beth was behind the bar in the Prince Albert while upstairs there was a village-hall meeting going on. She polished glasses, her ears cocked for the clomp of people descending the stairs indicating the meeting was over.

Not only did she want to be ready for the sudden rush of orders, she wanted to know if the committee had been happy about the decoration of the hall. They knew about the wedding, of course, and that something had had to be done smartish, but when they were used to maroon and dark green, how would they cope with the white? Beth knew there had been a mass trip to inspect it before the meeting.

She really hoped, for Rachel's sake, there hadn't been a rebellion. For although Rachel said she knew the paintwork couldn't stay white, she was hoping for a colour so light most people wouldn't even notice it had colour in it.

Rachel was first into the bar. 'A large white wine, Beth, and one for you too if you're allowed.'

Beth hesitated. 'Celebrating or commiserating?'

Rachel grinned. 'Celebrating. They loved it, basically, and are quite happy for me to choose paint colours. The architect sent in a written report about some structural stuff but he didn't comment on the colour scheme.' Rachel wrinkled her brow. 'It's Angus, apparently. I met him briefly when we were decorating.'

'Oh, yes, Lindy's brother-in-law. I must have missed him.' Beth placed a rapidly frosting glass of wine on the counter. 'I won't have a drink, thanks. I might give someone the wrong change.'

Lindy and her mother came up to the bar. 'Well, that went well!' said Sarah. 'Lindy? Glass of wine? Rachel? Oh, you've got one. Beth?'

Sukey came up while the drinks discussion was going on. 'Why don't you take a break when this lot are served, Beth? I'm sure you want to discuss the meeting and the wedding.' She sighed. 'I do hope I'm going to get extra trade because of it.'

'Of course you will,' said Rachel. 'As you know, there's going to be a keg each of beer and cider and wine provided but when that runs out, they'll all come over here.'

'Oh, good. Beth, just clear this lot' – she indicated the little queue of people – 'with me and then you can bunk off for a bit.'

Rachel made a dash for the big table and Beth saw Sarah hesitate before being beckoned to sharply by Lindy and Rachel. It wasn't long before Beth joined them, clutching a lime soda.

'The reason I'm butting in,' said Sarah, looking embarrassed, 'is that I've had a call from April.'

'Oh, God! Why?' said Rachel, worried.

'She's having trouble with her seating plan. She didn't want to mention it to Lindy, when she had a fitting.'

'Oh dear,' said Beth, summoning sympathy.

'She's hoping you can help her,' went on Sarah.

'I'm not sure we can really,' said Rachel. 'We don't know who anyone is. It's for the bride and bridegroom to sort out. And their parents.'

Sarah put a hand on Rachel's. 'The trouble is, April hasn't got a mother and her father is so tied up with the farm he can't help. And her fiancé isn't terribly involved in the wedding either. That's why she needs you three.' She hesitated, looking a bit embarrassed. 'I'm afraid I told her you'd be happy to help.'

'Well, I'm sure we can,' said Beth, who would do anything for Sarah, she was so unlike her own mother, so controlling and critical.

'But we won't know who anyone is,' persisted Rachel,

obviously unhappy. 'We could put ex-wives on the same table!' Then, realising she'd sounded a bit hysterical, she felt obliged to explain. 'Sorry, I really hate doing anything I can't do perfectly.'

Sarah laughed gently. 'It won't be ex-wives you need to worry about but who hasn't spoken to whom since nineteen sixty-four.'

Beth joined in the laughter. 'Oh well, it'll be a piece of cake then.'

'We'll need somewhere to have a final session with April, to sort out all the little tweaks,' said Lindy. 'And not my house because it's full of wedding dress and miles of bunting.'

'Bunting?' said Rachel, instantly concerned. 'I thought we were having boughs of greenery, not bunting! That's more suitable for summer!'

'I know, sorry! Don't worry,' said Lindy. 'I'm making sashes for the bridesmaids to unify their look, and I just meant all the material looks a bit like bunting at the moment.'

Rachel pushed her hair away from her face as if she were too hot suddenly. 'OK, I'm probably just panicking. There is so much to do!'

'There's nowhere big enough in my cottage,' said Beth. 'The table seats three when it's fully extended.'

'I wonder if Sukey would let us spread out in the upstairs room?' said Lindy. 'It's a bit cold up there but there's plenty of space.'

'Why don't you use your house, Rachel?' said Raff, who'd appeared behind them.

They all looked at Rachel. Beth realised she knew

Rachel really quite well, she lived nearby and yet she'd never been in her house.

'Erm—'

'Well? I really think the girls would like it,' said Raff. 'Especially now you can light the stove.' He looked round, twinkling wickedly. 'It's very – er – white in Rachel's house.'

'What?' began Lindy.

'It's wevet!' snapped Rachel. 'The colour is wevet!'

'Oh, sorry,' said Raff. 'But you could have the meeting there. There's lots and lots of space.' Then he'd moved off before Rachel could reply.

'I would really love to see your house, Rachel,' said Lindy.

'Yes, right,' said Rachel, who seemed to have gone a bit pale. 'We'll get together tomorrow, if that's all right. Will you be able to get childcare, Lindy?'

'Yes,' said Sarah. 'She will.'

Lindy put a hand on Rachel's. 'Really, we don't have to go to yours, not if you'd rather not. I totally understand about not wanting people you're not actually related to by blood coming into your space. I feel like that often.'

'It's fine. I love my house and I'm proud of it but sometimes I feel – judged – when people go in it.'

'We're none of us judgemental,' said Beth. 'And it can't be as untidy as Lindy's.'

Rachel laughed. 'It's really not at all untidy!'

Chapter Thirteen

Rachel removed the freshly ironed, antique Irish linen tablecloth she had just put on her refectory table. In spite of her desperate urge to cover the dark elm boards with a crisp protective covering, even she knew it was overkill. She folded it carefully. Beth and Lindy knew she was obsessed with white, but there was no need to ram the fact down their throats.

She got her white-wine glasses out of their box and put cheese straws and hand-fried crisps in white bowls. Then she giggled. The sort of evening she seemed to be preparing for was so different from when they went to Lindy's and sat where they could find a space in the tiny sitting room and drank whatever was available out of a variety of tumblers and Paris goblets. At one time she'd have been a bit horrified but now her elegant lifestyle seemed the odd one.

The spare bedroom upstairs was cleared for action so that April could have a final fitting for her wedding dress at the same time as they sorted out the seating plan.

Rachel felt almost exhilarated. It hadn't been an easy

assignment, the timescale being so short, but she felt they were pretty much on top of it.

When the doorbell went, Rachel found Beth and Lindy had arrived together. Usually she was wary of people coming into her space and making it look untidy but now she felt she wanted to show off her creation.

'Oh my God! It's amazing,' said Beth, looking round her. 'It's like it's in a magazine or something.'

'Rachel,' said Lindy, 'I'm now so embarrassed that you've been to my house, coming from this.'

'No, Lindy! I love your house,' said Rachel, putting a glass with an inch of chilled white wine in it into Lindy's hand. 'Your house is normal. Mine is like a sort of – shrine to whiteness.' She handed Beth a glass too. 'It's exactly how I want it, but who has a house exactly how they want it? No one normal, Raff would say. Now have a cheese straw, both of you, and note I'm not giving you plates to eat them off. That's progress for me. What time is April coming?'

Beth glanced at her watch. 'She should arrive any time now.'

April duly arrived, flustered and untidy. She had a bundle of files under her arm.

'Hello! I'm so glad I found the right house. I was worried I'd get lost.'

Rachel ushered her in, swanlike in her calm and poise. 'April, we're so pleased you could come. Do sit down. Here, at the head of the table. Wine?'

'God yes!' she said. 'Charlie dropped me off and is picking me up so I can get legless if I have to.' She glanced at Beth. 'He said he'd love to see you at the pub after.'

'That would be lovely, if we get it all done.'

'I brought all my lists of who's invited,' said April. 'My lot, Tristram's lot. So you can help me with the plan?'

'Of course we can,' said Rachel, hoping she was right. 'Now, who do you want on the top table?'

The day before the wedding, Lindy left her sleeping boys safe in her grandmother's house. She'd put a note under her grandmother's door explaining what she was up to and left the house as quietly as possible, the key to the van in her pocket.

The dress was perfect, the bridesmaids' dresses had been suitably upgraded by her expert needle, she'd even cobbled together outfits for the three of them to wear while serving at the wedding; it was either too late or too soon to do anything else wedding-related. So Lindy was going foraging.

Although it was going to be a very busy day, it wasn't really necessary for her to raid the hedgerows while it was still dark – there would have been plenty of time for her to do it later. But she preferred to go when no one would see her dragging plant life out of the hedges, snipping at garlands of old man's beard; basically stealing stuff.

Lindy had raided the hedgerows before for various reasons, but she'd never needed so much previously and she really didn't want to bump into anyone she knew. Rachel and Beth had offered to go with her but she had very little time on her own in her life and so she had refused. She wanted to be alone with her thoughts and the greenery.

She parked the van in a lay-by and had taken her

father's loppers, some secateurs and a roll of bin liners with her for the plants. If there were any berries about she'd take those too but she was expecting to use fake ones to add colour to her garlands. She had just snipped off a lovely long trail of ivy and was about to put it into her bag when she heard a noise behind her.

'Excuse me! What on earth do you think you're doing!'

Lindy shot round. The voice was loud and angry and panic shot through her. A tall figure, shrouded in waxed cotton and woollen scarves, was outlined against the mist.

'I'm picking ivy. It doesn't actually belong to anyone, you know, it's wild. Oh. It's you.'

Angus allowed a smile to disturb his stern expression. 'Well, technically, it does belong to someone. It belongs to me.'

Lindy was at a complete loss. She had deliberately driven miles from home to somewhere out of the way to find material for her garlands and now here was Angus. 'Really?'

He nodded. 'I own the land this hedge borders on.'

Lindy stared at him, trying to think of something to say. She was dreadfully embarrassed. He wasn't to know that she'd spent a lot of time thinking about him since that Sunday lunch but now she felt as if it was written in neon across her forehead. She briefly considered chiding him for the state of his hedgerows but knew hedges like this weren't supposed to be tidy. She also knew she should have asked permission to take the ivy but couldn't make the words come out of her mouth. She felt so caught out, as if she'd been stealing apples from a garden, not wild foliage from a hedge that really wouldn't miss it. She couldn't tell how he felt about it. He looked inscrutable – which was his default expression. 'Oh,' she managed when he didn't say anything helpful either.

'What do you want all that stuff for?'

'April's wedding. We're decorating the village hall with garlands.'

His expression relaxed. 'Oh, the wedding! Of course. I'd forgotten. The event that's going to encourage people to rent the hall as a venue?'

Lindy also relaxed a little. 'That's it. It'll look amazing when I've finished with it.'

'How much more stuff do you need?'

'Masses and masses. You'd be amazed how much you get through making garlands long enough for a hall. And it's going to go all round and possibly some across, too.' Although she'd known this all along, hearing herself say it out loud made her realise quite how enormous her task was.

'I'd better help you then.'

She bit her lip. She needed help, she really did, but it didn't seem fair. He had obviously been going somewhere; she couldn't hold him up. And she'd turned down Beth and Rachel when they'd offered help, sure she could do it all on her own. It had been a crazy decision.

'You'll get filthy and, besides, you can't see properly in this light and you never know when you're going to come across a briar that'll rip your palm open. You need gloves. It would be dangerous.'

'You've obviously done this before.'

'Yes, for the school and church sometimes but I don't usually need so much.' She allowed herself a bit of a

175

smile – a sort of apology. 'I always come here. It's so far away from home I'm not likely to be seen robbing the hedgerows by anyone I know.'

'Bad luck for you I caught you then. I wouldn't have, only I spotted the van in the lay-by and thought you might have broken down or something. I've just given hay to some sheep that are grazing on my land.'

'You knew it was our van?'

He nodded. 'Your van is famous locally. Although to be fair, this time it was the decals and fancy writing that drew my attention, not the hole in the exhaust.'

Lindy, who had stuck on the decals and had a propensity for guilt, frowned. 'We are going to get the exhaust fixed, really. It's only just appeared. Beth swore it was fine when she first had it.' She didn't elaborate on how annoying it had been to have something go wrong with the van so soon after they'd bought it. Beth had been mortified; she'd felt responsible. 'The boys helped with the decoration.'

'I can tell.'

He might have been teasing but she couldn't see his mouth properly because of the scarf that was draped round the lower part of his face. 'I'd better get on.'

'I'll go back to the house and get some gloves and give you a hand. I feel it's the least I can do.'

'What do you mean?'

'It's my ivy. It's only polite it should get to you as quickly as possible.'

As she watched him walk away, she wondered what he was really thinking. Did he think she was a bloody nuisance, and was only helping to get her out of the way

176

quicker? Or did he really want to help? Her mother said he'd been really useful over at the hall, taking quite a lot of time to work out what needed doing. Was he different from his family? His snooty mother and his brother who had very little sense of responsibility? She felt he was but how could she really tell?

She worked faster, determined to do her best before he came back. He might have been really kind but she didn't want to take advantage. His mother had once accused her of trying to trap Edward, to connect herself with their family. Although it had happened a long time ago, she hadn't forgotten. She didn't want Angus thinking along the same lines.

She had filled another bin liner before Angus came back. He had a ladder with him and was now wearing wellingtons.

'It's very kind of you to help me,' she said. 'You'd be perfectly entitled to let me steal your ivy without your help.'

'That's OK.' He set up the ladder against the hedge, testing it for steadiness.

'And shouldn't you be at work?'

'It's still early.'

'I suppose it is.'

'Do you want to climb up here?' he suggested, indicating the ladder. 'There's some lovely stuff.' He smiled. 'I'll hold the ladder.'

'I'm sure you don't need to,' she said, feeling single-mother proud and independent.

'I do need to. Trust me.' He smiled. 'I'm an architect who doesn't especially like heights. I'd feel a lot happier if I held the ladder.'

Sympathising, Lindy climbed up the ladder. There were indeed some very nice strings of ivy with neatly spaced leaves, just what she wanted for her wreaths. She gathered as much as possible and handed it down.

She climbed down the ladder and then up it again. She resumed lopping and tugging at nature's bunting, filling her black sacks as she went.

'Where are the boys?' Angus said as she pushed the last bag into the van.

'With Gran,' she said. 'We all spent the night with her last night so I was able to sneak out this morning without disturbing anyone.'

'Then have you time for breakfast?'

Every part of Lindy was certain she ought to get away from Angus – she found him far too attractive than was safe – and back home with her booty as soon as possible, so she was surprised to hear herself say, 'I have, actually.' Realising she'd accepted an invitation she'd meant to refuse, she added, 'I'd love to see your house.'

He laughed. 'It needs a hell of a lot of work doing to it but I'd be happy to show you round.'

As they walked back to the lay-by where they'd left their vehicles, Lindy was surprised to feel a camaraderie with him. Angus had always been the older brother, the one she'd had a crush on, but just for now he was someone she'd enjoyed doing something with. She wanted to see his house, too, to see how much work it really needed doing. It felt like a long time since Lindy had done anything that wasn't to do with the boys, the hall or April's wedding and she was enjoying the prospect.

She pulled the van up behind his in front of a large Georgian-style house covered with scaffolding.

'My goodness!' she said as she got out. 'Ripe for restoration, eh?'

He laughed. 'Indeed!' He stood looking up at his house. 'Actually, I probably shouldn't have bought it.' He paused. 'In fact I know I shouldn't. I just fell in love. I mean...' He smiled ruefully. 'I saw the potential. I don't think architects are supposed to fall in love.'

For a moment Lindy didn't understand this, and then she realised: architects shouldn't fall in love with houses because it would be unprofessional. That's what he meant. Somehow she couldn't help being disappointed.

He unlocked the huge front door and Lindy went in. 'My goodness!' she said again.

The hall was enormous. There was a double staircase leading down into it and there were fireplaces at either side. The dimensions were magnificent – it would make a perfect wedding venue – but, thought Lindy, only after about two million quid had been spent on it. It was a beautiful ruin.

'Correct me if I'm wrong – you're the architect – but wouldn't the technical term for a house like this be "money pit"?'

'You have the term exactly right. It's a money pit. And no, I haven't let my parents see it and won't until a few years and several hundred thousand pounds have gone into that pit.'

'They might mutter about the heating bills,' said Lindy with a smile.

'They'd do more than mutter.'

'Can I see some more?' Lindy realised she felt flattered. He was showing her something he wouldn't show his family.

'Come on then, but before you ask me, no, I'm not sure what I'm going to do with it when it's done. It's certainly far too big for a bachelor pad.'

'Oh well, I can help you there – it's a wedding venue! And a place for weekend courses, et cetera., if you want to do anything other than live in it?'

He shook his head. 'No, this house will have to earn its living. I couldn't keep it as a pet.'

He opened a door and ushered her into a grand drawing room, which had black mould covering the walls but a fine plaster ceiling.

'Heavens!' said Lindy. 'I'm sorry to be rude but how are you going to afford to renovate this house?'

'I'm going to do it in stages. The plan is to get some rooms usable, see if they can earn a bit of money and then go on to the next bit. I didn't pay a lot for it – the surveyor's report had a few issues on it that brought the price right down.' He paused to inspect a bit of wainscot that had come away in one piece. 'My first project is to get the chauffeur's cottage habitable.'

'Really?'

'So I can live in it and stop paying for accommodation. But I promised you breakfast. Come through to the servants' quarters.'

The kitchen was a joy. 'I love this!' said Lindy, looking round delightedly. 'The old range is still there. That amazing built-in dresser. And there's a sofa. You could live here quite easily with a few more home comforts

180

and a telly. I've always wanted a kitchen big enough for a sofa and a telly. As it is I've hardly got a *house* big enough for a sofa and a telly, not when the boys are home anyway.' She stopped, suddenly worried in case it looked as though she was complaining about her lot. 'I mean... I love my little cottage but you wouldn't need to do more than do up this bit for you to live in, if you wanted.'

'I think I might find it a bit spooky living in this huge house on my own,' he said solemnly.

Lindy didn't know if she was being teased or not. 'Maybe divide some of it into flats? Just keep the main rooms and enough for some accommodation?'

He nodded. 'That's what I thought. A house like this could be a home for lots of people. They could share the garden.'

'Aren't you much of a gardener then?'

'No! I'm not much of a cook, either, but I can do a bacon butty. Would that be OK?'

'Lovely,' said Lindy, her mind full of possibilities. She was glad it wasn't her house – her money pit – but she loved playing with its potential in her mind. 'Shall I make tea?'

They ate their butties sitting on the old sofa next to the huge calor-gas heater. It was really cosy. She was surprised to find herself relaxed in his company. He seemed genuinely interested in hearing about her life, and about Vintage Weddings, but they could also munch in silence; either was easy.

'So why did you buy this house?' she asked when she'd finished chewing. 'Apart from falling in love with it. Was it just because you could afford it?'

'Well, having fallen in love I did manage to justify it. Basically, it's not as bad as all that, structurally. It's a lovely house that shouldn't be allowed to fall down and I wanted a project, something I could do for myself instead of just for clients.'

'So it's not a speculation? You don't hope to do it up and sell it?'

'No. Maybe, if it's ever finished and I don't want to live at a wedding venue or whatever it is you think it should be, I will sell it. But that's a long way down the road.'

'And you don't feel daunted by the prospect of all that work, and the money?'

He considered. 'Some days I do. At others I just see the potential and get excited. Like now. Probably because you see the potential too.'

Lindy picked up a mug even she wouldn't have allowed in her house it was so chipped and stained and sipped from it. She felt pleased. Then she looked at her watch. 'Oh my God! I can't believe the time. I must phone my gran.'

She left Angus's house with her tea half drunk.

'You've got something in your hair,' said Beth as they surveyed the hall later that day.

'Is it alive?' said Lindy.

'Don't think so.' Beth removed the wisp of fluff from Lindy's fringe. 'It would be quite a rare species of caterpillar if it was, though.'

Lindy laughed. 'I'm shattered! But thank you so much

for helping, Beth. I really and truly couldn't have done it without you.'

Beth laughed. 'I enjoyed myself. But you're right, you couldn't have got those garlands fixed by yourself. They were so heavy.'

'And took ages and ages to make.'

'So worth it though.' They stared upwards, admiring the final effect.

Then someone else came in.

'Hi Lindy.' Angus looked at Beth.

'I'm Beth, another member of the Vintage Weddings team.'

'Oh? The Wedding Cake queen?'

Beth laughed. 'Currently I'm only doing the icing, but that's hard enough.'

'I bet.' Angus looked up. 'I had to see the finished result,' he said. 'And I must say it looks wonderful.'

Lindy smiled. It did look wonderful. The full, lavish garlands of ivy, old man's beard and sundry other hedgerow items were bound round with tiny fairy lights (one of Beth's eBay bargains) and looked magical against the whiteness of the walls and beams. 'We are pleased, I must say. It's turned out very well.'

'It has. And I have to say my hedgerows don't look any different, even though so much has been taken from them.'

'It'll grow again anyway,' said Lindy. 'At least I hope it will, or I won't have anything to raid for next time.'

He laughed. 'Well, I'll go now but I'll see you tomorrow.'

'Really?'

Angus nodded. 'I'm behind the bar. Sarah has roped in most of the committee to help. It's going to be fun pulling pints with Audrey.'

Lindy laughed. 'Audrey used to work in the Prince Albert years ago. She's probably a demon pint-puller.'

'Ooh, I'd like to see that!' said Beth. 'Perhaps I can persuade Sukey to get her in for a shift. I bet she can add it all up in her head and count back the change.'

Angus chuckled. 'I'll let you know. It'll be good fun, anyway.'

'I'm glad about that,' said Lindy and then hoped he didn't think she was pleased about him being behind the bar – just that the bar was going to be well manned.

They'd had a nice time together this morning. She didn't want to spoil that easiness by her girlhood crush coming back to haunt her, either by him finding out about it or, almost worse, it becoming a present-day crush. Goodness, life was complicated!

Chapter Fourteen

Beth answered her phone. It was the day of the wedding and she was trying to eat a banana squashed between two Ryvitas and dry her hair at the same time. It was Rachel.

'Beth? Any chance you could come over?'

'What? To yours? Why? Is there a problem?' A thought occurred to her. 'Please don't tell me April wants to back out!'

Rachel laughed briefly. 'I don't think so but she is really upset. Can you come?'

'If you need me, of course. But why is she upset?'

'It's her mother not being here on her wedding day; that sort of thing.'

Beth sighed. 'How sad. Tell you what, ring Sarah. Get her round there. She's a brilliant mother-substitute. But I'm out the door!'

As Beth arrived, April, wearing grubby jodhpurs and a ripped rugby shirt, was sitting in Rachel's white linen-covered chair in the sitting room, weeping.

It was not at all what Beth had envisaged for their first vintage wedding.

'I'm so sorry,' their bride gulped. 'I just can't help it.'

'It's fine,' said Rachel, sounding very calm. 'I understand. We all do.'

'It's natural to want your mother with you on your wedding day,' said Beth, feeling tearful herself. However difficult a woman's relationship with her mother was, she'd want her there. Beth couldn't help wondering how Helena would be when her turn came in a few months' time. Maybe it wasn't something you could predict?

'I thought I was over it. You know, grown out of needing a mother,' said April. 'But what with the thought of wearing her dress and everything, it all came over me.'

'Have you talked to Tristram about it?' asked Rachel.

April nodded but couldn't reply for a few moments. Then, in between gulps, she said, 'Yeah – a bit – but he gets fed up with me going on about Mum. He says he doesn't know what to do to help.'

'Men are like that,' said Rachel. 'They don't like you to have problems they can't solve.' She sounded as if she was speaking from experience.

'I know I'm tired and emotional – whatever that means,' sobbed April. 'But I can't stop crying!'

'I think I'll make some tea,' said Rachel, putting her hand on Beth's shoulder, passing on the comforting-baton.

'You will have to stop crying eventually, hon,' said Beth, 'because you can't sob your way down the aisle. It would look bad. But feel free for now. You don't have to start getting ready until...' She looked at her watch. 'Well, we've got a few minutes.'

There was in fact plenty of time but Beth was worrying about April's tear-streaked face. Her eyes and nose were red and swollen and she was looking anything but bridal. But maybe clever make-up could sort that out.

'Tristram says I just have to get over the whole Mum thing. She's dead and that's not going to change.'

Beth couldn't think of a reply. She just leant across from her chair to April's and took her into her arms. 'It's not too late to call it off,' she said.

To her surprise, this made April laugh. 'He's not that bad! I do really love him. He's just got about as much tact as my dad's old goat.' She pulled out a scrap of used tissue from her pocket and blew her nose, following up with a swipe from her hand, the tissue being totally inadequate.

Rachel came in with a tray with mugs, a special box with different sorts of tea bags, bowls for used tea bags and sugar and a little jug of milk. 'So, which kind of tea would you like? The kettle's just about to boil, so just choose and I'll make it.'

April seemed confused by the choice.

'I think builder's, Rach,' said Beth. 'I'd like that too.'

'Fine. And Beth? There's a box of tissues on the side.'

When Rachel came back with the filled mugs she gave one to April and offered a little bowl. 'Sugar?'

April shook her head. 'No thank you. But I wouldn't say no to a biscuit or something. I didn't have breakfast.'

'Oh, God! Why not? I can't cope without breakfast,' said Beth while Rachel rushed back to her kitchen on the hunt for sustenance.

'Nor me, usually,' April explained, 'but I had to be up

early to get the pony ready to go in the trailer and then I ended up helping them put the cart on the low-loader—'

'April! You shouldn't have been doing all that on your wedding day. What were your dad and – er – Charlie doing?' Beth was embarrassed to mention Charlie. She didn't know if April knew that she had been out with him a couple of times and was quite keen.

'Well, I get on best with Poppy – that's the pony – and Dad and Charlie were doing the heavy work. Tristram's going to help decorate it.' She looked at her watch. 'They'll be doing it now.'

'Actually, that's quite sweet. I'll forgive them all for making you work, now,' said Beth. She got up, glad that April seemed to be back to her usual down-to-earth self.

Rachel came back with a plate of shortbread fingers. April took one. 'I'm not sure it's the best breakfast but otherwise it would be muesli with nuts and seeds and that didn't seem appropriate.' She left the plate near April and retired.

'Um, Beth?' said April, when the first shortbread finger had gone down.

'Yes?'

'I wonder if I could ask you a favour?'

Now Beth looked closely at April she could see her eyes were still a bit swimmy. Maybe she wasn't as recovered as she'd thought. 'Anything!'

'Would you do my make-up for me?'

This was a bit of a shock. 'I thought one of your bridesmaids was going to do it?' It was one of the major economies: no make-up artist. They'd all been thrilled.

'Yeah, but the thing is, she did a trial on me and I

188

hated it. It was awful. I didn't look like me at all! Tristram wouldn't recognise me and Dad would disown me!'

'No, I'm sure he wouldn't. Not on your wedding day. Tristram won't recognise you anyway, if you're wearing a wonderful dress and not muddy old jodhpurs and his cast-off sweater!' Beth smiled to make sure April knew she was joking, eager to make her feel happy about her bridesmaid's make-up trial so she wouldn't have to do it.

April shook her head. 'Hang on. I've got a picture on my phone.'

Beth examined the photo. 'Mmm, I see what you mean,' she said after a few seconds. April looked like a woman who was well past the first flush of youth dressed for a night on the pull. Thick heavy eyebrows, caterpillar eyelashes, orange foundation and far too much eyeliner.

She picked her words carefully. 'I can see it isn't exactly a natural look, but won't your friend be terribly upset if she doesn't do your make-up?'

'I've done that part. I said I didn't like what she'd done and I'd find someone else. She said I wouldn't be able to find anyone else. She nearly stopped being my bridesmaid but she fancies Charlie so didn't want to miss out on coming to the wedding.'

'Oh,' said Beth, suppressing a pang of jealousy of the unknown bridesmaid. Then she cheered up. Anyone who could make April look like that when she was really very pretty couldn't have much clue.

'So I was hoping for something that made me look like me, but better. I've brought my kit,' said April, unaware of Beth's moment of suffering.

'Let's have a look.'

April's kit was half an inch of a kohl pencil, a dried-up mascara and some ancient foundation that might have explained the orange in her trial.

'Hmm,' said Beth. 'I'll go and ask Rachel what she's got.'

Beth found Rachel in the kitchen. 'This is a nightmare! April wants me to do her make-up and she hasn't got any, really. Have you got some?'

Rachel swallowed. 'Yes. I have. Some.' She breathed in slowly, through her nose and then breathed out again through her mouth. Beth recognised this was a coping mechanism and didn't rush her. 'I'm happy to donate it.'

'But you won't use it again afterwards?'

'The pencils I will because I can sharpen them but not the eyeshadow or the foundation. It's powder you see. I'll wash the brushes for April. I could use them again, then. I think.'

'Don't wash them now though. We'd need them dry.'

'Check with April that she doesn't mind using my dirty brushes on her face,' said Rachel. 'It would freak me out.'

'I don't think she's quite the same as you,' said Beth, smiling so as not to cause offence. 'I'll have to sort her swollen eyes out first.'

Rachel looked happier. 'I'm on the case. I've got wet cotton pads in the freezer.'

'You're brilliant. And can we borrow your laptop? YouTube, how to put on wedding make-up. I left my iPad on charge at home.'

'Of course. I'll bring it out.'

*

After April had eaten a surprising amount of short-bread and then some toast and Marmite that Rachel had produced, and had lain on Rachel's sofa with cold pads on her eyes for some time, Beth felt they couldn't put off the evil moment any longer. They had to get on with the make-up.

'OK, so what we're going to do is go through YouTube and find a look you like, then I'll copy what they do, step by step. Painting by numbers, easy-peasy.' She knew it wouldn't be this simple but she felt inspiring her bride with confidence would be a good start.

Some time later, after they'd all laughed at the many spoof make-up lessons to be found, they realised that to do a look as suggested by the make-up artists, you needed a whole range of brushes and a zillion shades of foundation. You also needed a ton more make-up than even all three of them could provide.

'We could ask Lindy to bring what she's got,' said Beth. 'If we ring her now we'll catch her before she sets out. But I don't suppose she's got much either. She doesn't wear it, really.'

'Well, let's just go for it,' said April. 'Why don't I just shut my eyes and you do it? I'm sure it'll be fine.'

Rachel closed her laptop.

'Hey!' said Beth. 'I thought I was going to copy it from YouTube, not actually do it freestyle!'

'Come on!' said Rachel. 'We watched enough of them – just do it!'

Beth glanced at her. Those were very un-Rachel-like words. She was impressed.

'OK. Let's get going.'

Actually, Beth found it was a lot easier than she expected it to be. Rachel's make-up was very high quality and she had a good selection of brushes. It only took a tiny bit to make April's youthful skin look glorious.

'What do you think?' Beth asked April, who had opened her eyes.

'Oh that's great!' she said, surprised.

'Not being orange is a good start,' said Rachel. 'What time is Lindy due to help April on with her dress?'

'You're the Clipboard Queen,' said Beth. 'Isn't it on your list?'

'OK, in about half an hour,' said Rachel, having checked. 'I'll get the stove lit myself. It's quite chilly in here, but it'll soon warm up.'

'Mm,' said Beth, who was concentrating on April and not really listening. 'Now, I can't remember, what comes next?'

'Be glad that the Clipboard Queen took notes,' said Rachel, on surer ground now. 'It's primer, foundation, spritz, concealer, highlighter, bronzer, setting power and blush. What have you put on, Beth?'

'Just a tiny bit of powder foundation,' said Beth.

'Put that all on me and I'd fall over with the weight of it!' said April, peering at Rachel's list.

'No danger of that,' said Beth. 'We have a bit of blush and that will have to do. I don't think you need concealer and all that stuff.'

'What about my freckles?' said April. 'Shouldn't we cover those up?'

'No,' said Beth firmly, who had them too. 'My dad always said, "A face without freckles is a sky without stars."'

'Oh, that's lovely!' said Rachel.

'OK, eyeshadow now, I think,' said Beth and she picked up a brush.

Sarah rushed in with Lindy about half an hour later. 'I'm so sorry I couldn't get here any sooner,' she said. 'I had to go and sort out some problems for a farmer on the other side of the county. Is April all right?'

'Go and see,' said Rachel. 'She's in the sitting room.'

'Wow!' said Lindy when they found her, the room cosy now the stove was lit. 'Amazing make-up! That friend of yours is really talented. Where is she? I'd planned to get here before the bridesmaids.'

'She's not here,' said April. 'She did a crap job and I hated it. Beth did this.'

'Beth did?' said Lindy. 'Beth? I thought you said you couldn't do things with your hands. First it's the cake and now it's make-up. I had a look at the cake, by the way, in the hall. It looks brilliant.'

'I watched a lot of YouTube videos to acquire both those skills.'

'Well, however you learnt it, it looks brilliant! It's another service we can offer our brides!' Lindy patted Beth's shoulder approvingly.

'No! Not again,' said Beth. 'It was far too nerve-racking.'

'But it looks so amazing!' said Sarah.

'That's because April is really pretty and has brilliant skin!' protested Beth but no one took any notice.

'I think we need a toast – the drinking kind, I mean,' said Rachel. 'I'll get the bottle.'

'Good idea,' said Beth. 'Shall I find glasses?'

There was a tiny pause. 'They're in a box in the second cupboard as you go in.' Rachel let out a breath. 'I am so relaxed about people being in my space now. I can't believe it.'

Rachel took a photograph of the bride wearing Rachel's towelling robe, all made up, waiting to put the dress on. There was no official photographer and guests had been detailed to take as many photographs as they could.

She took more when April had the dress on, with Lindy on her knees adjusting the veil and making sure all was as it should be.

'That's such a nice thing to do,' said Sarah, nursing her second glass of cava. 'Taking pictures of this process. It'll be a lovely memory.'

'I'm going to make it into a book,' said Rachel, 'and see if I can get guests to email me their photos so April will have a proper record.'

'That's so nice!' said Sarah, sounding very slightly as if she were going to cry.

'Please don't start crying!' said April. 'It'll set me off and I'll ruin my make-up!'

'I've got more cotton pads in the freezer, in case we need them again,' said Rachel.

'There is such a thing as being too organised,' said Beth.

'No there isn't,' said Rachel happily, crossing something off her list.

'I'll just pop along to the hall now,' said Sarah. 'You don't need me here any more and I'll make sure it's all ready for the reception. Then I'll go to the church. See you there!'

Then the bridesmaids arrived and Lindy could help them with their outfits. Beth felt awkward about meeting the one who had been supposed to do April's make-up and not just because of that, but because she fancied Charlie. She was quite a large girl and was wearing the make-up she had thought suitable for April: the heavy brows that started slightly too close together; the 'smokey eye' that actually looked like 'I-came-out-of-a-fight-the-wrong-side eye', so dark and smudgy was her make-up. Her lips were nude and shiny.

'Call that make-up, April?' she said disdainfully. 'You can hardly see you're wearing any!'

'That's the look we aimed to achieve,' said Beth, feeling protective of April in the face of this Amazon. She handed her a glass of cava.

The girl drained her glass and held it out for more.

Having served the other bridesmaid, Beth put only a tiny bit more in the glass thrust in front of her. This woman was a nightmare sober, what she'd be like drunk was too horrible to think about.

'Yes, I really like my make-up,' said April, sounding a little defiant. 'It's natural.'

'You'll look washed out in the photos. Just you wait and see.'

Beth gulped, wondering if this was true, then Rachel stepped forward. 'Actually,' she said, looking at her camera, 'I think she looks lovely. Not washed out at all.'

'Let's have a look!' demanded the Amazon.

'Sorry,' said Rachel crisply. 'Not until they're all properly edited and the bride and bridegroom have had a chance to look first. Now, if you two bridesmaids

195

would like to go upstairs to the bedroom on the right, Lindy will be up shortly to help with your sashes. Beth is available to do make-up should anyone need it, but do let's press on.'

She sounded so commanding and efficient, no one dared argue. They trooped upstairs like lambs.

'I don't know why I asked her to be a bridesmaid,' said April, leaving no one in any doubt who she meant. 'She bullied me at school and she's trying to bully me now. Charlie wouldn't look at her,' she added, sounding very un-bride-like in spite of her appearance.

'Never mind about her,' said Beth happily. 'Let Rachel take a few more pictures of you on your own before they come down again.'

Only April was dry-eyed when her father came to collect her to usher her into the little pony-trap that was now garlanded with more slender versions of what was decorating the hall. The pony had white ribbons threaded through his mane and his dark coat was as glossy as paint.

'She looks so lovely!' said Rachel, snapping away with the camera and sniffing.

'It is tragic that her mother isn't here!' said Lindy, clutching a sodden tissue to her nose.

'Oh, you two!' said Beth, a bit hoarsely. 'Let's have a cup of tea to calm down before we go to the hall. We've only got about an hour before they all get there, starving hungry and desperate for a drink.'

'At least we're not doing the food,' said Lindy. 'But we should make sure everyone knows where every-thing is.'

'Come on then. Tea and then get on with it,' said Rachel and led the way back into the house.

'Did you mind your house being filled with strangers wandering round in their undies?' said Lindy, gathering champagne flutes. 'I know it must have been a bit difficult for you?'

'Well, it was,' said Rachel, who was loading the tea tray, 'but you get to a point when you just can't fret about it any more. And I do like it when people like my house. It being beautiful and private isn't so satisfying.' Now she looked around. It was still a bit untidy but that seemed to be OK.

'And Beth!' said Lindy, having taken through the glasses and come back to tidy some more. 'Get you and the make-up! You did a really good job on April. You've got a hidden talent there.'

'Not hidden any more,' said Rachel. 'I've made a note. It's something we can offer brides now.'

'Oh, you and your notes, Rach!' said Beth.

'So how much are we earning from all this?' asked Lindy. 'I've got a horrible feeling my mum might have told April she can have it all for nothing.'

'Not at all!' said Rachel. 'April's dad slipped me an envelope with a cheque in it for a thousand pounds!'

'What? That's a huge amount of money,' said Beth. 'I thought we'd agreed five hundred.'

'Still very good value,' said Lindy. 'She got a dress, the bridesmaids made over, a venue, catering, make-up – all sorts.'

'Of course a lot of it was donated,' said Rachel, 'but what really touched me was he was paying more than we'd agreed because of the support we'd given his "poor, motherless little girl".'

'Don't!' wailed Lindy.

'Oh, don't take on so,' said Rachel. 'We've got to put on our outfits in a minute. And by the way, I paid myself back for the van.'

'I just hope Helena's wedding goes as well – as far as this wedding has gone. We really seem to have got a good package together. Something we can be proud to offer other brides, not just my sister.'

'We have, haven't we?' agreed Rachel. 'I'm so proud of us.'

'Me too,' said Lindy. 'Now let's get our kit on – see if our aprons fit!'

Chapter Fifteen

Lindy was delighted by how it was all going. Eamon and April had separately thanked them for arranging everything so well. The whole village was here helping out one way or another, everyone delighted to see the hall looking so attractive.

The catering team had done April proud and the wedding guests were all having a wonderful time. The paying bar was doing well, which would please Sukey, although Lindy realised it was mostly 'helping locals' – those doing the bar, helping with the food or generally finding something they could usefully do who'd have been drinking in the pub anyway, but they were certainly drinking more than usual. It was all good.

She was really pleased how attractive their outfits were too. With their full skirts and wide belts, close-fitting tops (models' own, as Rachel put it), little scarves round their necks, and ballet flats, they were all looking faintly like Audrey Hepburn, Beth especially with her short hair and huge eyes.

As they'd hurried into them and put on make-up (not

to be too outshone by the bride) they agreed they'd give a chunk of what they'd earned to the village hall fund. After all, so much had been donated by the village, it was only fair it got at least some of the benefit.

Lindy couldn't help looking back to how her life had been the previous year: happy enough but non-eventful. Much of what she did day by day had to be repeated the following day. Her boys were always a joy, of course, and her family warm and supportive, but it was tedious having to scrape every penny together for anything extra.

Lindy realised she had probably worked harder than any of them to make this wedding happen in such a short time but she had loved every minute. She felt for the first time ever her skills were really being used. Although she'd stayed up so late, got up so early, to get it all done, the result had been worth it: April had a really beautiful dress. Lindy was fulfilled. Vintage Weddings would supply what was previously lacking in her life. Then, for no reason, Angus flitted into her thoughts. She banished him rapidly. She mustn't read too much into a pleasant hour spent in his falling-down house drinking tea from a chipped mug.

'Lindy!' A voice broke into her thoughts. It was a woman who'd known her from her cradle. 'You've done wonders with this old place! Never seen it looking so lovely. Even in the old days it was always a gloomy building.'

'I didn't do it all by myself!' Lindy protested. 'I only did the garlands and things.'

'Don't say only. It looks terrific. In fact, I think we should have a dance in here – a hop, we used to call it

– while it's looking so good.' Mrs Jenkins was definitely a pensioner and yet she was obviously still up for a bit of a party.

'It might be a bit short notice to get it organised, Mrs Jenkins,' said Lindy, feeling a bit tired at the prospect of organising anything else quite so soon.

'The WI'll sort it. Raise some more money for the roof.' She frowned. 'I would have joined the committee only I've been so busy with my Eric's leg. Is your gran on it?'

'No. I'm sure she would have joined but she's quite often roped in to look after my boys,' Lindy explained.

'Oh well, I'm sure she helps from behind the scenes.' Mrs Jenkins looked upwards once more. 'I can just see the posters for that dance now: "Raise the roof to save the roof" or some such.'

Lindy watched smiling as Mrs Jenkins strode off into the crowd, heading for the chairman of the WI, who was wielding a teapot the size of a boulder. Lindy was reminded of something her mother had said: 'If you want something doing, get the WI to do it – they never fail.'

Sarah appeared just as Lindy was thinking of her. 'Oh, hello, Mum!'

'Darling! I'm so proud of you all. The hall looks amazing. You've done brilliantly. The boughs are stunning with the fairy lights. I was just wondering if we could arrange to have the quiz quite soon, while all this still lasts?'

Lindy laughed. 'I expect so but you'll have to fight Mrs Jenkins for the date. She wants the WI to organise a hop for the same reason.'

'Oh, good idea!' said Sarah. 'But I expect she means

more of a thé dansant, as Gran would call it. Tea dance to you and me. We could have the quiz the same evening.'

Lindy shook her head. 'Think of the clearing up! Also, all your quizzers will be exhausted from hopping. Better make it another night. The boughs will last for a bit. It's always so cold in here when the heating's not on, they won't drop for a while.'

'Oh, you're right. Of course you are. But will you join our quiz team? I might go for Saturday after next. I've asked Angus. He says he loves quizzes.'

Lindy had been known to say this too but really hoped Angus wouldn't think her mother was match-making. It was bad enough for her, but if he felt he was being pushed towards Lindy, it would be so desperately embarrassing she'd never be able to look him in the eye again. 'No, Mum, I can't leave the boys with Gran for another night, she's had them so much recently. Gran should go instead.'

Sarah shook her head. 'Not on a Saturday night, she won't.'

'Why on earth not?' Lindy suddenly worried that her grandmother was starting to feel her age and not want to go out during the evening. 'She's OK, isn't she? Having the boys so much hasn't exhausted her?' She said this before working out that her mother was unlikely to suggest Gran had them again if this was the case.

'She's fine. She's just very into the latest Scandi crime thing with subtitles.'

'That's silly. She could record it.'

'She does record it,' said Sarah. 'She says she needs to see it twice, so she can follow the plot.'

Lindy laughed fondly. 'She's amazing, but don't rely on me. I want to see how she and the boys feel about it. They've hardly seen me in daylight recently.'

'The quiz won't be in daylight, will it?'

'You know what I mean, Mum. They need to sleep in their own beds with their mum in the next bedroom.'

'Fair enough,' said Sarah. 'Oh, look, there's Bob. I'd better go and see what he thinks about bringing the quiz forward.'

Lindy set off to find Rachel to see how she was getting on. She hadn't seen Raff anywhere, which was a shame. While she'd thought her mother was mad trying to link up Raff and Rachel, getting him to walk Rachel home after that first meeting, he did seem to have had a good effect on her friend. She was much more relaxed about things these days. She'd still been incredibly efficient with amazing attention to detail, but the silly things didn't seem to bother her quite so much.

'It's all amazing!' said Rachel. 'It looks like a scene from a costume drama.'

'A contemporary costume drama,' Lindy objected. 'People are in modern dress.'

'You think?'

Lindy laughed. 'OK, maybe not modern dress for London but us yokels are happy enough with our threads. But, seriously, it does look great with all the people here.'

'It does,' agreed Rachel. 'They're going to do the speeches now, then we'll clear away the tables and chairs so people can dance. Do you think people will go to the pub while we do that?'

'I think they'll help clear away!' said Lindy. 'Everyone

seems to have taken on this wedding as their own, and they all want to help.'

'. . . and finally,' said Eamon, red-faced and relishing his role as 'father of the bride', 'I want you all to raise your glasses in a toast to thank the wonderful young women who made all this possible. Without them, April and Tristram would have had to get married in our old barn. As it is, we've got this magnificent hall. So, to . . .' He referred to a piece of paper. 'Beth, Lindy and Rachel, Vintage Weddings!'

There was a cheer that owed more to the amount of alcohol consumed than to enthusiasm for wedding planners, but they accepted their toast gracefully, even a little bit tearfully.

'It was a real pleasure to arrange a wedding for such a lovely bride,' said Rachel, when it appeared a reply was called for. There was a lot more cheering.

'Now!' said Eamon. 'On with the party!'

Lindy had been right when she'd said that people would help move tables and chairs. She, Beth and Rachel got together for a brief discussion. 'I've asked Joan if she'll start rationalising the food,' said Lindy.

'We'd better do some plates for the band. They'll be here any minute,' said Lindy.

'They're friends of April's dad, aren't they?' said Rachel.

'That's right. It's a wedding present to April, but if we're nice to them they might do us a good deal if we use them again.'

'Humph,' said Rachel. 'Let's see what they sound like

first. Not sure if I'm keen on Wurzle-alikes.'

'You're just so London and sophisticated!' said Lindy and then added, in broad Mummerset, 'You'll get used to our country ways soon enough, you see if you don't, my lover.'

Rachel gave her a push and handed her a pile of plates. 'You load up the band with carbs, then. Line their stomachs for a heavy night's drinking.'

'When I've fed the band would it be awful if I went home?' said Lindy.

'Of course not! You've been here since before dawn,' said Beth.

'Well, not quite – although it was an early start – but it's the boys, really. They're with Gran, and are staying the night. I'll stay there too; I know she doesn't really switch off and sleep properly until she hears me come in.'

'Oh no, that's fine. There are masses of helpers, after all. It's been so good.' Rachel sighed happily. 'I'm loving Vintage Weddings! It's been really challenging for me, you know, with my neurosis – never used to call it that! – but I've loved relaxing into life more.'

'I've loved it too! Vintage Weddings, I mean,' said Beth. 'Who'd have thought my sister getting married would have such a good effect on our lives.'

'It's turned my life around,' said Lindy.

They exchanged a group hug and then Lindy started loading plates for the band.

When she'd delivered them, overflowing with pork pie, sandwiches and chicken legs, to a very grateful band who'd just got through the door after a long journey, she went to get them drinks. She wasn't exactly sure what sort of music they played but she felt Rachel was probably right: they would play traditional folk songs, get slightly drunk and everyone would love it. Sophistication didn't go down well in Chippingford.

After what must have been a very hasty few bites of supper, the band struck up for the first dance.

'Oh, I love this one!' whispered Lindy, who found herself next to Beth. '"The Way You Look Tonight".'

Beth nodded. 'It was her parents' first dance, apparently. So sweet!'

The couple supported each other as they circled round and round, not attempting to do fancy steps or anything except show their love for each other. Lindy found a tissue and had a surreptitious blow before heading for the door as soon as everyone else joined April and Tristram on the dance floor.

But Lindy couldn't leave immediately. Before she could find her coat she was dragged on to the floor by a friend of her gran's. He'd definitely be a candidate for the hop, she decided, as he was very good at it. He also had a grip of steel. As long as they didn't both end up on the floor, all would be well. The dance ended and she thanked him profusely before he could even think of asking her again. Then someone else cut in and she found herself on the floor for yet another dance. She discovered she quite liked jiving although she couldn't really do it.

As she wiped her palms on her skirt she spotted Rachel being flung about just as wildly. While she did have a glassy stare and a fixed smile, she wasn't crying so it was probably all right. Beth was dancing more sedately with

Charlie. She looked as happy as anything. Beth hadn't talked about it much – obviously not wanting to jinx anything – but Lindy knew they'd spent a bit of time together and Beth was really keen on Charlie. She was so pleased for Beth. She'd make a brilliant farmer's wife. Then she smiled to herself – she was just like her mother, matchmaking!

Thinking she really needed a drink of water before finally heading off, Lindy went up to the bar. To her slight consternation, she found she was being served by Angus.

'Water's free,' he said, putting down a pint glass of it.

'Thank you.' She gulped some down, wishing she didn't feel so embarrassed. How hot and sweaty did she look? Had he seen her do-si-doing with a couple of elderly Lotharios? And she was wearing a costume she suddenly felt a bit self-conscious in.

'You look nice,' said Angus. 'I don't think I've ever seen you wearing anything other than jeans.'

Lindy didn't believe him. She couldn't possibly look nice when, basically, she was sweating like a pig, all her make-up was probably under her eyes and her hair was half hanging down from its once-elegant chignon. 'Really?'

'Yes. I don't think I've seen you wearing a skirt before – at least not for years.'

This felt like a challenge. She put her hands on her hips and looked up at him. 'Well, I've never seen you wearing pyjamas,' she said crisply. 'It doesn't mean you don't wear them!'

He smiled, apologetic. 'Actually, I don't.'

Lindy didn't have a snappy answer to bat back to him. She blinked at him for a couple of seconds and then found herself saying, 'Jolly good!'

Then, embarrassed beyond belief, she took her glass of water and left the bar area. She didn't want to know what he wore – or didn't wear – in bed. But now he'd told her she couldn't get the image out of her mind.

They'd had a nice time the other day, scrabbling in the hedgerows together, but she felt awkward now. She had loved her skirt and plain black top, she'd even liked the touch of eyeliner and mascara that Beth had applied with a newly confident hand, but it wasn't really her. It felt sad and wrong to be approved of when she was in costume. Jeans and sweaters were her actual uniform.

Also, no man had paid her a compliment for so long it felt almost like a criticism. And why did she care what Angus thought about her clothes? She felt so thrown by the whole thing she decided that this time she really would go home.

Lindy spent fifteen minutes saying goodbye to her nearest and dearest, which tonight included the bride's family and practically everyone else who was there.

She was halfway down the path from the hall that led across the village green when she heard footsteps behind her. She turned and saw Angus.

'Sorry,' he said. 'Did I give you a fright? I never know the etiquette about walking behind women in the dark. How do you let them know you're not threatening?'

Lindy shrugged. She didn't want to confess that in spite of her conscious mind knowing it was terribly

208

unlikely she'd get mugged by a wedding guest, the foot-steps had made her heart race. 'I don't know.' She felt like a teenager – a young teenager – flustered by being in the presence of a friend's older brother.

'So, can I walk you home?'

Such an old-fashioned thing to say. 'If you want to, but I will be OK.'

'I know you will but I wanted a chance to talk. Also an excuse to get away. Audrey was showing up my lack of pint-pulling ability.'

She laughed, relaxing. 'Maybe Sukey will have to get her in on especially busy nights.'

'Anyway, if I haven't given you a heart attack, I wanted to ask you about opportunities for me to be a bit more avuncular.' She stared at him. 'You know,' he went on, 'about seeing your boys more. Being a proper uncle.'

Lindy felt incredibly foolish. It wasn't that she didn't know what 'avuncular' meant, it was that for a few minutes she'd forgotten that Angus was related to her boys. She'd thought he'd been flirting with her, and she had flirted back. Now it seemed it was just because she was the mother of his nephews. She felt suddenly flat.

'I'm sure they'd love that. My dad does his best and although he's brilliant with them, they could do with someone – well, a bit more sporty. They do miss out not having a dad, rather.' The moment she'd finished speaking she realised she'd inadvertently criticised his brother. She hadn't meant to – although it was true.

'I'm not great at footie but I can play basketball,' said Angus.

'That's because you're tall. Cheating really.' Lindy smiled at him.

'It's why it's my chosen sport.'

'Sadly, there isn't a hoop locally, so you might have to practise dribbling or whatever it is football players do. But, seriously, whenever you want to take them fishing or something, let me know. I'll see what I can do to make it possible.' Suddenly she sighed. She didn't just want Angus to be a better uncle; she wanted something from him herself.

He must have heard the sigh. 'Lindy? Is everything all right?'

Lindy faked a yawn that turned into a real one. 'I'm fine. I'm just tired. This wedding has been a lot of work and a great deal of it quite last minute. Now I'm not stressing any more, I've sort of gone ping and so feel exhausted.'

He smiled understandingly. 'I bet. I picked a really bad moment. Could I have your number? So I can ring at a better time and arrange something?' He pulled out his phone expectantly.

Lindy gave it to him.

'Thanks,' he said, putting away his phone; then he held out his arm. 'Now, can I escort you to your door?'

Lindy took his arm. 'I'm grateful for the support. I'm out on my feet. But I'm going to my grandmother's house. Just a bit further away than mine.'

'I could carry you if you liked. Or give you a piggy back?'

He was laughing but she suddenly remembered a time when a whole gang of them had been messing around

210

after a barbeque. Angus had given her a piggyback then and Lindy had thought she'd died and gone to heaven.

'Better not,' she said, 'although my feet would appreciate it. Someone might see us and think I was drunk. Very bad for the company image!' She was pleased with herself for managing to sound so flippant.

'In which case I'll try to prop you up as best I can without sweeping you off your feet.'

Bit late for that, thought Lindy, who realised, unless she was very, very careful, she'd find herself developing a crush on him all over again.

'I won't be able to ask you for coffee or anything, as it'll wake my grandmother.'

'We'll say goodbye chastely at her garden gate then. Which somehow makes this all the more charming. Personally I feel old-fashionedness gets a very bad press.'

She laughed genuinely now. He was really nice and easy to be with. If they had been going back to hers, and the boys were sleeping somewhere else, she probably would have asked him in for coffee.

'When the weather gets better I'd like to take you and your parents, and your gran if she'd like it, to a pub for Sunday lunch, as a way of saying thank you for lunch the other day.'

'And the boys?'

'Of course the boys! And the pub I have in mind has a really good adventure playground-type thing in the garden.'

'Sounds perfect!'

They walked along in silence, his arm around her,

walking in perfect step together. All too soon they were at Lindy's grandmother's gate.

'This is it,' she said.

'Oh, shame. I hoped it was further.'

'Well, I didn't. I can't wait to get into bed.' Although it was true that she was aching with tiredness, she could have walked quite a bit further with Angus just then.

'So it's time to say goodnight,' he said.

'It is,' she agreed. A million scenarios flashed through her head. Should she kiss him on the cheek? Was he the sort of man who was used to this? Some men kissed everyone, it didn't mean a thing, but Angus's family were not touchy-feely. For Edward a kiss wasn't a casual gesture, it was a preliminary to sex.

But before she could over-think it any more, he bent and kissed her: on the cheek, but firmly – a proper kiss. 'Goodnight, Lindy.'

'Goodnight, Angus,' she said, not kissing him back. 'Thank you very much for walking me home.'

'It was a pleasure. I'll be in touch.' Then he turned and walked away.

On her grandmother's doorstep, hunting for her key, she rather wished he'd hung around longer. But as she finally got the key in the lock, she looked up and noticed he'd gone no further than a few yards. He was checking she'd got in safely but hadn't made a big deal about it. She sighed.

Once it all began and the wedding was obviously going wonderfully, Beth had started to really enjoy herself. Everyone had admired the wedding cake, which did look beautiful. Very slightly amateurish but, as Rachel had said, that added to its rustic charm. While privately she determined that the next cake she iced wouldn't have anything 'rustic' about it, she was satisfied. The delicate lace pattern had worked pretty well considering.

Beth loved to be really busy, to need to think on her feet and fly from task to task. She was just helping to cut the enormous pork pies into reasonable-sized pieces so that no greedy reveller decided he needed half of one when someone said her name.

'Beth? Is that you?' She looked up and took a moment to realise the woman she was looking at had been her art teacher at school.

'Oh, hello, Mrs Patterson. I didn't know you knew April.' Although how she would be expected to know this was a mystery.

'Oh no, we're old friends of Tristram's family, groom's side, but my dear! You look so different. Your hair. You've cut it.'

Beth noticed she didn't say 'had it cut' although since the first rebellious chopping off, she had gone to a hairdresser and a few times since. She put her hand to the back of her head protectively. 'Yes, well, felt like a change.'

'It looks amazing!' said Mrs Patterson, somewhat to Beth's surprise. 'You've always had lovely hair but when it was so long that was all one ever saw of you: the gorgeous hair. Now you see your enormous eyes. It really suits you.'

'Well, thank you! That's very good to hear,' said Beth happily. Her mother had always been so insistent that her hair was her main attraction; she'd always assumed that when she'd cut it off in a fit of rebellion no one would think it looked nice short.

'I always felt you were hiding your light under that bushel of hair.'

The compliment gave Beth the confidence to smile at Charlie when she saw him. He gave her a grin and an approving glance.

When the dancing started she accepted the arm of someone she knew from the pub. Charlie was doing duty dances but he winked at her when they met on the dance floor so she was confident that when he'd got through the people he had to dance with, he would be there for her again.

For a while she forgot about him and then realised, as she took a sip of the cider her current partner had handed her, Charlie was missing. He'd last been seen dancing with the Amazon, who looked a lot better now much of her make-up had melted off.

Soon her partner became amorous and Beth became too hot. She went to the Ladies, which was hardly more luxurious than it had been when she had first encountered it, just after Christmas. But now it was full of flowers and Rachel had added delightfully fragrant hand wash and hand cream and a scented candle, which, given there hadn't been time to do more, did make a big difference. She'd done her own share of decorating, of course, but it was Rachel who'd provided the finishing touches.

She examined her make-up and, newly into it, decided she had to apply a little bit more. Her make-up bag was with her coat, which she had put in a little room full of decorating materials, stuffed there by Beth and Lindy (when Rachel wasn't looking) to get it out of the way quickly. They had set up a makeshift cloakroom for the guests, but as it was a bit small, Beth didn't want to use up coat space intended for guests.

She found the right cupboard but the door was jammed. She gave it a huge tug, heard something crack and it opened suddenly. She switched on the light. There, on top of the dustsheets, discarded boiler suits and tins of paint, were Charlie and the Amazon. Beth shut the door as quickly as she could but not before she had seen Charlie's back and the Amazon sitting on the pile of tables. It was perfectly clear what was going on.

Then, realising she didn't want to go home without her coat, she opened it again. 'Excuse me!' She didn't look at Charlie; she didn't want to give him a chance to make excuses. She just pulled her coat from off the peg and then left, leaving the door open and the light on. It was their fault if the wedding guests saw what the bride's brother was getting up to with one of the bridesmaids.

'Oh God! What's the matter?' said Rachel as Beth nearly knocked her over in her hurry to get to the door.

'Don't want to talk about it. Do you mind if I go?'

'No – of course – but are you OK? Do you want me to come with you?'

'No! Thank you – really, I'll be OK. I just need to leave now.'

'But what's happened?'

Beth shook her head. She really didn't want to say but felt Rachel had to know. 'Charlie and the enormous bridesmaid. In that cupboard. Shagging.'

She then pushed her way through the people, avoiding eye contact with her ex-dance partner and got out of the door.

Beth didn't really know how she felt about anything, only that she wanted to get home.

In spite of her intention to wait, tears started to form and she blundered from the building half-blinded. She went bang into someone on her way out, and as her ballet flats had no grip on them she slipped alarmingly.

'Careful now,' said a man, catching her.

It took a moment for her to find her feet. She had to cling on to the man, who was swathed in a dark fleece, a big scarf and a flat cap pulled well down. His voice was soft with a touch of a brogue about it. She knew she should be wary of strange men who appear from nowhere but just then Beth thought she'd been through the worse that could happen and now she was only facing awkwardness.

She sniffed hard, hoping he couldn't see that she'd been crying. She didn't want sympathy. 'Thank you. Could have been embarrassing!' she said.

'Or painful.'

'Mm.' She yearned to wipe her nose but she knew producing a tissue would be like waving a flag saying, 'I'm crying.'

As the man didn't immediately go into the hall and she wanted him out of the way, she said, 'Can I help you? Are you a guest? The wedding's still going strong and there's lots of food left.'

'Is it a wedding? No, I'm not a guest. I just wanted to look at the hall.'

Beth wasn't thinking clearly but even to her this seemed odd. 'At this time of night? It's a bit late to be checking out a venue.'

He laughed. He had a very pleasing timbre to his voice, she noticed. ''Tis, but I saw the lights and thought I'd take the opportunity.'

'Well, go ahead. No one would notice if you went and had a look round.'

'So you're leaving the wedding?'

He seemed reluctant to move and unless he did, she'd have to push past him. 'Yup. No reason for me to stay.' She cleared the catch in her throat. 'I was working anyway and I'm not needed now.'

'Working as what?'

'Me and my friends organise weddings. This was our first. But we've done it now. I'm tired, I want to go home. But you go in, look around. Have some pork pie.' Get out of my way! she would have added if she'd been braver.

'I'll do that, then.' He moved at last.

Beth gave him a quick smile and set off down the path.

Beth was in such a whirlpool of emotions she didn't know which one was dominant. As she walked the rest of the way home, sliding along in her unsuitable shoes, wishing she'd retrieved her others so she could move faster, she was desperate to get inside her own front door so she could cry, or be sick, or maybe shout and scream.

Having got in she sat on the sofa in her coat and stared at the blank television screen for several moments, then she got up and switched it on so the picture in her head would be replaced by something else. Anything that happened to be on would be better than the vision of the

217

man she'd thought was her boyfriend rutting with that girl in the cupboard.

Two seconds later this drove her mad so she got up to turn it off. Then she went to the bathroom to have a shower.

As the warm water streamed over her head and body she tried to put her emotions in order of precedence. She was angry, desperately betrayed, an idiot. When the water went from warm to tepid, she turned it off and swathed herself in towelling, topping it off with her dressing gown. Then she went into the kitchen and rummaged through the cupboards until she found a sachet of hot chocolate.

She took the chocolate to bed with her, having shed the towels and pulled on her pyjamas. As she sipped she wondered if it would have happened – that terrible scene in the cupboard – if she'd slept with Charlie. A second after she'd had this thought she felt grateful that she hadn't. But as she finally burrowed under the duvet, praying for sleep and that she'd never have to see Charlie again, she wondered if things would have been different if she had.

And was her heart actually broken or was that physical pain in her stomach simply the result of a dirty great kick to her pride?

Chapter Sixteen

As it would be nearly teatime when the others arrived, Rachel decided to bake. It was three days after the wedding and pouring with rain. Beth and Lindy were coming round to discuss how the wedding had gone. Or, as Rachel described it, have a 'wash-up' meeting. Lindy had agreed to come as long as she didn't have to do any actual washing-up.

Before she moved to the country and learnt to loosen up a little, Rachel had rarely cooked – it made so much mess. But now she felt inclined to get out her traditional Mason Cash bowls, a recipe book and her scales, and release her inner Mary Berry.

She made madeleines in her special tins and laid them on a plate, and added a light dusting of icing sugar. She still needed things to be well presented but she wasn't as stressed when she made a mess and her clearing-up was less obsessive. Now, she discovered there was a lot of satisfaction to be had from producing something so elegant, so delectable, from a few ingredients and an oven. She was spared more philosophical reflection by the sound of rapping on the back door.

'Oh! What's that amazing smell!' said Lindy on the back doorstep as she pulled off her wellingtons. 'You've been baking. I didn't know you did that.'

'I haven't much, up till now. But we'll see what they taste like before we get too excited,' said Rachel.

'They look like something in a cookery book,' exclaimed Lindy. 'Your presentation skills are amazing.'

'My presentation skills have had a lot more practice than my baking but I did like doing them.'

'Can I have one?'

'Not yet! Not until Beth gets here.' Rachel frowned. 'I'm a bit worried about Beth, actually. Have you seen her since the wedding?'

'No,' said Lindy. 'Why, what happened?'

'I don't know if she'd mind me telling you—'

'I'm sure she wouldn't!' said Lindy, impatient for information.

'At the wedding, she found Charlie and the big brides-maid, in a cupboard – er – you know.'

'Oh God!' said Lindy as she took in what Rachel was saying. 'How awful! I'm sure Beth really liked him. How utterly horrible. Bastard.'

Rachel nodded. 'Horrendous. And now I don't know if it was OK for me to tell you.'

'I'll pretend you haven't, if you like,' said Lindy, who obviously didn't know either. 'So,' she went on, 'did you have a nice time? I didn't see Raff.'

'I'm not his keeper!' said Rachel and then sighed. 'He did say he might not be able to come. He was collecting an old fireplace or something from the other end of the country.'

'But do you like him?' Lindy obviously wanted the details.

Rachel bit her lip. 'I do like him. He's fun and he's kind, but I'm not ready for a relationship. And certainly not with him.' And before Lindy could say anything she added, 'It's not because of what he looks like or his clothes; it's just his – randomness. I like a bit of certainty in my life.'

'Setting up a business like Vintage Weddings with people you've only just met isn't a certain thing to do,' said Lindy.

Rachel found she was smiling. 'No. And yet it's been the best thing that's happened to me for years and years.'

'Oh, me too!' said Lindy. 'The best thing apart from my boys.'

Rachel had a second or two, before there was a knock at the door, to consider that if it hadn't been for getting pregnant, Lindy's career would have been very different – much more fulfilling. And yet she'd still think her boys were the best thing in her life.

'That'll be Beth,' said Lindy. 'We can find out more about Charlie – and eat the cakes!'

Rachel made tea and seated her guests round the table in the dining room.

'So, this is a wash-up meeting, is it?' said Lindy. 'I've never been to one before.'

'You probably have,' said Rachel, 'you just haven't called it that.'

'These cakes are wonderful,' said Beth. 'I didn't have lunch.'

'Oh, Beth!' said Lindy. 'Rachel told me what happened! I do hope you don't mind.'

Beth shrugged and took another cake. 'A close friend knowing doesn't make it any worse. I'm not sure if anything could make it any worse.'

'More to the point,' said Rachel, 'what will make it better?'

'Dunno. I expect in about ten years I'll think about it and laugh.'

'Don't wait ten years to laugh about it,' said Lindy. 'Ten months maybe, but ten days is better.'

'Oh, Lindy, I don't know. I feel so humiliated.'

'I don't know why you're feeling humiliated,' said Rachel. 'You're not the one discovered in a cupboard with your pants round your ankles.'

Lindy bit down hard on her lip. Rachel glared at her, knowing she was trying not to laugh.

Beth intercepted the glare and looked at Lindy. 'It's not funny,' she said.

'Oh, I know,' said Lindy. 'I'm not laughing at you; it's just the way Rachel said it, like she was a headmistress or something. It's just created a really funny picture in my head.'

Now Beth bit her lip.

Lindy was distressed. 'Honestly, Beth, love, I can imagine just how ghastly the whole thing must have been. You, discovering that fat girl with make-up smeared all over her face—'

'It was probably all over Charlie's face too,' added Rachel. 'She had enough on to supply an entire product range. "Slappers Are Us", or something.'

'OK!' said Beth. 'It's just a little bit funny. But what am I going to say to him if he turns up in the pub?'

'Would you like that pint in a glass or over your head?' said Lindy.

A little smile crept across Beth's face. 'Not sure I'll give him the choice.'

'He won't go to the pub for a while,' said Rachel. 'Not if he's got any sense.'

'Well, if he prefers that fat cow to me, he obviously hasn't got any sense,' declared Beth.

'And who wants to go out with an idiot?' said Rachel.

'Not me. That's for sure,' said Beth. Then she frowned. 'Not sure I want to tackle him about the hole in the exhaust in the van now, though.'

'Don't worry about it,' said Rachel. 'I'll ask Raff. He's sure to know someone who can do it at a very reasonable rate.'

'Oh! Thanks, you guys. You've made me feel a whole lot better,' said Beth. 'Obviously it still hurts like hell, but not as much as it did. But please, do not let me do that again.'

'What, fall in love with an idiot?' said Lindy.

'Fall in love with anyone,' declared Beth. 'Ever! Now, you'll be glad to hear that although I have been so miserable I could hardly move, I did do a bit of work on our website.'

'Really?' said Rachel. 'That's amazing! Not even workaholic me could have done that.'

'Well, I know, but I thought: Why should I let him take away everything, including the satisfaction I've got from Vintage Weddings?'

Lindy went over to Beth and hugged her. 'You're wonderful. Do you know that?'

'Yes, you are,' said Rachel. 'Working when you just feel you want to cut your throat is amazing.'

'I don't think I actually wanted to cut my throat, more, well... do something agricultural to Charlie that I won't mention in front of Rachel.'

'You mean cut his balls off?' said Rachel. 'I totally get that!'

Rachel picked up her clipboard. Things were calm now. Beth seemed almost back to her old self. Rachel knew she wasn't, really, but she obviously wanted to put the episode behind her and get on with the business in hand.

'OK, girls. The wedding: how was it for you?' Her pen was poised, ready to make notes.

'I thought it went brilliantly,' said Lindy. 'The hall did us proud. Everyone loved it, and the family were thrilled with what we did for them.'

'It was lovely of Eamon to thank us publicly like that,' said Rachel.

'April was thrilled with her dress,' said Lindy.

'There are zillions of pictures on her Facebook page,' said Beth. 'She does look amazing.'

'I thought our outfits worked well,' said Lindy, 'especially for you, Beth. You were channelling Audrey Hepburn—'

'Well, apparently Audrey Hepburn doesn't do it for Charlie!' said Beth, but with an air that made them laugh.

'Another indication of what an idiot he is,' said Rachel. 'But moving on...'

'Mum says everyone thinks we're miracle-workers,' said Lindy.

'We're not quite that,' said Rachel, suddenly a bit anxious. 'We had so much help from everyone.'

'But we learnt a lot,' said Lindy. 'We have skills now we didn't have before.'

'We can offer a make-up service,' said Beth. 'I might have to buy some more make-up though, if someone else wants me to do it.'

'We will have to think about catering in the future,' said Rachel. 'The village only did it for April because she's local, and her mother, and all. We should research people.'

'Or learn to do it ourselves,' said Lindy. 'Otherwise we'll have to use up all we're paid on the caterers.'

'We could add them to the bill,' said Beth. 'We can't do everything.'

Rachel sighed. 'I know we can't,' she said. 'But the food is so important. I hate not having control of it.' Then she felt embarrassed. 'Sorry, yes, I am a control freak. I will get over it!' The others laughed and Rachel went on: 'And it's so much easier to be neurotic if you don't have to hide it all the time. So I'm glad you guys know.'

'We'll find a caterer we can rely on,' said Lindy. 'And personally I'm so happy we haven't got to think about weddings any more. At least for a little bit. I'm completely weddinged-out just at the moment.'

'Me too!' said Rachel. 'Although I really loved it and seeing it all come together was amazing, I don't want to do it again immediately. Unless we got a paying client, of course.' She looked at her colleagues. 'So, let's make a list of what we need to focus on now.'

'We need to get the smell out of the van for a start,'

said Beth. 'I put up with it before but now it's going to remind me of Charlie.'

'I did notice a bit of a whiff the other day,' said Lindy. 'Like there's something rotting in the fruit bowl.'

'I think there's some trick with bicarbonate of soda,' said Rachel.

'I'll look it up,' said Beth. 'Next?'

'We need to finish doing the hall,' said Rachel. 'I know it looked fine – more than fine – but I am aware the decorating is nothing like finished. And then there's the kitchen. Even as a serving area it's disgusting.'

'Is it that bad?' said Lindy. 'I thought it was more or less OK. Inadequate, but not dreadful.'

Rachel regarded her sternly. 'I'm sure if anyone found out we were intending to hire it out and serve food they would close us down for hygienic reasons.'

'OK,' said Lindy. 'Add it to the list. But as well as doing stuff ourselves we must all get behind the fund to repair the roof. Like going to the quiz,' she added. 'My mother's making me go.'

'Are you good at quizzes?' asked Rachel.

'Not really, no. But she's invited Angus to be on our team.'

'He seems a nice guy. But do you think Sarah is up to her usual matchmaking tricks again?' asked Rachel.

'Probably. Anyway, if I'm going, you two must too.'

'I'll probably be working,' said Beth.

'Sukey might run a bar and let you work at it, then you can secretly tell us the answers,' said Rachel.

Beth laughed, looking genuinely cheerful now. 'Do you know how little I know about sport?'

'Everyone has a specialist subject,' said Rachel. 'Mine's how to avoid clutter and get rid of unsightly stains. Only those things never come up in quizzes.' There was a whistle. 'Oh, there's your phone,' she said to Beth. 'If it's Charlie don't answer it.'

Beth was reading the text. 'It's not Charlie. It's Helena. She's got a date for the wedding.'

'When?' demanded Rachel.

Beth looked up from her phone. 'April the twelfth.'

There was a tiny silence and then Rachel said, 'That's less than two months away.'

'Doesn't it interfere with Easter?' said Lindy, sounding as though she hoped it did. 'We could make her postpone it a bit.'

Rachel checked the diary on her phone. 'No. Easter is late this year.' She looked at Beth. 'It is very short notice. Can you ask her if she could put it back a bit? Even another month would help.'

Beth wrote the text.

There was a pause as they awaited a reply. Beth picked up Rachel's copy of *Interiors* magazine and flicked through it. Then Lindy said, 'This is getting frustrating. Why don't we try and Skype her? It would be good to see what she looks like.'

'Good idea – if she's somewhere she can Skype. I'll ask her.'

There was more waiting for Helena's reply. 'Just thought,' said Beth. 'You can Skype all right here, can't you, Rachel?'

Rachel nodded. 'All mod cons in this gaff.' She realised the thought of making a joke about her house would have been impossible to her only a couple of months ago.

There was a few minutes' hiatus while Rachel set up Skype and Lindy took the mugs and plate through to the kitchen and washed up. Rachel was aware of this but knew Lindy was sensitive to her washing-up foibles. It would be OK.

'Right, we're there,' said Rachel. Beth and Lindy rushed to join her and then there, on her computer screen, was someone who looked quite a lot like Beth.

'Hey, Hels!' said Beth delightedly. 'Long time no Skype. Why the hurry with the wedding? Are you up the duff?'

'Don't joke,' said Helena. 'Yes I am. And it would break Mum's heart if I went up the aisle with an obvious bump.'

No one spoke for a few tense seconds. Rachel cleared her throat and nudged Beth, who took the hint.

'Right, OK,' she said, 'I'd better introduce you to the team,' obviously still a bit shocked by her sister's news. She'd be an aunt by the end of the year! 'This is Lindy.'

'Hi, Helena,' said Lindy. 'Don't worry about being pregnant. I got married because I was pregnant.'

'Oh, and how did that work out?' asked Helena.

'Not well, but you've been together for ages. We were a bit of a one-night stand really,' said Lindy.

'And I'm Rachel. I'm in charge of the clipboard.' She waved it.

'So, Hels!' said Beth. 'This is a bit of a curveball. I didn't think you even cared what Mum thought about the wedding, which is why we're doing it and not her!'

'Since I've been away from home I realise I actually miss her. And really, it's not fair to dump it all on you.'

'But what about her wanting something completely different from what you want? You know: the big hotel? The eight bridesmaids you haven't seen for years? Her choir singing her choice of music? I thought you hated the idea of all that.'

'We've had some long chats and she's agreed it's my day and not hers. I think us both leaving home has made her realise how controlling she's been and she's changed.'

'Hmph!' said Beth. 'I'm not sure that's possible. Are you sure you're not going to lie down and let her take over? Just for an easy life?'

'Really. I'm not.' Helena leant forward. 'There's one suggestion I've totally said no to.'

'Oh yeah?'

'She wants me to wear her wedding dress and veil – to save money and because she loves it so. I told her that was out of the question.'

'Actually, Hels, that's one thing she might be right about. If I remember from the photos her dress would – well, it could hide a bit of a bump.' She stopped for a stunned second. 'Hey – you don't think Mum was preg—'

'No,' Helena interrupted her sister. 'I've done the maths. I wasn't born for a good year after they got married.'

'So have you told her you're pregnant? Congratulations by the way. I think it's lovely!'

'So does Mum! I was really surprised but I think the

thought of a grandchild mellowed her. She realised if she went on being like she has been all these years, she might never see it.'

'Ah! Love the thought of Mum being all gooey. Now we've got a van I should go and see her.'

Helena paused. 'You don't need to do that. She's coming over to see you. She wants to get involved with the wedding – but on our terms, not hers.'

Beth was silent for so long, Rachel felt obliged to step in. 'That's lovely. All help gratefully received, I'm sure.'

'Well, she can't stay with me,' said Beth. 'I've got no room!'

'I'm sure she doesn't have to actually stay in your house—' said Lindy.

'She'll have to stay in a B and B,' declared Beth. 'Lindy? You must know of a good one? My mum's a bit fussy.'

Lindy winced. 'Not in the village. Our one is a bit nylon sheets and loo-paper dollies.'

'Oh no,' said Helena from somewhere far across the world. 'Mum would have a fit.'

'It wouldn't have to be in the village,' said Beth, cheering up now she knew she no longer had to share the village with her mother, even at night. 'It could be quite far away – if you can think of anywhere.' She turned to Lindy who shook her head.

Helena joined in. 'Beth! I could find a B and B that's not in the village on the internet. But she wants to be really local.'

Briefly Beth thought about the pub but the two rooms were both occupied at the moment and they were very basic – not up to her mother's standards, that's for sure.

Rachel found her mouth opening and strange words coming out. 'She can stay with me. I'll be a B and B.'

'Cool!' said Helena, unaware of just how big a deal this was for Rachel. 'When can she come?'

'Um, Hels, we need to think about this,' said Beth. 'We've got a lot to sort out. Can we get back to you?'

'Oh, OK,' said Helena, much to Rachel's relief, who was in shock. 'Oh, by the way, Beth, she's found out about you cutting your hair.'

'How? You didn't tell her?' Beth was appalled.

'No! I promised I wouldn't but Mrs Patterson, who saw you, met Mum in Waitrose. Apparently you look great. I mean, I know that, but Mrs Patterson said to Mum you looked great.'

'Great,' said Beth faintly.

'Mum said Mrs Patterson was an arty type and obviously didn't believe her.'

'OK,' said Rachel, breaking in. 'Me and Lind will leave you girls to chat—'

In the kitchen Rachel bit her knuckle. 'What have I done? Why did I say Beth's mother can come and stay?'

'I don't know but I think it's a brilliant idea!'

'Lindy. I don't have people to stay in my house. Especially not difficult people like Beth's mum.'

Lindy laughed. She was obviously relaxed about it because she didn't have to have Beth's mother to stay. 'You do now!'

Rachel frowned. 'Actually, you know what? I just love the little details in a B and B. Fresh milk, not those cartons. Proper sheets, nice soap, you know? I think some part of me does want to open one. As a sort of test.'

Lindy nodded. 'I sort of know what you mean. Although you'd want to be careful you didn't get too neurotic about it. Not take it personally if the people don't like everything.'

'I think I'd be OK if they just didn't like the marmalade – although of course I would provide thin-cut and chunky. But if they discovered something awful, like a hair on the mattress, then I'd quietly die.'

'You wouldn't ever have a hair on the mattress, Rachel. You'd hoover the mattresses between visits.'

'Of course I would. Right, I've left my clipboard in the other room but you know we will have to sort out caterers, urgently. I thought we had a few months but obviously we haven't now.'

Lindy nodded. 'We can't expect the Good Women of the Village for Helena's wedding. I'll ask Mum if she knows anyone.'

'Oh, here's Beth,' said Rachel. 'We're just talking about catering. I don't suppose you have any clue what sort of food Helena wants have you?'

'Yes, I have,' said Beth. 'Canapés, then a sit-down do, three courses and cheese.'

'So is that Helena's choice or your mother's?' asked Lindy.

'Oh, Mum's! Helena says she won't do what Mum wants, but I know she'll cave if the pressure goes on.'

'Just as well Helena has Vintage Weddings to make sure she gets what she wants,' said Rachel.

'Yay, lucky Helena,' said Lindy. 'She's got us.'

'I was going to ask if anyone would like more tea,' said Rachel, 'but actually, I want wine. Anyone else?'

'What a brilliant idea,' said Beth. 'I'll get the glasses.'

Chapter Seventeen

'So, Rachel,' said Beth. 'Do you think you could have my mother – better known as Mrs Fussy Knickers – to stay? As a B-and-B owner?'

Rachel nodded. 'Actually I think I could. I really like a challenge and I think a touch of OCD is what you need to be really good at B and B. I'd move into the spare room and let my room so it would have the en-suite. Could be a nice little income source for us.' She paused. 'I'd only do it for people connected with the wedding. I couldn't have just anyone. And possibly only women.'

'You couldn't do that, Rachel.' Lindy was horrified. 'Not give up your bedroom. And if you did, it would be your money. The business couldn't take a share in it.'

Rachel thought how she could explain. 'I wouldn't do it if it weren't for the business. I don't need the money. I have a fairly regular income.' She considered what it might be like to have a stranger in her perfect bedroom and sighed. 'But everyone has to make sacrifices when they start up a business.'

'I know I've worked hard,' said Lindy. 'But I haven't actually sacrificed anything.'

'Nor have I!' said Beth. 'And I haven't done as much as you and Rachel, I don't think.'

'There's still time, girls. Beth might be forced to learn synchronised swimming so we can offer it as entertainment and Lindy, well, you've got two charming little boys. I'm sure we can find some way of making money out of them!'

As Rachel didn't often say things like that it took the others a few seconds to work out she was joking.

'But, seriously,' said Rachel, 'I so want this business to work. I'm prepared to do anything. It's the first time – ever, I think – that I've really enjoyed my work. Creating your own business and working for it is the way forward, I'm convinced.'

'Um, when we've finished our wine,' said Lindy, 'could we go and look at your room? Just make sure it's good enough?' she teased.

Rachel considered. It was white wine. 'You can bring your wine with you, I'm sure you won't spill it.'

'We won't!' they said in unison.

'This is so exciting!' said Beth.

Rachel tried to keep up as her colleagues headed for her bedroom. She was aware that they'd never been in there before; it had been her shrine. Now she was prepared to rent it out. How times had changed – or rather how she had changed.

No one spoke as they surveyed the room. An antique brass bedstead stood at right angles to the windows. Opposite was an antique pine wardrobe. An old washstand, in the same pale old pine, stood in between the windows. On it was a jug and bowl. There was a framed antique sampler hanging over the bed and a blanket box under the window added to the impression that the room belonged in a different century.

'I'm sorry about the mess,' said Rachel, because when she'd got up that morning she hadn't thought that anyone but her would see her room.

Lindy looked bemused and then said, 'Rachel, I don't think having your slippers slightly out of alignment under your bed counts as mess. You've seen my house – now that *is* messy!'

Rachel, who knew that yesterday's jeans were slung on the pretty Lloyd Loom chair, not visible unless you went right into the room, didn't agree with her. 'Your house is... homely, and if that's how you like it—'

'I like it to be homely but I don't like the mess. It's just something that happens to me,' said Lindy, sounding a bit crisp.

'My mother nagged me so much about being untidy, I've sworn I won't do it to my kids,' said Beth. 'I think it's a temperament thing – you either care enough to do something about it or have other priorities.' She paused. 'Can we see the bathroom, Rachel?'

'OK. We'll start with the en-suite, which is what your mother would use.'

This was much more modern but still minimalist and elegant. There was a row of glass jars with silver lids containing everything one might need to either put on or take off make-up.

'I love those!' said Lindy.

'They're jam jars really – not the kind they sell the jam in obviously – but I had collected a few and didn't know what to do with them until I needed something to put cotton buds in.'

'My mother would love this,' said Beth ecstatically. 'It's stylish yet comfortable.' She frowned. 'She does have quite a demanding list of must haves, I warn you.'

Rachel nodded. 'So have I. I'm a nightmare hotel guest. For instance, a radio by the bed and not coming out of the TV. I must get another one, so I can have one when your mother is staying.'

'Proper hangers,' said Beth.

'Fresh milk – either in a little fridge or in a thermos,' said Rachel.

'I'm just happy if the sheets are clean and there's a kettle and the pillows aren't too bad,' said Lindy. 'And no wriggling little bodies to share the bed with.'

'All my pillows are goose down,' said Rachel. 'And my personal pillow has a silk pillow case.' She frowned. 'Do you think I should provide this room with one?'

'No,' Beth and Lindy said in unison. 'Absolutely not.

After the others had gone, Rachel had just settled down in front of the television (usually hidden behind a screen) when the telephone rang. She instantly recognised the voice of Belinda, Raff's mother.

After some brief preliminaries Belinda said, 'Darling, when are you coming to sort out my china? It's getting a bit urgent. I can easily get in some house-clearance people if you don't want to do it.'

Rachel nearly shrieked, but then took a breath. 'No! I

do want to do it – if you still want me to. I've been very taken up with this wedding. We had to use the village-hall china and what people who made food provided. I only wish I'd time to sort it before.' Belinda's voice had been quite brisk and Rachel hoped she hadn't offended her by not going round sooner.

'I do know how busy you girls have been. The whole village is talking about how wonderful the wedding was. I don't mean to make you feel guilty for not sorting me out but I would prefer someone I know and like to do it.'

Rachel was incredibly flattered and mentally consulted her diary. 'I could come tomorrow if you like,' she said.

'Excellent! About nine? Too early? Too late?'

'Perfect,' said Rachel. She could postpone her client for the next day – he would be grateful for the extra time to find his receipts. A few clients had felt the benefit of the time she'd spent on the wedding.

'That's perfect for me too,' said Belinda. 'Now, do you need directions? I know you've been before but having no sense of direction myself, I always need to be reminded.' She drew breath. 'Or will you come with Raff?'

'Raff? Is he going to be there?'

'Oh God yes, darling! There's far too much for one person!'

Rachel swallowed, thinking of the rearrangement she had yet to make. Maybe she could ring back later and say she had to change the time? But she suspected that Raff would change the time too and still be there.

'Actually, directions would be good. You know – just in case.'

As she took down Belinda's instructions she couldn't help wondering why she was in such a hurry to clear her house. Maybe she wanted to put the house on the market? She determined that this time she'd find out why Belinda was clearing things now.

Up until that moment Rachel had managed not to think about Raff too much. There had been so much to think about with the wedding. Now she had to confront him – not literally, thank goodness – but mentally. Her feelings were so confused. Her sensible head told her she wanted nothing to do with him. He was bad news. Yet the rest of her – heart and body and possibly soul – was drawn to him. Why? She was almost frightened of him – not because he was dangerous but possibly because of the response he awoke in her. He pushed her out of her comfort zone and she both feared and liked it.

While she was conducting her own self-awareness course she realised that on a very basic level she fancied him. But that was OK. You were allowed to fancy unsuitable people, you just had to have more sense than to do anything about it. Let her head rule the rest of her and keep him at a distance. That's what she would do.

The following morning she was ready for the challenge. Raff had sent her a text suggesting he pick her up on his way to his mother's. She'd declined it politely. This way she could go home when she wanted. She wore old clothes and packed her boiler suit into a bag in case she needed it. She had really wanted to wear it but thought it might look rude, turning up in protective clothing to sort out some china.

She had flattened the back seats of her car and put in useful things. There were her banana boxes, gleaned from supermarkets and carefully saved for house moving, so strong and convenient to carry around. A leftover roll of bubble wrap, plus a bin liner filled with every piece of bubble wrap she'd ever used; some cardboard boxes, flattened, with lids, that were referred to as document cases; a tape dispenser and several rolls of tape. There was also a box of sticky labels and several Sharpie pens. Rachel knew herself to be an expert packer and house-mover. She'd not only moved herself a few times but she'd helped friends too. While Raff's mother – she must think of her as Belinda – wasn't, as far as she knew, moving, the skills required would be similar. She thought about a couple whose belongings she'd helped pack into a Transit van and felt that maybe now she could invite them to stay. Previously she had felt too anxious.

As she tapped the address into her satnav she realised she was excited. This was going to be a real challenge, sorting all that china. And the best part was, she could leave at any time if it got too much. And it was nice to be doing the journey in daylight: she could appreciate the scenery. It was so different, she felt, admiring it as a resident and not just a weekend visitor. She felt part of it now, not just a looker-on.

She was also excited at the thought of what she might find. She wasn't taking Belinda's offer of the china as a gift seriously. There might be some valuable things there, which she wouldn't be able to accept. Besides, people could be very generous about giving away things they thought were worthless but their mood could swiftly alter if the valuation changed.

'I brought some things that might help,' she said when she'd been warmly greeted and given a cup of very good coffee. 'Some boxes, bubble wrap, labels.'

'It sounds as if you've come well prepared,' said Belinda and Rachel wasn't quite sure if she should take it as a compliment.

'Well, you know. I thought they might be useful.' She sipped the coffee and it gave her confidence. 'Do you want us to work together? For me to help you?'

'Good God, no!' said Belinda. 'No. I want you to do it. If it were left to me it would never get done. And it needs to be done.'

Had Belinda been a jot less formidable Rachel would have asked her why, but she didn't quite dare. Then she decided this was ridiculous. The worst that could happen was that Belinda would ask her to leave, which would be sad but not exactly life-threatening. 'Sorry, but can I ask why? It would help if I knew what sort of time frame we have.' There, she'd said it. Now she could wait until the sky fell in – or not – depending.

'Raff's asked me too and I don't think he was satisfied with my answer,' she said. But to Rachel's huge relief she didn't seem annoyed. 'This house is far too big for me to live in on my own and yet I can't face leaving it. Ridiculous, I know.'

'So . . .' prompted Rachel.

'I thought I'd carve out a flat for myself in part of it and rent out the rest.'

'Oh, but wouldn't that be difficult? You'd have to

share your space with strangers. Goodness me, I've only just got used to the thought of people staying in my house for a couple of nights.' She made a face. 'Although I admit I am a bit odd like that.'

'It rather depends on whom I rent it to.'

Rachel regarded Belinda and decided that this was a woman with a plan. She baulked at probing further.

'I'll just get on with it.' Then, bravely, she added, 'I work better on my own, really.'

'I thought so!' Belinda smiled in satisfaction.

Rachel had fairly quickly worked out Raff wasn't there. There was no sign of his truck and she was fairly sure there was only one other mug in current use in the kitchen. As there were many mugs queuing up for the dishwasher this wasn't an easy call to make but Rachel felt she could relax.

'I knew you were the right person to do this,' said Belinda, adding cream to her coffee. 'As soon as I met you. I really didn't need Raff to tell me.'

Rachel made a sympathetic face. 'I hate being told things I know already. Now, where would you like me to start?'

'The dining room,' said Belinda. 'How do you want to do it?'

'What I suggest is, I make three piles: valuable things you might want to sell, things you'll give away to a charity shop, and things that aren't worth keeping. I'll decide which is which and then you can decide I'm wrong and that I've put a valuable antique or something of great sentimental value on the chuck pile.' She paused. 'Of course it won't be piles. I'll pack everything in boxes. Then, when you've made up your mind, I'll wash everything and pack it properly.'

'Goodness me! I'll let you get on then.'

Rachel was in heaven. She had Radio 4 on, was wearing her boiler suit and rubber gloves and had completely forgotten about everything except what she was doing.

She didn't know a lot about ceramics but went straight to the famous names in the world of porcelain. Someone had collected a lot of Mason's Ironstone and there was a certain amount of Clarice Cliff.

She began by sorting everything into sets. She decided – although she winced while she was doing it – to overlook chips and small flaws. She'd been there about half an hour before she realised she needed to know more about what she was dealing with.

She went to find Belinda in the kitchen.

Belinda switched off her KitchenAid. 'Can I help?'

'I was wondering if you had any sort of reference book about ceramics. It would really help me decide about things.' She noticed that Belinda had several bun tins with cake cases in them dotted about the work surface, balanced on piles of books and plates and the fruit bowl.

'Oh yes,' said Belinda, wiping her hands on her apron. 'I'm sure I've got one somewhere.'

Rachel smiled but wondered if, in fact, Belinda had a hope in hell of finding it amongst all the clutter. But to her surprise Belinda reached into a bookcase and pulled out the book straight away.

'Thank you,' Rachel said, hoping that her surprise wasn't obvious. 'This will be really useful.'

'Good,' said Belinda and went back to the worktop.

Holding the book to her chest, Rachel said, 'Would you mind my asking how you collected all this china?'

'No, I don't mind. It was mostly my parents and then aunts and uncles contributed more. When you have a big house people think it's OK to dump things on you, even if you don't really want them.' She smiled. 'But some of them are lovely. When I've downsized I'll keep only the best.'

'I'm sure there'll be some lovely things you'll want to hang on to, but if there's a particular pattern of china you like, or brand...' Rachel wasn't sure you described famous names like Crown Derby, Wedgwood and Minton as brands, but she couldn't think how else to describe them '...could set it aside for you.'

Belinda shook her head. 'Oh, I wouldn't select by pattern, I don't think.' She seemed to think this a very odd notion. 'Now run along. I've these cakes to get in the oven, then I'm going to cook us lunch. You'll need it!'

Rachel went back to the dining room, book in hand. She decided she didn't mind being told to 'run along' by Belinda. She'd said it with such charm it was almost a compliment.

Rachel carried on with her work. She was having a brilliant time. She loved sorting things, finding other members of the same family and putting them in groups. She'd long since stopped noticing how dirty she was getting, or tired, moving piles of plates and dishes from one place to another.

Her best find – one she thought she would accept if it

was offered – was a bit more Shelley china in the pattern of the set she and Beth had won when they first met. It was still in Beth's house and so far they hadn't had a chance to use it. It seemed a long time ago now.

She was getting to learn more about china too, what she liked and what she didn't. Even discovering, (courtesy of the book) that the Clarice Cliff was called 'Gayday' didn't make her like that, and Rachel put it all in one of her boxes. It included a teapot that was, she was fairly sure, perfect, and so would raise a decent amount of money. Belinda had reiterated that she didn't want the bother of selling things and that Rachel could have it all if she took it away, but Rachel couldn't accept that generous offer. She'd work something out.

She was just bending backwards to ease the pressure on her lower spine when Belinda called, 'Lunch!' Glad at the prospect of a break she headed towards the kitchen.

Just as she walked through the door Raff came in through the back door. 'Hello, my two favourite women!' he said and kissed his mother on the cheek.

Although Rachel had known he was expected she had somehow forgotten about him while she was lost in the joy of dealing with beautiful – and less beautiful – china. And it was still a shock when he came round to kiss her cheek too.

'Hey! Look at you, Ms Dusty Face!' he said, approval in his eyes. 'Sorry I'm late. I got caught up and couldn't get away.'

'Have you come to help, or just for lunch?' said Rachel, hating herself for not being able to think of the right witty response and ending up sounding critical instead.

'For lunch, and then to help. So, what's in the oven, Mum?'

Belinda chuckled. 'Fairy cakes. We're having soup and salad.'

'Sounds wonderful,' said Rachel, hoping she hadn't offended Belinda by sounding a bit off with her son.

'Sounds dull,' said Raff, 'but Mum makes salads even men like. Don't you?'

'So I've heard,' said Belinda. 'Now, Rachel, I expect you'd like to wash your hands. Down the passage, door on the right.'

Belinda had been tactful when she suggested that only Rachel's hands needed washing. She was filthy! Her face was streaked with dust and her hair was tangled with things that looked horribly like cobwebs. Quite how they'd got there she could only guess. She'd left her handbag in the kitchen and she couldn't go back and get it in order to reapply the bit of mascara she always wore, she'd just have to manage with water and the quite grubby towel. She felt irritated. She'd been so relaxed and happy before, when she was working, but now Raff was here and was making remarks and kissing her cheek, she felt as uptight and prickly as ever. And she thought she was past all that overreaction and spikiness.

Belinda put a glass of wine into her hand when she arrived back and she didn't refuse it. She took a large sip. It was delicious.

'Come and sit down,' said Belinda. 'Just move those books. There should be space.'

Rachel duly moved the books. 'Are you clearing out your cookery books too?' she asked.

'Oh no, although I ought to have a sort-out.' Belinda put a soup plate the size of a dustbin lid in front of Rachel. The contents were thick, full of vegetables and smelt divine. There was already a basket of bread on the table, which looked home-made.

'Do you cook a lot?' asked Rachel, willing Raff to come and sit down so she could start eating. Rachel was surprised he couldn't hear her mental chivvying.

'Not when it's just me, no. I live on toast and Marmite, but I like cooking for other people. Do start. Don't wait for Raff.'

Rachel lowered her spoon into the soup and then took a sip. It was delicious. 'Dinner parties and things?'

'Not much these days, but a friend is having a surprise party. Obviously she doesn't know that. I'm doing the food.' Belinda looked amused. 'Don't worry, it's at her house.' She turned round to her son. 'Do hurry up, Raff. Your soup's getting cold.'

When Raff joined them at the table Rachel realised that he'd been washing his hands in the sink – probably because she'd spent so much time in the loo.

'So, Rachel, have you been having fun?' he asked after a few mouthfuls.

Whether it was the wine or the soup Rachel didn't know, but she felt her spikiness fall away. 'The best fun I've had in ages,' she said.

'Hey! You said that when you were doing the mist coat,' objected Raff.

'That was also lovely,' said Rachel, considering, 'but this is a different sort of fun. About the same level of fun-ness though.'

'So have you found anything that might be useful for your business?' asked Belinda.

Rachel put down her spoon. 'Belinda, there is treasure in there and I can't accept it as a gift.'

Belinda sighed. 'You'd be taking it out of my house. Off my hands. I don't want it any more.'

'You don't have to keep it,' said Rachel. 'I'll take it all away and store it in my shed, and then Beth – she's one of my colleagues – will sell it for you on eBay.' She paused. 'Vintage Weddings will use anything that's not part of a set, or valuable, or whatever.' She picked up her glass for another sip of wine.

'Oh, darling!' Belinda was cross. 'That wasn't the deal at all. It works for me because I get rid of it. I don't want money.'

'Surely—' Rachel began. They had already had this discussion but seeing how much and how potentially valuable the china was, she felt obliged to protest again.

'Well,' said Raff, 'if you don't want the money, Beth could sell the china and the money could go towards the village-hall restoration fund. God knows it needs it.'

Rachel looked at him. 'Brilliant idea! And if you change your mind, Belinda, you could have the money instead. Or some of it,' she added, thinking of the huge amount of money the hall needed, just to get its roof repaired.

'Well, that sounds fine to me,' said Belinda. 'Have you room to store it all?'

'Well, we'll have to sell things we're going to sell fairly quickly,' said Rachel. 'But before we get rid of anything – even to use for Vintage Weddings – you have to go through and see what you want to keep.'

'I wouldn't want to let any large platters go out of the family,' said Belinda. 'In case we have any big parties.'

'Big parties here, Mum?' said Raff, frowning slightly.

'Or anywhere. You know, like this surprise party I'm doing the catering for.'

Belinda had mentioned this party before but now, hearing her use the word 'catering' gave Rachel an idea. 'Do you like catering?'

'Love it, as long as it's not too often. Why?' Belinda's blue eyes, so like her son's, were penetrating.

'We need a caterer, someone who'll do weddings. For April's wedding, the WI and people in the village did it but that was just for her. We couldn't expect them to do it regularly.'

'Well,' said Belinda, after what seemed to Rachel a lot of thought, 'I wouldn't want to do them too often and I would need a galley slave or two to help me, but otherwise, yes, I think that would be fun.'

'Oh my goodness. That would be amazing. If I've found us a good caterer—' Rachel began.

'You don't know she's good,' said Raff.

'She is! I mean, I am!' Belinda was indignant. 'Really, Raff. You know perfectly well I did Veronica's Golden Wedding do and had people begging me to do theirs.'

'I know,' said Raff calmly, 'but I knew you wouldn't tell Rachel unless I pushed you.'

'Obviously we'd find someone else if you didn't fancy it but we've got a wedding coming up in April, for Beth's sister, and we need someone really good.' Although she didn't say it she thought Belinda would probably be able to convince Helena and her mother to have a menu that would be easy to do, and not just one that was impressive.

'That sounds like a challenge I could rise to,' said Belinda.

'There is just one more favour,' said Rachel.

'Anything,' said Belinda.

'There's some china in the same pattern as the tea set I won in a raffle with Beth, when I first moved down here. It was in the village hall.'

'I remember,' said Raff.

'If I could have that, I'd be thrilled. Beth and I both would be.'

'Of course you can have it!' said Belinda. 'I thought I made myself clear!' Then to take any possible sting out of her words she went on: 'Now, this soup won't be as nice tomorrow. I insist you both have some more.'

Chapter Eighteen

'I think it's time you went home, darling,' said Belinda. 'It's too dark to see properly, even with all the lights on. And you must be exhausted!'

'There's just that one big cupboard over there I haven't been through…' Rachel began, and then put her hand on her back. 'Ow. Too much bending.'

'You need to get home and into a hot bath,' said Belinda.

'That does sound like heaven.' Now the thought was in her head she wanted to be in one, as soon as possible.

'Well, Raff has got most of the stuff in his truck but I don't suggest he unloads it all into your shed tonight. You've spend enough time humping boxes around.'

'And I might have to do some rearranging to make it all fit.' Rachel bit her lip. 'You are absolutely *sure* you don't want to have the money for the stuff we sell?'

'Rachel, darling, haven't we had this conversation? Having the space is reward enough.'

Rachel considered. While she knew Belinda wanted to make a flat for herself in her house and rent the rest, she felt there was something Belinda was keeping back. But Belinda had been kindness itself all day; Rachel couldn't press her. No matter: Raff would know what it was. She'd ask him.

At last, the convoy was ready, Rachel in the lead with Raff following with his truck full of china. Rachel pressed 'home' into the satnav and drove, and as she negotiated the country lanes she was dreaming of hot water and wine, in no particular order.

She was really tired but she'd had such a good day. As well as lots of lovely china they had discovered at least eight huge platters that would be really useful for events: Belinda's and for Vintage Weddings. There were also dozens of plates that didn't fit into proper sets, so Rachel didn't mind accepting them as a present.

In between Rachel sorting and washing (it had taken her a bit of time to convince Belinda that some of the really good stuff shouldn't just be shoved into the dish-washer) Rachel had had the opportunity to discuss Belinda's catering. Rachel was certain that Belinda would be able to convince Beth's mother to have the sort of food that Belinda could do well. The antique platters would definitely help. And privately she decided that Belinda being so posh would also help. She didn't voice this thought – she didn't want to be seen as a snob (although she accepted she was one) – but she felt it was true. If Helena was seen to be having a wedding where the guests ate off Spode plates (among other varieties of high quality) her mother would deem it a success, even if it wasn't the sit-down dinner with four courses she'd imagined she'd wanted.

Rachel couldn't remember a time, before now, when

she felt everything in her life was right. She wasn't craving to live anywhere different, with a different job and a different husband. She was in the right place, doing the right thing, and if there was a man in a truck behind her who caused a bit of stress from time to time, well, in every life a little rain must fall. In her case the rain was called Raff.

When at last all the china in Rachel's car and some of that in Raff's van was safely stored in her shed, she locked the door.

'Well, that's all done then,' said Rachel. 'Thank you very much for your help. No need for you to wait.'

Raff shook his head. 'Mum said I was to make sure you got in all right. She also said I was to run your bath. She feels bad about all the work you've done for no reward – as she sees it.'

Rachel laughed. It seemed a harmless enough offer. 'OK, run my bath if you insist. But you will have to leave before I get in it.' She put her key into her front door, slightly surprised the hall light wasn't on. She must have forgotten to turn it on. Never mind; better for the planet.

'Oh,' she said as she flicked the switch and nothing happened.

'No lecky?' said Raff, coming in behind her.

'Apparently not. I wonder what's happened?' She found the torch on her keyring.

'Would you like me to check the fuse box?'

'There shouldn't be anything wrong,' said Rachel, leading the way to the back of the house. 'I had it all rewired.'

'Well, the trip switch has gone,' said Raff, who now had control of the torch.

'Switch it on again then,' said Rachel. 'And you don't need to sort me out. I can do it myself.'

'You are joking, aren't you?' said Raff. 'If my mother found out I'd left you in the dark she would change her will in favour of the donkey sanctuary!'

'I won't tell her if you don't.'

He ignored this and flicked the switch. Rachel had been resetting her own trip switch for some years and yet she found she was relieved not to be on her own, in the dark, when she was so tired.

The lights came on. 'Hooray!' said Rachel. 'Thank you so much for helping me. And, really, you've done enough. You don't need to run my bath. I'll be fine now I can see.'

Raff looked down at her and shook his head. 'We need to find out what caused it all to go pop. What did you have on apart from the hall lights?'

'Well, nothing really. I'm meticulous about turning things off after I've used them. I didn't even straighten my hair today because I knew I was going to be working.' She sighed, aware she was cold as well as tired and dirty. 'I'll get an electrician in first thing. Now I just want to fall into the bath – or maybe just have a shower – and go to bed.' She realised she was on the verge of feeling tearful and really wanted him to go.

'Your wood-burner doesn't heat the hot water, does it?' said Raff, still studying the fuse board.

'No. It's an immersion heater – Oh.' A wave of despair fell over her. No hot water, no possibility of getting off the dirt of the day. She couldn't go to bed dirty, she just couldn't, not into her clean white sheets. She'd have to boil kettles and have a strip wash in her freezing bathroom, splashing dirty water all over the place. She'd never be able to get properly clean and the mess in the bathroom would be horrendous. She bit her lip. She really did not want to cry in front of Raff. She'd got her OCD so well under control lately but now she was tested to the limit.

'I'll just check it,' said Raff calmly, unaware of her turmoil. 'In the meantime, why don't you get some things together?' And he set off to investigate.

She prayed he wouldn't hear the tears that constricted her throat. 'What sort of things?' She called out to him. She couldn't think straight. Was he suggesting she find electrical screwdrivers and fuse wire so they could mend a possibly broken immersion heater?

'Pyjamas, sponge bag, electric toothbrush. You're coming to stay with me. Something is definitely wrong with it. I'll take a proper look tomorrow. You can't stay here tonight,' he added as he rejoined her in the hallway.

Just for a second Rachel allowed herself to imagine what that meant. Warmth, hot water and, even more briefly, the bliss of being looked after. But the thought of it put her into a panic. It would be Raff looking after her.

Then she thought of the alternative: lying in her percale sheets (put on only that morning) in sweat and grime. 'No.' She didn't know if she was saying 'no' to his invitation or 'no' to the dreadfulness of her situation.

'Would you rather stay here?'

'No.' It came out as a squeak. She forced herself to sound calm and logical. 'But I've got friends I can stay with.' Then she remembered that Beth didn't have a spare room and Rachel didn't sleep on sofas. And Lindy? Well, it would be the sofa or the floor in her house.

'So? Which friend?'

Rachel took a moment. 'OK, I realise that neither of them can really put me up at no notice, but I could go to a hotel...' The conversations they'd had about where Beth's mother might stay came back to her and how there was nowhere local she'd be able to tolerate. Rachel's standards were possibly even higher. Anyway, how could she turn up anywhere so filthy and untidy?

'Sweetheart,' said Raff, gentle but firm. 'I know this is difficult for you, but I have a spare room, hot water, food. I promise that I won't do anything you don't want me to and in the morning I will help you sort out your immersion heater. Now, just be brave, and come with me. I will look after you.'

It was the endearment that finally undid her. She burst into tears. Raff took her into his arms and patted her back while she hiccuped and sobbed. When the worst was over she pulled away. She swallowed and sniffed hard. 'OK,' she said quietly. 'It's really very kind of you, but...' She paused. 'How did you know I had an electric toothbrush?'

He produced a tartan handkerchief. She took it and blew her nose.

'I know you,' he said, taking the handkerchief back when she'd used it. And he looked at her in a way that made Rachel feel both very cherished and very nervous.

Raff lived in a long, low house attached to his reclamation yard. She instantly longed to get out her loppers and hack back the plant that covered most of the front of the house, nearly pulling down the porch it scrambled over. She could tell the outside needed repainting – maybe the rendering needed replacing too. But it was charming. If you overlooked the clutter of the yard that encroached from its designated area to the front of the house. Like mother, like son, she thought.

He unlocked the front door and she followed him into the house. It was warm, she realised, and light.

There was a fairly narrow hallway with rooms going off each side but Raff led her to the back of the house to the kitchen. This was new and if you ignored the view of the yard it was a lovely space, she realised. And all the fittings were real quality. It was a surprise and, looking at him, she saw he'd known she was going to be surprised and was happy that she was impressed.

'Nice gaff you've got here,' she said.

'Glad you approve. Now, why don't you let me show you upstairs?'

There was a staircase at the end of the kitchen, and going by the shape of the building she guessed it wasn't the only one. 'This leads to my bedroom and bathroom,' said Raff as they reached the landing at the top. 'This is where you're going to sleep. I'll be up the other end in the guest accommodation.'

'That sounds very grand,' said Rachel approvingly.

'It's a dump actually, but fine for me. I'm going to find clean sheets.' He opened a cupboard and began pulling out bedlinen. 'Why don't you check out the bathroom? Through that door there.'

Rachel went in and looked in the mirror. She really wished she hadn't. Tears had made the general layer of dirt took even more filthy. Still, it was too late. Raff had seen her like this and to frantically wash now would just highlight her insecurities.

She distracted herself by admiring her surroundings. This too was newly done. It was a bit more modern than her own en-suite but also had good-quality fittings. It lacked the high-end toiletries she'd put in her bathroom but in among the more generic products she spotted a bottle of Penhaligan's Douro. Hmm, expensive, she thought. Was it a present from Belinda? Or, more likely, a girlfriend? Or did Raff buy it for himself?

Rachel went through to the bedroom where Raff was pulling off the duvet cover. 'Do you want to eat first or wash?' he asked.

She hesitated. She didn't want to eat while she felt so dirty but she didn't want to have to put clothes back on after her bath. 'I'm not sure...'

'It'll take me a little while to cook. Why don't you have a bath and then come down in your pyjamas.'

It sounded so tempting. 'I haven't got a dressing gown—'

'Borrow mine,' he said. 'Now, if you don't mind, get the other side of the bed and tuck in that sheet.'

It was odd making up the bed with him. That was a task one usually did with another woman or a partner, not someone like Raff. Quite how Raff could be defined she wasn't sure. He wasn't a partner or a boyfriend but nor was he a friend in the 'just a friend' category.

The bed made, she ran the bath while Raff disappeared downstairs. As she slid under the water Rachel wondered, not for the first time, if there was anything as luxurious as lowering your cold, dirty body into water that was exactly the right temperature – in other words, very slightly too hot.

She couldn't resist submerging her head so only her face remained above the water, even though she knew she was now committed to washing her hair. She stayed there until she began to overheat, relishing the thought that although of course she would clean the bath after her, she wouldn't have to go to quite the lengths she did normally. That involved polishing it after it was dry to make sure there was no trace of cleaner left in it. For Raff she would just make sure it was clean. He wouldn't have the equipment – the special bath cleanser, the soft cloths – that she used on her own bath.

Although she had brought make-up with her Rachel decided it would be just too weird to put it on after a bath. She added the tiniest flick of mascara so as not to feel naked and then put on Raff's dressing gown.

It felt as though she was wearing a warm, masculine hug. It was a dark green tartan and was made of some sort of very soft, thick wool. It smelt of him: part Penhaligon, part Raff. If it hadn't been so warm and luxurious she'd have rejected it, it was so unsettling. She almost changed her mind about getting dressed, but the thought of putting on underwear, jeans, jumpers, when she was so warm and relaxed was just too horrible. She'd have to put up with being unsettled to be so wonderfully warm. She pulled on her own cashmere bedsocks she'd had the forethought to pack and prepared to join Raff.

He was in the kitchen putting the lid back on a casserole. Rachel decided if she'd arrived two seconds earlier she'd have seen him tasting it with the same spoon he was stirring with. She also decided not to dwell on it.

'Hello!' she said.

He turned and smiled. 'Hey. Look at you. You look wonderful.' Then he frowned. 'Forget I said that. I promised myself I wouldn't say or do anything to make you feel uncomfortable. But I will just add: I always knew I wanted to see you a bit more rumpled.'

It was very hard to know how to take all this. 'I'm not rumpled, I'm clean.'

'And you smell delicious.'

'I smell of very expensive aftershave.'

He laughed. 'Mum gave me that. She said she was fed up with me smelling of creosote and old buildings.'

'I can see her point.'

'Here, have this.' He handed her a vast glass of red wine and put his hand on her shoulder to usher her out of the room into the hallway. 'Go and make yourself comfortable. I'll bring it through when it's ready. Supper on our knees in front of the fire.'

Obediently Rachel opened the door indicated and went in.

She stood on the threshold for a few seconds, taking it in. It was warm and fairly dimly lit. The source of the warmth was easy to see: a huge tree root was smouldering in the fire, which had obviously been going for some time. The dimness was because the room appeared to be lit only by candles.

She made her way to the sofa, which was close to the fire, and sat on it. It was covered in sheepskin throws and was very soft. She soon found herself drawing up her feet and settling back. She took a large sip of wine and looked around her.

After a few seconds she realised Raff was a man who took his work home with him. Everything she could see seemed to have come from his reclamation yard, but nothing seemed perfect. The huge fireplace – beautiful pale stone – was cracked and had been repaired with something that didn't conceal the damage. The fire surround was tiled – Rachel recognised them as William de Morgan – but the tiles were all stuck together like crazy paving. Next to it was a bookcase that was made up of at least three different bits. Neither end matched the other and the shelves seemed to come from somewhere else.

She put down her glass on a table supported by a cherub more at home attached to a church and got up so she could look at everything more closely. It was like finding a book she was longing to read. She wanted to inspect it all.

She heard the door begin to open and fled back to the sofa and picked up her wine so he wouldn't know she'd been so nosy. As she assumed a position of complete relaxation she realised that absolutely nothing in the room was perfect, matched or themed. She should have found it an absolutely nightmare and yet somehow it was homogenous and worked in the way a patchwork quilt worked.

'I hope you're hungry,' he said, putting down a tray on the cherub table.

Rachel discovered that she was. 'Starving. That stew smells delicious.'

'I hope it is. Mum gave me a recipe. It's been in the oven all day. I realised I was good at cooking quick pastas and things but had missed out on the basics. Now I've got a range cooker I can let things cook long and slow.'

The thought that maybe there were other things he did long and slow shot through Rachel's mind like a dart. Fortunately he wasn't a mind-reader and need never know.

He handed her a newspaper. 'Put that on your lap. It's quite hot.' When the newspaper was in place he handed her the bowl and a spoon. 'Dig in. I'll get the bread.'

As the sofa was quite large and they had to share the table for their wine glasses and bread, Rachel didn't mind too much having Raff sitting next to her.

Part of her wished that her ex-husband could see her now, so relaxed in spite of so much being wrong. She wondered now if her desperate need for order and tidiness came from her desire to make her wrong marriage be right. Her ex wasn't a bad man but he wasn't right for her. She couldn't make him a better emotional fit so she altered everything she could alter.

Raff had put on some classical music. It wasn't loud enough to prevent conversation and it added to the atmosphere.

'More stew?' said Raff.

'No thank you, but it was delicious. Did you make the bread?'

He was pleased. 'Yes I did! Mum always used to make hers but she's stopped lately, saying she didn't eat enough to make it worthwhile. So I make it now and give her a loaf. I enjoy it.'

She sipped her wine. 'And you think she's really happy to do the food for Helena – Beth's sister's – wedding?'

'Oh yes. She'll love it. Not too often but now and again she loves to cater for a do. Cheese?'

'Um – I'd better not...'

'Oh, go on. Then we can have more wine.'

Rachel smiled. 'All right then.' She was happy here, curled up on the sheepskins, looking at the fire, among Raff's eclectic furnishings; she didn't want to go to bed just yet.

He came back with a couple of cheeses on a plate and a packet of water biscuits and knives. 'Do you mind sharing a plate? I've run out,' he said, handing Rachel a knife.

'Ooh, I think I know someone who can help with that.' Rachel couldn't help wondering which lot of plates she'd want him to have.

He laughed. 'I meant I've run out of clean plates. I haven't washed up for a couple of days.'

'I'll do it for you tomorrow,' said Rachel before she could stop herself.

He shook his head. 'I suppose I should be impressed that you're not running off to do it now.'

Rachel was quite surprised herself. 'I'm not that obsessive, you know.' Then she wondered why she cared what he thought. And not for the first time. She decided to change the subject. 'I asked Belinda why she wanted to sort her house out and she told me about making a flat in the house and letting the rest. Does she have a firm plan, do you know?'

'I think she has but she hasn't told me directly. I have my suspicions though.'

'What?' He looked at her speculatively and Rachel wondered if she'd said the wrong thing. 'Don't tell me if you don't want to. I don't want to pry.'

'You're not prying. I think she would like me to move into the house.'

'Really? But you've got this place. And you've obviously worked so hard on it.'

He accepted this compliment with a nod and a grin. 'I have, but I think she would think I could sell it and spend the money getting her house in order.'

'I think that's outrageous,' said Rachel. 'Quite unreasonable. Why should you put all your capital into a house you don't want to live it?'

'But maybe I do want to live in it, with the right person.'

Rachel didn't know where to look. 'Oh, well, it is a lovely house. I just thought – well – I would have thought your independence was important to you.'

'It is and moving into part of my mother's house wouldn't affect that, I assure you.'

Still embarrassed and not sure why, Rachel said, 'I'm turning my house into a B and B – only occasionally – so we can put up important people we're doing weddings for.'

'Oh? Will you like that?'

Rachel nodded. 'In a way I will. I love the details and it would be a challenge.' She smiled. 'Probably very good for me to have strange people in my house from time to time. It'll make me a better person.'

'I think you're just fine as you are.'

Rachel gave him a quick look and then turned her eyes away. His expression was extremely unsettling. 'Some people consider I'm a bit anal.'

Now he laughed properly, throwing his head back revealing his Adam's apple, something Rachel found rather attractive.

'You are anal,' he said, 'but also very brave.'

Rachel realised she was blushing. 'So far it's only Beth's mother I'm having.'

'Still brave. More wine?'

He filled her glass and she didn't protest.

'Tell me,' she said, wanting to divert attention away from her. 'How did you become the owner of a reclamation yard? I gather it's not because of any previously unrevealed anal tendencies.'

'Are you saying my house is untidy?'

'Not at all, but no one with OCD would have a house like this. Nothing matches, nothing is in sets; it's a nightmare.'

A flicker of what could have been concern crossed his features. 'I thought you liked my house? You said nice things about it earlier.'

'That's the surprising thing. I love it. It works. But it's not something I could ever have created myself.'

He laughed. 'Well, that's a relief.'

She looked questioningly at him. 'Why?'

'I wouldn't want to think you were uncomfortable, that's all.' His smile was noncommittal.

'So – to get back to my question. The reclamation yard?'

'It used to belong to my uncle, Mum's brother. I worked here in the holidays, had a talent for it – but more importantly I hated things to be wasted, especially beautiful things. '

'And all the things you have here...' She made a gesture, nearly spilling her wine.

'They're the leftovers. The things no one would buy.'

Holding her glass in both hands, she looked at him over the top of it. 'So, what's your favourite thing in this room?'

'Are you fishing for compliments?'

'No!' said Rachel hotly, although she knew deep down she hadn't been entirely disingenuous. 'I wasn't asking about animate objects. I was talking about things you've collected, chosen to put in here.' And you know it, she added silently.

He put his head on one side as if he didn't believe her. 'Well, if you push me, I think it's the cherub table.'

'Why?'

'I think because it's a very innocent thing but is a little bit smudged around the edges.'

'Oh?'

'Yes. There's something very seductive about smudged innocence.'

Just over an hour later Rachel was in bed. She couldn't believe he had made absolutely no attempt to even kiss her! What was wrong with him? More importantly, what was wrong with her? She'd been sitting on the sofa next to him all evening, practically naked if you overlooked knickers, pyjamas, dressing gown and bedsocks, and he hadn't made any sort of move on her.

Her indignation – and possibly the wine – made her chuckle. He had said he wouldn't do anything to make her feel uncomfortable but really, it was possible to take the whole 'gentlemanly restraint' a bit too far!

Chapter Nineteen

A couple of days after Rachel had been to Belinda's to sort out china, Beth had asked if they could have a Vintage Weddings meeting. Her mother had been on the phone wanting to discuss catering arrangements. Rachel had said the matter was in hand but couldn't come to a meeting until now, as she had paid work she had to catch up with.

Now Beth unlocked the doors to the pub for lunch-time opening. As planned, Rachel, Lindy and little Billy came in.

'Who'd have thought nice girls like you would be so desperate for a drink?' said Sukey from behind the bar.

'Do you mind me bringing Billy?' said Lindy. 'I couldn't get childcare.'

'No problem,' said Sukey. 'He's the customer of the future. There's a box of toys in that corner, Billy, why don't you have a rummage?'

While Billy sorted through the box to find a really good car, Sukey went on, 'Besides, there's no one else in currently, until the Probus Club get here for lunch. You can have your meeting.'

'Who are the Probus Club?' asked Beth. 'Or shouldn't I ask?'

'They're a club for retired businessmen,' said Sukey. 'They have lunch here once a month.'

'Oh, OK,' said Beth.

'Are you sure you don't mind Beth chatting to us for a minute? That's really kind,' said Rachel. 'We shouldn't be long.'

'Rachel,' said Sukey, ignoring her gratitude. 'Did I see Raff drop you off at your house the other morning?'

Rachel looked as if she was considering denying this but instead she just said, 'Yes. My immersion heater broke down. I had to stay the night with him.'

Beth and Lindy gasped. Not that they were shocked but they were a little surprised.

Sukey went on: 'So you and Raff...?'

Beth and Lindy looked expectantly at Rachel. Beth wondered how, in Rachel's mind, Raff had turned from the Demon King into someone you stayed with if you unexpectedly needed a bed for the night.

'Just friends,' said Rachel firmly. 'What does everyone want to drink?'

'Can I get you a truth drug, Rachel?' said Beth.

Rachel sighed. 'I'll tell you everything you want to know if you just give me a sparkling water with ice and lemon. The drinks are on me or, even better, on Vintage Weddings. This is a meeting and the firm should pay. As long as not you're not after double single malts.'

When Beth had organised drinks, including an orange juice for Billy, Sukey sent them all to sit down.

'There's nobody but you here now,' she said. 'I can

keep an eye on the pies in the oven for the pre-ordered lunch, so you get on with your meeting.'

Beth protested a little before promising to work an extra hour washing up after the lunch, and then they carried their drinks to a table.

'Why don't one of you light the fire,' suggested Sukey, 'and go and huddle round it for your meeting? It's freezing in here.'

'I'll do it,' said Rachel enthusiastically.

'Really?' said Lindy.

Beth wondered if Rachel thought being occupied with the fire would mean she could get out of telling them what had gone on with Raff. She felt a pang of envy. She was getting over Charlie, slowly, but she hadn't got used to not having a man to think about and feel she belonged to.

'It's one of my recently acquired skills,' Rachel said proudly and went to investigate the kindling box.

Whatever had happened with Raff, thought Beth, it hadn't left her a sobbing wreck, which was good.

While Rachel was kneeling in front of the fire, breaking up sticks and rolling up newspaper, Lindy said, 'So, tell us about you and Raff. And would you have told us if Sukey hadn't dobbed you in, so to speak?'

'I would have told you!' said Rachel, as if not telling them had never crossed her mind.

'I don't want a love life myself,' said Lindy. 'Too complicated with the boys and all, but I always want to know about other people's.' She pushed the thought of Angus firmly out of her mind.

'We should stick to business,' said Beth, feeling guilty. She'd called a meeting in work time and now they were just discussing Rachel's love life. Although she was desperate to know the details. 'I am supposed to be working.' She sent Sukey an apologetic glance.

'It's OK,' said Sukey. 'I want to hear too. I know Belinda is really keen for Raff to settle down and have children.' She paused as the other three all gaped at her. 'What? Why are you all looking so surprised? I'm a pub landlady. Of course I know everything!'

'But you don't know why Rachel stayed with Raff when she could perfectly easily have stayed with me, or Beth.'

'Not perfectly easily,' said Beth. 'My house is not set up for overnight guests, and nor is yours, to be fair.'

'And I will know everything in a minute,' said Sukey. Then she went into the kitchen, to check on the pies.

'So?' said Beth, when they were all settled. 'Tell us about the catering first. Then we need to know about Raff.'

'It's Belinda, Raff's mum. She does catering and according to Raff, she's really good.'

'Brilliant!' said Beth. 'I'll be able to tell Mum it's arranged.' A thought struck her. 'Hell. Mum's due to come tomorrow, isn't she? Will you have hot water?'

Rachel nodded. 'Yes, Raff sorted out a new immersion heater for me. Fitted and everything.'

'Brilliant! I'd hate to have to find her somewhere else to stay at this short notice!' Beth relaxed a little.

'OK,' said Rachel. 'Going back to Belinda and the catering, we might hire space in a commercial kitchen for her but I haven't discussed it in detail. We need to know what Helena wants.'

'I'll find out,' said Beth.

'Did you discover that Belinda did catering when you were sorting out her china?' asked Lindy. 'And how did that go?'

'Amazing! She's got so much stuff. We'll take what we need – she insists – and then sell anything she doesn't want in aid of the village-hall fund. Should raise a goodish amount.'

'Oh, excellent,' said Lindy. 'Well done you.'

'There's quite a bit more sorting to do though,' said Rachel.

'I'll help when I'm not tutoring the village elders to be silver surfers,' said Beth. 'But some of them are taking a while to get the hang of it.'

'It's nice that you're doing that,' said Lindy. 'Gran was very impressed when I told her what you were up to. She's a fairly nimble silver surfer herself,' she went on proudly. 'She's always shopping online and emailing her friends.'

'That's great,' said Rachel. 'Now, when are we going to know what kind of food Helena wants? Belinda will need lots of notice.'

'Rachel!' said Lindy. 'You have to tell us about you and Raff.'

Rachel sighed. Beth sensed that she did quite want to talk about it, in spite of appearing reluctant. 'Well, I spent all day sorting china. There's so much of it—'

'Can you cut to the chase, please?' said Sukey, who had rejoined them. 'My pies only need another ten minutes.'

'Oh, OK,' said Rachel. 'Basically, Belinda insisted Raff saw me safely home and it turned out that my immersion

270

heater had broken – as you know – so I had no hot water.'

'Immersion heaters are always going,' said Lindy, obviously speaking from experience.

'And I'm afraid I didn't deal with it well. I'd like to report that I got out my magic screwdriver and fixed it. Instead I had a bit of a meltdown. I was so tired! And absolutely filthy. The thought of not being able to have a bath... anyway, I got a bit tearful.'

'Don't blame you,' said Beth.

'So he took me back to his place,' said Rachel. 'Which is amazing.'

Lindy frowned. 'What? That he took you home? I don't want to shatter your illusions or anything but I think he fairly often takes women home.'

'I meant his house is amazing,' said Rachel. 'I'm sure you're right about the women.' She took a sip of water. 'Anyway, I had a lovely bath, he gave me supper, we sat on the sofa by the fireside and he did not lay a finger on me!'

'But I thought you didn't like him,' said Beth.

'So did I,' said Rachel, 'but I changed my mind. Obviously I wasn't looking my best, my hair all wild and no make-up, yet he seemed to quite like that look. But he didn't even kiss me goodnight. I was outraged.'

Sukey chuckled knowingly. 'He's not stupid, that Raff. He knows how to gentle a nervous woman into wanting him.'

'Hm, I'm not sure I feel gentled, but he is very...'

'Attractive?' suggested Lindy.

Rachel nodded. 'And he's good at fixing things.'

Lindy sighed. 'I love a man who does DIY. It's why I love my dad.'

'I love Grandpa too,' said Billy, who had joined them without anyone noticing.

'Quite right, Billy,' said Rachel. 'Anyway, that's enough about my private life. I'm more excited about finding a caterer.'

'Belinda is ace,' said Sukey. 'She doesn't do many events and only for people she likes but she can certainly cook.'

'Sounds perfect!' said Beth. 'And doesn't she live in a stately home? My mother will love her!'

'We all love her,' said Rachel. 'Especially giving away all that lovely china. Beth? Are you OK to put a few things up on eBay? Most of the stuff is in my shed.'

'I'll come and take photos as soon as I can,' said Beth. 'This is exciting. The only thing more exciting than buying stuff on eBay is selling it. Even if we're not getting the money ourselves.'

'That's brilliant,' said Lindy. 'Mum'll be thrilled.'

'And so generous,' said Beth, 'unless it's all rubbish.'

'No, it's amazing,' said Rachel. 'It should raise some proper money.'

'As should the quiz,' said Lindy. 'I do hope you both come. I can't get out of it and I'm hopeless at quizzes.'

'I quite like them,' said Rachel, 'but as I said before, I'm not good at sport.'

'We don't have to win,' said Lindy, 'we just have to pitch up.'

'I'll come if I'm not working,' said Beth. 'Talking of which – is that the meeting over then? If it is, I should get back to it.'

'Quickest meeting on record,' said Rachel, 'but I declare it over.'

After Rachel and Lindy and Billy had left, Beth washed their glasses and straightened the bar towels. She was thinking about Rachel and Raff. It seemed fairly obvious that they would get together and while she was very happy for Rachel, she yearned for something like that for herself.

It was obvious now that Charlie had been hopeless. And she'd stopped wondering whether he'd have stayed faithful to her if she'd slept with him. Why would he? He had no morals, otherwise he'd have thought, when the Amazon came on to him, 'Hey, I have a girlfriend, and she's here, right now, I'll say no.' But no, he'd said, 'Yes,' and maybe, 'Here's a cupboard.' She sighed. It was one thing to sort it all out in your head but it didn't stop you wishing things were different.

'Are you OK, hon?' said Sukey. 'You don't seem quite your normal cheery self.'

'Oh, it's nothing,' said Beth from habit and then realised that Sukey would get it out of her anyway and it might help to talk. 'Well, it's Charlie, actually.'

'Oh, him.'

'I thought ... you know ... I thought we were getting on well together but at the wedding he went off with the bridesmaid. The fat one, who bullied April when they were at school.' Beth realised saying all this out loud sounded quite funny and made her smile. 'He's been texting me non-stop but I just delete them.'

'Good girl! You can do so much better,' said Sukey. 'Trust me!'

Sukey had gone back to producing pie and mash

for the retired businessmen and Beth was rearranging the glasses in the dishwasher when the door opened. Looking up, she saw a male figure wearing a cap, a scarf round his neck and his collar turned up. It was quite a lot of clothes for the mildness of the day.

'It must be cold out there!' she said cheerily as he approached the bar. Then she realised she'd seen him before but couldn't quite place where.

'Hello, there,' he said. 'Could I have a pint of porter, please.'

Beth frowned. 'Sorry?'

'I mean stout. I'm sorry.' He frowned. 'Haven't I seen you – aren't you the girl I met running out of the hall the other night?'

Beth had realised who he was at about the same time. She put a glass under the appropriate beer tap. 'That's me.'

'Well, it's nice to see you again.'

She couldn't help agreeing although she didn't say anything. Something about him had piqued her interest even when she'd been so upset about Charlie that night. She took a sneaky glance at him. Without being able to see much of his face she couldn't really tell how old he was but she'd have guessed early thirties. And she couldn't tell if he was good-looking or not either, but he did have a nice voice.

'Do they have bands in here? To do gigs?' he went on.

'They do. Do you want to arrange something? I'll ask Sukey, she's the landlady.'

'Well, no need to do that right now.' He smiled and took off his scarf and cap. Now Beth could see he had a lovely smile.

'When we met before you were going to check out the hall. Was it any good? As a venue?' Then she worried that she'd remembered too much detail about their very casual encounter.

'It was fine but I'm not sure I'd want to do a first gig there. It's a bit too big, I think.'

'Acoustically?'

'I'm not sure about the accoustics – the wedding was quite noisy when I poked my nose in. I'd have to check them out but I was thinking – a new band – we might not get a big enough audience to fill that space. We are a bit out of the way here.'

Beth smiled. 'Not exactly the centre of the music universe. How did you find us out here in the sticks?'

'A mate of mine was passing through on his way somewhere, stopped at the pub, saw the hall, suggested I check it out.'

'Well, I'm sure if you did want to use the hall, we could get you an audience,' said Beth. 'We're trying to raise funds to repair the roof – well, repair everything really – so we'd love to rent it out. We'd help drum up the punters for you.'

He laughed. 'It sounds very appealing but I think I'd rather have our first try-out somewhere the punters are already.'

'What sort of music is it?'

He put his head on one side as if searching for a way to describe it. 'That's quite hard to say.'

'Well, I don't suppose it matters as long as it's not horrible,' said Beth.

'I promise you it's not horrible.'

'If you did a gig here, we'd all find out what it was like. I'll go and see if Sukey is free, so you can talk to her about it.'

'Thanks.'

As Beth went into the kitchen she wondered if an attractive speaking voice automatically translated into a good singing voice.

Having promised to keep an eye on the pies for Sukey, Beth hovered in the kitchen, washing up and occasionally peering into the oven, hoping that Sukey would persuade the man to do a gig at the pub. He was rather nice!

When she thought the pies really ought to come out of the oven or be turned off, she went back to the bar to tell Sukey.

Sukey was leaning on the bar looking entranced.

'I think the pies are done. Do you want me to do anything else?'

Sukey nodded, not taking her eyes off the man who had been talking to her in a low, soft voice. 'Yes, please. I can see them out of the corner of my eye, in the car park. They'll be on us in a minute.' But these words weren't accompanied by action.

'So, will you do their drinks when they come in? Shall I plate up the pie and mash?' But Sukey wasn't really paying attention.

An elderly man came into the pub and Beth gave Sukey's arm a shake. 'The Probus Club? They're here! We need to feed them.'

'Oh yes, of course.' At last Sukey came out of her trance. 'Let's do it.'

Once in the kitchen, Sukey said, 'Do you know who that is?'

'Should I?' Beth realised she'd missed something crucial.

'It's Finn! From the McCools!'

Beth was none the wiser. 'Do I know them?'

'Yes! They were mega. You must remember.' Sukey was insistent.

'Oh yes . . .' said Beth slowly. 'They were an Irish boy band?'

'That's right. Seven major hits and then they broke up and all disappeared. And this is Finn. He was gorgeous then but now – he's even better ten years later! It's so unfair that men just get better and better with age.'

Beth waited a few seconds for Sukey to get over this dreadful injustice and then said, 'He's got a new band and he wants to do a gig here.'

'I know! How amazing would that be!' Then she looked out of the window. 'Oh God, here come the rest of them! Let's get them fed.'

The next few minutes were too busy for Sukey to chat but Beth was aware she was on fire with excitement. When at last there was a moment, she said, 'So he can have his gig here, then?'

'He could have a pyjama party here and I'd say yes! Now get him another pint. Keep him here a bit longer so I can gaze at him. Golly!' She patted her brow. 'Now, hurry up!'

Not sure if she was now shy of approaching someone who had once been a celebrity or amused at seeing Sukey so obviously star-struck, Beth went back into the bar.

'Um, would you like another drink? It's on the house,' said Beth to the man she now knew as Finn, ex-member of a boy band. She assumed his surname wasn't actually McCool, like the Irish giant.

'Yes, please.'

Beth placed a glass under the relevant pump. 'And I'm sorry I didn't recognise you.'

He chuckled. 'You were just a child when I was first on the scene. No apology needed.'

Beth laughed. 'It's probably only me who hasn't heard of you. When were you – you know...'

'Famous?' He laughed again.

'No!' Beth was embarrassed. 'When you were at the height of your powers!'

He was really laughing now. 'Which power would that be, now?'

Beth wanted to say 'being really gorgeous' but now she could see he wasn't bald and had deep brown eyes with lashes as long as a cow's, he obviously was still gorgeous. She felt a mixture of excitement because she was talking to him and he was looking at her in a way that told her he was pleased with what he saw, and anxiety in case he was just another Charlie. And, she realised, as an ex-pop star he probably was worse than Charlie. He'd have a girl in every town he played in. 'I meant when were you top of the charts.' She paused. 'It's all right. I'll google you when I get home.'

'Can I google you? Otherwise I'll just have to ask a lot of questions. Starting with your name.'

'It's Beth. And are you flirting with the barmaid?' said Beth, brave because there was a bar between her and him.

'Not at all. I wouldn't flirt with you.'

She handed him the drink that had finally settled. What did he mean? That she wasn't pretty enough to flirt with?

'Should I be offended?'

'Not at all. Flirting is something you do with people you don't care much about. I'd like to get to know you properly.'

Beth gulped. She lifted the flap and went out to do her job. She was trying very hard not to feel flattered. He was a flatterer, like Charlie had been, and although he was definitely far better looking than Charlie, he was unlikely to be better behaved.

She came back with a loaded tray and felt pleased that he was still there. He was lovely to chat with because she wasn't expecting anything more than just a chat. He must have experienced his fair share of groupies. He needed to know she was not one of those.

The thought of this made her smile and although he didn't know why she was smiling he smiled back. He was certainly cheering up the lunchtime service.

Sukey, who'd emerged from the kitchen, was now chatting away about bands and music with Finn and another couple of locals who had come in. The conversation was getting animated. Beth could tell that Sukey would put her considerable PR talents into getting as many people to his gig as possible. Between her and Sukey, Finn and his new band would get a good audience.

She was back behind the bar, stacking the dishwasher, when she heard the pub door open. She turned at the sound automatically and couldn't believe her eyes. It was her mother.

Beth couldn't speak for two reasons. Firstly she wasn't due until tomorrow and she'd have to ring Rachel as soon as possible to warn her, and secondly it felt so wrong seeing her mother in these surroundings she had to check it was indeed her. Pubs were not Vivien Scott's milieu and she looked around suspiciously. Then she spotted her daughter and strode forward. Beth trusted her power of speech would return before she reached the bar.

'Beth! My God! I'd heard you'd cut your hair. But what a shock. You look ghastly. And you're working in a pub! No wonder you haven't got a boyfriend!'

Beth found she was smiling and in spite of everything she realised that she'd missed her mother, even her supreme tactlessness. 'Hey, Mum. Lovely to see you too. I wasn't expecting you until tomorrow.'

Mrs Scott leant over the bar and kissed Beth's cheek. 'Sorry, darling. That may have sounded a bit unkind, but I can't pretend I think your hair looks nice when it doesn't.'

'Lots of other people like it,' said Beth. 'Including me.' She paused. 'Can I get you a drink?'

Her mother frowned questioningly.

'I'm a barmaid, as you know,' said Beth. 'It's my job to sell drinks.' She knew perfectly well that Sukey wouldn't mind if she just chatted to her mother for a bit but she wanted to make it clear that she was independent and there was no shame in honest toil even if it did involve pulling pints.

Her mother squinted at the row of beer pumps. 'Um...'

'Have a gin and tonic,' suggested her daughter. 'With plenty of ice and lemon, like you have it at home. I'll make it a double.'

'I don't usually drink before six o'clock,' her mother objected. 'Unless I'm out to lunch, of course.'

'It is lunchtime. And you don't usually land on your long-lost daughter in a pub!' Beth would certainly have had a drink herself, had she not been on duty.

Beth felt her mother's eyes upon her as she prepared her drink. As always, she felt judged. She saw her mother eyeing up a bar stool suspiciously. Then she became aware of Finn, also watching.

Before Beth had worked out how best to help, he had jumped off his stool and taken hold of Beth's mother's elbow. 'Here, let me help you up. They're not designed for people with skirts, really.' Once he'd settled her securely on to a stool, he said, 'Hey, Beth. You didn't tell me you had a beautiful mother!'

Beth put down the gin and tonic. They'd barely chatted long enough to exchange their names let alone discuss their parents. He was doing this to help her out and she was grateful. Her mother sat up a bit straighter. 'So, who are you?' She addressed Finn with flirtatious sternness.

'I'm the man – one of them – who thinks Beth's hair is just great. It brings out her beautiful eyes, you see. Which I see she gets from you.'

Beth bit her lip to hide her chuckle. My goodness, he was good. Talk about Irish charm. Some may have kissed the Blarney Stone but Beth felt certain Finn had gone much further than that.

'You still haven't told me your name.' Beth's mother

was falling for the charm like a pet lamb at a farm park, eating out of his hand.

'I'm Finn.'

'And you and my daughter are...' she waved a hand towards Beth, '... an item?' She said the word as if it were foreign and should have had inverted commas around it. 'She never tells me anything, you see.'

Beth wanted to die. This was so embarrassing. Obviously her mother didn't know that Finn was some kind of rock god and had been a superstar but still... Yet she knew if she made an excuse to leave it would look worse.

'Ah, I wish!' said Finn. 'It's a bit early for that but let's just say I'm working on it.'

Beth wanted to kiss him. Not because he was so attractive but because he was so kind. He was going out of his way to stick up for her, having heard her riposte over her hair, to make her look good in front of her over-critical mother. What a nice man.

She smiled at him with gratitude. His returning smile reminded Beth that he'd been one of the hottest pop stars of his day and also why Sukey thought he had improved with age. Probably just as well she'd had a very recent injection of reality and wasn't going to take his flirting seriously, even if he had declared he wouldn't flirt with her.

'Well,' said Mrs Scott. 'At least things aren't quite as bad as I thought. My youngest fled the nest far too young and I really hated the thought of her being lonely.' Beth could have added 'and out of my control' but didn't.

'So, Mum!' said Beth when she'd judged her mother

had drunk enough of her gin and tonic to mellow her a little. 'What are you doing here a day early?'

'I'd have thought that was blatantly obvious! I've come to organise Helena's wedding! Starting by booking the church.'

'I'll need a place to stay tonight,' said Vivien Scott after she'd had another gin and tonic and had bought Finn a drink. 'Where are you staying?' she asked him.

Beth fervently hoped he was staying in a boutique hotel that wasn't too near but would provide her mother with all the comfort she demanded. Then she could send her off there and Rachel could relax.

'I'm staying with a friend a little way away,' said Finn.

Beth's mother turned her attention back to her daughter. 'It looks like I'll have to stay in this bed and breakfast you've booked me into.'

Chapter Twenty

❧

Lindy had delivered Billy to her grandmother's house and then gone back to Rachel's to look at the china that was now filling her shed. Thus she was with Rachel when Beth called and listened to the conversation from her end. Rachel was gulping and saying, 'OK,' rather a lot, she felt.

'What!' she said as soon as Rachel took her phone away from her ear.

Rachel licked her lips. 'Beth's mother is here. A day early. She's in the pub. She needs to stay here tonight.'

'Oh my God, Rachel!'

'Yes! I was absolutely relying on having the entire day to get her room ready before she arrived tomorrow night.'

'And of course I'll help.'

'Thank you, Lindy.' Rachel clutched on to her arm for a second, as if for support. 'Beth has tried to get her to stay in a hotel, somewhere like Bath, which has the sort of hotels she likes, but she doesn't see why she can't just rock up a day early.'

'You don't have to have her early. Beth would completely understand.'

Rachel, who seemed a little flushed, said, 'It's OK. I said I'd do it. It's a challenge, but one I can rise to.'

'But don't use your bedroom. Put her in the spare room, otherwise it's just too much upheaval.'

'No. I'd rather keep her contained.'

Lindy felt she could see the cogs of Rachel's brain turning, possibly selecting bedlinen in her head. She looked at her watch. 'What would you like me to do? Although I've only got half an hour.'

'I'll need about an hour and a half to make it all perfect,' said Rachel. 'If you could go to Beth and make sure she keeps her mother away for that long that would be great. And then maybe source some supplies?'

'You mean, go shopping?' Lindy couldn't help smiling. 'Of course. What do you need?'

'Croissants, freshly squeezed orange juice, good butter, local if possible, ditto bacon, sausages and eggs...' She paused. 'Do you think Beth's mother likes black pudding?'

'She definitely doesn't,' said Lindy instantly and they both laughed, aware she'd said this without having a clue as to Beth's mother's culinary preferences but instinct told them both she didn't. 'I can track down the other things but not black pudding. However' – she felt a moment of smugness – 'I could source a loaf of my grandmother's amazing wholemeal bread.'

'Brilliant! Croissants are so mega fattening Beth's mother won't eat them but I do have to provide them,

I think. How about jam and marmalade? Your grand-mother doesn't make them, does she?'

'She certainly does! And if she doesn't, she'll certainly provide a jam jar with a hand-written label on it that we could put shop marmalade into.'

Rachel shook her head. 'Lindy! I won't put the actual jar on the table. It'll go in my special jam dishes. Along with butter in curls – none of those nasty little packets – or would pats be better? Or balls?'

'Sweetie, I'm going shopping. You have a lot of things to do before you need to be worrying about what shape to mould the butter into.'

Lindy rang her grandmother to check that Billy hadn't exhausted her and could she have him a bit longer, and then asked very nicely if she could possibly pick up Ned from school and explained why. 'Obviously we'll pay you for the jam and marmalade and bread. You can charge top-end prices. I'll find out what those are.'

Her grandmother, mildly flattered to think her simple home-made offerings were going to contribute to a very exclusive bed and breakfast agreed to look out her pret-tiest preserves and to add a layer of seeds to the top of a loaf she'd baked that morning. And also pick up her grandson from school.

That evening, Lindy was just about to get the boys into the bath when her phone went. She thought about not answering it but instead ran down to get it. It might be Rachel having a crisis with Beth's mother. She couldn't abandon her.

It was Angus.

'Oh, Angus.' Lindy was surprised. And quite pleased – but terribly shy at the same time. She'd spent more time than was sensible thinking about him. Now it felt as though that's what had made him ring.

'Is that Uncle Angus?' said Ned. 'Can I speak to him? Please?'

The 'please' was accompanied by Ned snatching the phone and running out of the bathroom with it. As Billy had just climbed into the bath Lindy couldn't run after him and snatch it back. If she scooped up Billy now he'd scream the house down.

'Ned!' she yelled. 'Bring back my phone this instant!'

There was no response. She could hear Ned talking on the phone but not what he was saying. She felt completely helpless. If she shouted again Angus might hear and she'd sound like the very worst kind of parent. If she picked up Billy, ditto, and if she left Billy to grab the phone he might slip and drown while she was wrestling with Ned. She picked up a beaker of water and poured it over Billy's back. It was soothing for him and she hoped it would be soothing for her too.

Ned came back into the bathroom. 'Here you are.'

'Angus?' said Lindy into the phone.

'He's not there,' said Ned. 'He's coming round.'

'When is he coming round?' she asked.

'Tonight,' said Ned. 'He said if I gave the phone back to you he'd read us a story. Five stories, actually.'

Lindy didn't speak. She just got the children washed and out of the bath as quickly as possible. If the doorbell rang while they were still in it, she wouldn't be able to answer. She wielded the toothbrush, ignoring protests from Ned that she was using toothpaste that was for three-year-olds.

'Just open wide,' she said.

'Can't I do it? You always let me do it!'

'Not tonight. We're going extra specially fast tonight. If Angus is going to read you stories, he wants you to have clean teeth.'

'He's bringing toys,' said Ned, while Billy's teeth were being done.

'Goodness me. You are lucky boys,' said Lindy, wondering if Ned had actually got the message correctly. It all seemed to be going very fast, this uncle thing. Angus had played with them very patiently at her parents' house but now, to come round at bedtime with toys and promises to read bedtime stories – it was very unexpected.

Once the boys were clean, dry and in their pyjamas, sitting in front of the television for a bit of unscheduled viewing, Lindy tried to ring Angus back, to find out what, if anything, was going on. She really hoped he was coming round. The boys would be bitterly disappointed if he didn't. And she'd had enough of their father not turning up on time and having to make up stories about late planes and missed trains. She really hoped Angus was different. And not, she admitted, just for the boys' sake.

Fortunately, just as she was trying to find his number on her phone – quite what Ned had done to it before he handed it back she didn't know – there was a knock on the door. It was only after she'd got it open she realised she was probably smiling a touch too widely. It was only a casual visit, after all, not someone telling her she'd won a million pounds.

His returning smile was enthusiastic too, but also a bit surprised.

Lindy tried to explain. 'Oh hi! I'm just so pleased to see you because the boys were all excited and I thought Ned might have got it wrong and you were coming another day or not at all...' She trailed off.

'Can I come in?' he asked.

The way he looked down at her as he said this made Lindy's stomach clench. Instantly she was a schoolgirl again, with a hopeless crush on someone's older brother.

'Do – go through to the sitting room. The boys are there. Shall I put the kettle on?' She was still gabbling, she realised, and took a breath, willing herself to calm down.

Angus put down the old rucksack he had with him and went through to where the boys were sitting on the sofa, television ignored, looking up at him, already a favourite uncle.

'Uncle Angus!' they shouted and rushed to him.

'Hi guys,' he said calmly. 'Are we going to have stories, or what?'

'Stories!' they yelled.

'Then let's all calm down then.' He took his seat in between them on the sofa. Then he looked at Lindy. 'Do we have stories down here, or should we go upstairs, Lindy?'

Lindy had re-established herself as a sensible young mother. 'Two stories down here and then two when they're tucked up in bed,' she said.

She tidied up the kitchen while they were downstairs, overhearing him read to the boys. But when the two stories were over and he was marching them upstairs, she followed.

'Come on, boys, into bed now.' She switched on the night lights, drew the curtains, arranged the teddies. Then, to her enormous relief, the boys got in as calmly and obediently as if they advertising some child-centred product.

'OK, which book?' said Angus.

She handed him the current favourite and perched on the end of Billy's bed. Angus sat in the middle of the bed so both boys could see the pictures. He read to them in a calm, soporific voice. While he did this she thanked the Goddess of Mothers for making her often obstreperous children seem perfectly brought up, just for these few minutes. Then she added a prayer that this would continue. When the story was finished, she kissed both boys and tucked them in.

'We're going downstairs to have a cup of tea but I'll pop back up in a minute. There'll be a prize for the first boy to be asleep!'

'What's the prize! What's the prize!' said Ned.

'Something special from my bag,' said Angus.

'But what is it?' persisted Ned.

'If you go to sleep very quickly, you'll find out!' said Angus. 'And if you're both asleep, there'll be prizes for everyone.' He looked at his watch. 'Can you be asleep in ten minutes?'

'Yes!' said Ned, who lay flat and screwed his eyes shut.

'And you, Billy,' said Lindy. 'You can be asleep in ten minutes too!'

Then Angus and Lindy left the room.

Lindy didn't speak until they were downstairs. 'Well, that was the best bedtime ever! It's not usually that easy, I assure you!' She knew she could have pretended everything was always so calm but that would have felt like lying.

'I think it helps having someone they want to impress, their Uncle Angus in this case.'

She laughed. 'Yes, I think that helped a lot. Thank you so much for reading to them.'

'I loved it. It probably would get less fun if I was doing it every night but they were very good stories.'

'Oh!' said Lindy. 'And quite good boys?'

He nodded. 'Very good boys.'

She smiled at him, aware that she was being teased and enjoying it. 'Well, I said we were having tea so I'll put the kettle on. Unless you'd prefer coffee? Our other option is hot squash.'

'Actually, I brought wine,' he said, finding his rucksack and looking in it. 'White or red?'

Wine would alter the whole mood of the evening, turning it from a 'pop round, tea and biscuits' into something more like a date. She realised she hadn't ever had a man in her house who could be described as a date. She had been on some dates – forced into it by friends and family – but they'd never been in her house. She felt a shiver of something between excitement and nerves. She tried to suppress both. This wasn't a date, he didn't fancy her (did he?) and she was a grown-up now, not a silly adolescent.

'Red please,' she said. 'I'll get glasses. You go through to the sitting room.'

She tipped a couple of packets of value crisps into a bowl and brought them with the glasses. Then she quickly lit candles and turned off the main light. 'I always do this in the evening. It helps me overlook the mess.'

He laughed and started pouring wine. She opened the wood-burner and added a log. Then she accepted the proffered glass and looked longingly at the sofa.

'This is nice,' she said. 'But I must just check on the boys. They probably are asleep, but you never know.'

'I'll sort out the prizes,' said Angus. 'Then we can both relax.'

As Lindy ran upstairs she felt a hiccup of excitement. Relaxing, with Angus, wine and candles, was a very lovely thought!

'Right,' said Angus when Lindy returned, reporting both boys fast asleep. 'Let's see what we've got. These things were in the attic. There were also some beautifully painted toy soldiers, pure lead, so really not suitable until the boys can be trusted not to suck them, or put them anywhere near their mouths. I didn't bring those.'

'I'm glad. I'd have had to find somewhere to keep them until Billy was old enough and storage is a bit of a problem here.' She indicated the room; it was fairly tidy, but there were still boxes stacked in the corners, under the chairs and one stack even formed an occasional table.

'Well, they're just fine in my house. I'm clearing out the attic to get at the roof, which is when I found these things, but there's plenty of room for storage.'

'What beautiful words!' said Lindy. 'I can't think of any more beautiful ones just at the moment.'

He laughed and glanced at her. 'You're easily pleased.

Now, what about this? A child's tool kit but they're all real tools, just smaller.'

Lindy took the box. 'They're lovely! And in such good condition!'

'My grandfather had some very similar, but we were never allowed to play with them.'

'Too dangerous? They probably are lethal really.'

'I don't think it was that. My grandfather didn't want them messed around with.'

'Oh, that's sad.' Lindy took a sip of wine that, she couldn't help noticing, was far better than the wine she usually drank, and reflected how her own father loved teaching the boys things. 'But maybe you didn't express any interest in the tools?'

'Oh, we did but were firmly told they weren't for little boys when it was blatantly obvious they were!' Angus laughed but Lindy suspected he had been a bit hurt by this in the past. 'I loved carpentry,' he went on. 'Still do. And I'd love to show your boys how to use tools properly.'

'They'd love that! Mind you, the way they seem to feel about you, they'd love it if you taught them their times tables. In fact, a bit later on, I might get you to do that!'

Angus laughed. 'I'll have to make sure I remember them. And of course, they've got a grandfather who's much more hands-on than mine ever was.'

'But he hasn't got a perfect miniature tool set. And his carpentry isn't great either. Although he's happy to let them do things. Edward never liked Ned fiddling with his things. He used to get really upset.'

'Well, I suppose if they could have injured themselves...'

'No,' said Lindy, chuckling, although she hadn't felt like laughing at the time. 'I meant his Lego sets.'

Angus smiled. 'I remember. Not good at sharing.'

'He had other virtues,' said Lindy hurriedly, aware she shouldn't criticise Edward in front of his brother.

'Such as?'

'He was fun – at least at the beginning. But he had the whole parenting thing thrust on him when he was far too young.'

'So did you. You were younger.'

'I know but I'm a girl!' she said. 'We grow up faster.' She smiled to show she was joking but actually she felt it was true. Then, because she felt uncomfortable with the direction of the conversation – she didn't want to moan about her ex-husband to his brother – she said, 'Have you eaten?'

'Have you?'

'Not really. The boys ate with my grandmother. I usually just have toast or something if it's only me.'

'Can I make a suggestion? That I go out for fish and chips.'

'That would be great – but there isn't a chip shop in the village.'

'Since I moved into a house without much of a kitchen, I soon learnt where the chip shop is.'

After a brief discussion about what was required, he left.

While he was gone, Lindy went up and checked on the boys again, and then she brushed her teeth. Then she rinsed out her mouth so he wouldn't notice that she smelt of toothpaste. Back downstairs, doing a bit more clearing up, she thought about Rachel, about how, although she was sure he would, Raff didn't even kiss her.

She would be very, very surprised if Angus had even thought about kissing her. He was there as a kind uncle – a truly excellent one – not because he fancied her. He probably felt sorry for her: plucky little Lindy, made pregnant (twice) by his brother, and now bringing up the boys on her own. And thought it would be good for the boys to have a man in their lives, and not just a grandfather, who, however willing, was obviously a generation older.

One grisly scenario that fortunately she did manage to dismiss was a family conference: 'Angus, you've got to go and check on those boys. Make sure they're not little hooligans with ghastly accents. Being brought up by that girl can't be good for them.'

So, unlike Rachel, she wouldn't feel remotely snubbed if he didn't make any sort of move on her. She wanted him too; she was honest enough to admit that, but she didn't expect it.

Quite why she fancied him so much was probably because she hadn't had a boyfriend since Edward left; she'd had a major crush on him when she was a teenager and he was very good with her boys. He was also a good-looking man and very kind. Any woman in her position, lacking male attention, a single parent and really quite young, would be bound to be attracted.

She'd done quite a lot of tidying while she had these deep thoughts so when Angus arrived with vinegar-smelling packages, she was ready for him.

'I've got the plates hot,' she said. 'So, in the kitchen or in front of the fire?'

'The latter, please. Not having any sort of fire just yet, that sounds lovely.'

'It was so kind of you to read to the boys,' said Lindy when the fish and chips had been eaten and they were sipping mugs of tea. 'You do it so well.'

'I used to read to kids in a children's home when I was in Canada. I got roped into it by a friend who was an actor; he taught me how to do it. Expression, but not too much, not if you want them to sleep.'

'Well, you do it perfectly. My dad's quite good. I remember being read to by him as a child. He'd only read things he liked though, which were sometimes a bit too old for me.'

'What sort of things?'

'*The Jungle Book*, *Old Peter's Russian Tales*, *Wind in the Willows*. They're all there in the bookcase waiting for when the boys will appreciate them.'

Angus got up and went to where she indicated. He pulled out a book. 'I don't know *Old Peter*,' he said.

She laughed. 'Feel free to borrow it, any time.'

'I'm going to read it to you,' he said. 'Make yourself comfy on the sofa, put your feet up. And then listen.'

Lindy happily shuffled cushions around and pulled a blanket from the back of the sofa over her, making herself comfortable. 'I love being read to,' she said. 'This is so kind. But you're not to feel offended if I go to sleep.'

'Of course not. Now listen.'

She let the beautiful golden tones of his voice flow over her. His friend had taught him well. He did the voices but didn't exaggerate them so they sounded as if they were in a play. She closed her eyes.

*

She awoke to Angus gently pushing her head back on to a cushion.

'Sorry to wake you,' he said, 'but I thought you'd get a crick in the neck if you slept with your head forward like that.'

She shook her head to wake herself properly and found herself looking into his eyes. The next moment his hand was behind her neck and his lips were on hers.

It was heavenly to be kissed so tenderly yet thoroughly. She'd been on her own for three years and she missed that sort of physical contact. She had her lovely, cuddly boys constantly snuggling up to her, their little limbs tangling themselves around her, and her kind and affectionate parents who offered frequent hugs, but she missed this. She wanted it. She hadn't expected it to happen but now it was happening, she wasn't going to stop it.

Soon they were lying next to each other on the sofa kissing with more intent. He was, she realised, a much better kisser than his younger brother had been.

'I didn't mean this to happen,' Angus said, breaking free, sounding almost guilty. 'I mean, obviously I'm delighted it did, but it feels a bit... I don't know...'

She put her finger on his mouth. 'It's all right; you don't have to apologise. I would have told you if I wasn't happy about it.'

'Oh, good.'

The smile in his eyes was like sunlight after a long, bleak winter. It made her feel the most desirable creature in the world. She'd thought she'd never feel like this again – or not for a long time. She decided to go with it, let what happened happen and then just deal with the consequences. It felt so right.

Eventually, boldly, she said, 'Do you think this would be better if we carried on upstairs?'

'You mean, in your bed?'

'Yes! The boys' play mat is a bit small and scratchy and, besides, we might wake them up.'

He gently pinched the bit of her he happened to be holding. 'The bed it is.'

She was woken by the sound of a car driving away and realised she was alone. But the space next to her was warm so he hadn't been gone long. Her clock told her it was five o'clock. She sighed. He'd picked his moment – another hour and the boys might come in at any moment.

Relief and regret mingled to form a sort of happy melancholy. Her body felt different. She'd been on her own for so long that now it felt as if she'd had a very intense massage: very relaxed but also a bit tender. It would have been wonderful to wake up together but she wasn't greedy. She'd had a really wonderful time – unexpectedly – it wasn't reasonable to ask for more. She'd always said she didn't want a stepfather for her boys and that hadn't changed. Angus was a wonderful uncle, but she didn't want him to be a father to her boys. That would be way more difficult.

She got up to check on the boys and go to the loo and then went downstairs. There was a note on the kitchen table.

I didn't want to leave you but I thought it was probably

best, for the boys' sake. Please phone or text to say you're all right. You are so very lovely. A x.

She knew that whatever happened from now on, she would treasure that scrap of paper.

She felt really awkward about ringing him. Although he'd written that sweet note she felt embarrassed about having set aside all sense and just gone with her feelings. In her sane mind she would never have slept with anyone she'd only just met and hadn't even been out with. It was crazy.

She was fairly sure he wouldn't judge her but she did judge herself – even though she'd made her decision consciously; she hadn't slept with him by mistake. She did worry about looking as if she was a desperate single mother – she probably was a desperate single mother! She decided to text instead of phoning. *I am fine. I hope you are too. L x.* She'd thought about the kiss, not because she didn't want to give him one but because she didn't want to look needy.

Suddenly doubts came crashing around her – the trough that came after a wonderful peak. Supposing he thought she might try to trap him? That she'd seen a single man and would think: Here's a meal ticket? Should she tell him she was on the pill? Had she mentioned it last night? She couldn't remember!

When she thought about it more rationally she realised he probably wouldn't feel that, but the doubt remained, like a stone in a shoe, tiny, but also nagging and painful.

Grateful it was a nursery day for Billy as well as school for Ned, Lindy focused on being as normal as possible. She had only just managed to get the bags of toys out of sight. She put the KitKats on the side, their 'going to sleep quickly' prizes.

Her feelings about Angus were so incredibly confused. Part of her – a big part – was in danger of falling in love with him. He was gorgeous, kind, considerate, sexy – a wonderful lover. The rest of her was acutely embarrassed. Easy didn't describe her – how long had it been before she was inviting him into her bed? OK, he did kiss her first – she was fairly sure it had been him – but she definitely moved them on from kissing to sex. The thought of it made her cringe and she had to concentrate very hard on getting some Shreddies into Billy.

She had just come back from walking Billy to nursery when her phone went. Her heart leapt in hope and dread that it might be Angus. It was Rachel. She sounded relaxed and happy.

'Hi, Lindy. Are you free?'

'Pretty much – child-free too,' said Lindy, wondering if her friends would be able to tell that she'd had amazing sex since she'd last seen them. It seemed likely. You couldn't go through all that and still look the same, surely. If they did guess, she'd have to go into all sorts of explanations and she hadn't got it all clear in her own head yet.

'Excellent. Come over to mine then, help me out with the leftovers. Beth's mother's gone but she will be back. Beth's on her way so you come when you can. I just want to tell you what she told me she and Helena wanted. Of course it might all change when we hear from Helena, but I thought we ought to be prepared.'

There was no trace of her bed-and-breakfast guest in

the house but Rachel seemed extra energised.

She served large white cups of real coffee to them and offered a bowl of croissants, a dish of butter curls and some jam. 'Dig in,' she said.

'We will make crumbs,' said Lindy.

'That's fine! I have a crumb brush.' Rachel moved the croissants in Lindy's direction. 'I knew Vivien wouldn't eat them but they looked lovely on the table.'

'Christian-name terms already,' said Lindy. 'Good sign.' She took a croissant and reached for the butter.

'So, tell all,' said Beth, obviously relieved that her friend wasn't a gibbering wreck after her night with her mother.

'Oh God, I loved it,' said Rachel. 'I was born to be a bed-and-breakfast landlady.'

'But wasn't she terribly demanding?' said Beth.

'Yes, but I rose to the challenge. And I had very good bedlinen, and down pillows. It put me right ahead of the game.'

'She would have appreciated that,' said Beth, tucking in herself now.

'She did. Although I will develop a pillow menu for those who like something firmer or have allergies.' She paused. 'She absolutely loved your grandmother's bread, Lindy. If I was going to do this regularly, I'd have to have an order so I could always have it.'

As Rachel had paid Lindy's grandmother handsomely for the loaf, Lindy felt this would probably be fine.

'And the preserves. Excellent. What Vivien really appreciated was how local everything was. Thank you so much for sorting that, Lind. You'll have to tell me where you got everything. And, Beth, I ought to have a website if I'm going to do this. Can you sort that for me?'

'Of course. I can make a start now if you like. But didn't you hate having to give up your room?' asked Beth.

'Not really. But it was cooking the breakfast I found the most challenging – and enjoyable. For example, if I cooked everything to order it would take too long so I started off a couple of sausages and some bacon. I did the eggs just before she wanted them, of course. It worked brilliantly.'

'How much did you charge?' said Beth.

'Well, I had to offer family rates, seeing as she's your mother, Beth.'

'But she can afford—'

'That's what she said. She gave me a hundred and fifty. Said it was well worth it. I'm definitely going to have another en-suite put in. If I had three letting rooms that we could offer our wedding clients, it would be a wonderful service.'

'But not cost-effective unless you wanted to do B and B all the time,' said Lindy. 'Even I can work that out.'

'I think I would like to. Not all clients would be as wonderfully challenging as Vivien, of course, but if I charged high prices I'd only attract a really discriminating clientele.'

'You mean fussy so-and-sos, like my mother?'

'Exactly! I loved it,' she said again. 'Now, enough of the fun stuff. I need to tell you Vivien's vision for the wedding. She's coming back really quite soon. And she's bringing Helena! Back from her travels. Not the blushing bridegroom though. He's still organising their future lives.'

Beth's eyebrows rose at this mention of Jeff. 'I've had some ideas about the website for Vintage Weddings,' she said. 'But maybe it's a bit early to set it up?'

'I would have thought you could do one, if you wanted to,' said Lindy. 'I'd like to be referred to as Wedding Dress Consultant on it.'

'And I'll be Bed and Breakfast and General Nit-picker,' said Rachel. 'But let me tell you about Vivien. We know, because Beth told us, that she really wanted Helena to get married in the cathedral – apparently she could have swung it – with the cathedral choir, bells, real trees instead of flowers, like Kate and William: the works.'

'You can see why Helena asked me to do it,' said Beth.

'But Helena is having a change of heart, according to Vivien. Coming to realise there's lots to be said for an upmarket wedding.'

'She's not backing out from Vintage Weddings, is she?' asked Lindy, appalled. 'I mean I know not much has actually been set in stone but it was because of Helena that we got together to do weddings. Has she said anything to you, Beth?'

'Not a word, but don't panic,' said Beth. 'Helena might want something a bit grander than she thought at first she could have, given she'd spent the wedding money. But she won't go for the cathedral and real trees thing. Trust me.'

'Vivien said the same,' Rachel confirmed. 'They've missed the moment for the cathedral, so they're settling for St Mary's, which handily, is just here.' She exhaled.

'Vivien did want us all to go over to Little Netherbourne or wherever she lives, and do it all there, but I explained that was impossible.'

'That's a relief,' said Lindy.

'And I hope I've steered her away from too many posh canapés. They're very fiddly to do and I can't see Belinda wanting to make them.' Rachel seemed fairly confident. 'I told her a few canapés and a sit-down do is far better, more fashionable.'

'Is it more fashionable?' asked Beth.

'I have no idea! But more to the point, nor had Vivien and that's all that mattered.'

Lindy couldn't help noticing that Rachel had a bloom about her. Did she have a bloom about her too? And if she did, would they guess why? No, she told herself firmly, she was being neurotic.

'So there's nothing we can do immediately?' said Beth. 'I might as well do a website for you, Rachel, and for Vintage Weddings. I've got some lovely pictures of April's wedding I can use – you know, background shots. I'll have to ask if I can use recognisable ones. I should be able to use some of them on your site, Rachel.'

'Brilliant!'

'And when we've got a look we're pleased with – a logo and things – and everyone's happy with it, I'll get some cards done, brochures, things like that. Can I pop up and take some pictures of the bedroom and bathroom?' Beth went on.

'Go for it. It's looking lovely. The flowers I did for Vivien are still fresh.'

After Beth had taken her photographs and every

leftover had been eaten, Lindy and Beth headed off in different directions, replete and wondering what difference Helena's presence would make to the planning of her wedding.

Lindy was less concerned about this than the others – she had other things to worry her – and was pleased to bump into her mother. She wanted to tell her about Angus's visit – not everything, of course – but that he'd been, and read to the boys and been great, generally.

'Hi, Mum! What are you doing? Not at work?'

'No, not this morning. How are you? You're looking amazing. Really well. Any particular reason for that?'

Lindy knew that her mother couldn't possibly have any inkling about Angus but still felt embarrassed. 'It's probably because I've just had breakfast at Rachel's – eating up the leftovers.' She went on to explain about Beth's mother and Rachel's new-found passion to be a bed-and-breakfast hostess. 'I just wanted to tell you that Angus came round last night.'

'Did he? Any particular reason?'

'He was just passing but he was so nice. He read to the boys, and probably because he was there, they were good as gold!'

'They can be good as gold,' said Sarah.

'Yes, but we both know they're not always. I just hope Angus always has that effect on them.'

Sarah laughed. 'Yes. Too much to hope the change is permanent.' Her mother regarded her thoughtfully. 'Angus is a nice chap. Not at all like his brother.'

Why had she told her mother about his visit? Because she'd thought it would be a good thing to keep it all normal and in case the boys mentioned it, but it had only encouraged her mother further. 'I'd better rush, Mum. I've got some curtains to finish. I got a bit behind with everything, what with the wedding and all, and I want to get Mrs Jenkins's done before it all starts again. The bride is about to descend. And apparently she's coming round to her mother's way of thinking about how a wedding should be. I hope it doesn't mean she's turning into a Bridezilla. And I also hope that means she won't want me to make the dress.'

Her mother frowned. 'But I thought she wanted you to do it all for her on the cheap?'

Lindy shrugged. 'I'm not sure that's still the case. Now her mother's around the budget will probably change. They still need us to co-ordinate it all, sort out the food, the flowers, all those things.'

'Weddings were simpler in my day,' said Sarah.

'I know! Anyway, I must go. See you at the quiz?'

'Oh yes. And do bring the girls. We need as much support and as many teams as possible. Lots of people will just turn up and make teams on the night.' She made a face. 'Such a shame Angus can't make it. He left a message on my phone. He was very apologetic about it.'

This was a blow. 'Really? But Dad's really good at general knowledge. We'll be OK.' Somehow she made her words sound casual, as if she didn't care. 'But I must go.'

She went to her house as fast as she decently could. She didn't want to check her phone in the road, in case there was bad news on it. And if there was good news, she wanted to be at home to enjoy it.

Once inside the door she checked her phone. There was a text. *I'm away on an architectural emergency rescue mission. Be back ASAP. Meant to mention it before. Please don't feel abandoned. A x.*

After a few moments speculating on the other meaning for the word 'abandoned', Lindy decided she was fine about this. If he was away she didn't have to see him. She could enjoy the quiz perfectly well without him – of course she could.

Her family must never find out about her and Angus sleeping together, Lindy realised. They would be so worried that it might be a rerun of her relationship with Edward; or, worse, they'd see Angus as the solution to all Lindy's problems: tiny house, tiny income, fatherless sons. Whereas Lindy still felt exactly the same as she had done before about having a step-parent for her sons. Angus was lovely, he really was, but she wouldn't risk turning her life upside down for any man.

Chapter Twenty-One

❦

When the three girls arrived at the hall on Saturday night, it was buzzing with people forming up teams and buying raffle tickets. They followed Lindy to her parents' table and, rather to Lindy's indignation, discovered they were happily teamed up with another couple.

'Don't worry, Lindy,' said Rachel. 'We can form our own team. You said we can have up to six and maybe we can find someone who knows about sport before it starts.'

'So, how can we tell what one of them looks like?' asked Beth, knowing she was being facetious. 'Muscly legs? Dart-thrower's arms? Or just any sort of football shirt?'

'Football shirt,' said Rachel. 'Now where shall we sit?'

'I don't mind quizzes,' said Beth when they had found a vacant table. 'But I hate it if I feel I have to win. I never know anything.'

'Oh, we won't win,' said Lindy with confidence. 'There are a couple of local families who are wildly competitive – they always win.'

'Cool!' said Beth. 'I'll enjoy my night off and get mildly plastered.'

'You seem to have perked up a bit recently, Beth,' said Lindy. 'Any particular reason?'

'No, not really. Well, yes and no,' said Beth. 'A very nice man came into the pub the other day. Finn Something? He was in a boy band called the McCools?'

Rachel considered. 'I think I do vaguely remember them. They were good!'

'Well, he had planned to do a gig at the pub, but not for a while because Sukey's got some comedy festival coming up. But he checked out this place and thinks it's better. Can you imagine? A band, here!'

'That would be great!' said Rachel. 'Another opportunity to admire our wonderful paint job.' She looked up and suddenly frowned. 'That bit needs doing again.'

'Oh, don't worry about it,' said Lindy. 'It's fine.'

'You seem in the mood to enjoy yourself, Lindy,' said Beth.

'I am! I expect it's because my children are tucked up with my grandmother who's got her Scandi crime to watch and I'm out with my mates.' She shrugged. 'I don't get out much.'

Rachel raised her eyebrows. 'You don't. Now let's see what the raffle prizes are.' She looked at the list that had been left on every table. 'Oh, I see there's another tea set. It must be Belinda again.'

'Nice,' said Beth. 'It really must be your turn to have it, Rachel. And you'll notice I'm offering a computer lesson, though I don't suppose anyone will want it, given most people know I'll do it for nothing anyway.'

'Oh no,' said Lindy. 'People from outside the village come – a few anyway – they might want it. It's good advertising anyway.'

'That's what I thought. It won't be long before Rachel is offering a night in her B and B as a prize.'

'Good idea,' said Rachel. 'Now, we need to look out for stray people who might know about sport. I'm afraid I am a teeny bit competitive and would rather we didn't come last.'

'There's the family that always win,' said Lindy, indicating a group of people who had just arrived. 'And they've got their son over from the Forest of Dean. He's their ringer. He knows about pop music and sport – their only weak subjects. Damn!'

'I thought we didn't mind about not winning?' said Beth. 'I'll go home now if it matters.'

'It doesn't matter,' said Lindy. 'It's just a bit boring if the same people win every time.'

'Well, I was glued to the Olympics,' said Rachel. 'But I don't know a thing about football or anything like that. I'd better get some wine.'

'That'll help,' said Beth.

Score sheets had been handed out revealing the subjects. There was also a page of pictures of celebrities, which they gave to Beth to identify. Rachel and Lindy looked through the categories.

'Sport – well, we'll have to hope it's all Olympics stuff but it won't be,' said Rachel. 'Music? Either of you any good at that?'

'I can always hum along,' Beth said, 'but I'm not reliable on who did what.'

'History,' said Lindy. 'Dad always knows everything.'

'If it's outside my GCSE period I've no chance,' said Rachel. 'Tudors and Stuarts. How are you on art, Lindy?'

'I did it for GCSE and we did go to some galleries,' said Lindy. 'I could pick out *The Hay Wain* if I had to.'

'So could the rest of the world, including me. Beth, how are you getting on with those celebrities?'

'Not bad but I could do with some help.'

Lindy's mother came round selling raffle tickets. 'I'm thrilled we've got so many people here,' she said. 'Pound a strip. People have really gone to trouble to make up teams. Those new people – remember? Justin and Amanda? – they've got people down from London. They seem really up for it. Thank you, Rachel,' she said, accepting a fiver and handing over five strips of tickets. 'But they did donate the bottle of fizz as a raffle prize. Dad actually read the sports section of the paper last week, in preparation. Not quite sure what's made him so competitive all of a sudden.'

'We won't mind not winning,' said Lindy, 'as long as we get a decent raffle prize.'

Beth and Lindy were poring over the pictures of celebrities just before the start of the quiz when Rachel looked up. 'Hello! There's Raff. And he's got two mates with him. Is that Angus? And – hey, Beth – is that the ex-boy-band man you mentioned?'

'Oh my God!' said Beth and Lindy in unison. 'I think they might be the cavalry!'

'Only if they know about sport,' muttered Rachel.

Raff came up to their table. 'Sukey said you were here. Mind if we join you?'

'I haven't seen you for ages!' whispered Rachel.

Raff kissed her cheek. 'I've been away. I've come back.'

'Mum told me you couldn't come to the quiz,' said Lindy to Angus, suddenly in a panic in case she said something she shouldn't.

'I've been away too,' he said. 'And I also came back. I didn't want to miss the quiz.'

But the look in his eyes told Lindy it wasn't the quiz he'd hurried home for.

'And I've been in the pub all the time,' said Finn.

As Lindy looked across at Beth, smiling happily, she realised that possibly she had stopped thinking about Charlie and had found a very nice distraction.

Beth said, 'You guys don't know Finn. He's the – well, you know. We met in the pub.' She stumbled and failed to find a way to say who he was without embarrassing him.

'Does everyone else know each other?' asked Rachel.

Raff nodded. 'Angus and me go way back to when he used to live in the village and Finn, well, he's kind of a celebrity...'

'That you met in the pub,' added Finn, apparently wanting to be a man in the pub rather than an ex-boy-band member.

'As you're a kind of celebrity you can help me with these,' said Beth, slightly pink.

He picked up the pile of score sheets and shuffled through the subjects. 'Music, I'm all right on.'

Raff, looking over Finn's shoulder, said, 'I'm OK at sport.'

Angus said, 'No good on either of those but history and current affairs should be OK.'

Lindy glanced up at him and felt a pang of lust, possibly triggered by the word 'affair'. How many times did you have to sleep with someone before it was an affair?

'One last chance to buy a drink!' called the quizmaster, looking over at their table. 'And then we'll get started. Can you all decide which round you'll pick to play your jokers?'

Lindy leant in. 'OK, guys. I know a lot of these people. My dad will definitely want their team to go for history and the family over there – with the pale kid who looks like he does too much homework? – they'll go for music because that boy is a whizz at it and they reckon no one else will be able to do it.'

'Come on, now!' said Finn. 'If I can't do that round I've had nothing but a wasted life!'

'Depends on how you're using the word "wasted",' said Raff.

'We can use our jokers for the same rounds as other people,' said Lindy. 'As long as we get them all right as there's double points going.'

'Let's go for music,' said Finn. 'Between us we can do it.'

'Don't forget to put the name of your team on your jokers!' called out the quizmaster.

'What's our team name?' asked Lindy, pencil poised.

'Vintage Weddings, of course!' said Rachel instantly. 'If you guys don't mind?'

'Go for it,' said Finn.

Lindy was beginning to really enjoy herself and, judging by their expressions, Rachel and Beth were too. She could tell Finn liked Beth by the way he kept looking at her but Lindy knew it might be hard for her to trust a man again, so soon after the Charlie-and-the-Fat-Bridesmaid incident. Especially one who was so good-looking and with the glimmer of celebrity on him. And they were doing so well! Angus knew all the traditional general knowledge questions and thanks to Finn and Beth they got all the music and celebrity questions right. Sport was a high scorer too, thanks to Rachel and her knowledge of the Olympics, and Raff.

Courtesy of someone's clever laptop there was a scoreboard so they could see how they were doing and there were three teams neck and neck. The clever family with the ringer son called 'the Wilson Clan', the team who mostly came from London called 'WestEnders' and 'Vintage Weddings'. Lindy's family were only just behind.

'Oh my God, this is so exciting!' said Lindy. 'I didn't know I cared.'

'If we don't win now I'll die,' said Rachel.

'I do hope we win, then,' said Raff. 'My mother would blame it all on me if anything bad happened to you.'

'She donated another lovely tea set for the raffle,' said Rachel.

'Popular culture!' declared the quizmaster, who was answered by a loud groan from all the intellectuals.

'Come on, guys,' said Finn. 'We can do this. We just have to focus.'

'It might be just you and Beth,' said Rachel. 'I listen to the *Archers* and watch *Countryfile*.'

The questions were all fairly easy to begin with and

314

then came the clincher. 'Name all the members of the band Boystars and which instruments they played. And for an extra point – and it may prove to be a tie-breaker – what was unusual about them?'

There were general howls of dismay from the currently winning tables – including Vintage Weddings until Finn leant in. 'I know this!'

'You weren't in Boystars, were you?' said Raff.

'No! But we supported them in the early days,' said Finn. 'The unusual thing is, the drummer was the lead singer too.' He began scrawling names.

'Oh God, I want to win this so badly!' said Rachel.

'What's the prize, do you know?' asked Beth.

'It's usually a box of sweets and a voucher for a round of drinks for the winning team,' said Lindy. 'Sukey donates that. Mind you, it's usually actually held in the pub,' she said for the benefit of Angus and Finn.

'So not a holiday for two in the Caribbean?' asked Finn.

'Sorry,' said Lindy.

'Pass on your score sheets!' called the quizmaster. 'Let's see who's won this very tightly drawn battle!'

Lindy stole a look at Angus.

He hadn't paid her any particular attention but every now and again she'd caught him looking at her. She couldn't help remembering what had gone on between them and wondering if he was too. She'd promised herself that it wouldn't happen again – she couldn't let her carefully balanced life be disturbed by a man – but maybe if she slept with him again it would stop the other night being a one-night stand. That might be a good thing. While she'd sworn it was a one-off, she wasn't at all sure she'd be able to stick to her resolution.

'In third place...' The quizmaster hesitated for an agonisingly long time.

'Come on,' called Lindy's dad, 'this isn't one of those blasted talent contests on telly.'

'We have a tie.' He named two teams including Lindy's parents' team.

She clapped wildly.

'In second place, also a tie, we have the WestEnders and the Wilson Clan, so our winners are... drum roll please – sorry, you'll have to imagine that... Vintage Weddings!'

There was thunderous applause, some of it from the members of the team.

'Go and get the prize, Rachel,' said Lindy, nudging her friend. 'Go on!'

Rachel went up and claimed their prize. Then the raffle was drawn. Sadly, their table didn't win the tea set.

It was while people were gathering themselves and Lindy's parents were beginning to clear up that the senior member of the Wilson Clan came over.

'Excuse me, but are you chaps in any way local? It is traditionally a local quiz – or families of local people.'

'Come on, John,' said Raff. 'You know me well enough.'

'I'm local,' said Angus, 'and I've known Lindy since she was twelve years old.'

'And I came to the quiz because my mother donated a tea set and she said I had to look after Rachel here. If you don't do what your mother says, you're always in trouble,' said Raff.

'I didn't mean you, Raff,' went on Mr Wilson Senior, 'I meant this guy here, who I've never seen before in my life and seemed to have a lot of specialised knowledge on popular culture and music.'

There was a silence. Beth cleared her throat. 'He's with me,' she said, making faces so Finn would play along.

Finn put his arm round her as if to confirm this. 'And if you think she and I are just pretending to be together for the sake of this quiz – although the fact is I can afford to buy her drinks without the generous prize – you'd be wrong. I met Beth's mother only the other day. And as Raff will confirm, when you've done that, it's fairly serious.' He gave Beth a wink so subtle only she and Lindy noticed.

Mr Wilson stepped back, a bit embarrassed. 'Well, sorry to cause offence. I know these three girls have done a lot for this hall already. I was just wondering – but I can see I was wrong.'

'Bloody hell! What cheek,' said Rachel when he'd gone. 'Let's go to the pub.'

After they'd had their free drinks and another round, Lindy said, 'I'd better go. My gran will be listening out for me.'

'I'll walk back with you. My car's in that direction and I've got a very early start.'

It occurred to Lindy that he'd probably driven miles so he could come to the quiz when he'd said he couldn't to her mother. It made her heart race for a few seconds.

'Rachel,' said Raff, 'can I walk you home?'

'Oh, OK,' Rachel replied, looking girlish and excited.

'Where do you live, Beth?' said Finn. 'Should I put my walking boots on?'

'Just across the village green,' said Beth. 'You can walk me home but don't expect me to invite you in for coffee.'

Lindy and Angus stepped out into the night. He hooked his arm through hers and held it firmly.

'Lindy, about the other night—'

Lindy rushed in. She didn't want to hear him politely explain that it was a one-off and she mustn't read anything into it. 'Oh dear God, no! I completely understand! It was just—' Somehow she couldn't say the words 'a one-night stand'. Her only other one-night stand had made her pregnant.

'Hang on,' he interrupted her. 'What did you think I was going to say?'

Lindy realised she'd been quite wrong. Fear that he was like his brother, who would never have married her if she hadn't been pregnant and there'd been family pressure, had stopped her thinking straight. 'I don't know! That maybe you just wanted to be an uncle to the boys and not carry on – you know – carry on with their mother?'

'I was going to suggest we should just do some of the filling-in things, get to know each other bit more.'

'Oh.'

'I really didn't mean to... well, for us to... go to bed like that. I hope I haven't frightened you off.'

She had been worrying about this conversation ever since she'd woken up and found him gone. Now, she laughed gently. 'Honestly, I'd have put money on me winning the lottery before I thought that would happen.'

'What? Happening ever? Or happening that night?'

'That night,' she said softly.

'You'd have expected to have built the relationship up a bit before leaping into bed?'

'Definitely.'

'But it hasn't scared you?'

Lindy sighed deeply. 'Angus, I have to be honest with you. I loved what happened between us, really loved it. But I'm not in a position to have a proper, full-time relationship.'

'Why not?'

'Because of my boys. They're my number-one priority.'

'I wouldn't expect that to change.'

'But I don't know how they'd feel if I was sleeping with their Uncle Angus.' She blushed in the dark. 'I'm not sure how I feel about it either, really. It is a bit weird.'

'It's only weird because you're calling me Uncle Angus. It sounds – wrong.'

'It does.'

'But it isn't wrong, wouldn't be wrong, if we'd gone about things in the normal way. You know, a couple of dinner dates, a walk in the countryside with the boys, and then maybe a weekend at a hotel far away from everyone?'

'That sounds like heaven!' Then, realising that maybe she'd sounded overkeen, she added: 'I can't remember the last time I stayed in a hotel.'

'We'll do that then. Take things slowly, in the order they should happen, and we won't sleep together again until we've reached the right point. Not unless you want to.'

'Perfect,' said Lindy. But she really hoped the dinner dates and the walk with the boys wouldn't take too

319

long. She wanted to cut to the weekend-away-in-a-hotel stage immediately. 'My grandmother's house is just over there.'

'Then we should say goodnight.' He paused. 'A kiss on the cheek would be all right, wouldn't it?'

'Of course,' said Lindy. 'A kiss on the cheek is always all right.'

But somehow they both moved at the same time and the kiss ended up being on the lips and then their arms went round each other.

Lindy pulled herself away. 'Whoops!'

'Indeed,' he said solemnly.

'Now I'm going to say, "Goodnight and thank you very much for helping us win the quiz. We wouldn't have had a hope without you."'

'It was a team effort.'

'Well, you did a lot of it.'

'Not at all. Oh, by the way, one more thing...'

'What?'

'You are very, very lovely.'

Then he turned away, back to where he'd parked his car.

As Raff walked with her, Rachel made a decision. And she had to act on it quickly – it wasn't far from the village hall to her house. She didn't have time to think out what to say.

'Raff. I'm a bit worried about my immersion heater. I think it might break down at any moment. I know it worked perfectly well when I had Vivien to stay but I just can't stop worrying about it.' God, Raff, she prayed silently, please take over! I sound more insane than ever!'

Raff halted. 'Really?'

'Yes, and it's in my bedroom,' went on Rachel rapidly. 'And I know that's incredibly cheesy and obvious but it's the best I can do. I just can't do this whole seduction thing. It's too – difficult.'

'You don't need to seduce me, sweetheart. I'm already seduced.'

Much later, as they lay in Rachel's antique brass bed, between ironed, thousand-thread-count sheets, she sighed blissfully.

'That was the most lovely time. Thank you so much.'

Raff laughed. 'I almost said "the pleasure was all mine" but I'm very glad to know it wasn't.'

'I've never been much of a fan of sex before. It was more like something everyone did that I never really saw the point of. I hated the whole idea of being out of control. But now – well, being out of control seems like a good thing.' She paused. 'Only in the bedroom, of course. The rest of my life needs to be very controlled.'

'If you think sex only takes place in the bedroom you've still a bit to learn about losing control,' he said gently, kissing her shoulder, 'but there's plenty of time to explore the other possibilities.'

'How much time do you think?' Rachel was trying to stay relaxed and cool about the future but she couldn't quite manage it.

'I think approximately – give or take a few years – all the time in the world.'

She giggled. 'Cue music!'

Chapter Twenty-Two

Beth put two glasses of sparkling water on the table. 'Thank you so much for coming this morning, you guys. Such short notice too. But Mum and Helena Skyped last night. Mum was confirming some plans she made when she was here, and seemed a bit shaky on some others. It's all a bit urgent.'

'Of course it is,' said Rachel. 'Ten days!'

'Do we know if they want me to make bridesmaids dresses or – please God, no, a wedding dress?' Lindy sipped her water.

'Oh God, did I forget to tell you? You're OK, there, Lind. Mum's agreed to pay for a wedding dress separately – provided they can get one at such short notice. Apparently it's not just a matter of going into a shop and buying one.' Beth sighed. 'I did my best to help by looking online but really, unless you get something that's been altered to fit someone else, and they've rejected it, you've no chance.'

'I can't believe that!' said Lindy.

'No,' Beth went on. 'The usual time scale is about six months.'

'Goodness,' said Rachel. 'Let's hope with Vivien on the case they can speed that up about times a hundred!'

'So, Helena will accept help from your mother now?' asked Lindy.

Beth nodded gloomily. 'She and Helena are officially best buddies. Helena was caving in a bit before but now Mum's paying for a dress, she's following the party line where the wedding is concerned. The good part is that Mum is now a Vintage Weddings fan, mostly thanks to Rachel.'

Beth was actually a bit worried that her big sister and her mother would gang up against her. It could easily happen, now Helena had turned into the dutiful daughter of a pushy mum. Thank goodness they didn't know how much she thought about Finn. Then they'd really have an excuse to tell her off. She wouldn't admit to having fallen for him; that would be wrong – far too soon after Charlie. And after Charlie she wasn't sure she could trust her instincts, but she'd never felt like this before. What she'd felt for Charlie, real as it had been at the time, now seemed a bit pathetic. This felt like the real deal. But Finn would still be a bad boy in her mother's eyes even if he had charmed her a little bit. Sadly the good feelings she had towards him would have worn off at about the same time as the gin.

'So, bridesmaids' dresses?' said Lindy. 'I've got something in mind but if they'd rather buy them, I won't be at all offended.'

Beth shook her head. 'I'm afraid not, Lind. Mum was delighted to think they could have something specially designed for what seems to be a bit of a bargain.'

'We must put our prices up next time,' said Rachel, scribbling in her notebook.

'Do you mind, Lindy?' Beth went on. 'Trouble is, Mum saw pictures of April's dress and was so impressed. I know it's a lot of work for you.'

'Now you've flattered me into wanting to do them. But it's a lot of responsibility in such a small time frame. And flounces are very time-consuming. Just sayin'.'

Beth laughed. 'Don't worry! I promise you they won't involve flounces. I'm a bridesmaid and I'll boycott them. That said, Helena might want boning and a zillion hooks and eyes.'

'Oh God, seriously, Beth, don't joke. I've only got a chance of getting them done if they're really, really simple.' Lindy took another sip of water. 'But it would be a lovely project.'

'OK. I'll plead for simplicity. What does that mean, exactly? Mum and Helena really want your ideas.' Beth felt it would be easy to ask for something really plain and then find out it was really complicated to make.

'Well, I don't know what Helena wants or anything but what could be lovely and would fit in with the Vintage Weddings theme Helena originally wanted...' Lindy paused.

'You've obviously thought about this,' said Rachel.

Lindy nodded. 'I have. I – er – haven't been sleeping too well lately.'

Beth knew that Angus had been away and wondered if this was why Lindy hadn't been sleeping. She'd admitted to them both that her crush was very much alive and well, but Beth was sure there was more to it than that.

'So?' said Rachel, obviously keen to know about the dress.

'A sort of romantic tutu – a long one, that is. Here, I've got some images.'

Seconds later the women were poring over Lindy's phone.

'I like that idea!' said Beth. 'Sort of Audrey Hepburn again!'

'It suited you so well, Beth, and as I don't know the other bridesmaid I thought I might as well base it on you,' Lindy explained.

'That's lovely!' Beth was thrilled. Maybe she could somehow wangle an invite for Finn, so he could see her in her outfit.

'But wouldn't they take ages to get right?' objected Rachel. 'That very fitted bodice? And all those layers of net? I must say they are very pretty.'

'You could add ribbons round the neck and things, for the Degas look,' said Lindy.

'They are really lovely,' said Beth, 'and I'm sure Helena would love them. But why would they be quick?'

'I'd make them on to leotards. That would be the time-consuming bit, the bodice. But if the bodice is ready made, the rest is fairly easy.' Lindy smiled. 'How many bridesmaids is Helena having? I know she's kept changing her mind.'

'Well, now it's only me and Hels' best friend, Nancy. Thank goodness! Her other friends looked like being Bridesmaidzillas – if there is such a thing! Nancy is about the same size as me,' said Beth.

'But if you do it straight on to leotards,' said Rachel, 'won't the bodices look nylony?'

'Not if we don't buy shiny ones. Lots of them are matt. Velour, velvet – fabrics like that. I have researched this,' said Lindy.

'I think that's lovely!' said Beth. 'I'll try to convince Hels. But I suppose she might be worried about us looking better than she does.'

'I'm sure not,' said Lindy. 'Just don't go for white net or it could all be a bit *Giselle*. And get her to choose ASAP!'

'Brilliant!' said Rachel. 'Moving on? What else did you have to tell us about?'

'Oh yes, worse than the dresses really,' said Beth. 'Mum and Helena are coming down here tomorrow. They'll stay until the wedding. I did point out it's unusual to stay near the wedding venue that long, but they said it was different, I lived here and there were timing issues. They wanted to be on the spot.'

Rachel gulped. 'Where are they planning to stay?'

'It's OK, not with you. I told them they couldn't and Mum realised you haven't got room for them both. Sukey's got two rooms they could use if one of them had a bit of an overhaul. I'm going to give it a coat of paint when I can and make sure they're basically serviceable, but it would be wonderful if you could do the finishing touches, Rachel. You know my mother's requirements. Helena's not quite so bad, I don't think.'

Rachel scribbled and then sighed, sounding very happy. 'I'd love to! And if you need help with the decorating I'll make time. Then is it just a case of detailing and good bedlinen? Actually, I'll have a look myself after this.'

'Brilliant, thank you so much.' Beth looked at her list. 'OK, so when they arrive, Mum wants to meet all the suppliers.'

'Oh God, just thought!' said Lindy. 'Are you doing the cake, Beth?'

'Thank goodness, no,' said Beth. 'Can you imagine? Wedding cakes are stressful enough to do – they're so centre stage – but doing one for my mother? Me? The black sheep?' She shuddered and took a sip of water. 'Mum has chosen a posh shop in London to do it. It'll cost the same as a good second-hand car.'

'Blimey,' said Lindy. 'So who are the other people your mother wants to see?'

'The caterer, florist, Lindy, of course. She's organising her choir to come, so that's OK. The caterer is the most important.' Beth checked her list for things she might have forgotten.

'That's Belinda,' said Rachel. 'Raff's mum. The caterer, I mean.'

'Did you blush when you said Raff or did I imagine it?' said Lindy.

'I may have blushed. Just a little bit,' said Rachel, blushing a lot now.

'So did you and he…' Lindy persisted. 'I wouldn't mention it but Mum said she'd seen Raff's van outside your house really quite early in the morning.'

Rachel blushed some more. 'If you're asking if we've slept together,' she said, 'then yes we have. I didn't want to say anything about it in case it all went wrong. But yes, it was amazing. But of course it's very early days. Do we know what sort of food Vivien is going for?'

Lindy was obviously disappointed. 'Of course, if you don't want to tell us...'

'It's not that!' said Rachel. 'But this is a business meeting and we've got lots we need to get through.' She was still a bit fluttery in spite of her statement.

'But it was OK?' asked Beth.

Rachel nodded. 'More than OK, but we do need to stay focused!'

Beth studied her friend. There was a girl in love or she didn't know the signs. Rachel was finding it very hard to think about anyone or anything except the man in her heart and was struggling extra hard to do it. She recognised the symptoms because she felt she was beginning to feel like that about Finn. It didn't seem to matter that she'd only just met him, really, but she couldn't stop thinking about him. He'd been in the pub a few times and she was pretty sure he was interested, but could she be sure?

Rachel wrote something in her Emma Bridgewater, although Beth wondered if she was actually just doodling, so she didn't need to look up for a few seconds. 'But I'll go with Vivien to the meeting. I think she'll be bowled over.'

'Who, Mum or Raff's Mum?' said Beth.

'Vivien. Belinda is the real deal.'

'It's hard to think of Raff as remotely posh,' said Lindy. 'Obviously I've met his mum and we all know about her but Raff never seems like her son, somehow.'

'He's a rough diamond,' said Rachel.

'And are you the one to polish him up?' asked Beth.

'No,' said Rachel, a happy smile forcing itself past her

work-focused façade. 'I love him just as he is.'

There was a pause and then a wistful sigh. 'Oh, bless,' said Beth. 'Rachel's got a bit of rough.'

'He's not rough,' said Rachel. The smile was broader now. 'He's very gentle.'

'Oh God, you two!' said Lindy. 'Now it's me who thinks we should get on with this meeting. I've got to pick Billy up soon.'

'Next on the list is flowers,' said Beth. 'Is that you, Lindy?'

'No! Not me! I don't do formal flower-arranging, in church. Besides, I won't have time.' Lindy took a breath. 'I'll get Mum on to it. She knows all the WI and the Flower Guild. That'll be OK.'

Beth wasn't convinced. 'You know Mum will want stunning flower arrangements? A few chrysanths in a bit of oasis won't do, you know.'

'Don't worry!' said Lindy, possibly a little offended. 'There is a lot of talent among those women. They do demonstrations and some of them have done the flowers for Gloucester Cathedral!'

'Oh, Lindy, I'm sorry!' Beth was mortified. 'You know what my mother's like – I think I might be getting like her. It's probably catching.'

'Weddings do make everyone a little crazy,' said Rachel. 'I read that on the internet. It's absolutely true.'

'I know,' said Beth. 'But it's not supposed to affect the wedding planners!'

Lindy laughed. 'Don't worry about it. I do understand.'

Beth sighed and looked back at her list. 'I don't think there's anything else Mum expects us to do.' She looked up. 'I'll just ask Sukey if Rachel and I can have a look at the rooms. So if you need to get off, Lindy, you can.'

'Thank you,' said Lindy. 'And please let me know about the dresses as soon as you can. They will be fairly quick to do but I'll need to order the leotards and the tulle, once we know what colours we need.' She paused. 'You're sure it wouldn't be easier to just go to a shop and buy bridesmaids' dresses?'

'It might be, but the chances of finding anything anyone likes within the budget is nil,' said Beth.

'Oh, OK,' said Lindy, and kissed both girls goodbye.

A few minutes later, Sukey was minding the pub and Beth was showing Rachel the accommodation. 'So, what do you think?'

Rachel was examining the biggest bedroom, which had an en-suite. 'Basically, as you say, it's fine. It would benefit from a coat of paint.'

'If I don't have to do it to your amazingly high standards, I'll do that. What colour, do you think?'

'We've got some paint left over from the hall,' said Rachel.

'So, white then, is it?'

'Just for reasons of economy, Beth!' said Rachel defensively. 'We can add colour with the bits and pieces. I've got decorative thermos flasks for fresh milk, some lovely containers for cotton wool and things for the bathroom. Has Sukey got kettles? Does she know not to have packets of butter and jam for breakfast?'

'You know what?' said Beth. 'I think you should tell her about those things, not me. You know she's only rented the odd room out to men who aren't fussy. Angus

330

was no trouble. But having my mum and sister will be a much bigger deal. You can explain how it should be done.' She made a face. 'And she might not do it again however lovely it all looks when we're done.'

Later, Beth overheard Rachel saying, 'You know what's a really nice touch? A bottle of lavender oil next to the bed to help people sleep...'

Beth was disappointed she couldn't hear Sukey's reply.

Finn had told Beth after the quiz that he might not be around for a bit. She felt heartened by the fact that he'd told her his plans, and not just taken off. He had a lot to do getting his band together and so would be travelling quite a bit. She rather envied him. Beth had an unaddressed streak of wanderlust and although she was loving life in the village, there was a big world out there she had hardly seen.

Thus, she was very surprised to see Finn and two other men come in just before she was due to finish her shift.

'You know what they say about bad pennies,' he said, kissing her cheek. 'But the guys want to check out the venue. They're not convinced a village hall is the place for the relaunch. Although they liked that idea better than the pub.'

'Do you boys want a drink first?' said Beth.

Sukey appeared. 'They want a key,' she said. 'Finn rang ahead. Why don't you go with them, Beth? Make sure they don't wreck the joint.'

'Because I'm working?' suggested Beth, who did want to go but felt guilty knocking off early.

'You go,' said Sukey. 'I'll take over here. We're doing the bar for the gig so find a nice position for us – not too near the loos. It should be good for us.'

Beth took the key and led the way. She felt incredibly pleased to be with Finn again. She knew she ought to curb her feelings but she just couldn't. He was so nice to her – so polite. He had introduced her to the band as if she was someone important, not just the barmaid.

'I know we wanted somewhere small for our first gig together,' said Seamus, one of the members of the band. 'But nice as this is, isn't it a bit too much off the beaten track? Will we get an audience?'

Beth, who was checking chair numbers up the other end of the hall, listened attentively.

'I think we will,' said Finn. 'I've got to know some of the locals, who'll make sure we do get people through the doors.' He paused and looked in her direction. Beth was too far away to read his expression but she could see he was smiling. 'Besides, there's a record producer/agent in the area who could be really useful. This guy Raff who I met, he knows him and will bring him along if he's free. It could be really good for us.' He paused. 'We don't really want anyone who will still think of us as a boy band. We'd be new to this guy.' He sighed. 'As long as we're good enough, that is. Otherwise it would be a major embarrassment.'

'C'mon man! We will be. That'd be sweet. Who is he?'

Beth went back to counting, glad that he was so enthusiastic about the hall. And there would be a good audience for them. She and Sukey, and probably Raff too, would make sure of it.

After the band had finished their inspection Finn came up to her. 'Hey, Beth! Would you mind taking the key back? We've got to get off.'

'That should be fine,' said Beth, feeling inexplicably hurt.

'I really wish I had time to see a bit more of you,' Finn went on, making Beth pray he hadn't seen she'd been upset. 'When we've done our first gig together and it looks like it might work out, I want to really get to know you. At the moment I'm always flying in and out. But it will get easier.'

Beth shrugged. She didn't know what to say.

Then he put his hand on her cheek. 'You're sweet, Beth. Please don't run away until I have time to pay you proper attention.'

Looking forward to a plate of pasta and some gentle telly, prior to a very early start on the decorating in the morning, Beth was less than thrilled to hear Skype singing its merry tune indicating her sister wanted to speak to her. And why wouldn't Helena get to grips with Facetime? Still, maybe now wasn't the time to teach her how.

She connected and saw her sister was crying, looking utterly distraught. 'Oh God, Beth!' she sobbed. 'It's all awful. There are no nice wedding dresses I can have now. They all have to be made specially and there's no time. Mum will go mad. I'll have to walk down the aisle in a bin liner! And I daren't tell Mum! She'll go off on one. You know what she's like.'

'Don't panic. I'm sure there's a solution.'

'You don't know what you're talking about! Have you tried to buy a wedding dress with only ten days till the wedding?'

'No, and I know it's hard – very hard – but really, don't panic. There will be a solution.' She didn't point out that it was Helena's own fault for not getting round to it sooner.

'What?'

God, her sister was maddening sometimes. But Beth tried to make allowances for her hormones and wedding-itis that, according to Rachel, affected every bride to some extent. 'I don't know off the top of my head, Hels, but trust me, there is one.'

'It's all very well for you to say that, you're not getting married. And you're not pregnant.'

Deliberately not reminding her sister that she'd known she was getting married for quite a while and suggesting she should have done something about a dress sooner, she said, 'I'll ring Lindy. I might be able to go and see her and you can have a chat on Skype and see if she's got any ideas.' She wondered if in fact, she should have nagged her sister into doing it earlier, but buying a dress was the bride's job, surely?

'Do you think she will?'

'Yes. She's already had a brilliant idea for the brides-maids' dresses. She'll be able to explain better than me.'

'Oh thanks, Beth! I feel better now. I did buy a really gorgeous basque though. It's beautiful. Quite expensive but it'll make me look amazing. And I could just try it on and take it away. I didn't have to wait six months to have it made.'

'I can see that would be reassuring. What did Mum

say about not being able to buy a dress?'

Helena didn't say anything; she just picked at her nail.

'Oh my God, she doesn't know! I cannot believe she let you go wedding-dress shopping on your own!' For once, Beth wished her overbearing mother had been even more overbearing.

'She would have done only I didn't tell her. I wanted to sort out what I wanted on my own first, before she started having opinions.'

Beth sighed. 'I do get that. Listen, I'll just have something to eat and then Skype you from Lindy's.'

An hour later, having rung beforehand, Beth knocked on Lindy's door. Half an hour after that – Helena's Skyping never went to schedule – Lindy and Beth were in front of the computer.

'OK,' said Lindy, having been given – in colourful language accompanied by tears – a reprise of the fact that it was apparently impossible to buy a wedding dress in the time available. 'You need a wedding dress.'

'I could source something from the internet, second-hand, eBay, I'm sure I could,' said Beth, who felt Helena was being embarrassingly bridal.

'I'm not having a second-hand wedding dress! OK!' Helena was shrieking now.

'I could probably find you a new dress,' said Beth. 'A lovely dress, something you'd be happy to walk down the aisle in...'

Helena made a big effort and sniffed hard. 'Not on our budget. Mum said a grand, tops. I know it's really mean but we did spend the money she originally gave to us on travelling.'

'Hang on,' said Lindy, 'a thousand pounds is loads of money. Are you sure you can't buy a dress for that?'

Helena shook her head. 'Not in the time, and not anything I'd want to wear. It'll have to be the bin liner option. Can you do anything creative with a bin liner?'

'I can't do much with a bin liner,' said Lindy thoughtfully, 'but did you say you'd bought a basque? Can we have a look at it?'

She made Helena put it on – a process that was barely possible without a maid or a lover to help and neither were available to Helena just then, but somehow she managed to do it up and screw it round so it was more or less on.

'It's lovely!' said Beth.

'It is. It's perfect,' said Lindy. 'Would you mind if I turned it into a wedding dress? We'd just about have time for that. It would tie in beautifully with the bridesmaids' dresses I've thought up. Shall I tell you about them?'

'Just as well Skype is free,' said Lindy a little later. 'We've been on it for an hour and a half. I'll just check on the boys.'

Beth had made tea by the time she came down again.

'Both asleep, phew. They're in my bed but I'll move them later. Tea. Oh, you star, Beth.'

'I thought I ought to do something, seeing as my family are being a complete nightmare,' said Beth. She felt very responsible for the enormous trouble she was putting Lindy to.

'Oh, don't apologise. I'm loving it,' said Lindy. 'It's just what I like best. We are horrendously short of time and I'll need you to source the fabric for me, but this is going to be epic.'

Beth inspected her friend for signs of clinical lunacy. 'Are you sure?'

'Yes. This is what I love. And you've been amazing.'

'What have I done?' said Beth.

'You got Helena to decide about colours for the brides-maids as well as hers. You can order the tulle and as soon as it's here, I can get going.' Lindy frowned. 'When are your mother and Helena arriving?'

Beth looked at her watch. It seemed a lifetime had passed since their morning meeting at the pub. 'Tomorrow, but not till the evening, thank goodness. Me and Rachel are painting the bedrooms. Just the walls, not the paintwork. '

'Oh, yes, I'd forgotten.' Lindy didn't seem to care about this much. 'But I'm really pleased. I can't wait to get started.' She paused. 'Honestly, Beth, this wedding thing of yours has really given us a boost. We'll all have an online presence thanks to you. Rachel is so loving it all. She's going to be winning awards for her services to the B-and-B industry any minute. And I'm having so much fun. Really, before you came I mostly put patches on school trousers and turned up jeans. And if you've ever sewn denim you'll know how much fun that is.'

Beth sighed deeply. 'I'm so glad. Sometimes I think my family is a major pain.'

'Challenging is the word. But hey, what do you think about Rachel and Raff getting it together? Amazing, huh?'

'Oh my God!' agreed Beth. 'Has that girl been on a

337

learning curve. She's changed completely since she met him.'

'And what about you and Finn?' asked Lindy. 'He is very attractive.'

Beth couldn't help sighing. 'Well, I don't know if anything is actually going on, but I have completely got over Charlie.'

'Not surprised! Gorgeous Celtic ex-boy-band member versus farmer-with-no-self-control? No contest.'

'And I do think he likes me, but as he said, he's never here for long enough for us to go out or anything.'

'It's nice to be able to think about him though, isn't it? Or are you just too yearny?'

'I'm a bit yearny, but not too much,' said Beth, glad that Lindy seemed to understand. 'I have a hope that we might at least go out together, even if we don't end our lives together. I would like that, of course, but I realise it's fairly unlikely and that's OK.' Lindy sighed suddenly. 'So what about you and Angus?'

'It all got a bit out of hand, frankly.'

'Out of hand? Angus? Surely not!' Beth was amazed.

'It was me that got out of hand, to be honest. But we've agreed we're going to take things much more slowly now.'

Beth giggled. 'You dark horse, you! But how lovely!'

As she walked home shortly after this Beth realised it *was* lovely. Lindy worked so hard, she deserved a lovely steady man like Angus. She just really hoped it worked out for them.

Chapter Twenty-Three

'I cannot believe my daughter is going to walk up the aisle wearing nothing more than a bra and a bit of net. You can see her legs!'

Vivien and Helena, who'd not yet been in the village for twenty-four hours, were already getting everyone to run round in circles. Beth had had to spend time playing a hairdryer over the walls of their bedrooms to make sure they didn't get paint on their clothes.

Lindy, however, was calm. She was crouching at Helena's feet, checking for length, and was actually very pleased with how it looked so far. They were in Rachel's sitting room, summoned early by Vivien who was still furious with her daughter for buying a basque and not a dress. 'There will be many more layers of net,' she said. 'I've only had time to do a couple of layers.'

'The fabric only arrived this morning,' said Beth. 'Lindy's done brilliantly to get this far. It's only ten o'clock.'

Rachel, who had served proper coffee and home-made (by Lindy's grandmother) biscuits when everyone arrived, picked up Helena's hair, which was tumbling round her shoulders like a wet sheep and secured it on top of her head with a covered elastic band and some pins.

Lindy picked up a bit of ribbon and put it round Helena's neck. 'There,' she said. 'The Degas look.'

'Oh,' said Vivien, the wind taken out of her sails.

'Can I see?' demanded Helena. 'Everyone knows what I look like and I don't!'

'I'll go and get the long mirror,' said Rachel.

When she'd stood the pier glass in front of Helena, the bride-to-be regarded herself. 'Oh my God! That's amazing.'

Vivien stood beside her daughter and looked too. 'Actually,' she said after a long time, 'I think it might work.'

Beth began to applaud, Lindy joined in and Rachel said, 'I've got a bottle of fizz in the fridge.'

'It's a bit early, isn't it?' said Vivien.

'They always give you fizz at the best wedding-dress shops,' said Rachel.

'It is a bit early,' said Lindy. 'I'm going to have to really hurry up to get this dress done by next week. And the bridesmaids'.'

'Oh come on!' Beth pleaded. 'Let's have the fizz. My mother and my sister are agreed on a wedding dress. How often does that happen?' She frowned. 'Sorry, Mum, Hels, but I never thought it would. You never agree about anything. We should celebrate.'

'Are you sure it doesn't look like underwear?' asked Vivien as Helena examined her reflection from every different angle.

'It does a bit now,' said Lindy. 'But when you've got

all the layers and maybe gloves? A proper bit of ribbon round her neck, a veil—'

'She's wearing my veil,' said Vivien, and then cleared her throat.

Helena spun round. 'Am I, Mum? Did you mention that?'

'What a brilliant idea,' said Lindy. 'How very special. What sort of veil is it?'

'Silk net, fairly short, and I would be thrilled if you would wear it, Helena.'

Lindy looked at the bride's mother, who up until now had been as demanding and unreasonable as befitted her role. She suddenly seemed vulnerable and tentative.

Helena turned. 'I'll definitely give it a go.'

'Have you got it with you, Mrs – er – Vivien?' said Lindy.

'Actually, I have.' Vivien went across to her enormous handbag, which looked frighteningly designer to Lindy. She produced a carrier bag and from it a parcel of tissue paper. 'Here it is.'

'But, Mum!' said Helena. 'It's yellow!'

'It hasn't aged as well as I'd hoped,' said Vivien with a sigh.

'Could you dye the net to match?' suggested Helena.

Lindy cleared her throat. It had taken her and Beth a long time to choose exactly the soft creamy white that matched the basque and was really pretty. No way was she going to try dye it. 'Can I see the veil? Shall we try it on for size?'

Short and full, it made Helena look more like a ballerina than ever. 'It's perfect,' declared Lindy.

'The colour isn't.' Vivien sounded so dejected. 'We could have it copied, I suppose.'

'Would you mind if I had a go at cleaning it?' said Lindy. 'Of course I could make a veil in the same net as the skirt but it would be a shame not to use this one. Something old and borrowed at the same time.'

'You will be careful...?' said Vivien.

'I'll ask my grandmother to help,' said Lindy. 'She'll have some old-fashioned whitening remedy used by the National Trust or something, I know she will.'

'Well, that would be all right, I suppose,' said Vivien.

'Here comes the fizz!' said Helena. 'I must say, it might be early but I could really do with a glass.'

When the prosecco had been drunk and the champagne flutes washed and put back in their box, Lindy gathered her dressmaking materials and the veil and went to see her grandmother.

'Hello, darling,' Eleanor said. 'What can I do for you?'

'How do you know I want something?' said Lindy, kissing her grandmother. 'I might have just come round to see you.'

'That is possible, but given all the things you've got on your plate at the moment, not likely.'

Lindy sighed. 'Well, you are right, as it happens. It's this veil.'

'Bring it all into the sitting room where the light's better.'

'They really want to use it,' said Lindy. 'And Vivien, who is extremely bossy and a Mumzilla when it comes to her daughter's wedding, got all sentimental at the thought of her daughter wearing it.'

Eleanor took the veil over to the window. 'I think I could sort this out for you.'

'Could you? That would be so brilliant! When I suggested you'd know of some wonderful old cleaning method, Vivien was delighted. It's so precious to her but she does want Helena to look amazing and she will if the veil isn't yellow.'

'Leave me a scrap of the skirt material and I'll see what I can do.'

'How long will it take? You know how tight we are for time...'

'Well, when I've gathered the right herbs, when the moon is on her back and the nightingales are singing...'

'Gran! I'm serious!'

'Come back this afternoon. Actually, I've got the boys, haven't I? I'll have it done by the time you come to pick them up.'

As Lindy left she realised she had no idea how her grandmother intended to clean the veil and felt it was for the best. If she did know she'd only worry about it.

'Oh my God!' she said when she saw the veil later than afternoon, while the boys watched *Scooby-Doo*. 'It's white! What did you do with it?'

'You asked me to clean it,' said Eleanor reasonably. 'It's clean. What's the problem?'

'It's – er – very clean, Gran! I mean – whiter than – well, it was.'

'It was whiter than white,' said her grandmother. 'But

343

then I dipped it in a bit of tea to make it the same colour as the tulle you're using for the skirt.'

'OK,' said Lindy, realising that this was a good thing really, as long as Vivien never found out. 'How did you wash it?'

'Biological washing powder. Bit of bleach. Came up a treat. What?'

'Vivien will die. I'll have to tell her you did something else.'

Her grandmother shrugged. 'People did use to bleach things in the olden days. Now don't worry. All will be well. When Vivien sees how lovely her daughter looks in the veil she won't mind about anything else.'

'Are you sure?'

'Yes. I'm really sure. Your mum wore my veil. I cried when I saw her in it.'

Lindy put her arms round her grandmother and hugged her. 'Oh!'

'And I'll cry again when you find yourself a proper partner.'

Lindy suffered a pang of guilt. She had found a lovely man, but partner? 'You know how I feel about having a stepfather for the boys.'

'I do and I completely understand but I think you might have to relax your rules. Otherwise they're growing up without a father and that's not good, really.'

'They have a wonderful grandfather.'

'I know but it's not quite the same.'

'A stepfather wouldn't be the same.' Lindy felt pleased with herself for this. Her grandmother didn't nag but every now and again she told Lindy things she felt she ought to know.

'Ah! You got me. You're right. But think about it, Lindy. Those boys need a dad. And you're a lovely girl, very young. Too young to become a nun.'

Lindy walked home with the veil and the sample thinking about the 'nun' remark and wondering if she was being ridiculous and should really just let her relationship with Angus develop as her grandmother said. What was she afraid of? But splitting up from his brother had been difficult. And very hard for Ned. Billy had been too young to notice really. But if she got together with Angus and it all went wrong it would be a lot harder now they were bigger and more aware.

By coincidence – Lindy didn't really think she'd conjured him up – there was an email from Edward when she got home.

Hi, coming back to the UK for a few weeks. I'd obviously like to see the boys when I'm over.

As far as Lindy was concerned it wasn't obvious at all. He'd been back to the UK a few times and not once visited his sons. She knew this from something his mother had let slip. He just sent birthday presents if he remembered and that was that. She read on.

I'll be staying with Angus so will be able to take them out and maybe have them to stay over in his house.

Was Angus's house fit for guests? She didn't care about Edward but she didn't want her boys spending time in a house that was mostly a building site.

I'll ring when I get here next week.

Next week? Just before the wedding? That's all she

needed. She'd be far too busy and wouldn't want the distraction of wondering how safe her boys were in their father's hands. She had never worked out if she was, as he insisted, an overly anxious mother, or if he was a bit careless. And then there was Angus – that could be really awkward. Supposing the boys mentioned he'd read to them? Edward could well be funny about it. In fact, she suspected that he was only coming to see the boys now because Angus had mentioned something.

She banged off an email. *The boys would really love to see you but could it be after next week please? Things are so hectic here.*

She considered explaining about having to make the wedding dress and bridesmaids' dresses but decided not to. He wouldn't understand how her being busy meant she didn't want her boys out of their routine. As she signed off she wondered if she was indeed being neurotic.

Then she got out the net and began sewing.

The bridesmaids would be wearing the softest teal colour with wide satin sashes. Beth had sourced the leotards and fabric and Lindy was confident that they were going to look sensational.

The wedding dress was going to be harder because the basque was stiffer and although the skirt was going to be separate, Lindy was anxious in case they didn't look as if they were meant to be together. She went on sewing until her grandmother rang to ask her if she wanted her to feed the boys and keep them for the night. Guiltily, she accepted this offer and carried on working until Beth came round to have hers fitted.

*

Beth was excited at the prospect of trying on her bridesmaid's dress. She was also looking forward to spending time with Lindy, who was undemanding and entertaining company. She'd spent the day with her mother and sister and was more than a little fed up with wedding chat. It was probably inevitable but Helena and her mother seemed to think that having an amazing wedding was the most important thing in life.

Lindy pulled the door open before Beth's hand had even left the knocker. 'Oh God! Beth! Thank goodness you're here. I've just had a really panicky phone call from your mum. And they're coming over here now.'

'What was she panicking about?' said Beth, who'd experienced her mother's panicky phone calls before.

'I don't know.' Lindy was flying about her sitting room kicking boxes of things under chairs. 'But it was bad. She used the F-word.'

Beth was taken aback now. 'She used the F-word? My mother? I didn't know she knew it. At least, obviously she knows it because she gets so upset if anyone else uses it but I really didn't think there was anything in the world bad enough to make her say it.' Beth suddenly felt weak. 'It's something to do with the wedding and it's bad. I do hope Jeff hasn't called it all off! He's a nice man – really good for Helena.'

Lindy was dragging a Henry out from under the stairs. The hose disconnected from the machine's smiley face and she kicked it. 'That would be dreadful. To be left at the altar. But why would she come and see me about it? Thank God the boys are with my gran.'

'Here, let me do that. You might want to find mugs and things. She'll probably demand tea or coffee.'

There was no doubt about whom Beth meant when she said 'she'.

Lindy had forced the door of the cupboard under the stairs shut with the Henry inside when there was a knock at the door. Beth opened it to her mother and sister.

Her mother had obviously calmed down a lot since she'd phoned Lindy. There was no way a four-letter word would pass her lips now.

'I cannot believe this. This cannot have happened. It is a complete and utter disaster.'

'Oh come on, Mum!' said Helena. 'It's bad but no one has died!'

'That's a relief,' said Beth. 'What has happened then?' What on earth could it be that had caused such panic?

'Mum booked the church for the wrong date.'

'Oh my God!' said Beth, pressing her hand to her mouth.

'That is quite bad,' said Lindy.

'I did not book the church for the wrong date,' hissed Vivien. 'The vicar, who must have been drunk or on drugs when we made the arrangement, has booked the church for the wrong date. He booked it for the Friday, not the Saturday!'

'Did you notice anything odd about him at the time?' asked Lindy.

Beth winced for her friend as her mother turned her furious gaze upon her. 'He seemed perfectly all right but how he could make a mistake like that—'

'I'm going to make tea,' said Lindy, obviously desperate to escape the scene.

'I don't want tea!' said Vivien, as near to shouting as her personal standards would allow. 'I need brandy!'

Beth, fully aware there was no way in the world that Lindy would have brandy said, 'Just breathe, Mum. Sit on that chair and breathe in through your nose and out through your mouth.'

Having first removed a toy fire engine that issued an alarm call from under her, her mother did as her youngest daughter suggested, for probably the first time in Beth's life. She closed her eyes and took measured breaths.

'Cool!' whispered Helena to Beth. 'Where did you learn that technique?'

Beth shrugged. 'Dunno. Probably saw it on telly.'

Vivien opened her eyes. 'Are you telling me you told me to do something you've only seen on television?'

'But it's working, Mum,' said Helena. 'Keep on doing it.'

Lindy came in with a tray. On it were four mugs and a bottle of something that looked like Ribena. 'Sloe gin,' she said. 'The nearest thing to brandy I've got.' She half filled a tumbler with it. 'There you are, Mrs – Vivien, get it down you, as my dad would say.'

Vivien opened her eyes and took the glass and then a sip. 'Good God!' she exclaimed. 'That's strong.'

'It's neat gin really,' Lindy explained. 'With sloes and sugar. My grandmother makes it every year. I've got another bottle if you fancy taking it home.'

'It's all right,' said Vivien. 'Although it is quite calming, actually.'

'The thing is, Mum,' said Beth while her mother was fairly quiescent. 'We have to think what we need to do about this wrong date. Is it on all the invitations?'

Vivien nodded, clutching her sloe gin close to her.

'Well, that's OK, me and Dad'll just ring everyone and tell them the date is wrong. Maybe it'll cut down the numbers a bit, which is always good.'

'As long as they're your friends who can't come, Mum, I'll be very happy,' said Helena. 'Half the golf club have been invited.'

'If I'm paying, Helena,' said her mother through clenched teeth, 'it's not unreasonable for me to have some say as to who comes. When I got married I had no say in the guest list whatsoever! My own friends were only invited if they were the daughters of my parents' friends.'

Beth sighed. It was obvious that her mother looked back at those days with nostalgia. Personally she felt a bit of nostalgia for when it was all going to be handled by Vintage Weddings. Although, with her mother in charge, it would always have been extremely stressful. 'Is there a list of who's invited?'

'Of course. On the computer.'

'With their telephone numbers? Email addresses?'

'Of course not,' said Vivien, just as vehement. 'We had engraved invitations. They cost over five pounds each.'

'Blimey,' said Lindy. 'I thought there was a budget for this wedding.'

Vivien gave her a look. 'Some things I had control of.'

'Right,' said Beth. 'Have you spoken to Dad about this?'

'When was your father ever any use at a time like this?'

Beth was very fond of her dad and thought he was

just the rock she would need if she were as devastated as her mother seemed to be. 'I'll call him.'

She went into the kitchen to do just this and had a fairly calm conversation. Her father would immediately email all the telephone numbers and email addresses of the guests that he could find. Then they would divide the list in two and he would call one half and Beth the other.

'There's just one thing, Dad,' said Beth, squirming a bit. 'I'll have to do it from my mobile and...'

'I'll sort the bill out, love. You've got your mother to contend with.'

Beth went back into the sitting room, pleased with herself. 'It's OK, Mum. Dad and I will get in touch—' She stopped speaking as she witnessed her mother rise from her chair and walk across the room, looking as if she'd seen some terrible outrage.

'Is that my veil?' Vivien demanded.

'Yes,' said Lindy nervously.

'What in God's name has happened to it?'

'Mum! You asked Lindy to get her grandmother to clean it,' said Helena. 'It's fine. What are you worried about?'

'That veil was – is – an antique. And it's nearly white! What did she do to it?'

Lindy looked nervous but determined. 'You asked her to clean it and she did. She then dyed it so it matches the tulle for the dress perfectly.'

'Great. Thanks, Lindy,' said Helena.

Vivien didn't hear her daughter's approval. 'She dyed it? She dyed my wedding veil?'

'She dipped it in tea,' said Lindy, looking defensive. 'And now it matches the dress.'

'I don't know what to say,' said Vivien, sitting down again with a sigh.

Beth picked up the sloe gin and poured another good half-glass and handed it to her mother. 'Don't say anything. Drink this and calm down.'

'You sound exactly like your father,' Vivien muttered into the glass.

'Good! Dad's great and he's going to get us out of this mess.' Beth picked up her tea mug. 'Here's to Dad.'

When a script had finally been decided upon, one that didn't imply the change of date was in any way a mistake on Vivien's part – 'owing to an administrative error', which Beth thought was a bit of a mouthful – Beth began her telephoning.

Chapter Twenty-Four

At ten in the morning, two days later, Rachel was driving Vivien to meet Belinda. 'I feel I must check every detail myself,' Vivien had declared, ignoring the fact that the wrong date fiasco was down to her. 'I know we've agreed a menu, and you're here to make sure it all works, but I must be sure it's going to be right.'

Rachel felt it was her duty to take Vivien but she was very anxious. Both women were strong personalities and although she was strong herself she didn't know if she could umpire if they fell out. At least Raff had told her he was busy. He would be an added complication. The downside of being in love, she now knew, was that it stopped you thinking clearly. She needed to be on top of her game and if Raff were there she would only think about sex. She cleared her throat. 'I know Belinda is very much looking forward to meeting you.'

'And me her. She sounds . . .' Vivien picked her words. 'Fairly eccentric.'

Rachel nodded. She couldn't deny Belinda was that. 'How are you getting on at the pub?'

'Well, Sukey does her best, but her heart isn't in the business of B and B. She doesn't really do detail, not like you and I do.'

Rachel felt slightly ill to think she might be like Vivien – especially when she realised it was true.

'No, the pub is her business and what she really cares about,' said Rachel.

A little later, Rachel turned into Belinda's drive.

'What a beautiful house!' said Vivien, much to Rachel's satisfaction. Then she said, 'But why has it been let go so?'

Rachel had wondered the same thing and suspected it was a lack of money, but she felt protective. If money wasn't an issue, and Belinda simply didn't want her house decorated, restored and presented like she – and obviously Vivien – would have liked, well, it was her choice. 'It's a work in progress. Belinda has cleared out a lot of rooms recently. I expect she'll decide what she wants to do with it when that process has been completed.' She didn't explain how Belinda planned to create a flat in the house because it wasn't Vivien's business. She also realised she'd sounded dreadfully pompous but decided Vivien did that to people.

'It would be such an amazing project. I wonder if she'd sell?' Vivien's eyes sparkled at the prospect.

Fortunately Belinda appeared from the back door and Rachel didn't have to answer. She liked Vivien, admired her in many ways, but she felt this was out of order.

'Darling!' said Belinda to Rachel, kissing her cheek.

From behind his mother, Raff appeared. He also said, 'Darling!' but kissed her on the mouth.

Reluctantly, she pulled away. She hadn't seen Raff for

a couple of days and had missed him horribly. 'I thought you said you were busy!' she muttered.

'I changed my plans,' he breathed into her ear.

Rachel got a grip on herself. 'Belinda! Let me introduce Vivien Scott, the bride's mother. Vivien, Belinda McKenzie.'

'How nice,' said Belinda, 'Do come in.' Rachel made to follow Vivien and Belinda into the house but Raff caught her arm. 'Come here. There's something I wanted to show you.'

Brushing away the flicker of guilt she felt for not going with Vivien, Rachel allowed her arm to be taken and went with Raff round the corner.

Behind the house were what had once been the stables and now had been converted into workshops. There was obviously a flat over the top.

'Oh! What's this?'

'This is where I lived before I could afford somewhere of my own. It's nice but a bit small. Mum should rent it out.'

'Can I see?'

'Yes, but that's not what I want to show you.'

'But can't I see the flat first?'

He grinned. 'No. If we go in there, we'll get distracted.'

'I don't think so!' said Rachel. 'I'm working, really.'

He gave her a look. 'Even so. Now, come in here.' He opened the door to one of the many outbuildings.

Once inside he took her into his arms and kissed her thoroughly. Rachel found herself responding instantly and realised he'd been right about not showing her the flat. If there'd been a sofa to tumble on to, let alone a bed, they'd have been delayed for some time.

Sometimes she asked herself if she was in love with Raff or just in lust. And she wondered how it was for Raff, too. So far, neither of them had talked about love and it didn't seem to matter when they couldn't keep their hands off each other. But when she was alone, Rachel did wonder what she was doing with a gypsy playboy with dark curls and twinkling eyes who could seduce a woman with the flick of an eyelash.

'I want you to see these,' he said when they had straightened their clothing. He took her hand and led her to where there were boxes and boxes of tiles. 'I think these might look great round your fire surround. What do you think?'

'They look like Delft?'

He nodded. 'I think they're English. None of them are perfect but I thought you might like them.'

Rachel allowed herself a moment to remember the woman who'd would have preferred to have new, perfect tiles to the soft, blue-painted squares with nibbled edges and mismatched patterns. She picked one up. 'It's a hare.'

'They're charming, aren't they? I saw them and instantly thought of your wood-burner. If you like them, I'll put them in for you.'

'But they must have been expensive!' said Rachel, examining a tile with a small flower in its centre. 'They're in really quite good condition.' She put a hand on his sleeve in a silent thank you.

'Don't you worry about that,' he said, squeezing her to him again. 'Do you like them?'

'I love them!' she said, turning round in his arms.

He kissed her again. 'Good,' he said at last. 'Let's go and see what my mother is up to.'

Chapter Twenty-Five

After Lindy's night of hell, when her tiny house had been full of people, tulle and a fair amount of hysteria, she took advantage of her sons' absence to finish the dresses. She sewed almost continually for two days, spending the night at her grandmother's house so she could at least see her boys. She let them sleep with her in the big double bed. She didn't want them at home because of the amount of work she had to do, but she did want to feel their soft little limbs and hear their gentle breathing.

She had got them off to her grandmother's and was calling into the shop on her way home to buy emergency biscuits to restore her blood-sugar levels when she met Rachel, coming out.

'Oh, Lindy! So glad I've met you,' she said. 'Vivien wants another meeting. Beth's off on some IT emergency at a farm – Sarah asked her to help so she shot off. So we have to deal with Vivien.'

'Do we have to?'

Rachel nodded. 'I took her to see Belinda yesterday.'

'Oh, how did that go?'

'Well, actually, if Vivien got a bit bossy, Belinda knew how to put her in her place and convince her that everything was going to be absolutely fine. Vivien happened to notice a thank-you card signed by Lady someone or other and although she didn't comment, it all went a lot better after that.'

'So why does she want a meeting? The dresses are done—'

'I can't wait to see them.'

'—and the catering is sorted. So why a meeting?'

Rachel shrugged. 'She's a bit addicted to meetings, I think. But this time it's the flowers.'

Lindy, who was still tired from her sewing marathon, sighed. 'Oh! I thought the Flower Guild were doing them. They always do weddings. Mum said they were booked to do it. And I think we've done enough!'

'So do I,' said Rachel, 'but I think you need to be the one to tell her. The meeting's at ten, my house.' Rachel paused, possibly guessing that Lindy was about to refuse. 'You've been so great with the dresses, and you're the local one. You can tell her that the Flower Guild will be just fine. I don't have that knowledge and Vivien knows it. I've made some shortbread,' she added.

Lindy smiled weakly.

'Really? Well, I'd better come then.'

Lindy went home and checked her emails. There was another one from Edward. *I really want to see the boys this week – possibly tomorrow. I'll be staying with Angus. It'll be fine.*

Bloody Edward! Why did he have to see the boys at such short notice? And why was he staying with Angus?

He was her friend – her lover, even, sort of. How embarrassing; how awkward. The fact that the two men were
brothers was just coincidence. And knowing Edward,
if the boys told them how much they liked him, or
anything like that – and being boys they were bound
to – Edward would get jealous. He was so competitive,
especially with his brother; she remembered that from
before. And supposing Edward somehow picked up that
she and Angus had slept together? It might be the most
horrible disaster.

Still, she couldn't think about it any more now, she
had to deal with the meeting-obsessed Vivien. She
looked at her watch. She barely had time to make herself
tidy before she had to go.

Typically, Lindy felt, Helena wasn't present.
Apparently she was packing and heading off later for
some 'quality time' with her fiancé, Rachel reported. But
there was Vivien, ensconced at the head of the table. There
was a plate of shortbread on it that, so far, no one had
touched.

'So,' said Vivien. 'Who's going to do the flowers?' She
had a clipboard and a businesslike gleam in her eye. The
expected knock to her confidence caused by booking the
church for the wrong date apparently hadn't material-
ised. Lindy realised that as soon as she'd got over the
effects of the sloe gin, Vivien had got back on the organ-
isational horse, in full command.

Rachel, who also had her trusty notebook with her,
said, 'Lindy's our local, who knows everything. She'll
tell you about the Flower Guild.'

Lindy was aware of Vivien's fears that a small group

of women couldn't possibly provide anything good enough, but she was not in the mood to be bossed about. 'Our Flower Guild are excellent. They are very highly thought of in the county,' she said. 'Some of them have even done the flowers in the cathedral, for special events.'

Vivien frowned. 'Where do they source their flowers from?'

Lindy shook her head. 'I have no idea.'

'Because however good you are, you can't do much without decent plant material.'

As Lindy was used to doing quite a lot with stuff she'd gathered from gardens and hedgerows, she said, 'Really? I would have thought it was more to do with the talent of the arranger myself.'

Rachel shot Lindy a look. She was usually so amenable. She hurried to sound placatory. 'I'm sure we could find out for you, Vivien. Would your grandmother know, do you think, Lindy?'

Lindy shrugged. 'Or my mother, she'd know. But can't you just trust them?' She addressed Vivien.

'I trusted your grandmother, Lindy, and look what she did to my veil!'

Lindy wasn't having this. 'It matches the dress perfectly. Even you had to admit that.' Honestly! She'd worked so hard on the dresses and they'd turned out so well.

Vivien possibly realised she'd gone too far. She gave a regal nod. 'It did turn out a lot better than I expected. And the dresses are excellent. Really lovely. It's because you have such a good eye that I'd like your help with the flowers.'

Lindy realised she found this very gratifying, and

decided she'd been unnecessarily chippy. 'I'll find out who you should speak to, of course, Vivien.' It was the first time she'd managed to use her given name without calling her "Mrs" first. She felt proud.

Vivien leant in. 'Actually, Lindy, what would be really useful would be if you'd come to the flower market with me on Wednesday. I don't suppose Mrs Head of the Flower Guild would quite get the zeitgeist of the wedding in the way you have.'

'Oh, I'm sure she would though, if you explained.'

'Not at four in the morning, she wouldn't,' said Vivien.

'Why four o'clock in the morning?' asked Lindy. 'When most people are asleep?'

Vivien looked a bit embarrassed. It was obvious her features weren't accustomed to that particular expression. 'The market opens then.'

'What market?'

'Birmingham flower market. We'd aim to get there about five. I reckon it's about an hour from here. We'll go in my car a couple of days before the wedding. OK, that's sorted. Now, has anyone done anything about confetti?'

'What?' said Rachel. 'Did I get that right? You're expecting Lindy to get up at four a.m. to go with you to buy flowers?'

'She'd have to get up a bit before four,' said Vivien as if this wasn't an unreasonable expectation. 'I'll pick her up at four.'

'But why me?' Lindy protested. 'I've done the dresses.'

'Because you have the artistic eye, my dear. I couldn't trust myself to buy flowers without your input.' Vivien put a diamond-encrusted hand on Lindy's.

Lindy sighed. 'Oh, OK.'

As she walked home, Lindy wondered how she'd allowed herself to get bumped into that one. Getting up at four a.m. to go to a market with Vivien? The idea was horrendous. Vivien had flattered her into agreeing. She should never have fallen for it. But she did accept that it might be fun. She quite wanted to see Vivien with her high-handed ways of coping with market traders. Obviously they wouldn't be East Enders, it being Birmingham, but it could be fun. The email from her ex-husband had taken the shine off her day somewhat but as far as the wedding was concerned it was all good.

Beth was working at the pub and Helena was leaning on the bar with the air of someone trying to look sad about something they were really very happy about. She had just announced she was abandoning the hell that was preparing for the wedding for her fiancé.

'I realised we do need to practise our first dance, Beth, honestly we do,' she said. 'It would be so embarrassing if we messed up.'

'I do think you could have told us before, rather than just run off like this! Rachel and Lindy are having to face Mum alone about the flowers.' She frowned at her sister, who did have the grace to look a little sheepish. 'Anyway, don't you just hang on to each other and circle and end it all with a snog?'

The bride-to-be was outraged. 'No! I don't think so. It has to be really good. We've been practising for ages, actually, but he's bloody hopeless.'

'What does Mum think about you running off to

362

practise your dance?' Beth was curious as well as irritated. It would be interesting to hear what her mother felt about it.

'She didn't mind. She's seen the dance.'

'So what did she think of it?'

Helena took a breath. 'She suggested we hire a professional to do Jeff's bit.'

'No!' Beth couldn't decide if this was appalling or hilarious.

'I don't know if she was entirely serious but I think if I'd been up for it she'd have got Anton du Beke down here smartish.'

Beth came down on the side of hilarious. 'I'm not sure Jeff looks much like Anton du Beke.'

Helena shrugged. 'Well, you know Mum. Maybe she'd find another professional dancer who would be a better fit.'

'Seriously, Helena. Did Mum really not say anything about you just abandoning everything?'

'She said I was jolly lucky I had Vintage Weddings to sort things – and her, of course. And by the way, thank you so much for sorting out my wedding list. I just couldn't do that online thing.'

'All part of the service,' said Beth, who had realised that many bridal couples struggled with technical stuff even these days and so it was another thing they could offer. 'Anyway, you don't really need us now you've got Mum on board.'

'Oh God I do! I want someone to protect me from Mumzilla.'

'You want someone to do the work while you're off practising your fancy footwork.'

'Secretly rehearsing with Anton du Beke you mean...'

'Hm, if I were going to cheat on my fiancé with a ballroom dancer I'd go for someone like Brendan Cole,' said Beth. She giggled. It was nice to be just her and Helena, being sisters together. 'He's younger and sexier.' Then suddenly she was sighing as she thought of Finn. She'd been working on not thinking about him but sometimes the thoughts just rushed in.

Her sister heard the sigh. 'You'll find someone. There is someone out there for you...' She paused. 'Even if you have got short hair.'

Beth shoved her. 'Get outa here!' Then she stopped laughing. 'Hey, if you push off now, when are we going to have your hen do?'

'You know what? I've been thinking about that.'

'And? What do you want to do? Clubbing? A spa? It could only be just for a night. It's going to be a struggle fitting it in anyway.'

'What I want to do is wait till I've had the baby.'

'What?'

'It's not as crazy as it sounds, Beth. Currently, I can't drink, I can't even have some of the spa treatments – I've looked it up – and I thought: why not do it properly? Go away for a weekend somewhere, but when I can drink and have all the massages and things.' She made a face. 'I also get quite tired sometimes.'

Beth, who had been worrying about organising her sister's hen do, was relieved and a bit disappointed. 'You don't think you'll miss the baby if you leave it for a weekend?'

Helena shrugged. 'If I do, we'll take a house

somewhere near a spa and leave the baby with Jeff. But now? I'm not really up for it.'

'I was hoping for a spa. I was waiting for you to suggest it,' said Beth. She and Rachel had been redoing bits of painting in the hall and she had a stiff back.

'But when could we have gone? No, this way is better. I'm sure it is.'

'You're probably right.'

Helena got out her phone to check the time. 'I'd better go! Mum's running me to the station and you know how she has to be there half an hour early.'

Beth laughed, suddenly feeling a rush of love for her slightly crazy sister. 'OK, madam, you go and practise your Argentine Tango with Jeff.'

Beth was alone in the pub a little later when the phone rang. For a moment her heart leapt because she thought it was Finn – he hadn't said he would call but she was ever hopeful. Then she realised it was an older voice and the accent was more Glaswegian than Irish.

'My name is Mickey Wilson,' the voice said. 'I just wondered if you could give Finn a message for me?'

'I'm not sure when he'll be in again,' said Beth, just managing not to say 'when I'll see him again'.

'He'll be there for the gig?'

'Yes. On Saturday.' The day that was to have been Helena's wedding day had her mother, or the vicar, not muddled the dates.

'That's right. But can you tell him I can't be there for Saturday as I'm off to the States for a few weeks? It's a shame. I was really looking forward to checking out the band. I didn't want him to think I just hadn't turned up.'

Beth felt her mouth go dry. 'Are you Raff's friend?'

'Er, no.'

Beth cleared her throat. 'Then could I have your name again please?'

'Mickey Wilson. I'm a manager. I was going to check out the band, but my plans changed. With that line-up I think they could be great and I'd like to take them on but obviously I've got to hear them first.'

'But you won't be able to be there now?'

'That's it. I tried to get in touch with him myself but I get put straight to voicemail, which is why I'm ringing the pub. Tell him I'm really sorry. I hate to think I might miss a great new act. But I dare say I'll catch up with them sooner or later.'

Beth licked her lips. 'Listen, sorry if this is out of order – it's not really my business – but if I could get the band to play on Friday instead, would you come?'

'I would indeed. I'm really disappointed I can't see them. I think they could make all our fortunes.' He gave a regretful chuckle. 'I hate to see that pass me by.'

'OK. Leave it with me. I'm going to do everything I can to make sure the gig is on Friday.' Beth hoped Sukey would understand and forgive her for not doing her shifts at the pub and for having to set up a bar in the hall for Friday and not Saturday. She didn't even dare think about whether or not there'd be licensing issues.

'Well, that's grand,' he said. 'I'd be delighted if you could do that. Goodbye now.'

Sukey came in just as Beth was putting the phone down. 'What's up, kid?'

'It's the gig! Apparently a manager was coming to see them. Mickey Wilson.'

'Oh God, I've heard of him!' said Sukey. 'Rock royalty. He could really help them break out.'

'Well! We need to tell Finn and the others that they have to play on Friday, not Saturday, or he can't see them. He's going to the States!'

'Oh, well, that is a bit of a shame. But I don't see Vivien liking her wedding guests put into rows so they can hear a full set of Finn and the McCools.'

Beth's hand shot to her mouth. 'Holy hell! The wedding! How could I forget about the bloody wedding.'

Sukey gave a knowing shrug. 'Divided loyalties?'

'There is a way round this. There is. I've just got to think of it. Oh. Change the wedding venue. Easy.'

'Have you gone mad? Change the venue for a big wedding, less than a week to go? Honey! I'm on your side here, I think it would be amazing if Finn's band got heard by Mickey Wilson. He's a starmaker. But move the venue for your sister's wedding? Not a snowflake in hell's chance.'

Beth gripped Sukey's hands. 'If I can find a new venue, can you make sure we get punters for the band?'

'That's not the hard part here. Twitter, Facebook, the band's on those, we can get the word out. I'll sort that. No worries. But you find another venue? Really? Less than a week to the big day? Your mother's practically had one heart attack over getting the date wrong already. Do you really want to change the venue on her too?'

Beth bit her lip. 'If you tell anyone I said this I will kill you. But I actually think Finn's gig is more important. It's not like the wedding won't happen, it just won't happen in the hall. After all, it's the ceremony that's important – not the bash. As long as they end up married...'

'Well, you've convinced me,' said Sukey. 'But have you convinced yourself? And yes, you can go off now. I'll be fine.' She smiled. 'So what are you going to do first? Find a new venue or tell Finn?'

Beth gulped. 'I'll ask Rachel and Lindy what they think and then find Finn. Do you happen to know where he is?'

Sukey stopped smiling encouragingly. She sighed. 'I can't lie to you, I do know but – he's not easy to get hold of at the moment.'

'What do you mean?'

'I mean he's not answering his phone and they're not answering the house phone.'

'I gathered that from Mickey Wilson. But you know where he is?' Why was Sukey being so secretive and odd?

'Yes, but he made me swear I wouldn't tell anyone though he felt someone ought to know in case of emergencies. They're in a barn practising and they're dead scared of news of their relaunch coming out too soon. If they're not good enough they'll cancel. I think they're being a bit diva-ish, to be honest. But I've already had journalists calling to see if the rumours of the band re-forming are true. God knows how they ever heard of my little pub, but they did.'

'But this is really important, Sukey. Surely you could tell me?' She pulled out the pad and pen she kept permanently in her back pocket.

Sukey scratched her ear, and then said, 'I have to really, don't I? But if you can convince Finn you discovered the address during a Tarot reading, I would be very grateful.'

Beth nodded and at last Sukey accepted she was breaking her promise to Finn for a very good reason. She took the pad and began writing. 'It's about thirty miles away but not hard to find, I don't think. At least the village isn't. Good luck when you get there though. It's probably one of those places where a huge area is all covered by one postcode.'

Beth smiled. 'Not a problem. The van doesn't have satnav anyway.'

'OK,' said Sukey. 'You'll just have to do your best. Finn's mobile and the house number are down there. You might be lucky and get an answer. But I doubt it.'

Beth checked her watch. It was just after four. With luck Lindy would be back from picking the boys up and if she wasn't in she'd try Rachel. She wanted to see Lindy first because she lived nearer and was more likely to know of other venues.

What she hadn't reckoned on was Vivien being there. Poor Lindy!

'Darling! I just came round to check on the dress. I've got a little bit of decoration I picked up in an antique shop. I think it'll look lovely!'

Lindy gave Beth a smile that said, 'Thank God you're here!' and 'Can you take her away, please?'

'I think it might look a bit much on top of the basque, which is already quite elaborate,' said Lindy quickly, trying to shoo her hungry boys out of the sitting room.

'Beth!' she whispered urgently as she got to the door. 'Be an angel and give them a drink. They can have chocolate biscuits as it's a special day. But not in here, obviously.'

'God, I'm so sorry she's descended on you. What a nightmare.' Beth paused. 'The day is special why?' she whispered back.

'Because your mother is here, I've got both boys for once and they're starving. They could go into meltdown at any moment. And... I've got to take them to see their dad tomorrow.'

Beth put a sympathetic hand on Lindy's. 'Say no more. Come on boys. Tell me where the KitKats are!' A chocolate fix might be just what she needed too.

She had just worked out what sort of drinks the boys liked and was reaching for the biscuit tin when there was a yell from the next room; something had seriously upset Vivien – again.

Confident it wasn't anything Lindy had said, although she might be put out having her beautiful creation added to by random antique jewellery, Beth said, 'Stay here, boys, I have to check out what's up next door.'

'We are not changing the venue!' Vivien screamed into the phone as if to someone both foreign and deaf. She slammed down the phone as Beth appeared.

'I don't know what's got into Sukey,' said Vivien. 'She seems to be having some sort of turn. She thinks we want to change the wedding venue. Has she gone raving mad?'

'Um, no, Mum,' said Beth. She put her hand on her mother's arm, hoping it would be soothing. 'I was just about to tell you: we are changing the venue. But don't worry, it'll be fine!'

Lindy had thrust her hands into her hair and appeared to be attempting to pull it out. 'We're changing the venue? Since when?'

Now Beth had two near-hysterical women on her hands. 'Since – since a little while ago.'

'Why?' said Lindy, who at least had stopped pulling her hair.

'The thing is, Finn's band... A big agent – manager – impresario – was going to see them. But now he can't come on the Saturday, so they need the hall on the Friday. It's really important that he's there.' It sounded pathetic to her own ears; she wasn't surprised her mother didn't take it well.

'Nothing, NOTHING is as important as your sister's wedding!'

'I know, Mum,' said Beth soothingly. 'But it's the ceremony that's important, not the party! We can have that anywhere!'

'I have to say, Beth,' said Lindy. 'We've all worked very hard raising money and decorating so Helena can have her wedding in the hall.'

'But she doesn't *have* to have it there. It's going to be a fabulous wedding. It can be fabulous in a marquee. They're lovely,' said Beth with a mixture of desperation and pleading. If she had to convince Lindy as well as her mother, it was going to be tough. 'Some marquees can be made to look like ballrooms.'

This penetrated Vivien's anquish. 'A marquee?' she said. 'Um, that could work, I suppose. Actually I quite fancy that idea. The hall is definitely a bit – rustic. But what about the weather?'

'No need to worry about that. They'd put down covered walkways. It will be fine! Don't you remember Samantha Edwards' wedding? That was in a marquee in the middle of winter. It was brilliant!'

Vivien began to nod and Beth felt that maybe, just maybe, she'd been won over. 'It was a nice wedding. She married a very rich man.'

'We'd have to find somewhere to put it, of course,' said Beth, encouraged by her mother's reaction.

'Oh!' said Lindy. 'I think I know somewhere.'

'We need to make sure we can hire a marquee at such short notice,' said Vivien warningly. 'If we can't, that hall is mine!' She paused. 'I mean Helena's.'

'I'll be online researching in a second,' said Beth. 'I know I'll find something amazing. Mum? Maybe you should go back to the pub? Lindy will be wanting to feed her boys, get them to bed.'

'Oh, very well. But, Beth, you know me. I won't be fobbed off. If it's not a nice marquee in a lovely venue, convenient to the church – oh my God! I forgot. I must give my choir directions or they won't know where to come. I must fly. Can't stay here chatting.' And she was gone.

'Oh God, Lind, I am so sorry about my mother.'

'Actually, this time it's you making life difficult!'

But Lindy smiled as she said it and Beth didn't feel too bad.

'I know, I'm sorry. But why do you think Sukey told Mum about changing the venue?'

Lindy shrugged. 'Vivien answered the phone. I expect the shock of hearing her voice made Sukey blurt it out by mistake.'

'I'd better get back and start looking for a marquee.'

'Why don't you ask Rachel? Raff will know of someone,' said Lindy. 'Sure to. It's just the sort of connection he'd have. And I'll go and ask Angus if we can use his field. We will need to hire it though. He needs every penny he can get to restore his house.'

Just for a second Beth wondered if there was something in Lindy's expression that meant she cared more about Angus than she'd let on, but she was too busy to think about that now. She was on a mission. 'Of course. We can sort that. Now, can I have the van?'

'So what's your plan, Beth? Why do you need the van?'

'I'm going to find Finn and the band and tell them they have to change the date of their gig.'

'Beth to the rescue. OK.'

Beth suddenly frowned. 'But you'll need it, though, won't you? If you're going to Angus's to see if he's got anywhere suitable and ask him if you can use it?'

'Not till tomorrow. And don't worry. Edward is going to pick the boys up. I'll get a lift with them and I'll get back from there somehow. I can always borrow one of my parents' cars if desperate. You can have the van but I'm afraid it needs diesel.'

An hour later, Beth had passed the problem of the marquee over to Rachel, and filled up the van with fuel, grateful for the money that her father had put into her account. She wondered briefly if her mother knew her father had been subbing her from time to time and chose to ignore it. She'd always got on much better with him than with her mother. But since they'd been doing the wedding together she'd somehow understood her a little better. And now she no longer lived with her she didn't need to feel bullied. She was still a nightmare but somehow a less frightening one.

Beth was a bit anxious about setting off into unknown countryside. At six thirty in the evening it was already beginning to get dark and she reckoned she had about an hour and a half of daylight left. There was a map in the van, which was good, and she knew roughly in which direction she was headed, but trying to find somewhere in the dark was always tricky. It would get harder when she reached Newberry Parva. She might have to ask and there might not be anybody about. But what she was really worrying about was the welcome – or not – she might receive. Sukey had been genuinely reluctant to disclose the address, even when she knew why Beth needed it. Finn might be very angry. She was poking her nose into what was not really her business. She hoped he'd understand and be pleased once she'd explained but she couldn't rely on it.

At last she found the place. A group of farm buildings, all now obviously converted to something more lucrative than the housing of cattle and horses. There were big double gates that were locked and an entryphone. She contemplated the entryphone and decided it would be far too difficult to explain who she was if anyone but Finn answered. And he might refuse to stop what he was doing to come and investigate.

She parked the van in a lay-by and climbed over the gate.

Half expecting a pack of trained Dobermans to come rushing out at her, she was relieved when nothing happened. She was in. Now all she had to do was find out which building the band was in. Suddenly a dull throb began to issue from the biggest barn. Beth took a breath and made her way towards it.

As she got closer to the building the noise increased. She noticed thick electric cables emerging from under the door. This was definitely the one. But how should she proceed? Should she knock? Would they hear her? Should she wait for a break in the music and then knock? She decided to just open the door – if indeed it did open – and go in. It did.

It was dark and loud and she realised only the stage was lit; the rest of the space was in darkness. Not wanting to go up to the stage like a lone fan she decided to just find a corner and wait until they stopped for a break. There was probably a reason it was so dark and they would put the lights on soon. She felt a bit like Goldilocks breaking into the three bears' house while they were in. She hoped she wouldn't give them an awful fright when she appeared.

She felt her way to where some old chairs were gathered round a low table. She pulled one out and turned it so it faced the stage; then she settled back to listen.

At first she couldn't get a sense of the music, of what sort of music it was. Then she got used to the volume and realised it sounded great.

She had (being human) checked out Finn's boy band on YouTube and quite liked it – wanted to like it, probably

– but this was a much more complex, richer sound.

Then suddenly it stopped. She froze, as if she was playing musical statues. Should she come forward now? Or hope someone spotted her? She cleared her throat as loudly as she could but the sound coincided with a huge guitar chord. No one heard.

She decided to relax and just listen to the music. Eventually someone would notice there was stranger present and with luck she could explain why she was there before they threw her out.

She found it easier to concentrate if she closed her eyes, and she was really getting into the music. Finn, as lead guitar and vocalist, was really good. His voice was musical but with a hint of rawness that was extremely sexy. It was warm in the barn and as she relaxed she found the words became clearer and she thought she heard her own name. 'You're imagining things,' she told herself. But there it was again: her name, in Finn's gently rasping voice. Then suddenly the music stopped, but she could still hear her name.

'Hey, Beth,' said Finn. 'What are you doing here?'

Chapter Twenty-Six

Beth jumped. 'Oh my God! I can't believe I did that. I fell asleep.' She was in a dark and noisy place and for a moment was completely confused. She'd heard her name and there was Finn. But somehow he wasn't the Finn she'd been dreaming about. He was different. He was frowning down at her. He wasn't at all pleased to see her. He was very cross.

Finn nodded. 'But that's not the odd thing, really, though, is it? Why are you here?'

Beth felt she needed time both to work out how to tell Finn her news and to get to grips with the fact he was annoyed. 'The falling asleep in movies and things, it's really embarrassing. I never thought I'd do it here.' She smiled. 'Not a movie. Obviously.'

She got up out of the chair. She needed to be a bit more upright if she was going to have to explain herself.

'I'm assuming you didn't come here because you felt a bit tired and wanted a nap,' said Finn.

'No,' Beth agreed.

'So there was a reason? Because we are here to get

work done, not to socialise. And this was supposed to be a secret location. Sukey swore to me she wouldn't tell anyone. Why did she tell you?'

Beth sighed. 'There is a reason, a really good one, and if we could only go somewhere where there's proper light and it's not so noisy—' There was a huge twang of a guitar just as she spoke. 'I could explain.'

She realised that Finn was very, very angry and keeping it all under control. She realised she hadn't seen him in a working environment – his environment – before. He'd always been at the pub, or in a social situation. Now she'd invaded his space. She was hurt, though, that he didn't feel he could trust her when before he'd disappeared he'd said he wanted to get to know her better.

'We'll go into the house,' he said. Then he went back to the stage and presumably explained what had happened.

It seemed to take a long time to get from the barn to the house, although they weren't that far away from each other really. Beth was beginning to wonder if she should have come after all.

She'd been so convinced she was doing the right thing, being their messenger angel, dashing across the country in the van to stop them doing the wrong thing so they could have their big chance. Now it looked as though she'd made a horrible mistake. And if she had, literally hundreds of people would have every good reason to be extremely fed up with her.

Her mother for one. And Lindy and Rachel, who would have a lot of extra work because of the change in venue. Belinda, Raff's mother, doing the catering, would have further to transport things, although Rachel had convinced Beth it would be much easier to cook in a tent with rented equipment than in a kitchen that was really only a kitchenette. Then there were the guests, who'd already had to change the day but now the venue too. What a bloody nightmare. And all Beth's fault. They'd have to tell the guests at the church. With maps.

Finn opened a door that let them into the kitchen of a property that looked to Beth like a holiday let. It was a far larger, grander holiday let than the one she lived in but it bore all the signs. It also bore the signs of having been lived in by a group of men who had better things to do than tidy up after themselves. The worktop was strewn with dirty mugs and there was a heap of empty beer cans in a corner. A couple of empty bottles of whisky and rum were lined up next to the beer cans along with empty mixers. It wasn't as sordid as a group of drunken stags would have left it, but the inhabitants did not include anyone who was obsessively tidy. If she hadn't been so confused she'd have laughed – Rachel would have conniptions here!

'I'd better make some tea,' he said. But as he filled the kettle and switched it on, hunted for tea bags and opened the huge fridge to find milk, his expression was still grim.

Beth sat down at the huge kitchen table. He hadn't asked her to but she felt silly standing around. Although she was still embarrassed and felt guilty she was also beginning to feel a bit cross. Finn was being angry just because she was there, had broken the cordon of security he seemed to think was necessary. Why didn't he wait to hear her side of the story and then decide if she was as bad as he now seemed to think her?

He handed her a mug of tea, the tea bag still in it, and then took a seat. He pushed the carton of milk across the table. Then some semblance of manners came back to him. 'Oh, sorry. Do you need sugar?' Without waiting for her reply he got up and found a bag of it, hardened by drips of tea and coffee.

'It's OK thanks.' She fished out her tea bag and left it on the spoon before adding milk to her mug. She very much wanted to sniff the carton to make sure the milk wasn't sour but felt that would be too rude.

'So, why are you here?' he said.

Although she was longing to tell him, to put everything right between them, this felt very abrupt. She took a sip of tea before answering. 'I answered the phone in the pub. It was Mickey Wilson.'

He swung his head towards her and she was horribly reminded of a lion suddenly catching sight of its prey. She floundered on. 'He said he can't come and hear you on Saturday night. He's going to the States.'

He didn't answer immediately. He seemed to be taking it in. Beth realised she'd delivered more than just a simple phone message.

'Mickey Wilson? Rang me? At the pub? How did he get that number?' He got up and strode across the room and kicked the cans in the corner. They went everywhere. Beth had the impression that only very deeply entrenched rules about not swearing violently in front of women prevented a whole stream of invective.

Beth flinched. She was not expecting this. She was expecting surprise, some irritation that the date of the gig would have to be changed and maybe annoyance that she had come in person with the news. She was not expecting him to make such a fuss about her getting the call.

'Well, obviously I can't tell you that.' He looked for a minute as if he doubted her. 'I don't really know who Mickey Wilson is!'

Finn sighed deeply. 'He is an extremely important, influential man. With him at our backs we could go to the top. Straight away. No messing.'

'And yet you seem put out that he's rung you. That he's willing to come and hear you play on Friday instead.'

'I should think I'm bloody well put out. How did he know to ring the pub?'

Beth shrugged. 'You're not answering your phone, Finn. Mickey Wilson's calls went straight to voicemail.'

'I've had my phone switched off – it's distracting, like visitors,' he growled.

'OK, which explains why I'm here. I had to come personally, because there was no other way of getting in touch. And before you go off on one – again – I'll tell you that I told Mickey that you'd do the gig on Friday, as originally planned.'

'Isn't that the day of your sister's wedding?'

'Yes it is!' Beth roared back. 'But we've moved the venue. You can have the hall.'

He frowned. 'Run that past me again?'

'My sister is having her wedding party in a marquee now.' She mentally crossed her fingers. 'The hall is yours. I told Mickey Wilson he can still hear you. Sukey said that Twitter and Facebook will make sure you still have an audience. It's all going to be fine. The only bad part is you have a day less to rehearse than you thought.'

Finn sat back down. 'This could be a feckin' disaster.'

Beth yearned to ask why but sensed the answer would be loud and possibly a bit sweary. She got up and made herself another cup of tea instead.

'I'm going to have to talk to the guys about this,' he said, getting up. Then he slammed his way out of the door.

Beth didn't know what to do. She found a loo and washed her hands and spiked up her hair a bit with water, and then she went back to the kitchen.

Part of her, the part that worked as a barmaid and a tiny part that was close to Rachel and liked a tidy space, wanted to clear up. The rest of her refused to slip into the womanly role. If Finn had been pleased to see her, grateful for her coming in person with the message, she would have, without thinking twice. But that would make her look like a groupie, a mad fan who was prepared to do anything to get near their idol.

Annoyingly, her stand meant she had to entertain herself with a three-day-old copy of the *Daily Mail*. She could have just gone home, she realised, with her wounded pride, but her curiosity meant she had to know the end of the story.

She decided she'd have to pretend they were doing the gig on the Friday, even if they didn't. Otherwise it would be just too embarrassing.

Then the door opened and the band walked in. There were four of them, including Finn. He made introductions. 'Liam and Seamus you know, and this is Pat.'

The three men, about the same age as Finn, grinned at her. They were all good-looking and she wondered if they'd all been members of his original band or if anyone had been added. They also all sounded unnervingly like Bob Geldof.

'Pat, this is Beth,' said Finn.

'This is Beth?' said Pat, looking at the other two. They just shrugged.

'Yes,' said Finn curtly. 'She's come with news.'

'Shall we order a pizza? I'm famished,' said Seamus.

Finn sat staring into space while the pizza was ordered. They insisted on Beth having one too. Then they produced more cans of beer and handed them out.

'OK, let's have the news,' said Liam, who seemed a bit more in charge than the others.

Beth, who would really have liked a glass to drink her beer with, cleared her throat. 'It's Mickey Wilson—'

'The big man himself,' said Pat.

'He rang asking for Finn, at the pub where I work.'

'And what did he say?' demanded Liam.

'He said he couldn't be there to hear you on Saturday but he could on the Friday,' said Beth.

'But I thought we couldn't have the gig on the Friday because of some wedding?'

'I changed the venue of the wedding,' said Beth. 'It's my sister's wedding. She's now having it in a marquee in a field.'

'You did that?' said Liam. 'So we could have the gig on the Friday? And Mickey Wilson could hear us?'

'Yes,' said Beth, wishing, not for the first time, that she hadn't bothered. Finn had been fine at the thought of a producer mate of Raff's coming; why was he so against Mickey Wilson?

383

'But that's amazing!' said Seamus.

'What's amazing,' said Finn, 'is how Mickey Wilson got to hear about us at all.' He didn't sound exactly thrilled.

'God, man! Why are you so pissed off about it? It's feckin' amazing! Took me for ever to track him down. Pulled in all the favours to get his contact details.'

'So it was you, Seamus?' said Finn.

'Yes! And you should be delighted. And thank this lovely woman, Beth, for making sure he will get to hear us,' Seamus went on. At least the others seemed pleased, but it was a hollow victory for Beth when Finn was so angry.

'But are we ready to be heard?' said Finn. 'Wasn't the whole point about doing a gig in some tiny little corner of England so we could see what we sound like?'

'We do know what we sound like,' said Liam. 'And I think we're good.'

'But are we good enough for Mickey Wilson? If he hears us and we're not up to it, he won't listen again. He'll move on. We'll have lost our chance for ever.'

'Oh come on, stop being so melodramatic. We are good. We know we are. And we'll get better.'

'But we don't have what we used to have. We're not seventeen any more, and gorgeous!' Finn railed on.

Had anyone asked Beth's opinion she'd have said they were all a lot more gorgeous than they were when they were seventeen.

'It's only about the music now,' Finn continued. 'And is the music good enough?'

Beth looked longingly at the door. She shouldn't be

here. She couldn't contribute to the argument. But she did want to know if she'd moved the venue for her sister's wedding for no reason.

The pizzas arrived, were paid for and eaten. Many more cans of beer were drunk. No conclusions were reached. To relieve her anxiety, Beth cleared up. She loaded the dishwasher, jumped on the growing pile of cans and found a box to put them in.

Then she left. Just as she was about to close the door behind her, one of the band – she couldn't see which one – said, 'Oh, has Beth gone?' Then the arguing started again.

She headed for the van and then home. Finn had shouted at her and while the others seemed pleased about what she'd done, he certainly hadn't been. She felt her hopes shatter around her.

Chapter Twenty-Seven

Lindy awoke the next morning aware that something bad had happened the previous day. Then she remembered it was only that the wedding could no longer take place in the village hall they'd worked so hard to decorate and make nice. Bad, but not a catastrophe.

The hall had needed to be done up, there was a committee to make sure they raised the money and it didn't really matter where Helena's wedding bash was held. Of course, if the marquee plan worked out well it would be just as good for Vintage Weddings. They weren't tied to one venue. And if there hadn't been a real sense of urgency, the hall wouldn't be in the much improved condition it was in now.

Then she remembered that today Edward was coming to take the boys for the day and they were staying the night. This would be the first time they had stayed with Edward without her. This was the source of her gloom.

Living abroad made it difficult for him to visit, she granted him that, and he was quite good at Skyping them – well, once a month, anyway. But for them to actually spend the night away from her, with him, would be quite a big deal.

She tried to talk herself out of her despondency. It would be fine. They were older now and were very used to having sleepovers (as they called them) with her parents and her grandmother. And she was going with them, to make sure there was somewhere suitable for them to sleep, that there was proper food and, basically, there were no major health-and-safety issues she needed to worry about.

What would be worse would be if he wanted them to go and stay with him in Germany, with his current partner. It would happen eventually, she had to accept it, but she would fight it until the boys were quite a lot older.

And at least the practical side of things would be dealt with by Angus. She trusted him. She probably actually loved him if only she'd allow herself to entertain the thought.

She made herself consider it. What she felt was pretty much like love. It was only that she felt love was too dangerous at the moment. If she and Angus fell out her boys would be devastated. Better for them if he didn't get too close, too familiar a face in their lives. Then the fallout would be less.

But whether she loved him or not – whether she *wanted* to love him or not – she had to get in touch with him. She needed a field and she was confident he had one but she had to make sure. She'd only seen it through the hedge she'd been robbing, recently, for April's wedding. It might have a huge pond in the middle of it. But at least unlike the farmers that her mother, Sarah, would know, he wasn't growing anything in his field. He probably would be happy to rent it so they could put a marquee on it.

Her boys were still asleep and the little house was calm. This happy state wouldn't last long so she got up to make tea before the chaos started again. They'd been in bed late the previous night so with luck she'd have an hour.

As she drank tea and tidied and did all the other things mothers do while their children are asleep (which in her case included another look at that bit of decoration Vivien had wanted her to add to the wedding dress) she tried to get her head round the fact that she loved Angus. She might not want to, but she did.

It shouldn't have been a surprise really. She'd had such a crush on him years ago. She also knew that she wanted him, in every way there was. She'd proved that when she found herself leaping into bed with him about six weeks before it was decent. But love? How could she have let that happen? It should make her feel happy, she realised, but instead she couldn't shake off a feeling of anxiety. Eventually she put it down to the boys being with their dad, which was strange to everyone and bound to be a bit stressful.

Edward was late. Lindy didn't know why she was surprised – he always had been late for everything. But it was irritating all the same. She'd had the boys all packed and ready, in their favourite clothes (as opposed to their best clothes, which would have been silly in the circumstances) for ages and they were getting fed up and so naughty.

She'd worked hard on setting the scene for them, explaining that the man who usually appeared on her computer screen would be there in real life. He had done this before but a while ago, and Billy, the little one, mostly thought of his dad as being two-dimensional.

But the thing that convinced them was when Ned asked if Uncle Angus would be there. When Lindy said that he would, both boys began jumping up and down with excitement and packing their bags with their favourite things. So now they were all eager and ready and it was very annoying that Edward wasn't yet there.

As a backup, Lindy had rung her mother about possible fields, but, worryingly and unexpectedly, she couldn't think of a suitable one that was near enough. 'It's the flatness you need,' she explained. 'It's all so hilly round here. If there was a bit more time I'm sure they could put a marquee on the side of a hill but the wedding is on Friday.'

'Thanks, Mum,' Lindy had replied, praying that Angus's field was as flat as she remembered and that he would be willing to hire it out.

Her conversation with Rachel had been much more cheering. She'd confirmed that Raff did indeed have a hotline to a marquee company who owed him a favour and who had something suitable for this Friday.

'It's because it's out of season,' Rachel had said. 'And they can do all the pretty bits too. Carpet, tables, fairy lights, the lot. And...' Rachel had taken a breath and paused '. . . deluxe temporary loos. They are a bit expensive but not nearly as much as they should have been and I'm sure Vivien will pay. She won't want Helena, or indeed anyone, having to visit a Ladies that is not pleasant in every way.'

'Oh well done, Rachel. I never thought about loos, and of course they're vital. I'm happy to pee behind a tree myself but of course, the guests won't be.'

'There might not be time to do flowers,' Rachel had raised her eyes to heaven and then said, 'given the short notice, so I've also ordered some circles made of mirror we can put candles on. Cheap and effective.'

'Vivien will probably want pillars of jasmine and roses,' Lindy had said, very slightly resentful.

'Vivien will have what can be provided.' Rachel had been firm but Lindy knew she would do absolutely anything to keep Vivien happy.

'Don't forget we're going to the flower market,' said Lindy. 'We can buy material – using the jargon – there.'

'It's not just the material,' said Rachel. 'It's the time. You could buy up the entire market but you can't buy more time.'

'Of course not. Oh, Rachel. Is this going to be OK?'

'Of course it is,' said Rachel. 'I have every confidence. I'll get in touch with Sarah to see if the Flower Guild or someone could make posies in jam jars or something, but we do have to manage Vivien's expectations.'

'If only Beth wasn't on her mercy mission for the band she could talk to her mother.'

'Actually,' said Rachel. 'Vivien and I get on. All this will be better coming from me.'

By the time she and Rachel had ended the call, Lindy knew there would be flowers on every table even if every pillar were not twined with lilies and bougainvillaea.

Lindy had just told Billy for the seventy-ninth time that no, they couldn't do cooking, when Edward finally turned up.

'Hi! Sorry I'm a bit late. Took bloody for ever to fit the car seats. Are you sure they're really necessary?'

Lindy had forgotten that Edward always ploughed straight into conversations as if there hadn't been a large gap since they'd had the last one. In a way it was maddening but it did avoid some of the awkwardness.

'Yes, the seats are really necessary. Hello, Edward, you're looking very suntanned, and do you mind taking me with you? I need to ask Angus something.'

'Oh, sorry, Lind.' He pecked her cheek clumsily. 'You look well too. And no reason why you shouldn't come with but why don't you just call Angus?'

'It's a big ask. I need to do it in person, really.'

'Well, he'll be glad to see you. He seems to think you're some kind of angel: the brave little single parent abandoned by a churlish husband. That would be me.'

Edward said this without rancour and Lindy wondered how much of it was true. Did Angus think so well of her? It gave her a happy glow to think so. He wouldn't have said that about her if he just thought her an incredibly easy lay. Would he?

Because the boys had already been hanging round all morning and were overexcited at the thought of spending time with their dad and uncle, getting them into the car wasn't easy. Billy absolutely refused to be strapped in and Edward suggested, in his hearing, that it was OK to skip this part.

'Absolutely not,' said Lindy. 'Billy, darling, you know perfectly well we do not go in the car – any car including Daddy's – without being strapped in. Apart from anything else it's against the law. Daddy could go to prison.' Currently this prospect was pleasing to Lindy but she knew her sons would feel differently.

'Daddy says I don't have to,' said Billy.

'And I say you do,' said Lindy calmly.

'But daddies are the boss,' wailed Billy.

'Who on earth told you that?' Lindy was beginning to lose patience, if not with Billy, certainly her ex-husband. 'I've never heard such nonsense in my life.' With that she finally managed to put the fixing together with a satisfying snap. 'There we go! Now, I'll get in and put my seat belt on and we'll be off.'

'Will you stay with us all the time?' said Ned, obviously wanting the answer to be yes.

'I'll stay with you a little while because I want to ask Uncle Angus something.' It suddenly sounded weird referring to a man she'd slept with as an uncle.

'Oh, for God's sake!' said Edward. 'You've turned the boy into a complete baby.'

Lindy cleared her throat and looked out of the window. This was not the time to tell her children's father that it was not her fault they lacked a role model. And as she had the thought she realised that perhaps it wasn't entirely his, either.

She found she was extraordinarily embarrassed to see Angus again. There had been some texts, sweet ones, but seeing him in the flesh reminded her of the time they slept together. Would Edward be able to tell what had gone on? She blushed at the horror of it. It wasn't helped by the fact that the children had suddenly glued themselves to her.

'Hello!' she said gaily, trying to pretend that the situation wasn't incredibly awkward.

'Hi, guys!' said Angus cheerfully.

But the boys weren't yet up for cheerfulness. 'Hello, Uncle Angus,' they whispered.

Edward gave them an irritated look. 'Do you want a drink or anything? I've got special drinks in.'

Lindy remembered she hadn't mentioned not giving them things with too much sugar in – it would make them so hyper. But now was not the time. Fortunately, the boys shook their heads.

'Maybe Daddy would show you round a bit?' she suggested, trying to push them forward but unable to detach them.

'That's a good idea!' said Angus.

'Yes,' said Edward. 'Come and look at the tree house we've made for you!'

As they all trooped off, the boys at last attached to their father and not her, Lindy realised that Angus must have done most of the work on the tree house. Edward hadn't really been in the country long enough for much chopping and sawing.

The boys ran ahead with Edward and Lindy followed with Angus. She needed to ask her big favour.

'Angus?' she began tentatively.

'Lindy? Are you all right?' He was concerned, possibly because she sounded worried.

'Yes. I'm fine. I just need to ask you a favour and it's a big one.'

'Anything you need, ever, just ask.'

'You're so kind. But this isn't for me personally. It's a Vintage Weddings thing.'

'I assume you don't suddenly need an architectural report on a wedding gazebo?'

She laughed. 'No. Something much more prosaic!'

'So?'

'We need a field. And you have a flat one.'

'I have, but why do you want it? Not that you can't have it – of course you can, even though there's currently a tree house on it – but why?'

Lindy explained about the change of venue and the marquee. 'So can we rent it? I insist on your getting paid.'

'If you think it's suitable, of course you can. But it might need some clearing up first, apart from possibly moving the tree house.'

They hadn't reached the tree house yet but Lindy could hear her boys, who obviously had. 'That will be dreadful. When you've gone to so much trouble to build it for them.'

'Well, it is quite near the edge of the field. It might be all right. Do we have a marquee?'

She liked the 'we'. 'We do. Raff is sorting it. It might need to turn up quite soon.'

'Well, let's see if we need to start dismantling the tree house.'

They reached the tree house and Lindy saw that it was in the far corner, well away from the gate and so it could be left intact. The field was fairly level and as the marquee would probably have a floor, any little humps and bumps wouldn't matter. It was also large, and so had plenty of room for parking.

What was less good was the number of small ash seedlings and patches of brambles, which might be too large to be concealed under the floor.

'Do you suppose they'd be able to put a marquee up on top of those saplings and bushes?' she asked.

'I don't know. I would imagine the bushes wouldn't be a problem but the trees might be.'

'It's a lovely spot though,' said Lindy. 'Imagine a proper summer wedding here...'

Angus laughed softly.

Edward had left the boys clambering in the tree house and joined them.

'I think we'll probably need to get rid of all the little trees,' said Angus.

'Why?' said Edward. 'Seems a bit unnecessary!'

'We need to put up a marquee in this field. By Friday. For a wedding,' said Lindy.

'Really? Good God! Why didn't you tell me? Congratulations! At least you won't have to change your name, Lindy-Lou'

'Very funny,' said Angus, having glanced at Lindy.

'It's not actually us getting married,' she said, keeping her tone light.

'Not this time,' said Angus.

'What?' said Edward.

'Joking!' said Angus.

Edward scowled.

'I'm part of a wedding company,' said Lindy, trying

395

to cover the slight awkwardness between the brothers. 'I know I told you. We're arranging a wedding for this lovely woman.'

'When is the wedding?'

'This Friday.'

'You've left it a bit bloody late, haven't you?'

Eventually Lindy left her children with their father and walked back towards the house with Angus.

'Does he always call you Lindy-Lou?' he asked when they were out of earshot.

'Only when he wants to put me down.'

'I'll never call you Lindy-Lou then.'

Without stopping to think, Lindy said, 'It would be all right if you did it!' Then she shut her mouth and looked into the bushes as they went along the path. Angus said nothing.

They reached Angus's makeshift kitchen – which seemed a bit less makeshift than when she'd last seen it – and Lindy braced herself to ask Angus for a lift home. It had been arranged that he would take her but for some reason she didn't want to leave.

Just as she was steeling herself to do it, her phone rang. It was Rachel. Raff and the marquee man were in the area and wanted to check out the site. Lindy could get a lift back with Raff.

After they had all tramped over the field, sucking their, teeth they eventually said, 'No probs. Our flooring will go over most of this. We'll be here tomorrow.'

Although she didn't say anything, Edward being well in earshot, Lindy did realise how terribly short notice it all was. Maybe that was why she still had a bad feeling that was almost physical.

Yet being with Raff was always cheering. She sat up beside him in the truck and realised he was one of those people who would always find a solution, make things work or know a bloke who could. He was so perfect for Rachel. She was all organised and efficient with her ever-present notebook and he was 'make it up as you go along'. They complemented each other.

'Is the marquee going to be expensive, Raff?' she asked.

He inclined his head. 'Well, it's mates' rates, and it's too early for the main wedding season so the marquee's there doing nothing, but Mike will have to put a lot of guys on the job to get it up and running. So yeah, it will be pricey.'

Lindy swallowed. 'Well, the bride's mother will have to pay.'

'Not her fault she can't have the hall, though, is it? Even if she did book the church for the wrong day, or whatever.'

Lindy adjusted her good opinion of Raff. He was capable of saying worrying things. 'No, but it is Beth's fault, and Vivien obviously wouldn't expect her to pay. Or us, so I think it'll be all right.'

'I'll tell you what Rachel said—'

'Oh, do!'

'She thinks that Vivien will actually secretly prefer the marquee to the hall because it'll look posher. The hall is quaint and we like it but it isn't grand. A marquee can look grand.'

'Oh, God bless Rachel. I feel better about it now.'

'She's a good girl, Rachel,' said Raff.

Lindy looked at him with satisfaction. She'd been cross with her mother for matchmaking but she could see how very satisfying it was – if it worked.

She thought about Beth. She'd obviously fallen hard for Finn – or why would she go to such enormous, inconvenient lengths so his band could be heard by an agent, or manager, or whoever the man was? She just hoped Finn wouldn't let her down. Realistically, the odds that he wouldn't weren't great.

It seemed that Lindy had only just sorted out the house, feeling a bit tearful in the boys' bedroom seeing a couple of toys that had been left behind in the rush to get packed, when the phone rang. Oh, please let it be Rachel or Beth, suggesting they come over with a bottle of wine, or even that they go to the pub. For once she didn't need a babysitter.

She answered the phone with a smile on her face. It was Angus.

'I'm afraid there's been an accident. It's Ned. Nothing life-threatening but I think he should go to A and E.'

Lindy's mouth went instantly dry. 'What happened?' She was surprised and relieved to hear herself sound quite calm.

'He fell off the tree house.'

Lindy swallowed. This was no time to rage against tree houses, even if they were dangerous. 'Did he hit his head?'

'No, it's his arm. I think it's broken. I've rung Sarah.

She's coming to be with Billy, who needs someone. Edward is... well—'

Lindy interrupted Angus's struggle to describe his brother's emotions. 'So have you rung anyone – a doctor? An ambulance?'

'Yes. We've rung the ambulance service but decided it'll be quicker to take him in by car. I'll pick you up on the way.'

'Doesn't he need someone else in the car with him while you drive?'

'He's being really brave. He knows that his father has to stay with Billy until Sarah arrives. It's not a long journey, after all.'

'Angus, would it be possible for you to wait until Mum gets there? I just don't...' Could she say she didn't trust her three-year-old with his father, even for half an hour or so? It wasn't that she didn't think he'd keep Billy safe, but he might not keep him reassured.

'Yup. If you'd prefer that. Sarah is quite nearby, luckily. She'll be here in about fifteen minutes.'

'I'll wait here then.'

'It will be all right, Lindy. Trust me. Horrible for now but not dangerous in the long-term.'

Lindy suddenly wanted to cry. 'Thank you,' she whispered, hoping he couldn't hear the tears.

Chapter Twenty-Eight

In the end it was twenty-five minutes before they arrived. Lindy's house had never been so clean and tidy. She didn't want to ring anyone so her phone wouldn't be blocked if Angus or her mother needed to get through to her. So she cleaned, dusted, hoovered, pulled out the sofa and discovered an entire plastic army and a packet of biscuits' worth of crumbs. She was just about to start wiping down the skirting boards when the doorbell rang.

She rushed past Angus with a brief apology to get to the car. She pulled open the back door.

'I'm fine, Mum, really,' said Ned.

He didn't look fine. He looked green, as if he might be sick at any moment. Lindy got in next to him and then got out again. 'I'll fetch a bucket,' she said. As she ran she realised that the front seat had been occupied. Edward was there too. It wasn't unreasonable, Lindy realised, but it was an extra complication when she really didn't need it.

'Your mother is there with Billy, so I came to give Ned support,' said Edward when she returned with the bucket. 'Really I think it would be better if I took him. My girlfriend's a teacher and she says kids're much better if they haven't got their mothers with them. You have to remember with children it's important not to make too much fuss, she says. It only makes it worse. Angus insisted on fetching you. Said you'd arranged it.'

'Thank you, Angus!' said Lindy, squeezing in next to Ned. Annoyingly, Edward's teacher girlfriend was right about the too much fuss, but it was up to her to decide what was too much and what was just the right amount.

When they set off Angus said, 'We haven't given him anything to eat or drink in case they have to operate.'

'Right,' said Lindy, concentrating on sounding calm for Ned's sake.

'They won't have to operate!' said Edward. 'He's just fallen out of a tree house. Children have accidents all the time. There's really no need for this. His arm is probably just bruised.'

Angus ignored him. 'They're not busy at A and E. Sarah knows one of the sisters on duty and she said we'll be fine if we come now.'

'One of the joys of living near a small town,' said Lindy. 'A and E isn't the nightmare it is in bigger places.'

She was glad it was getting dark in the back of the car so no one, especially Ned, could see how worried she was in spite of her calm tones. She breathed slowly in and out and found it did help. She squeezed the little hand in hers. 'It's going to be OK, Neddy, really it is.'

'Of course it is!' said Edward. 'You're making a fuss, Lindy!'

Lindy could see Ned's face was screwed up, whether

with pain or the effort of not crying she couldn't tell. 'It's all right to cry,' she whispered, hoping his father wouldn't hear. 'If you want to. It might help.'

There was a loud exhale of breath from the front passenger seat.

'What might help,' said Angus sotto voce to his brother, 'would be if you shut up and let Lindy cope with Ned. She knows how to handle him far better than you do.'

'I'm so glad you're here, Mum,' whispered Ned, clutching her hand. 'Is it really all right not to be brave?'

Cursing her ex-husband with every cell of her body, Lindy said, 'Yes, darling. You don't have to be anything if you don't want to be.'

The sister was waiting for them when they arrived. It was Mrs Haslam, someone Lindy had known a long time herself, and Lindy found it hard not to cry all over her, such was the comfort in seeing a familiar face.

'Well, young man, what's happened to you? Being just a bit too tough, I imagine,' said the sister. 'You young soldiers, always flinging yourselves around as if you're Bear Grylls.'

Edward took all the credit. 'That's right! Ned's a little toughie, aren't you, son?'

Although deeply annoyed by this comment, Lindy was very grateful to Mrs Haslam – Sue. Ned adored Bear Grylls and she could have hugged her for somehow knowing that.

'Let's get you where we can see what's what.' She pulled out a wheelchair. 'Ever been in one of these before?'

'No,' said Ned.

'Hop in then. Time for a ride.'

'I'm sure he can walk!' said Edward.

'I'm sure he can,' agreed Sue, 'but he's looking very pale and we don't want him vomiting on my clean floor. Or at least I don't.'

'I'll get us some hot drinks out of the machine,' said Angus. 'Ned doesn't need all of us with him.'

Lindy felt that personally she did need 'all of us' if it included Angus, but couldn't really say that. Edward was being so unsympathetic. He might have been an awful father but he did love his kids. Why couldn't he be a bit more sensitive? She realised it was quite likely guilt.

'So, how did this happen, young man?' asked the sister.

Ned looked at his father. 'We were playing in the tree house.'

'I've built them a tree house at my brother's place. Me and his mother' – he glanced at Lindy – 'aren't together any more, sadly, and I wanted to make our times together meaningful.'

God, thought Lindy, he sounds like something out of a 'How to be a good dad even though you don't live with Mum any more' pamphlet.

'So, what happened, darling?' said Lindy, kneeling so she could hear the subtext. By now, given Edward's attitude, she was worried there was one.

'Daddy said I should jump down and not use the ladder. Ladders were for wusses.' Ned was whispering and not making eye contact. Lindy knew he was speaking the truth.

'Is that true, Edward?' she demanded, seeing him about to bluster and deny it.

'Well, of course, Ned got it a bit wrong. I didn't say—'

'Did you actually say ladders are for wusses?'

He thought about this. 'I might have done. But for God's sake! I didn't ask him to jump down and fall on his arm!'

'OK, this is no time to play the blame game,' said Sue. 'Now, would you mind if it was just Mum with him? Better not to have too many people.'

Edward walked out without a word. Lindy was fuming. She'd begun to suspect he had had something to do with Ned's accident; now it was confirmed.

'You're a very lucky young man,' said the doctor after what seemed like hours of painkillers, X-rays, checks and, finally, a visit from the plasterer for a cast.

'It's a minor fracture and should heal fairly quickly. You'll visit the fracture clinic and we'll keep an eye on what's going on in there. Keep giving the painkillers as he needs them, Mum. We'll send over the appointment shortly.'

Usually Lindy hated being called Mum by people who weren't her children but the doctor had been so wonderful with Ned she'd have forgiven him anything.

After thanking everyone profusely she and Ned finally found Angus. Edward wasn't there.

'Edward took a taxi back to my place. I'm taking you home,' said Angus. 'I took the liberty of ringing Sarah and said you'd call the moment you and Ned were out.'

'Thank you so much. What time is it? We seem to have been here for ever.'

'About nine.'

'I'll just ring Mum.'

Sarah told her that Billy had fallen asleep on the sofa and that she was going to take him back to her house and keep him there. Edward was heading up to see his parents a little earlier than planned – he felt he wasn't really needed any more, Lindy was so much better at these things. He was deserting them again, the moment he knew there would be no more fun and games in the tree house, Lindy thought resentfully, although a part of her was quite glad. And felt very relieved now she knew that both her boys were safe and happy. 'Now let's get you back. How does that feel now, Ned?'

'It doesn't hurt any more. But maybe that's the pills.'

'And we've got more if you need them, Ned, so it'll be fine.'

'I'm starving, Mum,' said Ned. 'Can I eat now?'

'Fish and chips on the way home?' said Angus. 'Come on.'

It was while Lindy was waiting in the car with Ned for Angus to emerge with their supper that her phone pinged. It was from Vivien.

Don't forget I'm picking you up tomorrow at 4.30 a.m. Stupid o'clock I know! Vivien X.

Of course, she had completely forgotten and realised she'd have to cancel. Her son had broken his arm. Originally the boys would have been staying with their father so stealing out of the house at 'stupid o'clock' would have been no problem. Now she'd need to find a babysitter and while her grandmother would probably step in, it would mean taking Ned over there now and she felt he needed his mother. She suffered a familiar pang of guilt for the amount of childcare her mother and grandmother did.

But should she see if Beth or Rachel could go instead? Then she remembered that they were on chopping and peeling duty for Belinda. They were going to have to hire ovens and hotplates for the do but, Rachel had said, it was a lot easier than trying to produce a hot meal out of the village-hall kitchen: Vivien had declared it a 'kitchenette' and made quite clear her opinion of those.

Lindy realised she was thinking about other things to avoid the problem in front of her. Vivien would have to go alone and she would have to tell her.

She had just started with *So sorry, my son has had a fall and broken his arm* when Angus came back and dumped three hot parcels on her lap. 'Problem?' he said, seeing Lindy's anxious expression. 'You OK, Ned?'

'I'm fine,' said Ned, and he did seem to be.

'I've just had a text from Vivien. I'd completely forgotten I was supposed to go to Birmingham flower market with her tomorrow. I was just composing my text. I hate to disappoint her, but also I was really looking forward to going.'

He started the car. 'Don't do it yet. Wait until we get home. It's hell trying to text people in a moving vehicle.'

'True. And if she answers immediately I'll feel obliged to reply and get a bit car sick doing it.'

'If you need to cancel, I'm sure she'll understand,' said Angus and they set off.

Once home, Lindy couldn't help being pleased about the cleaning and tidying she had done when she was in such a state, waiting for Angus to pick her up with Ned. It was a shame one could only work at that pace when in a state of high anxiety.

Soon the three of them were sitting cosily round the kitchen table eating fish and chips, Ned doing his best with one hand. Lindy said, 'I must sort out Vivien. Tell her I can't come. She probably won't mind going on her own. She'll need help to carry the stuff but I'm sure she'll snap her fingers and a porter will appear!' She dipped a chip into tomato ketchup. 'I can go to the flower market another time, of course, but somehow it's not the sort of thing you organise unless there's a really good reason or someone pushes you into doing it.'

'Why can't you go, Mummy?' asked Ned.

Lindy ruffled his hair, touched by his concern about her missing out on a treat. 'Because someone needs to stay here and look after you. I'd be going too early in the morning for Gran to come. Or Sarah.'

'Why can't Uncle Angus look after me? Billy's at Gran's so it would be just me.'

'Darling! Uncle Angus has to work tomorrow!'

'Actually, Uncle Angus hasn't got much on. I could work here.'

'Really? You could work in my house?'

'Well, don't sound so surprised. You have a table and an internet connection so I can pick up emails? Actually your house would be easier to work in. I won't get distracted by wondering what the builders are doing. Not that they would have been anywhere near where the boys would be, it's perfectly safe...'

Luckily Lindy was too distracted to worry about such

things, even if Billy were still at the house.

'If you're absolutely sure,' she said. 'And, Ned, you wouldn't mind?'

'I'd like it,' said Ned.

Angus seemed flattered. 'Well, that's settled then.' He paused. 'I would have to stay the night though. I don't fancy setting my alarm for three a.m.'

'Would you really do that? That is so kind. And are you sure you'd be happy, Ned? I could get Gran to come over in the morning. You'll probably be asleep most of the time.' She paused. 'It's really very sweet of you chaps to make it so I can have my treat.'

'That's all right, Mummy,' said Ned. 'Mummies deserve treats too.'

As this was a direct quote from her, Lindy could hardly argue!

Relief that there seemed to be such an easy solution to her problem made her ridiculously happy. Or was it the prospect of Angus staying the night?

Angus had popped out to the pub to buy a bottle of wine while Lindy was on the phone updating her mother and grandmother about what was going on.

'Do you think it's all right to have wine?' asked Lindy, eyeing the bottle longingly. Ned was asleep, propped up with pillows to support his arm. 'I'm just thinking: if there was an emergency with Ned, I'd need to be able to think clearly.'

'There won't be an emergency with Ned,' said Angus firmly. 'But you do have to be up horribly early, so I'd stick to one glass. I won't have any in case there is, actually, an emergency and I have to drive.'

'You're a very responsible person,' said Lindy, accepting the glass he handed to her. 'I'm very grateful.'

'That doesn't make me sound terribly exciting,' Angus laughed.

'Sometimes exciting is a bad thing,' said Lindy, thinking that, actually, he was exciting in all the right ways.

'I suppose it's because I'm the eldest. I was always in charge. Edward had more licence to run around and be silly. He's not a bad father, you know, but he doesn't get much practice. And his girlfriend, who teaches eleven -year-olds, seems to have given him unreasonable expectations.' His smile was rueful. 'I could see he was egging Ned on to be more and more reckless and knew it would end in tears, to use an old cliché. But I couldn't see how to stop it, apart from muttering to Edward.'

'Muttering doesn't work with Edward. Hitting him over the head with a shovel might have done the trick. But you couldn't have really done that.'

'Not in front of the boys, anyway,' Angus agreed. 'Such a bad example.'

Lindy put out her hand and held his wrist. She was suffering from both extreme shyness and a sense of total intimacy. She felt at once completely safe with him and too nervous to say a word of how she felt. To her embarrassment, she yawned, deeply.

'Bedtime,' said Angus. 'You've got a very early start.'

There was quite a lot of argument about who should sleep where. Lindy won. She was going to sleep in Billy's bed so she could keep an ear open for Ned. Angus felt she should have her usual bed because she'd sleep better.

Lindy found him a new toothbrush and there was a lot of embarrassing 'you go first' regarding the bathroom.

At no point through all this slightly awkward time did Angus make any attempt to kiss her goodnight or anything. It was as if they had never shared that cosy, lovely evening that had ended up in Lindy's bed. Lindy half liked him for not assuming they would just go to bed together, and half felt miffed because he didn't.

She accepted there were lots of reasons for it – most of them perfectly rational. They were being more like parents because of Ned's accident; she had to get up at four in the morning; the whole evening was just different.

But as she lay in Billy's little bed, snuggled up to a dinosaur, the room lit by a Buzz Lightyear night light, she felt a bit lonely. She'd been through a worrying time; she wanted to feel Angus's safe, warm arms around her, to take away the stress. But she wasn't going to be the one to initiate anything. She'd done it before and had suffered the embarrassment. She was not doing it again. Although it was nice to think of Angus asleep in her bed next door. She might soon find out if he snored or not.

She couldn't get to sleep. She knew it was because she had to get up early. Her phone alarm was set so all should be well, but she couldn't get off.

When she'd been through all the names of the children in her first year at primary school she decided she had to something more about it. There were some painkillers in the bathroom; she could even steal a couple of Ned's – he now had loads. That's what she'd do. She'd make hot milk to take it with and she'd be off in seconds.

She tiptoed about, not wanting to disturb Angus,

opening the childproof medicine as quietly as she could and then dropping the Calpol into the basin with a clatter that would have woken Sleeping Beauty.

Then, without letting herself think about what she was doing she went into her bedroom and hovered in the doorway.

Angus turned. He obviously hadn't been asleep either.

'I can't sleep,' said Lindy. 'Can I get into your bed?'

He flipped the duvet back. 'You absolutely can. I thought you'd never ask!'

Lindy's phone alarm must have woken Ned, which was just as well as she hadn't heard it. He came into the bedroom and switched on the light. 'Oh. Hello, Uncle Angus.'

Lindy and Angus blinked in the sudden light.

'So, are you going to sleep in Mummy's bed all the time now? Or just sometimes?'

Angus cleared his throat. 'Just sometimes. If that's all right with Mummy.'

Lindy tried to clear her head. 'Fine. Yes. I think that will be absolutely fine.'

'Cool,' said Ned. 'As long as me and Billy can get in too if we have a nightmare.'

'Of course!' said Lindy. 'You can always get in.'

'But we might need a slightly bigger bed,' said Angus.

Chapter Twenty-Nine

'Hey!' called Rachel when she spotted Lindy in the doorway of the marquee. It was the morning of Helena's wedding. 'Come over here! Help me with these jam jars!'

Rachel not only had a lot of jam jars that needed to be decorated, she had been extremely busy helping Belinda and generally keeping Vivien under control, but Vivien had mentioned that Lindy had been looking very well when she went with her to Birmingham flower market. Rachel wanted to know why. She was fairly sure it had a lot to do with Angus. Why else would the mother of a child with a broken arm be looking so upbeat?

Lindy dumped another box of jam jars on the floor beside the table. 'These are from Gran. And here are the scraps of lace she had. Have you got ribbons?'

'Zillions. Internet,' said Rachel. 'Beth got them. Fortunately that was before she and Sukey became un-official PRs for Finn's band. We have to hope they have moved the date of the gig otherwise they've done all that work for nothing. And of course now she's in full-on bridesmaid mode.'

'So, what are we doing?'

'Lace round the jam jars with double-sided tape. Here.' Rachel handed Lindy a roll. 'But some will have ribbons as well. Five jam jars to a table, so that's fifty.'

'Wow, Rachel! No wonder you're an accountant! You can do your times tables!'

'Don't be cheeky, you. Sit down and get going.' Rachel was pleased to be with a friend. She could be herself with Lindy. She had to be the consummate professional when she was with Vivien, and Belinda now treated her like a sort of daughter-in-law, so Rachel felt she had to live up to her expectations. But with Lindy she could just relax.

Lindy sat. 'I can't believe I'm doing flowers, though it is fun, and actually a lot more restful than fighting Vivien about the extra crystals on Helena's dress. Helena wanted them but Vivien said they were common. Obviously, I'm on the side of the bride.'

Rachel made a gesture. 'Unless you were with her at the flower market, in which case you let the bride's mother get totally carried away!'

'OK, yes, so I did. But to be honest, she'd been so... embarrassing – ordering everyone about and snapping her fingers – I felt I should encourage her to give big orders.' Lindy scratched at a bit of jam label that had got left on. 'And there was something so wonderful about whole boxes of beautiful flowers I got carried away too. The scent was amazing.'

'You liked it then?'

'Oh, I did. You heard about Ned? And Angus being a total star?'

'Word had got to me. So he was a hero?'

Lindy bit her lip, her gaze a bit dreamy. 'I think he still is a hero, actually.'

Rachel clapped her hands. 'I knew it. You are so right for each other. So, tell me what happened. Did you...?' Lindy nodded shyly. 'Go, girl! But how did you get over the "I can't even look at another man until my boys have left home" thing?'

'Well, I did fight it. I mean, me and Angus got together a little while ago – before the quiz.'

'Beth said something about that. We knew you liked him and it was obvious he liked you, right from the start. But why didn't you tell me?'

'Because it wasn't going anywhere – not then. It was just – well – sex.'

'Ah,' said Rachel, sighing slightly. 'Lovely sex.'

Lindy swallowed, obviously agreeing with Rachel on this point.

'So how did things move on?' While fairly loved up herself, Rachel wasn't going to let Lindy leave anything out.

'Well, it was Ned really. We were in my bed and I'd forgotten I'd set my phone alarm for four a.m., for the flower market. He woke up. Came in to me and there we were. He was so relaxed about it.'

'Oh, Lindy. I'm so pleased. I thought he was gorgeous and absolutely right for you. But...' She made a face. 'Raff is so wrong for me and look at us.'

'Not wrong for you at all.'

'So tell me all about the flower market then.'

Lindy smiled in reminiscence. 'Well, I was completely zonked – fell asleep on the journey – but being there was like…' Lindy paused, obviously looking for the right word. 'The best kind of sweet shop, when everything is really tempting, and you don't have to have just a few but a whole box, or bucket, or whatever.'

'Did you and Vivien stick out like sore thumbs?' asked Rachel, trying to picture Vivien, perfectly groomed even at four in the morning, surrounded by men in overalls with strong Birmingham accents. Her loud, cut-glass vowels must have stuck out like crystals in a sandpit.

'Surprisingly, not as much as you'd think! Vivien had been before and there were a few women like her ordering stuff. But I suppose posh women do do flower-arranging; we just don't associate them with markets – at such an horrendous hour in the morning.'

'It does sound fun, although I'm not sure I'd have got up that early to go.'

'I'd go again, if necessary. It was like a shop but giant-sized. A massive great warehouse full of great trolleys laden with boxes of exotic flowers, which looked like shops, with boxes and buckets full of wonderful stuff. Honestly, Rachel, it was enough to make anyone want to take up floristry.' She smiled. 'Not to be confused with flower-arranging.'

'Well, don't add it to your list of accomplishments until we have someone else who can do dresses. You do have such a strong artistic sense.'

'That's what Vivien said. It made me forgive her for calling a stallholder "my good man". OK!' Lindy regarded her current jam jar with satisfaction. 'Remind me, can I put any colour ribbon on? Is there a code?'

'No, we're going freestyle. Goes against the grain.

If it were my wedding, I'd just have various shades of cream...'

'Really?' Lindy squeaked. 'Surely not. I mean, you'd need *some* colour.' She paused and looked at Rachel sideways. 'Are you actually planning a wedding?'

Rachel, who planned her wedding whenever she felt that Helena and Vivien were doing something that didn't fit in with her aesthetic, shrugged. 'Not in real life, no. It's a bit early for that.' Then a sigh she didn't know was there erupted. 'Raff is lovely though.'

'He is. We're very lucky.'

'Do we know what happened to Beth?' asked Rachel. 'Apart from leaving us here?' She gestured at the marquee, bustling with people, promising to look sensational.

'Well, the gig is tonight. Poor Beth – she'd obviously be at the gig if it wasn't her sister's wedding day.'

Lindy became anxious. 'I do hope she and Finn work out. She must really care, or she'd have just let them do the gig on the Saturday and miss the impresario – or whoever it was needed to see them for their new career to be launched. She admitted it was probably madness but she couldn't help herself, she really liked him. I do hope it's different to Charlie this time.'

'I'm afraid it may not be, because the last I heard was when I got a very clipped message from her saying that she didn't know if the gig was even still on, she didn't care, and she might have known Finn would be another Charlie. She did sound rather tearful now I think about it. I haven't been able to get hold of her again.'

'Oh dear. And I haven't heard from her either. I think she's all right – at least we know she's alive. She left the van outside my house and posted the keys,' said Lindy. 'It is worrying,' she went on. 'But she's an adult. She has to live her life herself.'

They both added lace and ribbon to a couple of jars before Lindy, obviously wanting to think about something more cheerful than Beth's possibly broken heart, said, 'So, Rachel, when you're planning your wedding in your head, where do you have it? A hotel? A stately home? A marquee in a field?' Lindy looked around, admiring the developing glamour.

Rachel swallowed. 'The hall,' she said. 'Our village hall. It will be the only place for me.'

Lindy suddenly put her hand on hers and squeezed it. Rachel loved the fact Lindy understood, without having it all explained to her; why she, picky, OCD Rachel, would, if asked, have her wedding in a small, currently fairly rundown village hall when, in theory at least, she could get married anywhere.

'I feel the same,' said Lindy. 'It brought us together, that hall, made us create Vintage Weddings, which has been amazing for me.'

Rachel nodded and cleared her throat. 'We owe it. Not that Raff has asked me to marry him or anything. Maybe never will!'

Lindy seemed a bit tearful too. 'So, what do we do with the jars when we've decorated them?'

'Take them over to those women over there. They're the Flower Guild and the WI. They've raided their gardens for foliage and are doing a brilliant job. Take this lot over and see.'

The women had taken over a couple of large round

tables and were creating perfect little arrangements in every jar. Lindy knew several of them, it turned out. They were her grandmother's friends, or her mother's. They admired the little jars, and she admired how quickly they selected material, twisted them together with wire, and made something beautiful.

'These spring flowers are so lovely, Lindy,' said one. 'I love these little Wordsworth daffodils.'

'Yes,' agreed another. I've rather gone off those big fat King Alfreds.'

'Sorry,' said Rachel. 'But what are Wordsworth daffodils?'

'Oh! You know, from the poem. "I Wandered Lonely as a Cloud". They're like the wild ones,' the woman explained. 'The King Alfreds are those really yellow ones that you often see in formal displays.'

Rachel nodded. 'I totally agree. You women are epic.'

'She doesn't mean we're fat, does she?' one asked another.

'No!' said Lindy. 'And if she'd said you were sick, that would have been a compliment, too.'

Rachel had things to do. She opened her trusty Emma Bridgewater. 'Oh, give over, Lindy, you and your street talk. We need to check the ovens have arrived and it's all OK for Belinda for later. And I'm sure you've got a Swarovski crystal or two to adjust.'

Lindy laughed. 'I'm sure I have!'

Chapter Thirty

Meanwhile, over in Chippingford, Beth had opened her eyes and seen that at least it wasn't raining. That fitted in with the weather forecast on her phone. Good. All the family, and Lindy and Rachel, had been looking at weather forecasts on various websites for days and none of them quite agreed. Beth's had said it would be a lovely day, the kind you can get in April when everyone says, 'I expect this is summer.' She was going to trust hers.

For a few seconds she lay there, wondering how Helena was feeling, and Jeff and her mother? Were they feeling anxious? Excited? Or just wanting to get on with it? Then she wondered how Finn and the band were feeling. This was their big day too. It could be the dawning of a new career for them. Or it could be a small gig in a small venue and only a few people, drummed up by her or Sukey. She wondered why she cared so much, especially as Finn had made it perfectly clear she was persona non grata as far as he was concerned. But you couldn't just switch off your feelings for someone, not if you really cared, and she admitted that she did. And when you cared about someone you always wanted the best for them.

Feeling her loyalties torn between the two events, wanting passionately for them both to go well, she got out of bed and into the shower. She was not going to have her hair done by the hairdresser brought in by her mother. Having it so short meant she didn't have to. She was going to do it herself, thus saving money and, more importantly, the hairdresser's time. She hadn't actually told her mother this yet, but she would. Beth had never known either her mother or sister to be relaxed about what was being done to their hair. There might be requests for the whole process to be done again. Still, at least the hairdresser had been arranged by her mother. No one else could be held responsible if she didn't do a good job.

As she used the special shower gel her mother had given her and Nancy as bridesmaids' presents, aware that when it was gone she might never again wash herself in Floris, she determined that nothing, particularly her own private heartbreak, was going to spoil her sister's day.

Determined to count her blessings and not just feel miserable about Finn, she realised how lucky she was that, instead of turfing her out of their holiday house or, worse, wanting to share it, Jeff's parents had hired a huge mansion nearby. They had filled it with Jeff's grandparents, his aunts and sister. The thought of sleeping on the sofa while her sister's parents-in-law took the only bed had been worrying Beth on and off since she first realised it was a possibility. Luckily other distractions meant this had only recently occurred to her.

One of the band had left a message with Sukey to say

that yes, they would perform on the Friday – tonight! – but she'd heard nothing from Finn.

At least she knew now. He didn't care about her, didn't want her in his life, and that was that, otherwise why not get in touch? How long did it take to write a text? Just something. But no. Well, she'd be fine. It wasn't the first time it had happened, after all, and it probably wouldn't be the last. Not that she could really compare her feelings for Charlie with what she felt for Finn. But she'd been crazy. He was way out of her league. He just thought she was some sort of crazed fangirl, not someone he would ever consider having a relationship with.

She was obviously a bad picker. But bad picker or not, today she'd be a good bridesmaid and a good part of Vintage Weddings. And at least the other two girls seemed to have found good men who loved them. Lindy and Angus seemed to have got together quite quickly – she'd had an excited text from Lindy – but that was sweet. He was her first love, after all.

Clean, if not feeling quite as perky as her exterior appearance implied, she arrived at Rachel's house at the same time as the hairdresser and the make-up artist.

This would reassure her mother, Beth thought, as they introduced themselves. She set great store by punctuality and to be fair, Beth felt, on a wedding day you really wanted people to arrive on time. She was also grateful that her mother had turned up with more funds than Helena originally had. Otherwise it would have been her, Beth, on make-up duty, and this would not have been a straightforward gig. Doing April's had been fun, but then anything she did would have been an improvement on what that awful bridesmaid – in so many ways – had suggested.

As she smiled and introduced herself she imagined her having to do Helena's make-up with her older sister having ideas, her mother having ideas, and no one listening to her, little Beth, with her degree in subjects her mother either hadn't heard of or didn't approve of.

Still, things had changed. Her mother and sister had a lot more respect for her now. She decided if the make-up artist suddenly decided to run away, she would give her sister's make-up a go. And anyway, as the bride and the bride's mother had semi-permanent eyelashes applied, they didn't need a lot.

As no one answered their knock, Beth tried the door and found it unlocked. As it was a special day, and people would be coming in and out all morning, Rachel had obviously decided to set aside her fear of axe-murderers.

'Hello! Happy wedding day!' Beth called up the stairs, having let them all in. 'I've got Anna and Sophie with me! Hair and make-up!'

'Hi, Beth,' Rachel called down. 'Go into the sitting room. I'll be with you in a moment! I'm just bringing something down!'

Beth led the other two young women into Rachel's sitting room. It was prepared as if for a board meeting. Rachel's dining table was in there, with chairs around it. Three mirrors were propped up so three people could look at themselves at the same time.

'Useful,' said Sophie, the make-up artist. 'I'm booked to do four, right?'

Beth was about to say she didn't want her make-up

doing when they were disturbed by the sound of clonking down the stairs.

It was Rachel, manoeuvring her pier glass from her bedroom. Beth ran to assist her. 'I think it's important,' said Rachel, slightly out of breath, 'that we don't have to share mirrors more than necessary. That was heavier than I thought. And of course, much more space in the sitting room. Three people getting ready at the same time in my bedroom would be very crowded. Now – coffee? Tea? Orange juice? I've got croissants in a low oven, for when you get hungry. Also fresh fruit salad and whole-meal bread for toast.'

Beth, who knew Rachel had squeezed the oranges herself, said, 'I'm surprised you're not laying on a full English.'

Rachel's hand flew to her mouth. 'Do you think I should have? I could pop out for bacon the moment the shop opens; I've got some organic free-range—'

'I was teasing!' said Beth. 'We don't want anything greasy round the dresses.' She took the opportunity to introduce Sophie and Anna.

'Coo-ee!' called Vivien, opening the door. 'Bride and bride's mother alert!'

'Hi, Mum, Hels. What have you done with Dad?' said Beth, hugging first one and then the other.

'He's at the pub, doing a few last minute things,' said Vivien.

'So,' said Beth. 'Do I win a prize for getting the weather right?'

'Not yet, darling,' said her mother crisply. 'We've a few hours before we know what it'll be like getting to the

423

church and my weather forecast suggested there might be showers.'

As the church was so near Rachel's house, it had been decided not to have a car to transport the bride to it. A two-minute walk across the village green and you were there.

Vivien had thought this sheer folly but had, to everyone's relief, suddenly given in.

'So,' said Anna. 'Who's first?'

'The bride,' said Rachel, 'she's the most important. The shower does reach to the basin and I've put a chair there but you might be better without it.'

'Don't worry!' said Anna. 'We can manage. As long as you have running water . . .'

Rachel barely had time to smile at this pleasantry before Vivien said, 'Shouldn't the photographer be here by now?'

'I don't think she's booked until eight thirty, Mum,' said Helena, 'and I'd rather not be photographed in my rollers.'

'Oh, that's a standard now, love,' said Anna, ushering her client up the stairs. Indeed, while Helena was seated at the dining table, having rollers the size of soup cans put in her hair, the photographer arrived.

'Hi, guys!' she said blithely. 'I'm Chrissie. Just forget I'm here. But not until I've had coffee,' she added, taking the mug from the tray that Rachel had just brought in. 'Remind me who everyone is? Bride's mother, bridesmaids?' she said, looking round.

'Just me so far,' said Beth. 'There's another one expected.'

'Cool. So who else—'

Before she could finish her question Vivien had produced a list from her handbag. 'I think you'll find that quite easy to understand. I've given you details of what those people are wearing to make it easy for you.'

'Hey, Mum, did you really ask everyone what they'd be wearing?' Beth felt this was going a bit far even for Vivien, but of course she'd never seen her mother be a mother of the bride before. She was bound to be even more controlling.

'No one minded, sweetheart. Most people have got their outfits sorted weeks, if not months ahead.'

Anna had fixed up a hairdryer with a hood over Helena.

'Now all I need is a copy of *Hello!* and a cup of tea,' said Helena.

'Oh,' said Rachel. 'I haven't got *Hello!* but I do have a *Grazia*—'

'I was joking, Rachel!' said Helena. 'I was – Oh, it doesn't matter. I would like the tea though, if you wouldn't mind…'

'Coming up! So, what kind? Earl Grey? Lapsang? Builder's? Or I've got any amount of herb teas, rooibos…'

Beth feared that her mother and sister were likely to take advantage of Rachel's desire to make everything perfect. She hoped she wouldn't have to wade in and protect her. But at least she felt capable of doing that now.

Along with Helena's tea, Rachel served coffee and croissants.

'You won't want to eat when you've got your dresses

on and had your make-up done. Better have something now,' she said.

Obediently, Beth took the offered plate and then a croissant. She knew Rachel had gone to a lot of trouble to get really nice ones, and that there was champagne in the fridge for later. She really had attended to every detail.

Beth was aware that Rachel was studying her and she had a suspicion why. Beth really didn't want to talk about her humiliation today of all days, when she had to be bright and perky, and wondered if there was a way she could get Rachel to understand this without actually telling her. Anna took the dryer off Helena and felt the rollers. 'Hmm, still not dry. I'll just get my other hairdryer in for your mum.'

Beth helped Anna with this. 'Rachel, you have so many sockets. It's amazing.'

Rachel nodded. 'Call me obsessive but I thought: While you've got the electricians in, you might as well have as many sockets as possible.'

'I wouldn't call you obsessive,' shouted Vivien from under the dryer. 'And having someone who pays proper attention to the important things in life is very reassuring on a day like this.'

'Absolutely,' said Beth. She wouldn't have to stick up for Rachel after all.

Sophie wiped croissant crumbs off her fingers with the napkin Rachel had provided and looked around for a potential victim. Her eye lit on Beth. 'You're not having your hair done, are you? In which case, shall I do you now?' she said to Beth.

Beth was horrified. She'd once had her face done in a

department store and ended up looking like a doll with too much make-up on. 'Oh, no, I don't wear much make-up. I'll just do my own,' she said. 'I am quite good at it.'

'Oh, go on. Let me practise on someone,' said Sophie. 'You'll find it relaxing. And you can always take it all off if you don't like it.' She glanced at Helena and Vivien, still having their hair dried. 'Those two will be a while yet.'

'There's another bridesmaid on her way ...'

'Just sit down,' said Sophie soothingly, guiding her to a chair with gentle hands. And somehow Beth found herself seated in front of a mirror having her face stabbed by moist sponges.

Anna took Helena out from under the dryer and applied a hand-held one to the rollers. 'Does your hair always take this long to dry?'

'I'm afraid so,' said Helena.

'You should have tried drying her sister's hair before she cut it all off,' said Vivien. 'That took an age, I can tell you. It was such lovely hair.'

'It's lovely now,' said Sophie as Beth was in no position to reply herself. 'Look how glossy it is. Like a well-groomed horse.'

Beth laughed. 'Well, thank you for that!'

'You know what I mean,' said Sophie, unrepentant. 'Now close your eyes again.'

'Actually, that is lovely!' Beth said when Sophie had finished. 'I just look more me somehow.'

'That's the look we aim for,' said Sophie. 'But you have got amazing features. Huge eyes and great skin. And that glossy, glossy hair!'

Vivien studied her younger daughter. 'I must admit, now I've had time to get used to it, your hair does look quite stylish. And you look lovely.'

Just for a minute, Beth was overcome. She went over and kissed her mother.

Sophie smiled, satisfied that she'd done a good job. As the door opened, she clapped her hands. 'Hooray! Another bridesmaid. I'll do your make-up before Anna grabs you, if you don't mind.'

Rachel caught up with Beth while she was washing mugs. Rachel had, of course, a dishwasher, but Beth knew, the rate they were drinking tea and coffee, it would never cope.

'Beth? Are you OK?' demanded Rachel, drying mugs.

'Yes. I'm fine. Don't want to talk about it today though!' Beth prayed Rachel would read the subtext and not press her. 'The band are performing tonight. I do know that much. Sukey has promised to text me throughout the evening, to let me know how it's going.'

'You don't think you could leave the wedding and go?'

'No, I don't. You got my text?' As Rachel nodded but didn't comment, she went on, 'Honestly, I'm not sure I'd be welcome. Finn was really angry with me about it all, said I'd interfered in something I shouldn't have. I really thought...' Beth raised a hand as Rachel was about to voice her indignation. 'Please, not now.'

'OK, I understand.'

But her voice was full of sympathy and Beth knew sympathy might make her cry. 'And will you tell Lindy too? I just want to focus on the wedding, and be jolly an

428

light-hearted. If I start talking about my feelings I may not be able to do that.'

Rachel patted Beth as she reached for another mug. 'Understood. I'll tell Lindy.'

Lindy arrived shortly afterwards, sewing kit and extra bits and pieces at the ready to make sure the dresses were perfect. 'Hi! she said gaily. 'Everyone OK? I've got Rescue Remedy in case anyone's nervous.'

'We're all nervous,' said Vivien. 'I'm relying on a glass of champagne. Rachel?'

'On its way,' said Rachel, appearing with a napkin -wrapped bottle.

'Why are you nervous, Mum?' said Helena, who was still having her hair done. 'You don't have to do anything now. You've done it all. Thank you so much.'

Vivien suddenly gulped and reached for the box of tissues that was on the table. 'I'm frightened of crying too much and everyone will think I'm not happy about the wedding. I was worried at first but I know Jeff's a really lovely boy and will take care of my little girl and first grandchild.' She blew her nose. 'And you girls: you've shown me that it's possible to have fun – even when you're organised.'

Rachel and Beth took champagne flutes out of their boxes as quickly as possible. There was a pop and seconds later Vivien had a glass of champagne. 'That's better,' she said, having drunk half of it. 'I'll be fine now.'

There was a whirl of activity all morning, people delivering things – flowers, presents, shoes for the bridesmaids that had got delayed in the post, the music for the first dance – and then, suddenly, there was a silence. Helena was having flowers put into her hair and Anna was taking her time. Chrissie had nipped over to where the groom's party was getting ready at Raff's house, which was declared more fun than the mansion, and everyone appreciated the sudden moment of quiet.

Beth ran her hands over the top of her skirt. Lindy had done a great job with the dresses. She and Nancy really did look like ballet dancers, attendants to the main act, which was Helena in her stunning corset, with layers of palest tulle and the occasional crystal to catch the light.

'Can I just say,' said Helena, 'how absolutely amazing you've all been? Mum, Beth, Nancy, my bridesmaid, Lindy for the dresses, Rachel for organising everything, and of course Dad.' She raised her glass of orange juice. 'Sorry I can't toast you in the real thing but I'm really off it right now being pregnant and all, but it has been *so* fun.'

'It has actually,' said Beth.

'I've loved it!' said Lindy, who had even taken sewing Vivien's bra strap to her dress with equanimity, such was her obvious delight with the world.

'It's been the best thing that's happened to me since, well...' Rachel seemed not to know quite what the best thing that had happened to her lately was, as there was a lot of choice. 'Well, I've loved it.'

Just as they were all becoming teary and possibly a tiny bit drunk, Helena's father arrived. 'Come on, love, time to go!'

Helena glanced at Rachel's old station clock, which ticked steadily. 'Not yet, Dad. For one thing, my hair' not finished and for another, if I go now I'll be ther about fifteen minutes early! It's only a three-minute walk to the church.'

'And I need to be there first, Ted!' said Vivien. 'And Lindy. So we can adjust the dress.'

'We should be there too!' said Nancy. 'As bridesmaids.'

'And it would be good if her hair was done,' said Anna. 'Sorry it's taking so long.'

'Oh!' said Beth suddenly. 'What's your blue thing? I know you've got Mum's veil, which is old and borrowed, and new everything else, but what's blue?'

'Oh come on, love,' said her dad. 'It's only superstition! You don't really need anything blue.'

'Yes she does!' said a chorus of women.

'Lindy?' said Vivien.

'Um – I'm sure I've got a bit of blue ribbon I could sew—'

''S'all right!' said Sophie, having burrowed in her huge tool chest full of make-up. 'Blue nail varnish. On her toes. It'll only take a second. Oh, she's not wearing sandals, is she?'

'Ballet flats,' said Rachel. 'From Anello and Davide. One of Beth's eBay finds.'

'Well, do hurry up!' said Ted, looking at his watch.

'Chill, Dad!' said Helena, who was having her toenails painted. 'We've got ages!'

'Actually, we haven't,' said Vivien. 'Can you get a hairdryer on to those toes? I know no one's going to see them, but it would be better if they didn't smudge. And we do have to leave. Oh! Darling! Your hair looks amazing. Let's just put on the veil.'

'Where's the fire, Mum!' said Helena.

'You know your father is a stickler for punctuality.'

'Is he?' Helena seemed surprised to hear her laidback dad described as a stickler.

'I'm not normally,' he said, 'but in this particular instance, could I get you all outside?'

Rachel went to the front window. 'Oh my God!'

Chapter Thirty-One

There, outside Rachel's front door, on the village green, was what Georgette Heyer would have described as an equipage, Rachel realised: a horse and cart in other words. But one so beautifully polished and gleaming and elegant in every way.

Two black horses, easily as glossy as Beth's hair, stood like statues waiting for orders. Up on the box were two men dressed, as far as Rachel could tell, as Colin Firth in *Pride and Prejudice* only with bowler hats. One of them jumped down when he saw the front door open. It was Raff.

Rachel knew perfectly well how much she fancied Raff but seeing him in tight breeches and a well-fitting coat, looking as if he'd been born to wear such figure-flattering clothes, was a shock. She really did feel her knees weaken.

'I'd like to say "Your carriage awaits", but actually it's Elena's carriage,' he said, having bowed and touched his whip to his hat.

Rachel couldn't speak; she was still getting over the shock. What could she say that wouldn't reveal exactly how gorgeous he was? Did he need his head turning any more than it was already turned? Probably not. She cleared her throat. 'I'll tell her,' she said and then added, 'You're rocking the breeches, Raff.'

He made it to the front gate in two strides and swept her into his arms. When he stopped kissing her he said, 'That's better.'

Fortunately for Rachel, he steadied her as he released her. Unfortunately for Rachel there was a round of applause from most of the wedding party as she came to. And she rather thought Chrissie had got a good few shots too.

'Hey! Who's getting married here?' called Nancy.

'Is that for me?' said Helena, hardly able to speak from emotion. 'Oh, Mum! It's always been my dream to go to my wedding in a horse and carriage.'

'I know, darling,' said Vivien. 'I saw the scrapbooks.'

'I just never thought it would happen!'

'Well, come along and get in!' said Ted, who also looked, Rachel now noticed, very good indeed in his striped trousers and tailcoat.

Rachel and Lindy watched the carriage depart and the rest of the wedding party hasten across to the church on foot. Chrissie was jogging alongside the carriage, and also taking pictures of the bride's mother, holding her magnificent wide-brimmed hat and talking to Beth.

'Sorry to be vulgar,' said Lindy, 'but doesn't Raff look well, phwoar is the only way to describe it, in his coachman's outfit?'

'He does. I didn't even know he knew anything about horses.'

'He has a lot of skills,' said Lindy. 'And one of them is being able to dress up like Mr Darcy and not look a complete plonker.'

'Indeed,' said Rachel, thinking of other things he was good at although she was trying not to.

'I'd better scoot, to make sure I'm there to adjust the dress and veil and things,' said Lindy. 'Are you coming?'

'I will if I have time. I need to go over to the venue to make sure everything is OK there.'

Lindy looked at her watch. 'I reckon I've got about five minutes before I dash to the church. Did you manage to speak to Beth? I didn't get a chance. How is she?'

Rachel sighed, coming down from her private cloud. 'Not great, frankly. She's heard the band are doing the gig tonight and not tomorrow, but nothing from Finn. He was livid with her apparently. She's gutted, obviously, but determined not to spoil Helena's day.'

'Oh, poor love!' said Lindy.

'She said to tell you but she didn't want to talk about it.'

'God, I totally understand. Nothing worse than people being sympathetic when you're trying to stay in control. Oh, look, the carriage is going round again. And look at Beth, she looks stunning. She might be unhappy but she's not showing any signs of it. Good girl. And see, loads of locals have turned out. It's all so amazing. We have done well.'

'We've done lots of things well, you and the dresses mostly, but if Vivien hadn't suddenly unlocked the chequebook it wouldn't have been quite so lavish.'

'We could have done the horse-and-carriage thing

though,' said Lindy. 'But, sadly, Beth's ex Charlie would have been driving, which would not have been good!'

Rachel nodded. 'Hey, they're slowing down. You'd better dash.'

Rachel nipped in ahead of the bridal party, just so she could see what the church looked like. It was amazing. The flowers were just what anyone would have wanted: generous, original and all looking as fresh and spring-like as possible. The smell of them was quite something. Helena and, even more importantly in some ways, Vivien would be thrilled. And the church was packed, echoing with excited voices as the guests waited for the arrival of the bride, together with a slightly nervous-looking Jeff.

She popped out again. She knew the service sheets were perfect – she'd checked them herself a hundred times – and the ushers were busy handing them out to the last stragglers hurrying embarrassedly into the church. She met Vivien and Lindy in the porch, ready to make sure the bride was as perfect as she could be. Helena, Nancy and Beth arrived with Ted and as he and Raff handed them gently down from the carriage she saw Vivien dab at her eye. Raff winked at her and she felt her heart turn over.

'You all look beautiful!' she whispered and then she dashed home to collect her car and head for the marquee.

It was hard, she realised, trying to be a wedding co-ordinator while suffering from sexual obsession. Of course Raff couldn't have guessed the effect turning up like that would have had on Rachel but he didn't have to kiss her. It was true they hadn't seen each other for a few days but still. She'd never felt like that before with anyone. Sex in her marriage, when it was going well, was pleasant and companionable, but it wasn't like it was with Raff. That was completely different: passionate, unrestrained and left her exhausted with happiness. With a huge effort of will she turned her mind to the reception.

She parked her car next to the row of rather disreputable vehicles that defined them as belonging to 'staff'. There was an area of the field designated for guests, which would be fine as long as it didn't rain and get muddy. Rachel had lined up a friend of Raff's to be on hand with his tractor in case anyone needed pulling out. Fortunately it didn't look as if he would be needed today. It hadn't rained for a few days and was unseasonably warm now. She set off towards the catering kitchen, which was next to the marquee, and spotted Angus with Lindy's two boys. She called and waved and they changed direction to meet her.

'Hi, Rachel!' said Billy.

'Hi, Billy!' she replied. 'Ned. How's the arm?'

'This is our Uncle Angus,' said Billy, pulling Angus forward. 'He's our other daddy.'

Taken aback, Rachel spoke without thinking. 'Oh. Something happened to the old one?'

'He's still our daddy,' explained Ned. 'Billy has got it wrong. Uncle Angus isn't our daddy but he does sleep in Mummy's bed sometimes.'

Angus shrugged and laughed, obviously not knowing what to say in the face of this.

There was worse to come. 'When Mummy and Uncle Angus are married,' said Billy confidently, 'Uncle Angus will be our daddy then.'

'Cool!' said Rachel, giving Angus a sympathetic smile.

'Boys, why don't you check they've got the tables up in the marquee?' said Angus.

'OK!' the boys called and ran off, his broken arm not seeming to slow Ned down by much.

'So, Angus, anything you'd like to tell me?' Rachel knew she had to see Belinda in a very few minutes but she couldn't resist teasing Angus a little.

'They're great kids and I love them, but talk about embarrassing.' He became more serious. 'I really hope that eventually Lindy will consider making an honest man of me but it's early days yet.'

'Great!' said Rachel. 'You're a very lucky man. So are you and Lindy going to live here?' Rachel indicated the large dilapidated mansion a little way away.

'Eventually. It needs to be habitable first – for a family, not just me.'

'Well, let me know if you want any help with your colour scheme when you get to that stage,' said Rachel. 'I love a paint chart! I can recite lots of them by heart.'

'Um...'

'Of course if I have anything to do with it, it will be Fifty Shades of White.'

Angus laughed. 'Are there that many shades of white?'

'Oh yes, and the rest. And I'm not even joking. Now, I'd better make sure Belinda's coping all right.'

'The last time I saw her she had everyone running round her as if she was the centre of the universe.'

'Perfect!' said Rachel and went off to see for herself It was only then she remembered that Angus was ar architect and probably had ideas about colour scheme himself.

Belinda was indeed holding court in the catering tent. She was delighted to see Rachel. 'Darling! How lovely. I can't tell you how much fun I'm having in this adorable little space. And the ovens! Everything cooks so quickly.'

As one of the courses was slow-cooked pork, this gave Rachel a stab of anxiety. 'So, how's it all working?'

'Everything is cooked. We just need to crisp up the top of the pork – crackling, you know – and the spuds. And the veg will all be refreshed once the starter is served.'

'Which is...?'

'Smoked salmon. We're doing the bread and butter now and keeping it fresh. And there's masses of bread and cheese for later. Ken brought round enough for a couple of armies and their camp followers.'

Rachel's brow furrowed. 'Goodness, I didn't know there was going to be an evening do. It's never been mentioned. I hope that hasn't put you to too much trouble?' Rachel felt decidedly uncomfortable not being in full control but then that's what happened when you had a slightly loose cannon like Vivien involved.

'I think it was all last minute, but Ken's a marvel and a saint and came up with the goods. Obviously we've known each other for years.' Belinda frowned. 'It's all going to be fine, no need to worry.' Then, possibly to distract Rachel from the parts of the event that had escaped her control, she said, 'Did you like Raff in his groom's outfit?'

As a distraction, it worked. Rachel nodded. What did you say to the mother of your boyfriend about the effect his costume had on you? However much you liked her, you couldn't talk to her about sex – especially if it involved her son. 'It did suit him. It came as a wonderful surprise to the bride to see that beautiful carriage waiting for her.'

'Raff was able to get a good deal for Mr Scott. Sadly the happy couple won't be able to come here in it. It's only about fifteen minutes by car but would take ages in a horse-drawn vehicle. But nice to have the carriage for the journey to the church.'

Rachel nodded. 'Apparently it had been Helena's dream since she was a little girl.'

Belinda opened an oven and peered at the contents over the top of her reading glasses, then she closed it again, obviously satisfied. 'And what have you dreamt of having at your wedding since you were a little girl?'

'Oh, I've been married before.' She sighed. 'I suppose now I dream of it working out better second time round.'

Belinda chuckled. 'I think you can rely on Raff for that.'

'Belinda! It's far too early to start saying things like that. We're not engaged or anything. We haven't even been going out very long.'

Belinda was not remotely embarrassed. 'I know and I shouldn't try to rush you but I've a feeling ... well, if you want a very expensive dress, for example, you should start saving.'

'Honestly!' said Rachel, blushing and laughing and leaving the kitchen before Belinda became more outrageous.

The marquee looked magnificent. It had been shaping up very nicely when she and Lindy had been doing the flowers, but now it was as beautiful as any venue could be, given it was basically a tent. For a moment Rachel wondered if her dream location for her fantasy wedding shouldn't be in a marquee and not the hall. Not that she was planning it or anything. Of course she wasn't. Then she allowed her imagination to picture her and Raff in Regency costume, her in a bonnet, him in his tight breeches. Then she shook her head sharply. She was not, not, not thinking about her own wedding! And certainly not now when she had Helena's to pay attention to. She looked around the marquee, searching for possible imperfections. She couldn't see any.

The fragrance of the spring flowers was lovely. The five jam jars on each table looked so extravagant. And although the Flower Guild had said there wasn't time to decorate the marquee itself very much, they had found time to wind swathes of net and ivy and narcissi from the centre, covering the supporting struts. The roof was tented with net and tiny lights that gave the impression of being in a fairy palace.

The man responsible came up to Rachel. 'I'm Jim. Is this OK for you?'

Rachel had to take a couple of seconds to make sure she wasn't going to cry before she could answer. 'It's sensational!'

Jim nodded. 'That's what we like to hear.' He looked around. 'I am pleased. As you know we had very little time but the pea lights and net work very well.'

'It's just so pretty,' said Rachel, sighing. Then she frowned, aware that her rigid standards seemed to have been melted by some flowers, some fairy lights and a bit of tulle. 'Now, I must check the cake is OK.'

'Bit late now if it's not,' said Jim, who was fatherly and, Rachel decided, one of those people who always made you feel everything was going to be OK.

'I need to check anyway,' said Rachel.

Again, fresh flowers were the theme. Three tiers of white cake (which theoretically exactly matched the tulle of Helena's dress) were separated by layers of flowers, white freesias, narcissi and very pale primroses. It was a classic design: slightly old-fashioned, but perfect. There was a ribbon effect, with bows to mirror the design of the dresses with their Degas embellishments. Rachel sighed with satisfaction. Vivien might have selected one of the most expensive wedding-cake producers available but the effect was stunning.

'So what do you think?' asked Jim, obviously taking a personal interest.

'I think it's lovely. And the colour is perfect. The cake designer had a sample of the fabric. We didn't have much time, as you know. But I love it. She's done an absolutely amazing job.'

'It's one of the nicest cakes I've seen, and I've seen a few.' He smiled. 'It's going to be a terrific wedding.'

Rachel suddenly noticed something she hadn't been expecting. 'Why is there a stage? We're not having live music.'

'Oh? Are you sure?'

'Well, yes! This was all arranged at very short notice. We barely had time to make a tape and it's only got their first dance on it, plus a few of their favourite songs.' Beth had done her best with everyone's iPods, including her mother's, and thought all bases were covered.

Possibly sensing Rachel's concern, Jim shrugged. 'Ah well. No extra cost anyway.'

'That's OK then. Maybe we should get the happy couple to go up there to do their first dance?'

He inclined his head in agreement. 'Slightly depends on what sort of dance they're planning to do. Are they doing the full *Strictly* thing? Or just hanging on to each other for dear life?'

'I'm not sure. They did skip off at the last minute, telling us it was so they could practise, but who knows? Maybe they just practised hanging on! It's a shame as Helena's dress lends itself to dancing.'

'There are steps to the side of the stage so she could get up and down easily enough.'

Rachel checked the steps and then had a final wander round, tweaking some tulle, sniffing some flowers, generally feeling very satisfied.

She went outside to find Angus and the children. He was invited to the wedding as there was plenty of room – not all Vivien's extensive guest list could manage to come after the change of date. She wanted to make sure the childminding facilities were adequate. There weren't many children coming but Rachel wanted them to be safe and happy. With Lindy's help, Beth had arranged for a couple of local mothers to bring toys and be on hand to feed and entertain the younger contingent. Vivien had not been keen on the idea of children rushing around enjoying themselves.

Then she looked at her watch and realised she had to make herself tidy. She wanted to be there when the first guests arrived, to help hand out the champagne.

Chapter Thirty-Two

Beth stood at the back of the tent, sipping a glass of water. She felt tired, not only from running around being a bridesmaid and generally helpful, but tired of being cheerful. She wanted to go home and hide under her duvet, possibly eating chocolate, and get over her broken heart.

It wasn't really broken, she realised that. She and Finn hadn't had a relationship, really. He'd been kind to her and, of course, she had a major crush on him, but it was silly to think her heart was involved. And yet it was. She'd driven back through the lanes, late that night, thinking he hated her. It had been so bleak, so soul-destroying. She'd set out full of optimism, full of the conviction she was doing a good thing. She was helping Finn and his band.

And when she'd got there it had all been thrown back at her. Finn didn't want the band to play for Mickey Wilson, however influential he was. Raff's mate would have been fine, but he wasn't so important. But he didn't think they were ready for someone so influential. So instead of helping him, she'd actually made the band argue and him hate her. She thought again. No, he probably didn't hate her, that would imply he cared and he blatantly didn't care about her personally. She was just an irritant. She was wondering if her mother and sister would ever speak to her again if she sloped off before the end when Rachel and Raff came up.

'Hey, Beth! Come and dance!' said Rachel, who seemed very bubbly. Raff had changed out of his Mr Darcy outfit but still looked gorgeous in trousers and a shirt, with quite a lot of buttons undone.

Raff took her by the hand and together they went nearer the front, by the stage. 'Have a dance. Who chose this dreadful music?' He smiled.

Beth found herself smiling back. 'You know I did the tape. And it's grand music.'

'Dance to it, then.'

Beth noticed that Rachel looked radiant. Love would do that to you, she realised. And maybe one day it would do it to her.

And there was Lindy, dancing with Angus, looking like love's young dream. Beth hated herself for the pang of jealousy she felt for her friends. They deserved happiness and lovely boyfriends. She decided it wasn't jealousy; it was just that it highlighted her own loneliness.

She'd been quite cut up about Charlie. It had been a shock seeing in him the cupboard with the fat brides-maid. But she had forgotten about him quite quickly after she met Finn.

Lindy and Angus moved so the five of them were

445

together now. It was kind of them, thought Beth, but really she wished they'd just let her be miserable on her own.

Her sister was gazing up into her new husband's eyes as they dragged each other around the floor, and her parents were also dancing, looking at each other almost as if it were their wedding day and they were newly in love.

Then suddenly Rachel grabbed her hand and pulled her in tight, as if she were a child who might run into the road. Someone turned the music off. Beth assumed it must be Raff, since he had disappeared, but as Rachel wasn't rushing off to do anything about the absence of music she must know about it.

Raff appeared on stage. He tapped the microphone and then spoke. 'Ladies and gentlemen, as if this wedding wasn't special enough already, it's about to get more special. A wonderful new band – fresh from its very first, very successful performance in the village hall tonight – has chosen to perform for you all and I know sometime soon, when you can't switch on your telly without seeing them on it, you will all be able to say, "I heard them before they were anyone, and I didn't even have to go to Glastonbury to do it!" I give you – Finn and the McCools!'

Now Beth understood why Rachel was clutching her so tightly. Rachel knew she'd be out of there so quickly no one would see her move if she weren't virtually hand-cuffed to her friend. As there was absolutely nothing else she could do, Beth had to stay put. If she'd gone to see them in the hall she could have stayed out of sight. No chance of that here. And a part of her was thrilled. From what Raff had said the gig had gone well. She really hoped so, and that something good had come out of her meddling.

It took a while for the audience to get quiet so they could begin. The wedding guests might well all have been paid-up members of the Finn and the McCools' fan club judging by the reception they gave them.

At last, after a bit of fiddling about with amps and instruments, the music began.

Beth was concentrating so hard on not crying or giggling hysterically or generally making a public spectacle of herself that to begin with she didn't really hear the music. She glanced across at Helena and got the impression she'd had something to do with this. Then she relaxed and began to hear what the rest of the wedding guests were hearing.

They were loving it. The band had that sort of raw, skilful, poetic raunchiness that got hold of your insides and either twisted them or made them melt. And however much you didn't want to, you found yourself moving to it.

'They are good, aren't they?' shouted Rachel.

Beth nodded. 'Thank God, they are! Did you know they were coming?'

Rachel shook her head. 'Only about half an hour ago. Helena told me. Raff had asked her if it was OK. She was delighted, of course.'

'So I should hope!'

'And they're perfect for a wedding, even though they must be exhausted after their gig,' Rachel went on. 'Sad they probably won't do any more weddings after this or—' She stopped. 'Look at Helena and Jeff. They're really getting into it!'

For a couple who'd basically copped out of the first dance in spite of apparently going away to practise they were really giving it some. Beth remembered Helena saying that before they went travelling they'd gone to a couple of jive classes. They must have remembered more than they thought they would.

The crowd seemed relieved when the band brought the tempo right down. They'd all been dancing with enthusiasm but now needed a bit of a break. Finn took hold of the microphone. 'Just to give you all a little rest we're going to sing a new song for you. It's a slow one so make sure you're dancing with the right partner.'

Tears sprung into Beth's eyes. She had no partner, not even the wrong one. She wanted to escape but she was hemmed in by people. Pushing and saying 'excuse me' wasn't the way to keep people from looking at her. She was right in the middle of the crowd; she'd just have to stay there and cope as best she could.

The song started with a few bars of fiddle from someone at the back. Finn kept the microphone and started singing. He was looking out at the crowd of wedding guests, his expression wistful. Beth could hear sighs from all around her. 'Putting him on my To Do list right now,' said one of Helena's bawdier friends.

Beth looked at her feet. It seemed safest.

At first she wasn't really listening. She didn't want to hear Finn's voice being plaintive, singing a song that might well be a 'first dance' song in the future. She jus didn't want to cry. And then she heard the chorus. 'Hey, Beth!'

Her eyes flew to the stage. She'd heard that line before but she hadn't realised it was a song; she'd thought it had been Finn talking to her. And maybe it still was Finn talking to her!

Before she had time to properly listen to the words or work out what the song was about, Finn got rid of the microphone and left the band to carry on without him. He jumped off the stage. Terrified and confused, Beth stared down at her feet again. She knew he was coming in her direction and was trusting in the old trick: if she couldn't see him he couldn't see her.

'Hey, Beth!' he said and her eyes flew open. He was standing there, a rueful smile in his eyes and a hopeful smile on his lips. 'I've been a monster. I never meant to hurt you. Of all the people in the world I wouldn't want to hurt it's you. I care about you. Forgive me. Dance with me.' Then he swept her into his arms and off her feet and held her so tightly she couldn't breathe.

Either he didn't trust her not to run away or didn't think she was a very good dancer but he held on to her as he swayed to the music. 'Dearest girl,' he breathed into her ear. 'I'm so, so sorry.'

Beth became aware of the people looking at them, and at first she was embarrassed. Then she began to smile. She was in the arms of one of the most attractive men on the planet.

'Let's go somewhere we can talk,' he said, still holding her.

He put his arm round her, clamping her to his side,

weaving through the wedding guests and out of the marquee. Beth was aware of clapping and it made her giggle.

'We need to go where we won't be disturbed,' he said when they were outside.

'This is where Angus lives. I don't know it at all.'

'It's all right. I know where. Over there. There's a tree house. Raff said something about it. There are lights.'

'But doesn't the band need you?'

'Not just now it doesn't. Although of course I might live to regret those casual words. Mickey might sign up the band without me. Though he liked us well enough.'

'Let's go back then,' said Beth, thrilled to hear that their future was assured but suddenly worried in case it all went wrong now.

'Bollocks to going back. Now I've got you I'm not going to let you go until I've apologised.'

'OK then.'

'But will you be warm enough? We don't want you catching a chill. I'll give you my coat.' He stripped off his leather jacket and put it round her. It felt wonderfully warm and it smelt, beautifully, of him. 'All right?'

'Perfect,' she said.

'I'm so grateful – lucky – that you came with me just now. You could have slapped my face, the way I've treated you.'

Beth hooked her arm in his and they set off in the darkness towards the flickering lights. Watching them get nearer she felt they symbolised hope. They weren' steady, but they were there. Maybe she and Finn coul find happiness together. 'Well, thinking about it, I di turn up unannounced when you didn't want to be interrupted. It wasn't really your fault.'

'It was. I was a complete eejit. An eejit with no manners.'

'I'm prepared to put it all down to artistic temperament,' said Beth.

With a shout of laughter, Finn picked her up and swung her round. 'Never heard such a load of old cobblers, although' – he put her down again – 'maybe it is a good excuse and I'll accept it.'

'To be honest, I think I'll forgive anything. You wrote me a song.'

'I did. And a very good song it is too, if I say so myself.'

They reached the tree house. 'This is the house that Ned fell out of and broke his arm,' said Beth.

'Raff told me. But I'll make sure you don't fall out of it. I'll stand here until you're safely up. And maybe give you a shove from behind if it looks like you need it.' He laughed gently. 'I'm kind of hoping you do need a shove.'

She clambered up the ladder as carefully as she could, not wanting to damage her dress. She *didn't* want a shove. It might spoil what was turning out to be a magical moment.

The tree house was a little cramped for two but they snuggled in next to each other. Someone – Beth suspected Rachel – had hung wired jam jars with tea lights in them to the branches, so they didn't take up precious space. It was so incredibly romantic.

'Your dress is taking up rather a lot of room,' Finn complained, putting his arm round her.

'I'm not taking it off. I've only got a leotard on underneath.'

'A leotard? Good Lord.' Then he turned her face towards his and his lips came down and he kissed her for a very long time.

They forgot the cramped conditions and Beth forgot everything as they concentrated on each other and just how they liked to kiss.

They were disturbed by an urgent voice. 'Finn! Man! You have to come back! The crowd is baying for your blood!'

'Really?' said Finn, pulling away from Beth with reluctance.

'Well, not your blood exactly, but they want you to sing. I think you should come back.'

Beth sensed he was torn. He wanted to stay with her but also felt he owed the band. 'Come on,' she said. 'Let's go.'

She would have to give his jacket back but she really wanted to keep it, for ever, as a lovely reminder of this night.

'Give us two minutes, Liam!' Finn called down. 'We just want a private word.'

'Have a private dictionary if you need one!' said Liam. 'I'll see you there.'

'Beth,' said Finn urgently. 'Before we go back in there I just want to say – I don't know what I want to say really. It's such early days – we hardly know each other but want you to know . . .' He paused. 'You are really specia to me and . . .' He was obviously finding this difficult. 'looks like the band might be going places and we migh have to be apart quite a bit. But it would really make me happy... God, this is so difficult!' He exhaled. 'I don't really know what I'm trying to say but I would be so thrilled if you'd come back to Ireland with me, to meet my family.'

Beth was fighting tears. Although he was finding it difficult to express what he wanted to say, she had no difficulty in understanding. Of course he couldn't make promises but just the fact that he was trying to say something and – importantly – wanted her to meet his family was enough for her. 'I'd love to go to Ireland. Will I see a leprechaun?'

'I guarantee it.'

Their exit had caused something of a stir. When they came back into the marquee people were waiting for them. Someone even threw some confetti (dried delphinium petals, sourced by Rachel). The band had stopped playing – obviously having given up waiting for Finn – and Beth's selections were back on the iPod. The bride and groom had disappeared. Beth realised she'd missed Helena throwing her bouquet and that she didn't mind a bit.

'Darling!' said Beth's mother, obviously full of champagne and wedding spirit, parting the crowds like the Red Sea. 'You got carried away by this gorgeous man! It was like something out of a film!'

'It was,' said Lindy, following the path created by Vivien's progress through the crowd. 'Just heaven!' She kissed Beth's cheek. 'Are you OK?'

Beth's shining eyes should have reassured her. 'We went to the tree house.' At that moment Rachel came up

453

to join them, her arm in Raff's. 'Did you put the tea lights in the trees?'

'Might have done,' said Rachel. 'It was the Vintage Weddings thing to do.'

'Oh, Vintage Weddings!' said Lindy. 'They are so great.' Angus came up from behind and put his arms round her. 'They've turned our lives around.'

'Are you thinking of adding a dating service to what you can offer?' said Angus.

'Certainly not!' said Rachel. 'Why would we?'

Raff gave her an affectionate squeeze. 'It seems to have got you three fixed up.'

'Only by chance!' protested Rachel, turning round to Raff, but he kissed her so thoroughly she forgot what she was protesting about.

'Well, however we met them,' said Lindy, 'we're all very lucky. And even without our blokes, Vintage Weddings is still amazing!'

'It is!' said Beth.

'Absolutely!' said Rachel.

'Do you girls want me to get some drinks so you can have a toast?' said Angus.

'No, let's dance!' said Lindy. 'Look what's going on on the dance floor!'

The band members, freed from their instruments, had all joined in the dancing with abandon. Liam was dancing with Vivien and they were twirling each other round like professionals.

'Hey!' said someone. 'That bride's mother is a diva on the dance floor!'

THE END

LOSE YOURSELF IN THE DELICIOUSLY ROMANTIC NEW BESTSELLER FROM

On board a 'puffer' boat in the Western Isles of Scotland,
Emily is spending an idyllic summer at sea.

But it's only for a summer, and Emily knows that
soon she must return to her single life and her career
in town as a midwife.

But she has not counted on the new friends she is making.
Or the fun she is soon having.

Or the attraction she is starting to feel for Alasdair,
the handsome local doctor …

Turn the page to read an extract...

Chapter One

Emily regarded her rucksack, currently sitting on top of a vessel that looked like an overgrown bath toy. It had a large funnel and high wheelhouse – which must have its view obscured by the funnel, she realised – and a high bow that went down to the water in a straight line. A mast rose near the bow, painted yellow, with wire rigging coming from it. The rest of the boat was smartly painted in red and black and, had she not been travelling for about six hours, would have made Emily smile. She'd forgotten that Scotland was quite so far away from the South-West of England.

'I shouldn't have come,' she muttered. 'I shouldn't be about to take a summer job – something I might have done when I was a student. I'm thirty-five, with professional qualifications. It's ridiculous!'

But then she looked around her and saw the July sunshine sparkling on the sea, the islands set off against blue sky, the mountains, and, nearer, a very pretty harbour – Crinan – edged by brightly painted houses and what looked to be a nice hotel. She remembered the

1

scenery – first from the bus and then the car journey – and thought she might well be in the most beautiful spot in the world. It wasn't raining, and it seemed that currently there were no midges. All good enough reasons to join her rucksack, which had been flung on to the boat by the dark and almost entirely silent man who'd picked her up from Lochgilphead bus station. She'd made this mad decision, she'd better follow through.

She stepped aboard the puffer, described to her by Rebecca as almost a family member. In fact it was an old cargo vessel, one of a fleet built during the Second World War, designed to deliver everything that the Highlands and Islands might need, from farm equipment to groceries, livestock to whisky. Many years ago it had been converted to carry passengers. It was powered by steam and, according to Rebecca, had a lot of character. Emily's job was to cook for the passengers now Rebecca, who owned it with her husband, James, and ran it as a thriving business, was no longer able to, being so pregnant.

Emily had rented out her house, arranged to take all the leave due to her, to be followed by a sabbatical for when her leave ran out. This done, she got the plane and two buses and now was here.

'Hello!' she called. 'Anyone at home?' As a midwife she was used to letting herself into houses where there was a lot else going on but this was different. All was silent.

She stayed on deck for a few moments longer, drinking in the view and letting the stress of the journey fade away before deciding to go below. There must be someone here

Rebecca had warned her she would be shopping and James was organising a coal delivery, but had definitely said there'd be at least one crew member on board to greet her.

She found a flight of wooden steps leading down to what would have been the hold but was now the first level of accommodation and descended. 'Anyone in?'

Still no answer, so she looked about her, deciding to make herself at home if there was no else to do it.

There was a long, polished mahogany table, which, going by the brochure Rebecca had sent her, was where everyone ate together, passengers and crew. Now it had a large bowl of fruit on it and a pile of unread newspapers. On one side there was a built-in wooden seat with comfy-looking cushions and, on the other, a bench. Looking at the length of these bits of furniture told Emily she'd be cooking for a lot of people. It had been a long time since she'd worked in a café, producing vegetarian lasagne for twenty, and she hoped she hadn't lost the skills.

The rest of the saloon (described as such in the brochure) consisted of built-in sofas arranged around a huge wood-burning stove. Although it was a warm summer day, it was smouldering gently, giving off a pleasant, aromatic smell as well as warmth. There were paintings on the walls (bulkheads – she mentally corrected herself) and plenty of woven woollen throws and cushion covers, all with a definitely Scottish feel, which added homely style and comfort. There were steps that obviously led down to the guest cabins below and all in all gave the impression of being a sociable and cosy space.

Although tempted to make herself comfortable beside the wood-burner with a colour supplement, Emily felt she ought to explore the galley, which would be her place of work. After all, if the worst happened and the maternity unit at home was closed, or she had offended too many important people, it might have to be her job next year as well. Goodness knows what she'd do in the winter, when the puffer didn't operate.

On the way to the galley, she allowed herself to be distracted by a painting. As most of them were, it was of the puffer, but in a different setting to the gentle, distant islands and hills where it now lay. In the picture the mountains were nearer, majestic, almost over-powering. The puffer was gallantly under way, steam streaming from its funnel, obviously fighting against a stiff breeze. Emily was just struggling to read the title of the piece, which was in tiny writing underneath, hoping it would give a clue to the location, when there was a loud rustling noise. She jumped. 'Hello?'

There was no reply, just more rustling.

Oh my God, thought Emily, rats! I'm alone on an old boat and there are rats! She had a fear of rats people described as irrational. She didn't think it was irrational at all; they were vile, disease-ridden creatures who urinated as they ran. Rebecca had never said anything about rats. She'd have to spend the night on a rat-infested ship. Well, she couldn't. She'd have to decamp to the hotel.

Movement caught her eye, sending another stab of panic through her. It was in the galley and although she really didn't want to actually see the rat, she found he

4

gaze drawn to the sound. There was a plastic carrier bag in the sink and it was heaving.

She screamed. Not loudly, but loud enough to make someone laugh. A girl appeared from where the galley turned a corner. She was younger than Emily, and very pretty, with a cloud of dark curls and a curvaceous figure, revealed by jeans and a tight sweater. This girl had obviously been keeping out of sight, waiting for Emily to be alarmed by whatever was making the noise.

'They're prawns,' the girl said scathingly. 'Langoustines. We bought them this morning. Don't say the new cook Rebecca brought in is frightened of shellfish?'

Emily, who was good at people, realised this girl was not happy to see her and wondered why. Had she thought she could do the job and resented Rebecca for bringing in a stranger? She feared she was going to have work hard to get on with her. Well, she'd just have to do it.

'Hi, I'm Emily. No, I'm usually fine with shellfish but mostly they're not still alive when I deal with them.'

'Only the freshest is good enough for us.' The girl spoke possessively, obviously proud of the puffer's high standards of produce.

'And what's your name?'

'Billie,' she said.

Emily nodded. 'I've come to help Rebecca out, as she's quite near to term.'

Billie frowned slightly, and Emily realised she'd used a rather medical expression but she didn't patronise Billie by explaining. She'd work it out.

'Rebecca didn't need to get anyone else in. I could

5

have managed. I've got loads of energy – I'm not pregnant! Or she could have got someone else to be galley slave.'

Emily winced inwardly at the expression but suspected it was what they called the cook's assistant on the puffer. She didn't need to worry about it being politically correct or not. 'Well, maybe we can work together? Sort of a job-share? So both do both jobs?'

This seemed to soften the expression of resentment on Billie's face. 'That might work. Only of course you won't know how to help out on deck like I do.'

'Is that part of the galley slave's job?'

'There is a deck hand. Drew. But when we're doing a difficult manoeuvre, or coming alongside or something, it's useful to have extra people with fenders.'

Emily smiled inside. Billie was using technical terms that Emily didn't quite understand, but like Billie, she would work it out without having it explained. 'Will I have to learn how to do that?'

'Oh yes.' Billie's expression doubted her ability.

'Would you mind showing me round? As Rebecca and James aren't here.'

'OK.' She wasn't enthusiastic but she'd do it. 'So, this is the galley, obviously.' Billie waved a casual hand. 'It's small but there's a bit of extra space at the back. Quite useful. Two of us can work at the same time. You have to be tidy.'

Emily was a very tidy worker in the kitchen. Rebecca knew this from when they'd worked together. It was one of the reasons Rebecca had wanted her and not someone she didn't know. They'd made a great team.

'I'll show you where we sleep,' said Billie. 'Bring your bag. Have you got any more luggage?'

'No.'

'Cool. There's no room for more than the basics.'

Emily followed Billie up on deck and across to a metal hood that Billie pulled back as if she was opening a tin of sardines.

Underneath was what looked like a dark tunnel but then Emily noticed rungs. There was a vertical ladder downwards.

'You go down backwards, always,' said Billie. 'I'll take your bag.'

With the ease of practice, Billie got hold of Emily's rucksack and swung herself down on to the ladder and disappeared. Emily took a breath and then, trying to remember Billie's technique, somehow got herself on to the ladder and down it.

'Oh God,' she said, before she could stop herself. 'Rebecca didn't sleep here, did she?'

There were two built-in single bunks with lockers underneath. A bank of netting over what was obviously Billie's bunk held toiletries, a bottle of water, magazines, a book. Right at the end of both bunks was a space big enough for a rucksack as long as it wasn't big or full.

'Of course not. She's in the owner's cabin. Although that must be a squash now she's the size of a whale.'

Rebecca was almost seven months pregnant so this might not have been much of an exaggeration but as Emily hadn't seen her yet, she didn't comment. 'So I'm in your space now?' she said instead. 'I am sorry. I can see now why you weren't thrilled to see me.' The cabin was small for one; for two, the space would be – was – very restricted.

Billie shrugged, acknowledging what Emily said was true. 'Just hope you don't need to get up in the night for a pee.'

'Er – where are the bathrooms?'

'In the hold. There are three. Oh, and one under the wheelhouse but the boys use that usually. Bit pongy.'

'I can see I'm going to love this job,' said Emily seriously. Now she could see why Rebecca had asked her if she still liked camping when they were going through the details together. But actually, she didn't let things like cramped conditions and far-away facilities bother her. If she could get Billie to unbend a bit more, it would all be fine.

'Emily!' roared a familiar female voice. 'Did you get here all right? Alasdair promised he'd picked you up OK.'

Emily set off up the ladder, bursting with joy at the thought of seeing her old friend. 'Becca!'

Both women floundered towards each other clumsily, Emily because she'd tripped over something and Rebecca because she was pregnant. They hugged tightly.

'Oh! It's so lovely to see you!' they both said at once.

'You haven't changed a bit!' said Rebecca, standing back to look at Emily. 'Although you've got highlights now. Your hair was always so dark.'

'When I started going prematurely blonde I decided not to fight it and have a few more streaks put in.'

'Otherwise, you're just the same. Haven't grown or anything.'

Emily laughed. 'The same can't be said for you

8

although apart from being the size of a house, you're still the same Becca I was a student with.'

'I am huge, aren't I?'

Emily nodded. 'Are you sure that baby's got a few more weeks in there?' Emily hugged her friend again; any doubts she might have had about coming dispersed.

'Fairly sure!' They both laughed from the joy of being together after so many years.

'So, have you shown her round, Billie?' Rebecca asked as Billie appeared.

'A bit.'

'Well, let's have a cup of tea or something then I'll give you the complete tour.'

'If the tour could start at the loos, I'd be grateful,' said Emily.

A little while later, Emily and Rebecca were sitting in the saloon with mugs of tea and a plate of home-made biscuits. Emily had a notebook and pencil at the ready. Billie had gone off somewhere, to Rebecca's evident relief. Emily suspected her friend wanted to tell her things about Billie she couldn't say in front of her.

'You're sure you don't want lunch?' said Rebecca, picking up a biscuit and taking a bite.

'I had sandwiches on the bus. And at the airport waiting for the bus.'

'That's OK then. Now, let's run through what you need to do. The passengers are arriving at about five. Tea and cakes will be served. Then, dinner at about eight? There's an honesty bar but James will give them he welcome speech and the first drink to get them in the mood. I've made you two massive lasagnes – enough for twenty—'

'Oh!' Emily felt a stab of nostalgia in among scribbling notes and 'first-day' anxiety. 'Do you remember those ones we used to make at the café? Sold like hot cakes!'

'I use the same recipe for the vegetarian one. We ask people to tell us if they're veggie but sometimes they forget so I always do options on the first night. There are a load of baguettes for garlic bread . . . James'll cook the prawns for the starter – they're his speciality although he doesn't usually cook so don't get used to it . . .'

Rebecca continued talking about how everything worked until Emily had three pages of notes.

'So, tell me about Billie,' said Emily, putting down her pencil. 'Why didn't she get my job? It would have been easier to find an assistant, wouldn't it, and let her be the cook?'

Rebecca exhaled. 'Well, apart from me really wanting you to come . . .'

'I could have been a galley slave.'

'Billie is great in many ways. She's brilliant on deck. She can steer and even humps bags of coal, given half a chance. But she's not so great in the kitchen. She's sloppy and although she makes great cakes and biscuits she can't make bread. Can you make bread?'

Emily shrugged. 'I watch *Bake Off*; I can follow a recipe.'

Rebecca frowned slightly. 'Oh. Oh well, I expect you'll pick it up. Or I could make it at home and bring it in.'

Emily shook her head. 'No, I'll learn to make it. I've looked at the schedule. It'd be a poor show if you have to drive all over the Highlands and Islands to bring us bread in your condition.'

'And will you be able to cope with Billie? She's tricky! And I'm so sorry you have to share such a tiny space. I didn't mention it on the phone because I thought you wouldn't come and I so wanted you to.'

Emily did her best to hug her friend but was mostly prevented by her bump. 'It's fine. I can manage and, most importantly, I can get through the night without needing a wee.'

'Which is more than I can do,' said Rebecca gloomily. 'No sooner does the baby finally stop kicking and keeping me awake so I can drop off than my bloody bladder wakes me.'

'At least now you can catch up during the day and get some proper rest. Archie and Henry are old enough to understand if you need to fall asleep on the sofa while they watch that thing about dragons.' Emily caught up on children's TV while doing home visits. It was handy.

'Actually, the thought of curling up in front of the TV with my boys is absolute bliss. Not having to worry about the childcare rota is also bliss.'

'And you won't have to worry about me and Billie because we're going to job-share, so I won't be telling her what to do, just making tactful suggestions.'

Again, Rebecca frowned. 'Well, good luck with that.'

They finished going through everything that was expected of Emily and Rebecca gave her a thorough tour of the galley. The langoustines still heaved and rustled in the sink in a worrying way but Emily was used to them now.

'If ever a fishing boat offers to sell you anything wonderful, abandon the menu plans and buy the fish. The petty cash should have enough in it for that but if it doesn't, tell James and he'll sort it.' Rebecca leant against the counter, taking up the entire gangway. 'I love that spontaneity. It wouldn't work for some cooks but although I like having a plan, and I like knowing there are five dishes I could make without having to go shopping, I really prefer it if something lovely comes flapping on to my worktop, demanding something a bit special.'

'I went on a fish course once, with an old boyfriend, so that excites me too.' Emily realised that Rebecca didn't only need her cooking to be left in safe hands, she wanted the ethos to be passed on too. 'This is going to be great. Perfect for me. I'll be so busy I won't have time to brood about what's going on at the maternity unit. I'll have to think about food all the time! And how lovely is that!'

'Lovely,' agreed Rebecca, much less enthusiastically. 'Now bring me up to date on your love life. Have you left behind a broken-hearted lover?'

Emily giggled. 'No! I may have left someone who would like to see himself in that role but he wasn't doing very well.'

'So you don't have a love-life currently?'

'No.'

'That's good. I'd hate to think of you pining while you're up here working.' She paused. 'What did you think of Alasdair?'

'Who?'

'The man who picked you up from the bus station.'

'Oh! Well, he hardly opened his mouth for the entir

trip from the bus station. I assumed he was the local taxi but he wouldn't accept any money so—'

'Did you fancy him?' Rebecca asked before Emily could finish her sentence.

Emily put this down to hormones. Rebecca would never usually have said this about someone Emily had barely met. 'No! I just want to know why he gave me a lift if he's an elective mute. It must have been torture for him. In fact I could tell it was.'

'Don't take it personally.' Rebecca paused, obviously thinking how best to put what she wanted to say. 'He's James's brother. I told him you'd be tired and probably wouldn't want to chat.'

'Really?' Emily was astounded. 'When have you ever known me not want to chat?'

'Well, you'd had a long journey and you know how tiresome it is having to tell people what you do and things.'

'Why on earth should I mind telling people what I do? I'm proud of it.'

'I thought you might have felt a bit awkward, in the circumstances,' Rebecca explained.

Emily wasn't quite convinced by this but as she didn't greatly care, she just said, 'No, I'm cool about it. I didn't do anything wrong, after all.'

'No, well, back to business, I've made a cake for tea today.' Rebecca seemed eager to get off the subject of why Emily had suddenly dropped her career and come up to Scotland. 'The passengers will be here at about ve, so they get tea before James's welcome drink at even. Then, as I said, dinner at eight. That's in case

13

anyone has difficulty getting here on the first night. We have it at about seven usually.'

'That's fine. And you've cooked that already so I just do garlic bread and make a salad?'

Rebecca nodded. 'There's one guest I must tell you about. She comes every year with her son. He disappears into the engine room for the duration, being a steam buff. She sits and knits and helps with the washing up.'

'So passengers help with washing up? Don't they come away to avoid household chores?'

Rebecca shook her head. 'No, this is different from most holidays. People come because they want to get involved. There's no obligation, of course, but they enjoy it. It's different from doing it at home. And Maisie, who I just mentioned, she loves coming. I worry about her getting about as she's no spring chicken, but there's always someone to chat to, and it's time with her son. At mealtimes, anyway.'

'I look forward to meeting her. I love old people. There's always so much behind the wrinkles and dodgy hairstyles.'

'I'm so glad you said that! Billie gets a bit impatient. She says we should have an age limit. In some ways she's right, getting people on and off is a struggle sometimes, and I do worry about the steepness of the steps going down to the accommodation, but in other ways this is a perfect holiday for them. And Maisie loves it so, as long as she can come, I'm happy to have her.'

At last Rebecca managed to tear herself away, almos content that she'd left her beloved puffer galley in sa hands. Emily familiarised herself further on her own, locating utensils that were her personal essentials, glad that Billie still hadn't come back from wherever she'd gone.

When she did come back, Emily handed her a mug of tea with 'Chief Cook' printed on it. 'So, how are we going to divvy up the chores? I'll do tea so I can practise getting to know the clients—'

'Pazzies. We call them pazzies – short for passengers.'

Emily nodded. 'Cool. And we'll do dinner together? I need to jump in at the deep end, I think.' She smiled. 'Not literally, obviously. I'm not that great a swimmer.'

Billie didn't smile at this feeble attempt at a joke. Emily bit her lip. If her companion in the galley was going to be so taciturn it was going to make for a far from jolly time.

Before she could dwell on this further she heard boots on the steps and looked up to see James, whom she nearly didn't recognise now he had no beard, and a younger man coming down.

She came out of the galley at the same time as Rebecca appeared from the sleeping quarters to do the introductions.

'James! You remember Emily, don't you?'

'Of course! How could I forget? The prettiest of our bridesmaids.' He embraced Emily warmly.

'I was the only bridesmaid, James,' she said, hugging him back. He'd grown a little bit fatter since his wedding but he still had huge charm. It was easy to see why he was so successful at a business involving people.

'But still pretty,' he said. 'I remember your lovely smile. Now, let me introduce the first mate, Drew.'

A young man in jeans and a sweatshirt with 'Puffer Crew' on it stepped forward. 'Hi, pleased to meet you. I'm usually referred to as the deck hand but I'll take the promotion.'

Another man, a bit older, wearing a boiler suit and a big smile, appeared and put out his hand. 'And I'm Bob, chief engineer, often known as McPhail, after the Para Handy stories.'

'Hi, Drew. Here's your coffee, black, two sugars,' said Billie. 'It's how he likes it,' she added to Emily, proprietorially, as if only she would get it right.

'It's instant coffee and I'm very happy to make it myself,' said Drew with a grin that made him very attractive.

Emily intercepted Billie looking at him and diagnosed a bit of a crush. 'That's good to hear.'

'Well, welcome, Emily! It's lovely of you to agree to have a Highland summer with us,' said James. 'Now, is there time for a cuppa before our guests arrive?'

As tea was made and 'crew cake' produced, Emily suddenly remembered that Alasdair, her silent taxi driver, was James's brother. They were very different. James's accent was English and a bit posh and he had an easy, friendly charm. Alasdair was silent, but had had a slightly Scottish burr in the very few words they had exchanged. She had thought that Alasdair was good looking, in a brooding sort of way, although she wouldn' have dreamt of saying so to Rebecca. It would only hav given her ideas. Still, Emily realised she had mo important things to think about now than the differenc between the two brothers . . .

A SUMMER AT SEA

NOW AVAILABLE IN HARDCOVER